Over and Under

AN ACCOUNT OF A YOUTHFUL JOURNEY IN A DISTANT TIME AND LAND

Richard Ward

RolyPoly Press

OVER AND UNDER

CONTENTS

Man was made for Joy and Woe;
And when this we rightly know,
Thro' the world we safely go,
Joy and Woe are woven fine,
A clothing for the soul divine.

~ William Blake ~

1

Goodbye to girlfriend > An angel in black > Shotguns, sunshine, soaring bridges > The lion topples backwards > Telegraph phantasmagoria > Triadic fantasies

It is the spring of 1972 and I am driving cross-country to work off a broken heart caused by a girlfriend running off with a rock and roll band—the second time a girlfriend has done this, you know, with a band. I thought things were all right at the time with this girl but on the other hand as wild as she is I knew it was impossible. We were supposed to meet in The Canal Zone, a little beer-drenched dive frequented by hippies, clam diggers, construction workers and displaced mystics, the proprietor a garrulous Ginsberg look-alike given to wearing dirty T-shirts, ripped jeans and flip-flops, reputed to have an IQ of 180, constantly pushing his heavy glasses up the bridge of his greasy nose, serving drinks and rapid-fire commentary to the drunken clientele, who once in the town parking lot at night under a gibbous moon and single spotlight mesmerized several dozen curious onlookers with a brilliant performance of *Krapp's Last Tape*, a performance that has become the standard by which I judge all others.

I work construction and arrived late to see her (met the previous summer on the beach, a late hot afternoon shimmering purple and blue, the ocean heavy, silver and slick, the small waves shattering globs of mercury, both of us by coincidence tripping on acid, spying her a hundred yards away in a black one-piece walking towards me with her long-boned body, small pugnacious breasts and sandy loins covered with wet seaweed, smiling in that othergalactic way of hers that had nothing to do with the cosmos or swamic visions, simply too much LSD—*"Ah've had too much LSD,"* she'd say in that baby doll South Carolina drawl that gave me an instant hard-on—smiling I could tell that far away at me alone, all the intense lubricant swollen energy of the world gathered in that smile to smite a hapless wanderer instantly lost yet again deeply in another hopeless cul-de-sac) dancing topless by herself in the trance-like orgiastic state I had seen before, eyes rolling back in her head, great ecstatic smile, throwing her forearms up into her face and kissing them wildly, moaning and laughing at the music, her love of self, for all I know quivering in complete extended full-body orgasm (I never asked her about this state—I was mystified and in awe), her thick black hair swinging in sweating ropes, her taut white breasts mocking my proprietary illusions, dancing in some internal rhythm not much connected to the music but close enough, strong enough, crazy enough so that she was her own force and it hardly mattered to her or anyone else, being the phenomenon that she was, is. All the males were insane over her, wanted to fuck her madly, throw away their girlfriends, their wives, their lives for one taste of it, and the crazy thing is she—was—my girlfriend. At least for several months she was, and I knew she was fucking other men (and women) because my friends told me but I didn't care because this was the sweetest and scariest I had ever had it and the friends who told me were jealous and knew I was lost but still they wished, some of them anyway, that they were me.

Anyway she was dancing in her frenzied Dionysian way very drunk in front of the band facing the four of them, three guys and a girl, a Grace Slick look-alike who seemed to have a special thing for my girlfriend, really in a state, drunker, wilder than I had ever seen dancing like mad up there by herself. We had this date but what was transpiring didn't quite fit the image of demure sweetheart waiting at a table for me nursing a Shirley Temple. If I were the lusty crazed Viking we (males) sometimes wish ourselves to be I would have let out a roar, pushed my way through the crowd, picked her up over my shoulder and carried her out the door midst the tumultuous ribald cheering but I did no such thing and instead stood shakily at the bar drinking a worthless beer and watched the spectacle as the blood drained from my head and my balls shrank to the size of M&Ms—they just melted right away. My friends were too embarrassed to look at me. The room swirled like a carousel in my head and I clutched at the bar. I wanted to hate her but I was too crushed, cursing myself for falling under the spell of this drunken wild sex creature and unable to do anything but stand paralyzed and watch her while everyone I knew discreetly turned their backs or drifted away until I was standing by myself pathetic and emasculated. My foreman whom I hadn't noticed ambled over in his greasy overalls, drunk already, and threw his great arm around my shoulders and yelled in my ear through his whiskered toothless face and his words drew me out of my trance, "Forget it, Sam, she's crazy!" and I sort of came to and turned around and ordered two shots of tequila from the bar's owner who looked at me sympathetically, poured two overflowing glasses and waved me off when I tried to pay. I gave one of the shots to my foreman who as usual was enjoying himself immensely while pointedly not looking at my girlfriend, which I much appreciated, and we clinked glasses and drank the tequila. I thanked him and slunk out of the bar, the music fading, night sounds of summer taking over, passing cars, crickets, the blood congealing in my brain, feeling like death, like doom, like turds floating in tired dishwater. I had to leave, get out, vanish.

***

Two days later in a blasted and bleak state of mind with no plans other than to head to Berkeley and impose myself on a friend of a friend, a certain Pinchas Lieberman ("Pinky"), formerly of Queens, I am headed for the West Coast in my gray '59 SAAB, Rosalina, purchased two months earlier from the bar's owner for $250, which has no upholstery, only springs, and no starter but runs pretty well, the starting accomplished by pushing the tiny car from the driver's side, jumping in and popping the clutch or parking on a incline and letting it roll and doing the clutch thing again. Just outside of Elizabeth on the Jersey Turnpike, two hours into my trip, the car begins steaming and slows to about 25 mph. It is Sunday but there is no sun only gray Jersey overcast and grit but at least the traffic isn't too heavy and I and my Rosalina limp off the turnpike into a desolate industrial neighborhood thinking this is as far as my escape gets, some shit isn't it, my mind as wasted and gray as the blighted scene we've stumbled into, not knowing what the hell comes next, ruin, abandonment, addiction, degeneracy, death. Anything but going back. But this is too much. I will hitchhike if necessary and leave the poor car right here in some rubbish-strewn alley for whores and their somersaults, drunks and addicts for their sleep and vomit, tires stripped, windows smashed, maybe the engine hoisted away by someone else's desperate petard. Terrible thoughts. But I can't leave the little sweetie, little Rosalina. It is only steaming, still running, albeit limpingly, surely a radiator problem that might be fixable if only I can find a garage somewhere and I do have about $500, not a disreputable sum, more than enough to get to Oakland and back, even fix a little radiator if necessary. It is Sunday though and how the hell can anything good come of such a barren Sabbath in such a lifeless place? Nothing but hard-edged ruined industrial violence. Elizabeth.

As if to answer my bleak ruminations, the car sputtering down an empty street, steam hissing up through the cracks in its hood, temp needle buried in red, a full thundering shot, a 12 gauge I know instantly because I used to hunt, echoes through the streets clapping and roaring like a sonic boom and seems to lift the sick little car several inches off the pavement and causes me to duck instinctively, actually thinking that someone has fired at me from the doorway or window of one of these wicked factories out of the dead nineteenth century. Hunched and looking around I see nothing—no gaping holes in the car or myself. I turn left on Columbus Street. Dead ahead a salvage yard with its gates wide open and a small stocky man standing with a shotgun looking at me as I drive steaming like an autoclave in his direction. Maybe he shoots me, raises his gun at my windshield and pulls the trigger when I get within ten yards, a nice tight pattern leaving a hole the size of a volleyball and me on my way to Sleepy Hollow, but I am willing to take the chance, don't care really if he shoots or not, one way just as good as the other.

Well, he doesn't shoot, just stares and steps aside as I pull into the place, the SAAB groaning and hissing and I the car's equivalent, my mind several gaskets gone but both of us relieved, amazed really, that we have stumbled into such a place, grateful that there is an ambulant conscious being within a radius of five miles, that an establishment that specializes in wrecks like mine is open on the Lord's quiet day. Several questions though like who is this character dressed in black like Paladin carrying (and firing) a shotgun, a nice one from the looks of it, over and under, is he the least bit inclined to help me or even could he and then the biggest of all questions will the car after breaking down only two hours into my escape make it all the way to California—and back? It seems he is the only one here and I am somewhat heartened by the sympathetic slightly amused expression as if to say he has seen the likes of this before, wheezing clunker, no upholstery, desperate tatterdemalion at the wheel sitting on a piece of plywood (but still young, a whole lifetime to straighten things out) hoping against hope to squeeze a few more forlorn miles out of the little Swedish joke he is driving, probably the fourth or fifth owner and likely the last, and here's an opportunity to pick up a few bucks for himself on a Sunday when all he has planned is some idle hours blasting holes in cars and adjusting the brakes on his truck.

I turn off the engine and get out, catching my shirt on a spring and ripping it under the arm. Motherfucker. It's a pretty nice shirt. Blue Italian short-sleeve from Macy's three years before. He ambles up to the car. "Fuckin' radiator, eh? Open dat fucker up." I duck back into the SAAB, pull the cable and the hood pops open. Holding the gun in his right hand he pulls the hood forward and up in the odd way SAABs open, exposing the tiny lawnmower engine and the toy-like radiator that isn't steaming any longer probably because there is no water left. He sticks his thick grimy middle finger in his mouth and touches the radiator. It sizzles and snaps and he draws the reconnoitering digit back abruptly and whistles. "Whoo, dat fucker's hot! You aint got a drop of fuckin' water left. Probly a leak. Let it cool down. We'll check it out." I am now at the mercy of this little man in black, Antonio Vanzetti—and I immediately think of old Bartolomeo and his pal Nicola—who apparently likes to spend a few hours on Sundays with his beautiful Beretta over and under with inlaid stock and ventilated rib nailing the seagulls that flock for some reason in great swirling numbers over the decaying wrecks at Columbus Street Salvage and Wreckage, risking the $75 fine for shooting one, who finds and welds the pinhole in my radiator and charges me all of fifteen bucks, laughing at my car and marveling at my balls and insanity for even thinking about driving across the country in such a degenerate contraption, certain of catastrophe: "I *guaranfuckintee* you aint gonna make it in this thing. But hey, a guy's got balls, he's a little crazy and maybe a guardian-fuckin'-angel sittin' on the dashboard, so who the fuck knows. You be sure to send me a fuckin' postcard if you make it. I bet you don't make it as far as Harrisburg. Five bucks says you don't make it to California—on second thought, no bet. This whole thing's crazy enough you might make it. But comin' back? Forget it. Never gonna happen."

I agree to send him a postcard and heartened he marvels at my *balls* since after the affair at The Canal Zone I am wondering if I have any at all worth mentioning and if I will make it out of Jersey much less to Harrisburg. I leave the yard, the SAAB cool and happy for the moment, looking in the mirror as Antonio Vanzetti raises his gun and fires out over the massive wasteland of wrecks and wheeling seagulls, a farewell salute, a military sendoff for my heartbreak mission impossible.

***

Old Vanzetti was onto something though as I make it to Harrisburg that night and sleep with a blanket thrown over the springs in the back inside a sleeping bag actually feeling pretty good. Harrisburg is depressing, dirty and wet but I sleep soundly and rise in the morning still bleak but somewhat hopeful, take advantage of a decent stretch of empty parking lot and push the SAAB, jump in, pop the clutch and continue my southward chug on 81 to Knoxville and points west. I want to see this part of the country. The Appalachians are spectacular and Davy Crockett's song is right about Tennessee, the greenest state in the land of the free, and in a small village gas station as I pump the SAAB's little tank full of gas two hillbillies in a beat-up pickup roar through with rebel whoops and wave a rattlesnake in my face, dead or alive I don't know.

Just west of Memphis I cross an Erector Set bridge and see the Mississippi River for the first time, wide and muddy with the spring runoff. That night I pull off the road near Clarksville, Arkansas and the next day, somewhere west of Oklahoma City I pick up two scruffy white kids hitchhiking to Albuquerque with some of the hippie thing but will knock you over the head with a cinder block if they need cash for some Thunderbird or marijuana if they are so inclined. About 100 miles east of Albuquerque a snowstorm blows in suddenly straight out of nowhere and the SAAB goes spinning off the freeway into a kind of field, the two kids jumping out laughing and throwing snowballs. The engine thankfully still running, the boys push and I drive back onto the road, the storm disappearing as fast as it comes. We spend the night in Albuquerque at friends of the hitchhikers in a small adobe house and I dream of shotguns, sunshine and soaring bridges spanning blue waters. I know when I wake that I am going to make it.

***

The snowstorm in Albuquerque has knocked me into a different consciousness and with a surprisingly good sleep and leaving before dawn the SAAB and I motor through Arizona feeling the West for the first time and then Californee and the Mojave desert, the ride through the mountains to Morrow Bay with the bubbling emollients of SPRINGTIME in full-frontal assault transporting me into the emerald pages of a children's book with everything in H.O. scale, the tiny orchards, farm houses, grazing horses, cows, winding streams glinting under a benignant sun. And then the grand twisting ride up Highway 1 from Morrow Bay driving like a person obsessed, determined to make it to Oakland that evening with my eyes peeled for California beauties and Henry Miller, the little SAAB Rosalina with a glimpse of Valhalla at last, the magnificent skull-bending vast liquid blue wilderness on one side and the mysterious lonely interior on the other, both full of death and strange haunting intimations of a sort of liberation I have never felt before. California. On a turnout in Big Sur overlooking the Pacific hundreds of feet below reclines a large sculpture looking for all the world like an absolute Henry Moore, which seems under the circumstances completely normal. Maybe Henry Miller put it there. Finally the spinning chrome tractor-beam carbon monoxide madness of San Jose pulling me into the *Bayaireeya*, dazed, still with fevered heart, somehow locating Lieberman's apartment in Oakland through a dilapidated screen door banging shut shaking his hand and staring over his shoulder at a picture of a smiling man pointing at me with a large handgun.

***

Though I am in somewhat of a haze arriving in Oakland the next day walking around Berkeley puts me in a different state altogether with its color, anarchy, beautiful hippie girls, the ever-present aroma of marijuana and revolution suffusing the atmosphere up and down Telegraph Avenue. I gravitate immediately to the Caffè Mediterraneum where I nurse a tall glass of fresh-squeezed orange juice and clutch my notebook, an anchor in which I essay surreptitious portraits of Crumb characters already famous, doodle, scribble bad haikus and attempt half-heartedly at a diary resulting in disjointed formless gibberish. The pain of the ruinous night at The

Canal Zone is slipping away after a day of Berkeley sunshine, orange juice and bra-less hippie chicks at the Caffè Mediterraneum but I am still in a haze, eventually tiring of the Med and scrawling uselessly in my notebook, taking instead to wandering around other parts of the city.

At this time in my life I think vaguely of becoming an artist and I am particularly enthralled by Vincent van Gogh, so much so that it is a small wonder I hadn't returned to The Canal Zone the evening of my ignominy and handed my wild girlfriend a piece of my ear as Vincent had famously handed a piece of his neatly wrapped to a prostitute who promptly fainted dead away, though his sad mutilation was precipitated by yet another quarrel with the ruthless Gauguin and not public sexual humiliation. On the morning of my second day in Berkeley I happen into a well-known metaphysical bookstore on Telegraph and am struck immediately by a character a bit older than me with an orange blazing beard, straw hat and a wild almost violent energy that I recognize instantly. He isn't doing anything more dangerous than reading Paramahansa Yogananda but the sparks are flying off him sure enough and I know this is the real thing and not the pathetic misunderstood tragic artist of popular sentiment. I am glad to see him reading some Eastern stuff because Christianity hadn't done any favors and as I inch closer to absorb some of that galactic energy (I once sat in front of "Starry Night" at the Museum of Modern Art for an hour staring fixedly at the painting as a museum guard eyed me nervously) I can see he has lost none of the legendary powers of concentration that carried him through night sessions of café painting in Arles with candles burning in his hat for illumination or doggedly painting one canvas after another in a rocky olive grove while the vengeful *mistral* raged and pushed at his sanity, sometimes blowing his work off the easel into the air like stringless whiffling kites (deuced difficult to get in a day's work sometimes, wasn't it, Vincent?) crashing and careering off into rocks and ravines.

I am standing two feet away pretending to look at books in the same way I might stand next to a beautiful girl in a similar situation, my energy not up to competing with his as he neither moves nor looks up nor gives the slightest indication of being aware of my presence. Looking out of the corner of my eye at his bristling orange beard, mystic cheekbones and intensely focused blue eyes under the talismanic sweat-stained straw hat I struggle to think of something to say. I move away a few steps at which point he looks up and smiles into my eyes with the most oceanic blue intensity, a brother, comrade, soul-connection and I am overwhelmed but show nothing but the reciprocation of his smile with as heartfelt a one as I can muster. He returns to his reading and my head is spinning a little to be standing next to someone who looks so much like one of my heroes.

I back off a bit and pick up a book on Tibetan sexual arts but still observe him surreptitiously, the enormous intensity, chewing the hair below his lip, the small inward smile flitting across his vulcanian physiognomy, riffling through the pages so feverishly it might be a flipbook illustrating the progressive stages of enlightenment from callow pink hedonist to withered sadhu. I cannot let this opportunity pass because of the resemblance and the challenge is to see how I might somehow connect in a more than superficial way as it is an occasion that will likely never present itself again though obviously he doesn't go by V. van Gogh and I wonder intently what in the hell his name might be. He is so clearly of a northern type that I can probably rule out the Afro-Asiatic, Indo-Iranian or Sino-Tibetan surname but anything is possible in this blenderized world, my only hope being that it isn't something like Steve Jones or Rob Smith (apologies) but even so it doesn't matter as it is the essence that counts, not the label or the price tag, though you have to wonder for example if George Washington had been called Ralph Cramden, to cite just one possibility.

Inconsequential ruminations, these, and in any case I don't care what the hell his name is and in a moment of boldness as I know it to be one of those small circumstances of time and connection that vanishes so ruthlessly I move respectfully to his side and excusing my interruption and effrontery proceed as how it is a metaphysical bookstore and all and how van Gogh is a great hero to me I can't help but remark on his uncanny physical similarity to the great artist and a certain kind of energy as well, purely coincidental of course but his resemblance is actually quite remarkable, just thought I'd mention it. And by the way my name is Sam.

I stick out my hand and he grabs it in a strong warm grip that reminds me of Vincent's "draughtsman's fist" and tells me that his name is Paul, Paul Avery (absolutely acceptable), and how, yes, he's been told many times of the resemblance, the irony being that his first name is the same as Vincent's great friend, competitor and tormentor. He hasn't much interest in art but does love literature and in fact is writing a book about fathers and sons, mentioning his own father and how there is a lot of "unfinished business" between them and that through writing hopes to resolve some of these issues although it is a topic that obviously transcends the merely personal and who knows where it will all lead? I concur that this is the essence of the creative process, that one has certain intimations and impulses but no more of a map than that, indeed a map might be harmful, that it is the surprises, back roads, dead ends, accidents and unforeseen destinations that mark a truly creative journey.

As we speak I think of Vincent's troublesome relationship with his own father (I have done a lot of reading about Vincent), the minister and stern moralist who hadn't the slightest notion of who this person was that bore his name and resemblance, who frightened him with his compulsions, sincerity, moodiness, intensity, oddness, social awkwardness and intelligence. We sons all have problems with fathers, Paul says, and whether aware of it or not these problems frequently are transferred to one's country, particularly if the country fits a masculine paradigm as ours surely does. Here I interject a few observations about van Gogh, how his was a personality at war with itself, comprising the dominating father rigid and cold in the service of morality, the crucifix wielded as inverted phallus, the benighted mother, repressed, almost certainly sexually frustrated in that Calvinist household, and while saying these things I am struck by the surrealism of talking to one so closely resembling the very man whose famous personality I am dissecting, one of my great heroes, half expecting to be interrupted with demurrals or something stronger: "Listen here, old fellow, that's not it at all. You've a hell of a nerve talking about me like that. You don't know a deuced thing about any of it and you'd be better off speaking of baseball, or something more manageable." But no, he listens politely, even with interest, his head bent forward, eyes clear and comprehending, holding the still-open book with his left hand and stroking his whiskers with the other, not giving any outward sign if he agrees or not with what I am saying but occasionally shooting me looks with those high-powered blue eyes that unnerve me a bit but I hold on determined to stay with the moment and show him that I know a thing or two.

He is my height and stockier, his hands large—that "draughtsman's fist"—but there is really nothing physically remarkable about him nor does he emanate any discernible muscular energy the way an athlete or a violent person might, in fact knowing Vincent's temperament (this guy is close to really being Vincent to me right now) and ultimate psychological fragility, though he is clearly in good health, I feel a physical protectiveness towards him, wanting almost to put my arm around his shoulders the way my Friar Tuckish foreman had done that awful night at The Canal Zone, an oddly parental feeling to be sure, and the more I am aware of it the smaller and more vulnerable he becomes, although every time he fixes me with one of those broiling genius looks my head spins and I lose track of my thoughts, his frailty vanishing, replaced with something indestructible and superior.

**

We go to the Caffè Med continuing our conversation at a small round table in front, the sun striking the bottom half of his face like a reflection from a shard of yellow mirror, his beard glowing orange, the blue eyes shielded under the straw hat flashing like signal flares when he raises his head. He speaks rapidly and brilliantly and at times I literally hold on to the edge of the table for fear of slipping off into a territory where I have no moorings, so unequal to his buzz-saw intellect do I feel, his passionate skimming flights of imagination, his depth of erudition. He talks of philosophy, the Augustinian concept of grace and how there really is no such thing as free will (something that interests me), that some supposedly are preordained through the "whim" of God (nonsense, there is no God, he says) to attain this dubious notion of "salvation," which in some sense is related to the Eastern idea of nirvana, though the former is transcendent and the latter temporal and why would it be, he wonders, that over here we shoot for the great airy beyond, chalking up this mortal coil as a bad dream and over there they tie fifteen-pound weights to their dicks and stand on one foot for six years and smile seraphically. Maybe it's all the hashish they smoke, I offer, hoping to add a fraction to the discussion, that I might be seen as slightly more in his eyes than a saltshaker or napkin sitting insensate on the table in front of him. He speaks of his love for St. John of the Cross and his *Dark Night of the Soul*, the mystic visions of suffering and renunciation, closer, he says, to the Indian sadhus than any other Christian outcropping. I have no idea.

He talks about literature and philosophy, his favorite Indian divinities, the great quarrel between Vishnu and Brahma and Shiva's intercession as a pillar of light with no beginning or end, the *jyoitirlinga*, and how though Shiva is known as the destroyer it is really his creative aspects that are celebrated, how the raised phallus, the *linga*, is worshipped as an object of creation. At one point I make a trite observation about how in American culture the phallus is more commonly associated with destruction and domination, nuclear missiles the obvious example, and he nods, saying something like yes, hmm, and continues, having decided early on it is clear that I am a nice enough fellow but that it is his own words in this particular pairing that are of interest, presenting no real problem for me as I thoroughly agree. In my current condition it is easy for me to imagine I am sitting with Vincent van Gogh, and if he wants to expound at length on the divine dualities of Shiva, the frightening Kali, manifestation of Shakti, with her severed heads and bleeding skulls it is fine with me. I am glad to see that he has (this version of Vincent) gotten thoroughly into the Eastern thing since as I had mentioned Christianity was the shits for him in the long run as far as I was concerned, nothing but hair-shirt provincial exclusionism and hypocrisy, most glaringly illustrated by the hard-assed philistinism of his father though in the end there was love, it cannot be denied. Falling completely into the fantasy for the moment, I want to ask him about his life, his relationship with his parents, Gauguin, the expressionists, the *mistral*, absinthe, Arles, the gentle postman Roulin, his love for Millet, Sien, his cigar-smoking prostitute girlfriend who had treated him so cruelly, his love for Hokusai and Hiroshige, the kind doctor Rey, his brother, his state of mind at the end, but of course I don't, how ludicrous, this is *Paul Avery*, not

Vincent van Gogh, so I keep these questions to myself and half-listen to his rapid-fire incandescent monologue, struggling to keep up with the hair-pin turns, swoops and straight-aways, observing, in a sense, as I might a giant slalom or *grand prix* event, able to understand the general form and direction but keenly aware of my limitations and content with my seat on the sidelines.

He goes on about the incarnations of Vishnu, the preserver, as Krishna, Buddha, Jesus and so forth, and I briefly wonder was Vincent then an incarnation of some other great soul, perhaps even Vishnu himself, at the same time pulling back to take in the whole scene at the Med, the innocent sun-dappled exuberance of youth, the old-world energy and excellence of the swarthy cooks slicing avocados, sautéing onions, frying bacon, burgers, ham, chopping, dicing, buttering, smearing, toasting, dancing, shouting, laughing, cursing, unabashedly eyeing the fabulous hippie chicks and their untrammeled cantaloupe breasts, the crude, masculine humor in Italian, Spanish, Greek, Portuguese, Romany, Ladino, whatever it is, Yugoslavian, and, for whatever reason, perhaps the presence and energy of Paul together with my fevered state of mind, the whirling succulent energy of the youthful clientele, the ribald tumescent brutal force and professional efficiency of the Mediterraneum cooks, the graceful warm sunbeams slanting through the windows with their twin offerings of light and warmth, illuminated dust motes floating like miniature spaceships, the susurrus and laughter of the relaxed foraging crowd, the clank and clatter of dishes, glass and silverware, all of it together lifts me out of my seat somewhere between floor and ceiling and I float at a forty-five degree angle, head down, like some enraptured Chagallian peasant lover in purple blouse and green pants while *shtetl* livestock float by outside mooing and oinking down Telegraph and I am overwhelmed with the kind of awe and giddiness that overcomes a person two or three times a decade, if that, usually with the help of drugs or some outside stimulating agent or agents. That's okay. Whatever forces at work on me the experience is no less extraordinary because of it. If I were in Vietnam experiencing all the sex, drugs, rock and roll and violence a body could ask for would my consciousness be any less valid than if I were sitting on a bed of nails or under a bodhi tree wrestling with demons and houris? If the truth lies at "the bottom of a bottomless pit" then what is left? Style? Glamour? Deceit? Force? Permanent illusion?

***

Paul Avery pauses in his monologue and looks around the restaurant as if coming up for air. He has been talking with animation and intensity for more than an hour, completely absorbed in the pinball wizard working of his seemingly brilliant mind—seemingly brilliant because much of what he says is lost on me, indeed, produces in me this trance-like state as I float above the table despite gripping its edges tightly. This cat may be mad but it is the sort of "madness," I fancy, that afflicted Vincent, born of a fertile, overheated intelligence bubbling in a deep pressure-cooker loneliness. Any warm conscious audience served to release the valve and his thoughts shot out like hot steam, which of course only increased the wariness of those around him. Most likely fled or, sensing his vulcanism in the first place, never approached. This is why, I think, he regards me in that moment of coming up for air with a glimmer of warmth and appreciation: I am still around. Not only that, I suppose I convey the impression that I am following his words and more or less understanding them, though doing a woeful job as participant. I would have to be a Gauguin or Abbie Hoffman to get a word in edgewise. Then we'd see the "sparks fly," as Vincent used say, and no doubt the very hairs on our heads would burst into flames. But alas I am filled with helium, watching brightly colored farm animals float by above Telegraph Avenue.

I figure a person such as the one sitting before me has a void the size of the Grand Canyon inside him and a stack of well-used pornographic magazines stashed in his closet and surely the hard intense way he stares at the girls in the Caffè Med seems to confirm this. He burns holes through their peasant blouses and tank tops into their lovely breasts, no bones about it. I look as much as he does but his frank aggressive manner embarrasses me and I desist for the moment, discomforted by his need and unadulterated longing that seems to turn these basically innocent, fun-loving girls into raw meat. Painfully and obviously underneath it all he is one of love's desperate supplicants, poor Paul/ Vincent, and suffers no less now as then, writing heartbroken letters to his brother every night after painting for ten sun-baked hours in the middle of some stony ravine fringed with twisted dry olive trees, the hot *mistral* blowing his canvases into the air and his sanity to the very edge of the world.

As I am thinking this, watching Paul as he speaks but not hearing his words, his eyes take on a radiant deeply affectionate luster and I turn and look up at a large extraordinary woman of the type that is sometimes referred to as "handsome," not the Madison Avenue or Hollywood ideal but to some tastes, including mine, particularly breathtaking and sexual. She is dark, with a hint of Anna Magnani, a little older than Paul, probably in her early thirties, wearing a blue work shirt unbuttoned to the tops of dizzying unencumbered breasts and dungarees wrapped around full declamatory hips. I sense these physical details without really looking, as it would be rude to the ultimate degree. The connection between Paul and Vincent is obviously fanciful, at least I know this much, but I indulge the fantasy a bit more to feel happiness for him, Paul/Vincent, because it is pure justice that one who had suffered so much and strove so doggedly should at last receive a taste of earthly pleasure of the profoundest sort—if indeed this is his *amorosa*, as the vibes that pass between them so strongly suggest. I sense a certain quiet behind the counter where the swarthy lascivious cooks normally whistle, jabber, sizzle, slice and dice and know without looking that they are ogling the woman who stands behind me now talking to Paul about dinner plans for the evening (after Paul has politely introduced us. Her name is Carmen. Carmen!), which I find disorienting in its normality after the crackling enfilade of psychology, literature, philosophy and theology that has issued from the coiled personage across from me and that has swept me into such a surreal limbo-like state. They graciously invite me for dinner and of course I accept. Paul gives directions and writes down his address and then excuses himself and he and Carmen leave together, saying they will see me later.

***

Dinner at Paul and Carmen's is a continuation of the careening monologue at the Caffè Med over a great bowl of spaghetti with Carmen's rich winey tomato sauce, warm bread drenched in garlic butter, fresh salad with California artichoke hearts and a gallon of good Chianti. Chick Corea provides background music while Paul talks about the differences between Mencius and Confucius, how Mencius, like Marx, focuses on material conditions, that the people's material needs be well provided for, and how one cannot expect anything approximating a moral order if a part of the population is impoverished. Carmen contributes a warm nurturing counterpoint to Paul's relentless intellectualism. She wears a dark simple dress, cut very low, and red espadrilles. I am hopelessly blown away and try not to show it though they both know and accept it good-naturedly. I guess they are used to it. Carmen is a painter of intensely colorful portraits and landscapes. A portrait of Paul hangs in their living room, looking not at all like the resemblance to van Gogh I expect.

"Mencius knew about human nature," says Paul, filling our glasses for the fourth or fifth time, using two hands to hold the gourd-like bottle. We have finished with the spaghetti and salad and Carmen's serving an incredible cheesecake she has made. "I would love to arrange a meeting between him and Marx. They'd agree on the primacy of material conditions but would clash on governing paradigms. Totally different traditions. In the *Meng Tzu* he actually talks about cooperative farming—wait a minute." He gets out of his chair with the sort of rapid impulsive movement that I am beginning to understand as a signature characteristic, scans the huge bookcase of glass blocks and two-by-eights painted white that stands against the living room wall like a Univac, retrieves a book, sits down so quickly it is if he has never gotten up, takes a gulp of wine, wipes his mouth with a red cloth napkin, belches—Carmen good-naturedly reproachful from the kitchen—and opens the book.

"Here. 'Each square *li*'—that's a unit of measurement—'of land should be divided into nine plots, the whole containing nine hundred *mou*.' Another measurement. Just a second." Paul jumps up again and comes back with a yellow legal pad and stubby green pencil. He pulls his chair closer to mine and draws a diagram with his strong right hand, a square divided into nine equal parts, the middle square marked "public field," and two of the other squares labeled "100 *mou*," indicating the size of the squares. It is a hastily scribbled affair but I am fascinated. "The central plot is the public field, and the eight households, each owning a hundred *mou* farm, cultivate the public fields in common. Not till public work is finished may they resume to attend to their private affairs. Sounds familiar, doesn't it? Of course it does. So Mao was influenced by Mencius—at least a little bit."

Paul rubs his hand briskly through his medium-length carroty hair, fixes me with his blue eyes and takes another deep drink of wine, almost emptying his glass. "Goddammit, that's what's missing, don't you think, Sam? A little communal effort. We all want to be a part of something, don't we? At least some of the time, don't you think? It's the communal farming thing with Mencius. And his intuitive understanding of Yeats' center not holding—how things fall apart if not tended to. Confucius knew this too—how alike we all are but through laziness or neglect or sinister conscious design we are manipulated into drifting away from each other and from our innate goodness. And now we're living in our little rat holes so disgusted with the whole thing we're getting ready to blow it all up." He finishes the bit of wine in his glass, pours another and takes a drink. I wonder exactly what he meant by "sinister conscious design" but I don't ask, having a fair idea of my own.

I stay for several more hours, with Carmen bringing out the marijuana and rolling papers, the three of us on the living room rug, an old Oriental, propped comfortably on fat richly-colored velour and corduroy cushions, sinking into a warm stupor kept afloat by Coltrane, Monk, Evans and late Beethoven quartets, like so many late-night sessions with conditions such that your receptivity to the music is deeply tuned in, the stereotypical handful of stoned hipsters grooving to every nuance from motif and rhythm to each playful note and excursion, reminding me of an evening in college at an old Trotskyite's tiny record-filled apartment beneath the Williamsburg Bridge with a bunch of young radicals sitting in a circle around a water pipe of glowing hashish taking a magical mystery tour of the leftist's jazz collection. Somewhere around two a.m. he pulled out Coltrane's *Meditations*, which most of us had never heard, and slyly slipped it on to the spindle—he had the hipster's sense of moment—and for the next 40 minutes or so our stoned circle was swept away into the tumultuous land of the mystic saxophonist, all of us in the end deposited onto the safe sweet shores in one enervated body with something like love connecting us. Music can do that. Afterwards we walked down the sidewalk that bitter cold winter morning arm-in-arm singing the *International* ("Arise! ye starvelings, from your slumbers!"), the freezing junkies and trolls under the bridge staring at us bemusedly.

***

Though I have no comrades to walk arm-in-arm with I feel pretty good walking back to Lieberman's apartment after the evening with Paul and Carmen. Paul and I have agreed to meet for coffee in the morning at the Caffè Med. New York seems like another continent or lifetime but when I get to Lieberman's apartment I am transported directly back for here is the SAAB sitting forlornly in front reminding me of the wasted heartbroken state in which I had fled. It is as if the desolate interior of the car mirrors my own, stripped bare, all sharp cutting edges, no padding to soften my bones or deflect the grit and wild winds. At least the floorboards are without holes and the little thing runs, though the tires are near bald and of course the starter is broken, which certainly has a symbolic resonance when I reflect on it. With the distractions and novelty of driving across, arriving in Berkeley, meeting Paul and Carmen, the small adventures I have experienced, I have been diverted enough to forget for the moment my true, deeper condition, which is not simply the minor wreckage of a short-lived albeit intense fling with a daft sex kitten who had arbitrarily booted me out of our rapidly-moving pleasure machine. Clearly I am not one of the world's well adjusted, though reflecting on the world and those who seem to be in charge I wonder what the hell that term means, exactly. Certainly I am not confusing Lieberman with what it means to be well adjusted. He and his friend, Jerome, a lanky piece of hard-edged rawhide from Cody, are sitting at Lieberman's kitchen table sniffing powdery lines through a rolled bill from a pie tin with a bottle of Jack Daniels three-quarters finished, as are they, both in surly temper smoking Marlboros cursing everything under heaven from the weather to motherhood. I had met Lieberman once briefly back East and don't expect the vile dyspepsia but of course take it in stride as I have essentially imposed myself on him and unless I want to spend the evenings in the foothills or in the back seat of my car I had best get along to go along or not getting along go alone. Jerome, who lives in Oakland and is Lieberman's partner in a small construction business, rises unsteadily from a paint-spattered wooden chair and sticks out a large calloused paw, "So you're the fuckin' dip-shit faggot artist type from the effete degenerate East!" I allow as how I'm not so sure about the artist type which elicits a violent bout of resinous choking laughter and a resounding whack on the shoulder along with boozy manic commands to join them for a drink and a line or two. Reluctantly, I sit, fairly reeling from the difference between the warm peaceful confines of Paul and Carmen's and this sulfurous space of biliousness and simmering violence. Jerome is a long cowboy type, not bad looking but with vague intimations of what I imagine an eighteenth-century Liverpool ratter to look like and his hostility is all but jumping out of his pores. Lieberman watches with an amused expression on his pale puffy face, leaning back, a burning Marlboro between his yellow fingers.

"So," Jerome commands. "Who's the best fuckin' American writer? You have ten seconds to answer."

I look up at the bare ceiling light and then at Jerome, who regards me with an expression of smug savage triumph, as if he has

had a long successful career of ferreting out Easterners and exposing their assumed cultural superiority for the pretentious, sniveling,
yellow-bellied bullshit that it is and I about to become another un-
suspecting calf seared by the business end of his cultural branding
iron. I wonder what the consequences will be if I wait more than
the allotted ten seconds and also what writer he has in mind. I have
no idea who the hell the best American writer is. I look at Jerome
for signs of intelligence in his mocking steel-gray eyes and come up
with no clue. He might a fucking genius for all I can tell, a Ph.D.
from Yale who did his dissertation on the oral traditions of nine-
teenth-century nomadic possum skinners of the Dismal Swamp.
Actually he looks like he could have been one of them and this is
what makes me a little nervous about going beyond the ten-sec-
ond limit. On the other hand, who the fuck is he to jerk me around
like this? Just as I can't tell if he is an idiot or genius I don't know
if he is kidding with me or not. Lieberman's expression is of little
help, his amusement indicating either pleasure at my discomfort or
Jerome's out-of-the-blue literary challenge or both—or perhaps he
is simply in his own space enjoying a private joke. There's enough
of the Irish in me though to get a bit of an attitude when someone
puts me on the spot, even if there is a possibility that my debating
opponent might pull out a skinning knife in reinforcement of his
position, which I am not sure Jerome won't do. And so I drag my
heels and screw up my face in a caricature of deep thought and allow the seconds to pass, looking at Jerome, the pitted surface of the
grimy yellow table, the light bulb, the screen door at the back of the
small rancid kitchen, at Lieberman, whose expression subtly reveals
the recognition that I am engaging in a bit of my own play and finally, after about twenty seconds, I say, "Well—I don't know—how
about Melville?"

"Melville!" Jerome explodes, bringing his fist down on the table, "are you fuckin' kidding me? He wrote one good book, that was it—one fuckin' book—*Moby Dick*. All the rest was bullshit."

"OK then," I say, more amused than startled by his vehemence, "who the fuck is the greatest American writer?"

"Zane Grey. Zane fuckin' Grey is the greatest American writer, bar none. Period. *Riders of the Purple Sage* is the G-A-N, baby."

"G-A-N?"

"Great American Novel. Everything you want to know about America is in that fuckin' book. It's the essential mythology of the West and America. For one thing he's the greatest landscape writer. For another he's a great psychologist. For another he understands the horse. If you want to understand America you need to understand the horse, and I don't mean the equestrian sidesaddle faggoty Eastern bullshit. And tell a story? No one could tell a story like Zane fuckin' Grey. I bet you never read any Zane Grey, did you?"

No, I respond, actually I've never read a Zane Grey book. But he's very popular in the East, I know that much. I still don't know what to make of Jerome but he is beginning to remind of General Jack D. Ripper. Essential bodily fluids might be the next topic out of Jerome's mouth. Understand the horse.

"Tell me," I say, and I can see Jerome tensing ever so slightly, a subtle wariness of countenance, the effete Easterner about to ask a captious literary question. "What about the horse did Zane Grey understand and what does it tell us about America?"

"That's easy!" exclaims Jerome, as if a seventh-grader put on the spot and asked about something he'd primed for. I am happy I have asked the right question and genuinely interested in what he will say. "You know all about Freud and the horse, right?" I don't really but I nod. I am a little surprised to hear Jerome mention Freud but then with this guy I remind myself to be prepared for anything, including physical assault. I hope he won't press me for details about Freud and the horse and I run through a quick list of banalities should he ask. "Well, Grey took Freud one step farther. The horse is the great civilizing power of Europe in the New World. Just as the European used the horse to conquer and civilize so did the Americans use the horse. The horse is the symbol of masculine civilizing power—the great all-conquering father, destroying and fucking everything in its path and leaving order, peace—and Christianity—in its wake. The horse is the symbol of bloody destruction, insemination and immaculate, all-powerful Christian order. The horse is the passion, resurrection and glory of Christ, the same way nuclear missiles are today. The meek, contrary to what Jesus said, shall not inherit the earth. The great symbol of our time is the proud rearing white stallion in full erectile splendor!"

I look at him, blinking. Lieberman laughs and slaps the table, causing the pie tin to clatter. The whiskey sloshes back and forth in its bottle. The ceiling bulb flickers. Jerome seems to have grown larger sitting in his chair, his blue eyes glowing. He looks like fucking Charlton Heston. I am speechless for a few seconds but at last find my tongue.

"Zane Grey said all that?"

"A careful reading of his books will reveal all that and more. I did a paper on him in college. It blew the professor away. IT KICKED ASS! A chick professor. I fucked her in her office one time too. That's the only reason I wrote the fuckin' paper—to set her up, you know? It got her all hot and bothered and she asked me up to her office and I bent her over the desk and gave it to her from behind. *Riders of the Purple Sage*, my friend. The great American novel. Professor Swilling. From *Coon-necticut*. How sweet it is."

"*Coon-necticut?*"

"A little known fact, my friend. There's more coons in Connecticut per capita than any other state. Don't ask me why. Liberal welfare laws probably."

I decide to press this. "Was she Black, this Professor Swilling?"

"Are you kidding? I don't fuck niggers, my friend. I bet you do, though. I bet you fuck niggers up the ass. Come on, tell us. You're among friends."

This is too much. I don't know what to do. I've gone too far with this guy. Big mistake. He's not an idiot, this is plain. A demented kind of low intelligence, sticky enough to be dangerous. And meaner than a rattlesnake with a *pulque* hangover. I yearn for the safety and friendship of Paul and Carmen's instead of being trapped in this bizarre anachronistic Western scene. All that's missing are the playing cards, the pile of silver in the middle of the table and the six-shooters at our sides. I feel like Marlon Brando in "The Appaloosa" sitting across from Chuy Medina, the scorpion scratching in its box. Lieberman watches closely, not really sure himself what is going to happen but emanating a cold curiosity.

Jerome leans back in his chair coolly appraising me, waiting for my response, clearly not concerned should this little absurdity rise to another level and probably hoping that it will. He has determined right away obviously that I am no physical threat, that he can take me, and he is probably right. Though capable of obstinacy I am no fighter. Jerome, on the other hand, behind the whip-thin cowboy handsomeness, has the look of one sadistic hombre and for the first time I notice the long scar on his chin and feel more keenly the lonesome frigid winds whistling through his barbed wire Wyoming soul. I think of Curley in *Of Mice and Men* and picture myself slumped over and bleeding in the corner spitting out pieces of my teeth, an image that conflicts with my natural proclivity towards self-love and preservation. This being the case I decide that the only recourse is to diffuse the situation and a reply such as, "Better a nigger's ass than your mouth," which actually does go through my mind, might not be the wisest form of repartee under the circumstances and so twirl my mental Rolodex in search of a response that will puncture the poisonous balloon inflating rapidly and squeezing us into a corner and retain for me a modicum of self respect.

All of this passes fairly quickly through my mind and before Jerome derives any sort of satisfaction in perceiving an awkward or fearful hesitancy on my part, something I am loath to allow as I feel a genuine and growing revulsion for this pop-up character smugly leaning back in his chair before me while his puffy, pasty ghoulish friend quietly waits for something truly unpleasant to transpire, I say, "You know, actually, Jerome, I get the feeling that I'm not really among friends. I don't know you at all. But I can tell you're a real sportsman. You're having some sport with me, aren't you? Obviously you're a clever fellow. Very impressive. On top of it all, you're named after a saint." And here, not-so-gentle reader, is where it happens. A familiar impulse, which some might call suicidal, comes to the fore, a form of pure stupid bravado shoved rudely forward by a fear that is ashamed of itself—a hapless bystander pushed out of the darkness suddenly into the spotlight on an amateur-hour stage. It has gotten me into all sorts of trouble and on a couple of occasions nearly eliminated altogether. And so, taking a deep mental breath, fully expecting to end up in the critical care unit of a hospital that I hope isn't too far away, I say, "Saint Jerome. He's the patron saint of assholes, isn't he?"

While not having planned any clear defensive maneuvers I know that some form of self-protection is going to be in order and though Jerome is likely whippet-fast when sober thankfully his reflexes are mucked-up in drugs and alcohol as evidenced not only by his clumsily-delayed physical response but also by the reorganization of his facial features in stupefied spluttering realization of what I have actually said. At first there is a moment of blank incomprehension, as if my words are those of a record in reverse, then the understanding and rage, his face becoming so twisted and dark with fury that I am in that instant reminded of Spencer Tracy in Dr. Jekyll and Mr. Hyde, awed by the comparison and reflecting that Jerome with a little coaching might have a future in the movies. But superseding my thoughts on the possibilities of Jerome's cinematic career are more pressing concerns about my own future as a living intact human being and in an electric flash I'm out of my chair and picking it up as if suddenly finding myself inside a lion cage. It sounds a bit ludicrous, I know, but what am I supposed to do? Two things then happen more or less simultaneously that work to my advantage: Jerome, in sputtering and thankfully inebriate rage, instead of springing out of his seat to deliver upon my person his standard mayhem somehow manages in his Rumplestiltskin-like eruption of anger (and I am sure in his Rumplestiltskinism a prime component of the standard mayhem is a good stomping with the battered, shit-thumping, pointy-toed, sharp-heeled cowboy boots he wears) to propel himself in the opposite direction and topple backwards in his chair landing in a disjointed bony clatter on Lieberman's kitchen floor bellowing and cursing like a drunken syphilitic gunslinger and Lieberman, in sudden alarm at the potentially homicidal turn events have taken, probably not too keen on scrubbing the blood, likely mine, from his kitchen floor and perhaps realizing the lateness of the hour and the remodeling job he and Jerome are two weeks behind on, rises abruptly from his chair and in two agile strides that belie his pastry-like slumping physique is astride the blustering cowpoke still trying to disentangle himself in a red rage kicking his legs and flailing his arms with murderous intent, at the same time whirling around and yelling at me to get the fuck out and then directing his attention back to his thrashing friend delivers two quick stinging slaps to the face—whack, whack!—just like that and I stand dumbfounded, momentarily paralyzed, then drop the chair and indeed get the fuck out, backing out of Lieberman's kitchen, down the little hallway and out the screen door, glancing at the photograph of the smiling man with the gun as I exit.

I wait across the street for about fifteen minutes until Jerome staggers out the door, stumbles down the sidewalk and climbs into his large red truck which after several attempts he finally manages to start and then goes lurching and rumbling off in a noxious cloud of smoke that hangs in the air long after the truck disappears. I cross the street and cautiously knock on Lieberman's door. He greets me coldly and explains that his friend is wont to get exited now and again and while I can spend the night I have to leave in the morning. This is fine with me though I don't know what the hell I am going to do. I decide to worry about it in the morning, which, as the clock in Lieberman's living room indicates, isn't too far off. I lie down on Lieberman's couch and listen as he pours another drink and the smoke from his final cigarette of the night drifts over me like gas from an adjacent battlefield as I, weary doughboy, try to capture a few hours sleep.

***

The next thing I know it is daylight and in Lieberman's kitchen a scrawled note instructing me to make sure the door is locked when I leave. I take quick stock of my mental state and decide that I am nowhere near ready to return home and in fact feel no desire *ever* to go back though of course I have to if for no other reason than simply to put my meager affairs in order, touch bases with a few friends, say goodbye, etc. I have no prospects anywhere but feel towards the East something similar to how I would feel about a used condom lying on the gutter. The East is old, crowded, polluted, played out. Jerome had used the right word, *effete*, though I am sure he had used it for connotations of femininity whereas I feel there is nothing effeminate about the East but rebel at its frantic, blood-sucking madness, the same old act endlessly and pointlessly reprised: not beating but *fucking* a dead horse. *The West is the best*, said mad Jim, and a lot of us believe it.

But there is good in the East as well. There is art, culture, painting, and sculpture. Van Gogh appeared to me one day at the Guggenheim Museum in one of his impressionist paintings and turned my life upside down. *So this is how he saw things*, I marveled, somewhat naively, mistaking a painting style for an actual perceptual reality. It didn't matter. I had taken the bait and swallowed it whole, desperately needing something, anything, as an anchor in a world spinning off its moorings. Van Gogh was the pagan tragic figure I was looking for, the patron saint of the lost and lonely, a figure with whom each had a private, special relationship.

So I read some books, read his letters and begin to draw, but never give it the passion or energy Vincent would have required at a bare minimum. I always seem to get sidetracked by one thing or another and my life follows its usual pattern of somnolence interrupted by anxious moments of effort that last until my eyelids became droopy all over again.

I find myself now in one of these anxious moments compounded by a big thrumming ache in my heart that is, I sense, though still painful, beginning to transform itself into something else that I don't fully recognize but feel might actually hint at something helpful, or at least different. Meeting Paul Avery, I decide, is auspicious, a signpost of moment and change. Whether or not I have anything more to do with him—and I am to see him at least once more in an hour's time at the Caffè Med—his appearance signals to me that whatever path I choose it is time to get onto it fairly quickly—no more farting around—though there are heavy lessons to be learned, I have no doubt. Perhaps I can rededicate myself to art, take up drawing and painting in a more serious way, but as soon as I think about this something like a feeling of doom clouds around me and the efforts of art seemed empty to the ultimate degree. Something larger bumps up against me with the soft menacing insistence of a nightmare and I know I will have to deal with it. Name it and deal with it.

I close the door and face the Berkeley morning—a marvelous fresh blue sky filled with promise (I'm still young!)—but any thoughts of starting the SAAB are squelched immediately as there is no exit from its space. I don't want to leave it in front of Lieberman's apartment, don't want to see him or Jerome again, but I will have to wait until later and hope that the car in front, a red Porsche convertible, will be gone and no other vehicle taking its place. In the meantime I will saunter around Telegraph in the warm spring sun soaking up the colors and hippie chicks, riding the swell of the bittersweet energy I am feeling, the glorious expanse and possibilities of life right here in the golden west heart of it all, at the same time one foot in the usual tar pit, the dread miasma, a tattered hero pulled this way in vernal wonder and stiff searching pecker, spun that way by his dragging foot, perhaps tarred and feathered for good measure (the foot, that is). An agreeable image, and an apt one.

In any case I head towards Telegraph, stiff pecker and all, bowsprit straight, through the gloriously uncertain beckoning waters of a warm Berkeley morning, even if one's anchor drags a bit. And warm and beckoning these Berkeley waters are, my head spinning, visual platter filled with *bonbons* of every imaginable variety.

Ah, Berkeley! For the moment at least, Lieberman and Jerome, my uncertain future, my *petites misères du cœur* are forgotten as any young relatively healthy male's would be under the salubrious circumstances, the colors everywhere like a soft slow motion explosion in a flower shop, acid yellows, saffron (*I'm just mad about saffron!*), apricot, lemon, flaming reds (commies everywhere!), crimsons, rose, pinks, malachite, turquoise, azure, aquamarine, cobalt, indigo, silver-swirling tie-dyed (*So many fan-tas-tic colors!*), emphatic, rapturous, ecstatic—a bearded young man wearing a green top hat and American flag overalls handing me a joint and a piece of halvah wrapped in wax paper, saying, "Peace brother," a forbidding group of leather-clad Afro'd Black Panthers talking loudly in the middle of the sidewalk so that I step onto the street to go around them, nodding at one who looks at me, a slightly chubby goateed fellow wearing a black beret and not-so-dark sunglasses that reveals a bit of friendliness behind them, nodding back, as it were, with his eyes, the music issuing from windows, doorways and storefronts, Dylan, Hendrix, Doors, Beatles, Stones, Ravi Shankar, Cream, Donovan, Simon & Garfunkel, The Byrds, a balding bearded man in an embroidered white Indian shirt with a lei of golden marigolds wearing thick black-framed glasses (is it Ginsberg?) playing a droning tambura-like tune on a harmonium, a stone-faced cop glaring at the world and his uniformed impotence, a clutch of bald, diaphanously saffron'd *Hare Krishnas* chanting joyous mantras banging their glittering tambourines, and all the girls, ah, the girls, everywhere coming at you like a tide of crystals and floating perfumed fruit, the wonder of them, the incense thick like honey, marijuana smoke, tribal musk, the head shops, seemingly one on each block with their oddly assertive, furtive vibe, the paraphernalia, the posters boldly proclaiming the new gospel: *Turn on, tune in, drop out! Fuck authority! Fuck anything that moves!* The record stores with their psychedelic Art Nouveau album covers and colorful swirling subliminalisms, all these head-spinning, retinal-snapping, soul-succoring vibes of affirmation and rebellion transmitted and received—where else?—on Telegraph, of course, and all this before 10 a.m., the time I am to meet Paul at the Caffè Med. Invigorating stuff, this, and when I am finished walking around and enter the café to see Paul and Carmen seated at the same table as the day before smiling warmly in greeting I am feeling pretty good indeed.

Over orange juice and bagels I relate my adventures at Lieberman's as my two new friends sit wide-eyed. Paul, it turns out, had read *Riders of the Purple Sage* in high school and liked it. Appalled and fascinated by my descriptions of Lieberman and Jerome they laugh uproariously when I tell them how Jerome had toppled over backwards in a red rage and how Lieberman ("Pinky") had leaped out of his chair and slapped his friend while I stood crouching with the chair in my hands. I embellish things a bit, as I usually do, especially for Carmen's sake. I am hopelessly ass-over-teakettle smitten with this incredible female whose full-throated laughter at my descriptions of Lieberman and Jerome are so stunningly sensual and womanly it is all I can do not to swoon directly away. Just as I was holding on for dear life in the face of Paul's brilliant speeding locomotive soliloquy the day before I am now dizzy with lust and wonder at his beautiful companion. The occasion finds her in a simple black cotton sweater whose top buttons lay carelessly undone opening into one of the many vistas of heaven a woman's body has to offer, a *barranca* into which I hopelessly fall. I try not to look and do a manageable if not flawless job. A certain amount is acceptable, even desired. I recall how ardently Paul had stared at the females less than twenty-four hours earlier and notice that he still looks, but not as brazenly. Carmen pays no attention to his occasional wandering gaze. For me every other woman in the café is obliterated.

After the revivifying saunter on Telegraph and the replenishing of my bodily fluids (Jerome! Jack D. Ripper!) with the Caffè Med's incomparable fresh orange juice along with a crunchy, richly buttered cranberry bagel, I am in as fine a fettle as I have been for some time, even though tired and having no idea what comes next in my life. The warmth, openness, agreeable clatter and youthful energy both cerebral and sensual of this particular restaurant, the salutary effects of the California sunshine, the buzz, still with me, of all the happenings of the last twenty-four hours, my two friends—all of this instills in me a renewed sense of resolve and at the same time a certain relish for the open road that lies ahead. I have had a taste of the West and I like it. I know I will be back, probably soon. My resolve is to focus once and for all on art and to unravel the various twists, loops and knots of my being, which will open the door to love and happiness, or so it is said. Paul and Carmen seem to me like some sort of ideal California bohemian couple and I am in awe of them. In truth I feel unworthy of their friendship and flattered by their interest in me. They are highly distinctive people and while in appearance might be considered ill matched once you spend some time with them you recognize their symmetry and strength as a couple. They look at me together and smile and the combined power of their attention is enough to make me blush. Paul seems about to say something, hesitates, then speaks.

"I have a proposition."

For a fleeting moment I fantasize about taking care of Carmen while Paul goes away on a long trip. This would of course mean staying at their house and inevitably leading to an affair that would resolve itself in open, Aquarian fashion (*why can't we go on as three?*) upon Paul's return. Suppressing this involuntary bit of irreverence in an instant my heart is nevertheless beating fast in response to Paul's "proposition," a heavily freighted word if there ever was one. What is he about to propose?

I raise my eyebrows and try to act nonchalant. "A proposition. Go ahead."

"I propose to accompany you on your journey back east. I'll pay for all the gas and promise not to drive you mad with my chatter. The only thing I ask is that you make a slight detour to Jacksonville."

"Jacksonville?"

"I mentioned that I am writing a book on relationships with 'the father'—father as parent, father as country, father, even, as god. More specifically, the problematic aspects of this relationship. More specifically yet, the problematic aspects of this relationship for men. I told you also that I've been estranged from my own father for number of years, eleven to be exact. As part of the writing of this book and also as part of my own healing process I've decided on an attempt at reconciliation with my father. It might make for a fitting last chapter, or epilogue. We can take our time going across or hurry along, whatever you like. I'd be partial to going slowly, seeing a few sights, but that's up to you. When we hit Jacksonville you can head north and I'll fly back after visiting with my father. Who knows, maybe I'll turn around and head back immediately. I hope not but it's a distinct possibility."

I like the idea at once. Paul is a great guy and interesting company. Plus, he will pay for gas. The SAAB will be a lot easier to start with two people. This development satisfies my need for an immediate plan, and not only that, seems a fitting way to inaugurate the next phase of my life, which I hope will be directed and fruitful. Paul is on a quest himself and is way ahead of me in terms of its formal purpose: He is writing a book: He has his subject matter. He is older than me, extremely intelligent and well educated—he had mentioned in passing the night before that he had gotten his BA in philosophy at Berkeley, a credential that impresses me. I had dropped out of college my senior year, convinced that the revolution was imminent and such bourgeois things as degrees would soon be irrelevant. I am still hoping for the revolution though it is beginning to seem less likely. Nixon's "silent majority" feels more substantial than mere rhetorical invention, an increasing weight that burdens us in various ways throughout the culture: the wretched war still going strong, the dark Machiavellians running the country as typified by Nixon himself, the continuing void created by the loss of Malcolm, Martin, RFK and so many others, the increasing visibility of Christian fundamentalism as a cultural and political force, the growing militarism and heightened surveillance of dissidents, the sobering and dismaying fact the country has re-elected the troublemaking sociopath (*four more years!*) in a landslide. We are beginning to feel outnumbered.

2

An exuberant push east > Mr. America's ignominious retreat > Lil-liputian attack > The saving charm of Rosalina > Katzenjammer Kids'
acid queries > The mighty Jambo

I spend the night at Paul and Carmen's, the next day occupied with getting ready for the trip. The following day, Rosalina refurbished, a heavy canvas tarp across the springs in the back seat, another piece of plywood over the springs of the passenger seat and a small green alabaster statue of Ganesh on the dashboard contributed by Carmen, forty-eight hours after announcing his "proposition," Paul is pushing the plucky girl down the block as I sit in the driver's seat, ignition on, transmission in second gear, foot depressing the clutch as we roll along rapidly picking up speed, propelled by the exuberant strength and energy of my newfound companion.

Let it be happily noted that the only thing depressed in little Rosalina this morning is the clutch as I have all but forgotten the heart pangs and humiliation caused by my hothouse South Carolina dizzydoll and I am filled with energy myself and the clear *tabula rasa* excitement of fresh beginnings. My brief sojourn in purgatory is over and actually had been by the time I hit Albuquerque heading west and felt for the first time with certainty that I was going to make it to California. I even feel that once back on the East Coast I might have another crack at old Lulu Delilah and to hell with the syrupy sticky business of the heart—be damned with it! And don't you know my master compass stirs with these thoughts, pointing east no doubt.

Paul has us up to about 12 mph and pushing like Deacon Jones ahold of some hapless blocker and I pop the clutch and the little car slows and then coughs into four-cylindered puttering blue smoke animation, Paul letting go, throwing his arms up in celebration and whooping as I brake, gun the tiny lawn-mower engine and raise my fist outside the driver's window. Carmen in jeans and denim work shirt watches in front of their house with folded arms and a small smile on her sensual Mediterranean face. She has packed a cooler with two loaves of homemade bread, a jar of honey, two jars of *Deaf Smith* crunchy peanut butter, three cans of brisling sardines, four cans of tuna, two packets of beef jerky, three bars of Swiss dark chocolate and six bottles of Guinness Stout: We are ready to go.

Paul wants to see the Watts Towers in LA and get there via Highway One and so after goodbyes to Carmen and a trip to the gas station for fuel and the cautionary check of tires, battery, oil and radiator, thinking of Antonio Vanzetti in Elizabeth shooting seagulls at the wrecking yard, recalling that he had wanted me to send him a postcard, which I purchase—a picture of seagulls flying above a trawler at Fisherman's Wharf—and then just like that we are over the dizzying bridge into the Monday-awakening city through Daly City, Pacifica and onto the highway.

My companion has been unusually subdued since leaving Berkeley but just south of Half Moon Bay he begins to talk about his father, who had quit his job teaching engineering at Loyola of Chicago in 1960 and moved his family to Jacksonville to take a job in a private firm. Paul was 15 at the time, unhappily torn from school and friends, already at loggerheads with his increasingly troubled father turned bitter and distant, much closer to his mother, a kind, gentle woman stricken by a mysterious respiratory disease, part of the reason for the family's move to Jacksonville. Paul's younger sister Anabel was twelve at the time. They were, and still are, very close. Paul's father, a brilliant man, had become increasingly restricted emotionally, unable to communicate with his children, much less show affection. He loved Paul's mother deeply but foundered in the face of her deteriorating condition, overwhelmed with fear and burdened with the demands of his new job. As a result Paul assumed much of the responsibility for the physical and emotional care of his mother.

A year after the move to Jacksonville Paul's mother died and his father's drinking grew worse. Having lost whatever closeness they'd had, Paul, extremely unhappy, and his father, grieving over the loss of his wife, drinking heavily and prey to violent rages, clashed incessantly and fiercely. At the end of February, 1962, before completing his junior year of high school, Paul left for San Francisco. His sister, with whom he had kept in touch over the ensuing years and who eventually moved to Philadelphia, stayed with her father, whose drinking continued but within limits that allowed him to function.

Little Rosalina functions too, purring like a kitten at the teat, claws gripping the road, the Pacific slipping by on our right, a massive sapphire expanse as flat as a parking lot, the sky a delicate robin's egg blue at the horizon. Around noon we arrive in Santa Cruz and decide to stop at The Catalyst, one of Paul's favorite spots, where he treats me to a roast beef sandwich and a glass of lemonade. The Catalyst, a cavernous building filled with hippies, is great, pleasing me as much as the Caffè Med. A scruffy elongated hippie straddles a tall wooden stool on stage and plays Dylan songs on a harmonica and guitar, sounding remarkably like the man himself.

I tell Paul about hitchhiking a couple of years earlier with a girl-friend on Interstate 89 in springtime New Hampshire, the nasally troubadour picking us up in a green Mustang top-down convertible with a big sprawling Mama Cass type in the passenger seat, both drinking Canadian ale in green bottles, driving from New London to Lebanon at 100 miles per hour as the wind pressed the skin of our faces back, our hair lashing like little whips, the world an emerald blur. He never said a word and hardly looked at us—just picked us up and dropped us off. Paul listens distractedly, his mind captured by the hippie chicks floating by like so many lissome angels, their voices in sweet chorus echoing from the ceiling and drifting to earth like flower petals or butterflies.

"I love this place," says Paul. "Let's go."

***

A few minutes later driving south on Pacific Avenue, Paul at the wheel, Rosalina pulls to the right and the thump-thump-thump of a flat tire announces itself, the mocking leaden sound of entropy, of hope and progress deflated, of suddenly realizing that I have not checked the spare (all the way cross-country without knowing its condition), flashing back to the first leg of my hegira and the pin-hole in the radiator on the godforsaken Jersey Turnpike and the an-gel in black, Antonio Vanzetti, shooting at the wheeling seagulls.

"Shit."

Paul pulls over and we get out, dumbly looking at the flat, scratching our heads, balls, ears, scanning the horizon for divine in-tervention. I dread opening the trunk because I am certain the spare will be flat and sure as hell it is, so much so that the inner circum-ference of the tire pushes easily away from the rim and no gas station in sight, just an empty lot, a few homes with some kids outside playing and looking at us suspiciously.

This turn of events apparently invigorates Paul who begins springing up and down on the balls of his feet as if preparing to take the field for the opening kick-off. Unexpected car troubles always depress me and this instance is no different. I have been known to walk away from crippled vehicles and not look back, but this is not one of those occasions—a little too far from home for one thing and for another of course there is Paul. Besides, I like my diminutive Rosalina. Though bent, beaten and stripped bare she is a doughty little vehicle and I feel as if we have forged a pact between us. We have made it to California and we are going to make it back—together. Then she might be ready for Valhalla, but no sooner.

Paul continues to jump up and down like a human signal flare, barking "OK!" at the apex of each jump as if with one final spring he might take flight in search of a decent spare. I am a little taken aback by his enthusiastic response to this minor misfortune and reflect that this might be one of the first things that Paul is teaching me—not just a reflexive energetic response to adversity but an *enthusiastic* energetic response, even a joyful one. Indeed, his attitude is infectious. I don't know if it was Paul's beloved Mencius, or Confucius, or what Chinese sage it was who said that opportunity arises from trouble, but maybe it is this awareness that fires Paul's determined bouncing.

I had noticed a few minutes earlier that the two kids who had been playing in the yard of the house we are parked in front of, a white two-story Betty Crocker affair with garage, bracketed by a couple of large sycamore trees, had run inside and I can see someone peeking at us from behind a curtain, which makes me a bit nervous especially as there is a flagpole in front from which dangles a limp American flag. Though only a few blocks from The Catalyst I sense we are in enemy territory. Bad enough that we are in a beat-up car pulled over to the side of the road, but our appearance, inno-cent enough in our own minds, invariably conjures up associations with the Manson family for the sort of people with Betty Crocker houses and flagpoles in their front yards.

Sure enough, as Paul and I discuss options for dealing with our predicament—the most sensible being one of us walking back to The Catalyst and finding out where the nearest garage is—a Santa Cruz police car (a Santa Cruiser?) turns the corner, pulls up be-hind us with its lights flashing and a young cop as straight and stiff as the flagpole in the yard and almost as tall, gets out and strides towards us behind silver aviator sunglasses and starched, sharply-creased uniform, everything about him razor-edged spit and polish, thick creaking leather and hard glittering steel, his rigid unsmiling face as sharp as the creases in his pants. I look over at the house and the two kids and a man whom I assume to be their father come out-side and stand beneath the flagpole, the guy with his arms folded righteously across his chest, the kids gawking and excited, the three of them looking like Mississippi crackers at a lynching. It is small so-lace at the moment to reflect on the good fortune of not being black. The officer, close enough that we can read his name on the rectan-gular chrome-plated nameplate pinned neatly above the department badge—B. Nichols—close enough to detect his smell, a mixture of Murphy's Oil Soap, leather and peppermint, towers over us.

"Which of you is the owner of this vehicle?" he asks, his hard-edged granite features impassive as Rushmore, the voice deep, nasal and monotone. There is something scary about this guy, something that smacks of the technician in a dank cellar room with a chair, bare light bulb and curious gadgets hanging from the walls. This is a guy who doesn't allow his emotions to get in the way of his work. I see the alcoholic parents, the older brother who had committed sui-cide at seventeen and him, the star high school athlete who played with a cold, rigid intensity, the submissive girlfriend since tenth grade now his timid wife, the shame and fury in a dense icy ball inside his gut, a guy who follows orders even if it means arresting his parents. Officer Nichols, in short, is not one to be messed with.

I look past him and see that the children and their old man have moved a little closer, the kids now very quiet and serious as if for the first time seeing the rope being removed from the old rusted pickup, passed from one set of white hands to another, sensing the heightened anticipation of the crowd, inching closer in the dark turpentine woods. Well this is one Negro not really inclined to let the noose slip over his head without a question or two. I look directly at officer Nichols' sunglasses and see my distorted reflection, all nose, cheeks and forehead, the usual four or five days' growth of beard, goatee, an unsavory character whose appearance marks him guilty before uttering even a syllable in self-defense. In fact this is clearly one of those situations where each word deviating from the utterly simple negative or affirmative followed by the obligatory honorific results in a corresponding raising of the temperature in the oven of the law. Fully aware that my own and Paul's goose rests in this very oven, I proceed anyway. Since when does a flat tire warrant an aggressive flashing-light response from the local protector of persons, property and constitutional rights? Foolish question. Vestigial indignation. Nevertheless, one speaks.

"Is there some kind of a problem, officer?"

"I repeat. Which one of you is the owner of this vehicle?"

Suddenly to my surprise and alarm Paul moves towards the cop, who tenses, regarding him coldly. "Officer. Listen. We're law-abiding citizens who've had the misfortune of—"

"Stop right there," says the cop, raising his left palm at Paul and placing his right hand on his holster. The man on the lawn takes a step forward, motioning for his children to stay put. A breeze kicks up, stirring the flag. An elderly couple in a red Lincoln slowly drives by, staring. "Both of you turn around and put your hands against the car. Now."

Paul and I look at each other, our expressions mirror images, a combination of apprehension, outrage and helplessness. I am sure officer Nichols will search the car and I wonder if anything is inside that I don't know about—a joint or roach left behind from the previous owner's tenure or something Paul has stashed without telling me. Maybe he has something in his backpack. We turn around and put our hands against the car in the ritual posture of subjugation and humiliation that proclaims your guilt and helplessness, that you are, effectively, with your rump to authority and your hands immobilized, taking it up the ass and you had better grin and bear it otherwise sterner measures will be employed, make no mistake. This is how it is most of the time anyway cop or no cop and an extra dose of bitter medicine meted out to those who get too frisky or take it upon themselves to ask too many questions, all of this falling under the heading of "knowing your place," we being made to understand ours in no uncertain terms as B. Nichols pats us down and, determining that I am the "owner of the vehicle," stares long and hard at my license and registration as if his intense scrutiny might transform these documents into palpable forgeries, grounds for making our day even more unpleasant. He finds nothing untoward and hands my papers back matter-of-factly. Then he commands me to open the trunk. Paul, fuming under the indignities, can no longer contain himself, "Officer, there are no grounds for a search. We've done nothing wrong. We don't have any drugs. If having a flat tire warrants treating us like criminals and searching our vehicle then the United States is in worse shape than I thought it was. What you are doing is a clear violation of our Fourth Amendment rights. I'm sure you know that."

"Requesting the owner of a vehicle to open the trunk does not constitute a search, sir. However, if the owner refuses the reasonable request of a police officer, that does constitute grounds for suspicion, legal search and possible arrest. Now, sir," he turns and looks at me, his face inscrutable and stony. "If you will please open the trunk." It is pointless and foolhardy to argue with this robot and I look at Paul trying to communicate my extreme desire that he hold his indignation in check. Paul is so agitated I fear the cop will take this as a sign of guilt or use it as an excuse to pull some shit. I walk to the back of Rosalina and open the trunk, which has nothing but dust, lug wrench, jack and flat spare. The cop stoops and peers in, his nostrils flaring as if sniffing for drugs, then stands straight, looking beyond me. "Are you in possession of any illegal substances? Drugs? Contraband of any sort?" I reply in the negative. Perhaps he feels the need to ask these questions as a cover for his blatant harassment, though likely he has responded to a call from Mr. Righteous American who in turn had responded to an alert from his fearful children, themselves conditioned by an insular rigid view of the world reinforced by family and an authority of which B. Nichols is an integral component, the muscle, a neat little self-perpetuating, self-regulating, self-protecting, self-satisfied mollusk-shelled circle, Nixon and Agnew's "silent majority."

***

The cop's officially proclaiming his legal mission as a search for drugs results in an aura of legitimacy that descends upon this mean-spirited charade like a shroud. Because of our appearance, age and the condition of the car we are automatically under suspicion. There is a certain logic in this and combined with the tremendous weight of the law we feel a terrible impotence—in spite of the clear unfairness and questionable legality of the cop's actions—all the more humiliating with virtuous onlookers and passersby regarding our plight with silent satisfaction. The wind picks up and the flag in front of the house rolls and reveals its colors. The youngest child, a girl with blond curls and dressed in a pink sweat suit, leaves to go inside and her older brother steps alongside his father who places a protective arm around his shoulders. Officer Nichols moves to the driver's door and orders me to open it, which I do as casually as possible. He bends his tall frame at the waist and looks in and I am thankful for Rosalina's diminutive size because it is obviously difficult for B. Nichols to insert himself and look around without discomfort. As such his examination is cursory at best and I breathe a silent sigh of relief when he pulls out despite the fact that I don't think there's anything incriminating inside the car.

A minute earlier I had noticed a gray pickup with two teenage boys inside drive slowly by checking out the situation. Now as the cop withdraws from the car and slowly straightens himself—as if suffering from an old back injury—the truck drives by again, the boys this time staring less obviously, playing it a little cooler as officer Nichols regards them impassively. I have the feeling they know each other. Meanwhile Paul drifts closer to the man and his son attempting to engage them in conversation, to no avail. It's unfortunate, I hear him saying to the two of them, that law-abiding citizens experiencing an ordinary misfortune should be treated like common criminals. He'd been raised to believe that America is better than that: instead of being objects of harassment and suspicion travelers experiencing trouble in America were supposed to be the recipients of kindness and generosity. He is feeding them a line like nobody's business I am sure and probably doing it mostly for the sake of the poor brainwashed kid, conditioned to fear strange people like us. Forget the old hidebound prick of a father but maybe he can plant a seed in the kid.

Anyway I sure as hell never heard anything about Americans being particularly kind and helpful towards those experiencing ordinary distress. The myth maybe but rarely the reality. Americans are *supposed* to be that way, the friendly open people, the smiling WWII GI dispensing chocolate bars and chewing gum to Italian urchins, but since adopting some of the lineaments of the counter-culture I have seen a different side of the smiling friendly ordinary Americans that Nixon talks about with so much studied sincerity. At the beginning of my junior year in college I sprouted a goatee and started wearing wire-rimmed glasses, which apparently possessed properties that enabled me to perceive aspects of people's personalities I hadn't noticed before. Putting on those glasses—and maybe sprouting the facial hair to go along with them—announced at least superficially a set of values and a certain political stance that presumably accompanied them that was apparently the equivalent of showing these silent righteous Americans a picture of Jane Fonda giving Patrice Lumumba a blow job.

The man and his son, obviously uncomfortable with Paul's attempts at communication, shift their feet, the boy looking up at his father for some kind of clue, the father in turn staring at the cop as if in silent entreaty to rescue him from this brazen fiend whose actual intentions no doubt are to ritually sacrifice him and his wife and sodomize his children in the name of Timothy Leary, Charles Manson and Ho Chi Minh.

"Step back to the car, sir," says officer Nichols to the obvious relief of Mr. America and his son. Paul turns and walks back to the car muttering about the unfairness of the situation and the irrational fear that grips so many of his countrymen. To my surprise the cop tells the man and his son to return to their house, that there are no problems here, everything under control, etc. and they meekly walk away, striking such a pathetic posture that I actually feel sorry for them. The poor fucker can't even watch his tax dollars at work from the sanctuary of his own lawn standing under an American flag. I notice the gray pickup has pulled over a block behind us and then as if someone has flipped a switch officer Nichols seems to lose interest and after a few more questions and in essence telling us to get out of town before sunset, folds his long frame into his cruiser, turns off the flashers and rumbles slowly away.

"Sonofabitch!" says Paul tensely. "That guy is an asshole. We might as well be Black driving in the South. And that guy with his kids! Jesus!"

At that moment the pickup with the two teenagers pulls alongside and the kid on the passenger side, a stocky-looking guy with a crew cut and dark-rimmed glasses sticks his head out the window. "Are you guys okay? What did that pig want? We know the guy. He's a major fucking asshole."

"You can say that again," says Paul going through his backpack to fish out a tin containing a pouch of Bugler and some rolling papers, an aspect I haven't seen before. A cigarette sounds good about now. I smoke about one a month. Paul puts the tin on Rosalina's hood and begins to roll a cigarette and the kids turn to whisper to one another in the truck no doubt about the obvious.

***

Their names are Jake and Terry and right away they ask if we want to get high with them—killer stuff, they say, homegrown. We politely decline, especially with the lingering scent of officer Nichols in the air. We ask if they know where we can get our tires repaired and Jake, the stocky bespectacled one, offers to fix them at his uncle's garage. They park the truck in the spot officer Nichols has vacated and descend on the SAAB like an Indy pit crew, using the truck's heavy-duty jack to keep little Rosalina elevated while the repairs are effected. This is a huge implement that seemingly could lift a tank and my little Rosalina floats in the air like a petite majorette on an elephant's trunk. I volunteer to stay with the car while Paul goes with the boys to fix the tires and they throw the flats into the truck's bed and tumble in, Paul between them, driving off in a roaring tire-squealing commotion, exactly the thing I fear in front of the house of the freshly-emasculated Righteous American sent skulking with his son by the stone-faced officer Nichols.

I peer nervously for any signs of moving curtains and hostile eyes, wondering how the man will react but there is nothing. A stillness seals the neighborhood like plastic wrap, no voice of man, fowl, beast or machine ruffling the atmosphere. Rosalina, with her front wheel missing, the monster jack thrusting her up and over into the air, the desolate condition of her interior, looks like a candidate for the junk pile and I think of Antonio Vanzetti's clucking disbelief in her ability to make it cross country let alone negotiate a return trip. I have to admit it indeed looks like a dubious proposition and from the perspective of the children and their father I can see how my car, judged by the usual standards, might be cause for some alarm. I doubt it would have made much difference if we had emerged wearing gray flannel suits and carrying briefcases. The car is enough to do us in.

I figure I have about an hour's wait before Paul and the boys come back with the tires nicely sealed and inflated so I take my battered copy of *The Wretched of the Earth* from the glove compartment. I've been working on it for two years. I am on page twelve. At six pages a year I will finish the book in fifty-two years. I read the same sentence about eight times (of course it is Sartre's preface—maybe things will get better once I get into the actual text) and find myself staring up at a cloud formation resembling a dog's head that turns into a trailing pair of Wile E. Coyote ears and then into a fairly startling replication of the stripes on the American flag. It must be the jet stream or something up there because down here Mr. America's flag dangles like a dishtowel. I think about Mr. America. He looks older than me by about eight or ten years which would make him young for Korea but right at the most ideologically impressionable age during the McCarthy inquisitions. Whatever the demerits of my own upbringing rabid anti-communism was not one of them, being reared in an atmosphere of laid-back New Dealism and post-war triumphalism with its calm imperial assumptions. Communism was aberrant and possibly dangerous but McCarthyism was an embarrassment, like a pile of sludge on a fine new carpet. I was too young for McCarthy but not immune to the general phobia and brainwashing and until the late sixties never thought much in a critical way about the role of my own government in the suicidal *pas de deux* referred to as the "cold war."

For me it has all unraveled with Vietnam and the ludicrous "domino theory," staring into the faces of so obviously mendacious butt-ugly politicians and protectors of the republic's honor and safety like LBJ, McNamara and Hoover to name but a few of the more noteworthy. Now somebody like my Mr. America here looks upon those faces and listens to their words in feverish and trusting obedience believing in every forked utterance and roused to a fearful angry pitch because of them. As Dylan puts it all good ordinary Americans are only pawns in the cynical games of the masters which to me makes Mr. America a not unsympathetic figure, his life filled with the trials, frustrations and suffering common to all lives. Surely he loves his children, works hard, lends a helping hand now and then, adheres to the usual loyalties, is relatively honest. The failing is perhaps that these good Americans like their counterparts in Nazi Germany are all-too-willing to allow their rulers to decide life and death matters of policy and state for them, weakly acquiescing in the face of this authority in the name of an unquestioning obedience and ingrained feelings of inferiority, all disturbingly Germanic in my mind which may explain why we so readily call some of them Nazis. Ratchet the tension a few notches and we with our deflated, dilapidated vehicle are subject to more than mere harassment, which naturally complicates my feelings about Mr. America. What is the right thing to do in this situation? Fancying myself something of a revolutionary, which I do, shouldn't I knock on his door and introduce myself? Show him that I am not quite the monster he assumes I am? Try in some way to "explain" myself? To share our fears and opinions and endeavor to humanize ourselves in the eyes of the other? What would I say? "Ah, excuse me, sir, I just wanted to introduce myself and to let you know that though we differ in ways that seem poles apart, underneath it all we are exactly the same." Of course. Absolutely. But I don't really have the balls or the energy for this is the hardest work of all, breaking down barriers, trying to communicate. The difficulty is letting go of the desire for others to see things our way. Ultimately I have to admit that I am every inch the righteous American he is. Does this mean that I have to compromise my beliefs to reach an "accommodation" with him? If he is pro-war for example am I obligated in fairness to grant a certain validity to his opinions even if I think our government's policies are murderously despicable? My obligation is, I decide, to try to *understand* his opinions and grant them validity as originating from the sacred ground of his person. And then go from there. I have the hope that people are essentially decent as Anne Frank touchingly believed and all that is needed is a good dose of consciousness. But how is this consciousness to be delivered? And isn't it the height of conceit to presume myself the bearer of such golden fruit?

***

I am awakened from these ruminations by the slamming of the front door as the two kids step out onto the lawn eyeing me and at the same time I see one of the living room curtains pull slightly aside. I replace the book in the glove compartment and return their glances warily as they've re-emerged from their home in disturbingly different fashion than that in which they had fled at our appearance. The boy, who is about eight, wears a real WWII Army helmet that wobbles on his head like a salad bowl, chinstrap buckled, and carries a toy rifle slung over his shoulder. A brown canteen, another Army issue, rides his hip like a giant polyp. He looks like he means business. His sister, a couple of years younger, still wearing her pink sweat suit, looks less certain of her mission but her weapon, a small bow and a handful of rubber-tipped arrows, alarms me more than her brother's toy rifle. If I am to be the object of an assault I have more to fear from her missiles than the boy's auditory simulations though his imagination as a male and elder will be of more murderous intent.

He leans over his sister and imparts what are apparently instructions as she looks over at me several times ominously nodding her head as he speaks. If this is going to be a battle I should make some plans of my own but I can't think of anything other than preparing myself for the psychic onslaught of small children acting out my destruction and possibly some sort of dignified retreat if things get too close, although I don't know what this can possibly entail. I feel apprehensive and hostile and all my sympathetic feelings towards the kids' father and thoughts of communication fly out the window. Does this sonofabitch countenance his children coming out for ritual play killing because I am here? Does he get off on it? Encourage it? Surely he didn't tell them to do it. No, likely it is the boy acting on his own conditioning and instincts and also as surrogate for his emasculated father. Just what does the little fucker have in mind?

They seem to arrive at a plan and the boy unsnaps the canteen from its holster and takes a swig and then hands it to his sister who carefully puts down her weapon and with both hands takes hold of the object that is as big as her head, wipes its mouth on her sweat shirt and swallows, almost gagging, spilling a good deal of the stuff down her neck. It seems to be red, maybe Kool-Aid. She hands the canteen back to her brother and picks up her weapon. The boy takes a great deal of time and care holstering the canteen. They exchange a few more serious words, glance at me and go in opposite directions, taking up positions behind the sycamore trees at either end of the house. As long as they stay behind the trees I am all right because I can see them and it is certainly too far for the girl's arrows to reach.

My biggest fear is something happening at close quarter for then not only will the arrows be in range so will their little hate-filled psyches and faces, a distressing prospect for which I have no answer. The boy unslings his rifle and gets down on his belly, peering around the tree and lining me up in his sights. It is hard to tell if he is aiming at my head or chest. Probably chest because that is what they teach. The girl fits an arrow into the small bow and in an archer's stance draws back the string and aims at me. There is a moment of quiet tension. I feel like a large insect, a cicada or cockroach, trapped in the web of two small deadly spiders working in concert. If I stay perfectly still they might not shoot but any movement will vibrate the web and their venomous darts will sting me through, and so I remain motionless for a few moments leaning against Rosalina's rear fender, the apex of a deadly triangle in a kind of suspended animation. But the tension is too ridiculous and a kind of indignant absurd anger takes me over. Resisting the urge to battle-charge one of them (Whom would I charge? The boy, of course) I take a step forward, as if a feint, which elicits a kind of ululation from the boy and a second later a small rubber-tipped arrow arches into the air and falls harmlessly about half-way between me and the girl, followed by a volley of rifle fire coming from the other end of the house, a lethal panoply of explosive sounds employing the full range of the young patriot's diminutive but murderous vocal apparatus from harsh soft palate semi automatic rounds to full-bore glottal staccato machine gun fire to plosive heavy artillery shells, more than enough firepower to annihilate a platoon of VC, NVA, Russians, Chinese, Cubans, Black Panthers, Hell's Angels, Jews, Arabs, homosexuals, hippies—whatever despised target I represent—coming from this one tiny concentrated source of—what? Fear? Hatred? Patriotism? Good old American fun? Between rounds he calls out cryptic signals presumably communicating with his sister who launches two more arrows that land a little bit closer. I am reminded of mortar fire and how the gunners "walk" their rounds closer to the target. "Tango Yankee Lima! Tango Yankee Lima! Do you read? Roger! Murdoch! A-Seventy-Five! A-Seventy-Five! Air Support! Air Support!" The boy yells into an imaginary walkie-talkie, on his back while doing so, then rolls onto his belly and resumes firing.

Meanwhile the girl crawls forward to retrieve her three spent arrows, a look of desperate purpose on her soft cherubic face, blond curls bouncing with the effort, her round little bottom raised in a posture, I reflect, likely recapitulated in less warlike pursuits ten years or so hence. She is a cute little thing, no doubt about it. She grabs the arrows and scrambles back to the tree on all fours, her little fanny bouncing provocatively. Curse me. If daddy has the binocs out and sees me staring at his baby's rear end he will dust off the Mauser and finish me off for good, no question.

The boy increases the level of fire—as I say at a murderous pitch to begin with—probably covering his sister's scramble for her arrows, and as she reaches the tree he stops firing and scampers like a troglodyte around the back of the house and seconds later takes up with his sister behind the tree and begins discussing the next round of attacks. They have softened me up with the artillery and now it is time for some kind of assault. In fact they *have* softened me for I feel anxious and more than a little angry at these kids, ludicrous to let them get to me I know, but we are looking at something a little deeper than mere play here. I am an object of fear and hatred and if I am in say, Randy Creek, Arkansas and have somehow managed to survive the encounter with the cop then daddy and the kids will see to it that I am well and proper cared for. No, daddy won't be inside peering through the synthetic curtains while his children pop the *hippeh* with plastic guns and rubber-tipped arrows. So while I can be thankful for longitude and latitude and their effects on social interactions I am acutely aware that it is only a matter of inhibition—that at the bottom of things lay the same murderous intentions.

***

I look down the road in the direction the pickup has gone and long for its reappearance. Reinforcements. Rescue from the young Americans who have run off behind the house and then moments later appear again hurrying along in opposite directions, the girl hiding behind the tree formerly occupied by her brother who runs through the yard of the house to my right and crosses the street disappearing in a wooded lot behind me. A pincer movement. They have me surrounded. The boy whoops from the woods, the girl answering. I fold my arms and lean back against Rosalina trying to look unconcerned. I decide to keep my eye on the girl as she wields the more dangerous weapon. Her new redoubt is closer and though likely still too far for her arrows to reach they can now come close enough that I am obliged to increase my level of vigilance. Gauging the length of shots from her former spot I estimate that now the arrows will land about fifteen feet away but an extra strong or wind-assisted shot will come closer and might even hit me, a breach of space with disturbing implications. Sure enough she launches an arrow that flies much higher than her previous efforts, floating lazily in my direction, almost in slow motion, for a long pregnant moment suspended in its apogee like Kubrick's thighbone-as-space-craft-as-child's-rubber-tipped arrow and landing scarcely five feet away, within spitting distance.

This is followed by more war yelps from the woods. I am now faced with a dilemma. I can seize the arrow—depleting her ammunition by one-third—but by doing so risk an anguished communication to headquarters (daddy) that the bad person outside is stealing her toys, which might really land me in Randy Creek, or I can let the arrow be, hoping that it is close enough to me that she might not have the nerve to dash in and retrieve it. I decide to let it be for the moment, a tactical decision in keeping with my larger strategic design, which is to hold my position with as much dignity as possible and to pull out as soon as reinforcements arrive. As I think this a commotion and familiar sound effects behind me signal a resumption of the boy's attack as he charges out of the woods helmet flopping, canteen bouncing like a buffalo's testicle tied to his waist and assumes a full-frontal stance, his face contorted in a Richard Widmark snarl, cutting loose with as ferocious an enfilade as he can muster and then hitting the ground. At the same time the girl fires another arrow that smacks against Rosalina's front fender above the empty tire well. Then with a studied calm she steps out from behind the tree, takes two steps forward, kneels like some wicked little Artemis and fires an arrow that speeds directly towards me. This latest shot is not of the lazy arcing variety as the two before but travels a lethal line parallel to the ground shoulder high and after an amazed millisecond watching the approaching projectile I jump aside just before it hits Rosalina's rear window. None of the arrows has stuck. At the same time as the arrow hits Rosalina's window I sense something behind me and I turn to see the boy letting go with a baseball-sized dirt bomb that tumbles towards the car's roof, every detail standing out clearly, the chunk of brown earth floating, turning slowly, small pieces flying off, gray pebbles packed like shrapnel, the boy pitched forward in a follow-through balancing on his left foot, the huge brown helmet thrown down over his eyes. My heart sinks as I follow the trajectory of the bomb, for now I will have to respond. This is an actual physical assault with harmful intent and I am hamstrung by the age and size of my adversaries and by the fact that I am on their turf and daddy backing his troops like the implied threat of a nuclear arsenal.

The bomb explodes on Rosalina's roof, a shower of dirt flying over my head as I duck behind the car. I pop up to yell at the boy only to see another dirt grenade heading in my direction causing me to duck again and with my attention thus directed the girl races up behind me and seizes one of the three arrows she's fired. The second bomb hits the side of the car just below the window. I'm looking at real damage here, trapped in some kind of pitiful-giant syndrome. I can leave but the kids might vandalize my car, its ragged appearance encouraging them to further mayhem. An arrow whizzes by my head and clatters in the street.

That's it. I go onto the road and retrieve the missile—the boy running back into the woods—and then return to Rosalina and pick up the other arrow. Now unless there are more inside I have two-thirds of the little creep's ammunition. I look at the pink pussycat standing behind the tree. "If you stop shooting at me I'll give these back to you," I say, holding the two arrows in my outstretched left hand. The girl turns and runs into the house. A moment later daddy exits the front door and strides towards me, his daughter walking behind him glaring hatefully. He is a hostile-looking fucker, growing more formidable as he approaches, putting me in mind of the kid who pinned me in 30 seconds in my first high school wrestling match, stocky rather than tall, short brown hair, red face, some kind of motorcycle T-shirt, pale blue jeans, boots. He comes right up and puts his face close to mine. "Give my daughter back her arrows," he says, his breath smelling of beer. The boy is out of the woods and positions himself next to his sister, holding his rifle with his left hand, his helmet pushed back on his head, a regular Alan Ladd. The three of them stare at me. Closer to Randy Creek by the moment.

"Look," I say, looking the pumped-up fellow in the eye, "my car has a flat tire. It's getting fixed right now. The spare was flat too. We'll be out of here soon. I was just standing here and your children attacked me. Your son's been hitting my car with dirt bombs and your daughter's been shooting arrows at me. For no reason." I look at the girl. "Here are your arrows but please don't shoot at me any more." I hand the girl her arrows and she takes them sullenly. I return my gaze to the man, whose attitude seems a shade less threatening. Maybe he figures his kids have done enough damage. Hoping to capitalize on this I press forward. "I'm sorry if I've caused any trouble. My friends should be back any minute and we'll be out of here. I should've checked the spare but I didn't. We're on our way cross country." The man squints and moving only his eyeballs looks at Rosalina, then back at me.

"Cross country? In that?"

I have him. Rosalina has a way of eliciting sympathy, incredulity and amusement even in the hardest of hearts, excepting of course the law. Whatever suspicion and hostility he harbors towards Paul and me is mitigated by the sheer homeliness of my little car and the absurdity of it making such a long trip. That along with grudging admiration (*"But hey, a guy's got balls..."*) for the lunatic captain of such a rickety vessel. Either that or pity.

"Well, it made it from New York and now I'm on the way back. Although as you can see we haven't gotten off to a very good start."

The man looks at the car closely and shakes his chunky head, a bit of a smile softening his features.

"You must have a guardian angel watching over you." This is what Antonio Vanzetti had said, only a bit more colorfully. "A SAAB, eh? My sister used to have one of those things. Put about 300,000 miles on it. Sorry about the kids. They get a little carried away sometimes. Hey, do you mind if I take a peek at the engine?"

I go around to the driver's side and pull the cable, the hood lurching forward in its peculiar way. The guy pushes it open and smiles when he sees the tiny engine. "Ha! Look at that little sucker! I couldn't even run my lawnmower with that thing. How fast does this go?"

"About forty uphill and eighty down. Sixty on the straights."

Now he is smiling openly. "Well I'll be damned. You really *are* crazy!" He looks at me appraisingly for a moment and his expression assumes an attitude that seems almost sympathetic—and something more, a hint of wistfulness, perhaps. "Hey, good luck with your trip."

I hadn't been aware my sanity had been in question but reflect perhaps that's just the way it is with folks like Mr. America about my type and the hell with it. I probably *am* crazy to drive cross-country in Rosalina. In fact, thinking about my mental condition when I left Long Island, I have to agree. He sticks out his hand and we shake, one economical downward motion of the sort that communicates truce and a certain respect. Something about Rosalina and me has gotten through. As for my part any show of compassion or friendliness from one of Nixon's silent majority is like a celestial choir opening up in full-throated aureate splendor. I feel like crying and hugging the guy but of course I honor the formalities. There's some goodness in him obviously and maybe he acknowledges something in me. Hell, I even like the kids and I smile and say goodbye as they walk away, though just before the three of them enter the house the boy turns and levels his rifle at me, for which he receives a smart cuff on the back of his helmet from daddy.

***

So just to sit and wait. Maybe there is hope after all. Maybe my notions about "getting through," communicating on a basic human level, are not so ridiculous. I realize that my feelings about human nature fluctuate too wildly. What I need is some kind of leveling outlook. Just what the hell is "human nature" anyway? It is obvious that much of what motivates people's behavior is ignorance and fear. Exacerbating this are the cynical machinations of those at the top, the ones making the rules, whose interests are served by increasing the divisions among the rest of us.

I retrieve *The Wretched of the Earth* from the glove compartment and try reading but keep sliding across the words. But then my eyes hit a sentence and engage as if gears slipping into place. *"Our Machiavellianism has little purchase on this wide-awake world that has run our falsehoods to earth one after the other. The settler has only recourse of one thing: brute force, when he can command it; the native has only one choice, between servitude or supremacy."* There is nothing subtle or ennobling about white colonialism. So much historical slaughter by the whites. My own country has assumed the blood-soaked colonial mantle from Europe and is killing Vietnamese wholesale. Try talking about this stuff with Mr. America. Colonialism. Machiavelli. Capitalism. Racism. Pawns in their game. There has to be a way to get through—but how?

Now around the corner comes the gray pickup, the three companions crammed in front, all smiling broadly. My spirits rise immediately. On the road again. The truck careens up behind Rosalina and they spill out like Keystone Kops, Jake and Terry retrieving the tires fairly bursting with new air, rolling them towards Rosalina. Their eyes glisten and together they smell like they have been dancing around a bonfire of marijuana.

"Sam!" Paul pumps my hand and claps me on the shoulder. "How the hell are you?"

The boys and Paul are ripped, no question, and in great infectious spirits. Paul has really hit it off with Jake and Terry and after his enthusiastic warm hello he informs me *sotto voce* what great guys they are. I agree. They are wild, funny, wisecracking and immensely likeable.

They are also physical opposites—Jake, stocky, bespectacled, with dark buzz-cut hair, Terry, well over six feet, long blond hair, all arms and legs flying in different directions. As controlled and economical as Jake's movements are, Terry's are reckless and a bit alarming, yet they work together as poetry, a natural choreography that comes from a long history of god-knows-what escapades together and obviously a shared love of working on cars. Their non-stop high decibel chatter and enthusiasm along with the breakneck speed at which they operate evokes an on-the-edge roller coaster giddiness in me simply from watching. They make me smile and laugh outright, as they do Paul. I secretly dub them the Katzenjammer Kids. They seem to get a kick out of us as well, amused at Rosalina and impressed with the craziness of her cross-country round-trip. They have us pegged as head-in-the-clouds hippie intellectuals, warmly addressing Paul as Lao Tzu (obviously he has laid some Lao Tzu on them) and asking me twice if I have any acid. I tell them no both times but talk about Timothy Leary's visit to my college, dressed in white Gandhian homespun sitting cross-legged on the stage telling us to "turn on, tune in and drop out" while his sandalwood incense suffused the auditorium. They have tripped numerous times and say it's easy to get acid in Santa Cruz. They don't believe I have only dropped acid a few times and Paul never, though he has ingested much psilocybin. They fill us in on the Righteous American, whom I now like, and officer Nichols. RA's name is Mike Garrity. He works for PG&E and his wife died of cancer six months ago. I am relieved, hearing this sad news, that we have exchanged at least a few friendly words. His wife was an elementary school teacher and Mike has been drinking a lot since her death. Officer Nichols ("Brad") on the other hand is a bona fide "prick," a former high school athlete—I was right on that one—turned cop, about six years their senior, which would put him close to my age. He is married (right on that one too, though they don't know if she is a childhood sweetheart) and has a small child, a girl. He has pulled them over "about sixteen times." Santa Cruz is a small town, says Terry.

Jake and Terry have the tire on in a minute flat and Rosalina is four-to-the-ground ready to go. It is nearly four o'clock. The boys want us to stay and go to a beach party with them this evening, ample dope, numerous kegs, barbecue and lots of really fine chicks. I am unsure but Paul's enthusiasm convinces me. Why not? We are in no particular hurry and I am amenable to Paul's idea of letting things take us where they may. We get in the car and follow them to the beach, where we will hang out and wait for the party. Paul, in almost manic spirits, talks incessantly as I keep a wary eye out for Officer Nichols. The boys pass a joint back and forth as they drive ahead of us at a slow pace. "Look at them, Sam. There's a real purity there. And what does this country do? It fucking grinds them up and spits them out. Jake is going to enlist in the Marines like his father before him. Terry wants no part of the service but thinks he'll be drafted and go to Vietnam. He's waiting on the lottery." And how did Paul avoid going? "I applied for CO status and spent two years working in a mental hospital. A very grim, difficult time. The staff was almost as crazy as the inmates. That's when I started reading Chinese philosophy, to keep from losing my mind."

I think of Vincent in the sanitarium at Saint-Remy and how he complained of the stress of living with his fellow inmates, many of whom, unlike him, were genuinely crazy. I too had applied for CO status but never followed through. Draft counselors turned me on to a sympathetic and enterprising shrink in Boston who administered tests that certified you as crazy. I took the first part of the tests, which cost a hundred bucks or so, but then before going back a couple of months later for a second round the lottery was instituted and I got a good number. I was out of school and home free. The year before—my junior year—I had driven my roommate to Toronto. People do all kinds of things to get out of this sickness. Another guy I know looked up some kind of anal-retentive-obsessive-compulsive disorder, fasted and dehydrated for a week, shaved his body hair and rubbed his skin raw with Brillo Pads before the physical. It worked. I know someone else who shot the little toe off his left foot. That is pretty common, supposedly, shooting off the little toe. If you have money and connections you don't have to go to such extremes.

***

"The building itself was something out of a gothic horror novel, cavernous, dark, squalid—a warehouse for the souls of the damned trapped in wasted bodies. I worked twelve hours a day, six days a week, most of the time cleaning shit, mopping floors, wiping down the walls, changing beds, restraining hysterical, crazed people. Believe me, there were times when I wished I *was* in Vietnam. But I made it and I never killed anyone. At the end of my duty I was transferred to a VA hospital. In some ways it was worse. I was appalled at the suffering, the waste of young men's lives, the callousness of the orderlies, the lack of equipment and proper care. The injuries were horrific, absolutely horrific. Beyond imagining. They make you pay for your fucking CO status, believe me, but still it's nothing compared to what these guys experience. And then you go outside into the ordinary world and the contrast couldn't be more staggering. You understand more clearly than ever the *billions* of separate realities comprising human existence—separate worlds closed off from one another—and it dawns on you in a frightening way the utter tenuousness not only of what we call society but of human existence itself. You wonder what holds everything together. Clearly it's survival, the survival instinct that brings people together because alone man does not survive. We have the social contract. But there seems to be a competing, counter-survival instinct that seeks to destroy everything."

"Is it tribal?"

"Yes, I think that's part of it. Tribes competing for dominance, space, resources. Of course such competition is outmoded now. There are too many people in the world for this—too many horrible weapons. But I also think there's something to Freud's notion of Thanatos, the death wish—and I think particularly now, in the modern age, this destructive urge comes from the lack of significance people feel, the lack of purpose. There's a diabolical pleasure in the spectacle of destruction—I mean, fortunately in most people it's passive, but what about the Herman Kahns and Robert McNamaras of the world? The rational ones. What about LBJ? Nixon? Kissinger? Curtis Le May?"

"Bombs away with Curtis Le May."

"Exactly. What about Hitler? The death camps? Dresden? Tokyo? Hiroshima? Nagasaki? Nanking? Thanatos on a grand scale. So yeah, there does seem to be a conflict in the human soul—*agon,* the classic struggle between opposites, from which comes *agony*. The Greeks, bless them, still the greatest of all—after the Chinese, that is."

"What *about* the Chinese? Does such a struggle exist for them? For Mencius? Lao Tzu? Confucius? What about Mao?"

"Aha, grasshopper, good question," says Paul, still smelling strongly of the dope he and the boys had just smoked. "The struggle exists, but not quite in the same way." Paul swivels and looks at two hippie chicks. "God damn, look at the fucking women in this town!" Rubs his beard briskly. "The Greeks were full of this passionate drama. Nobody loved the spectacle, the clash, the turmoil, took such almost morbid delight in human foible and folly as the Greeks. 'War,' said Heraclitus, 'is the father of all things.' For Heraclitus anything in life that was meaningful came from conflict. And from this we get our Western notion of art, with its complexity and drama—and of course tragedy. Look at the basic structure of plot in literature and drama, it's all about conflict and its resolution, happily or unhappily. We get that from the Greeks. Nobody loved a good knock-down-drag-out like the Greeks. And of course the Romans and the English and the Americans. It's the same story told over and over again, with as much spectacle and bloodshed as possible. Now the Chinese—that's a slightly different story. Though naturally the basic elements remain the same. We're all human beings, after all, not much difference *there*, but the Chinese—how can I say this—the Chinese—"

And here, Paul, as if taking on the meditative mood of what he is attempting to articulate—the essence of which or at least some of it, I know, not easily put into words—becomes still and stares out the window a moment before speaking. We are near the beach and can see the ocean.

"The Chinese are a product of ethereal landscape, great rivers, cavernous gorges, vast dimensions and deep silence, of elastic time bending back on itself, which brings us to the interesting question of how circumstance and environment shape philosophy. The Chinese were equally aware of the duality of human nature, equally aware of our weaknesses, and yet the method for resolving these conflicts couldn't be more strikingly different. Why? What makes a human being in one part of the world come up with a method of dealing with the turbulence, contradictions, and flaws of his nature, a philosophy in other words, in a completely different way than a human being, essentially the same in all other regards, in another part of the world? Well, I think it has everything to do with the environment, circumstance, chance and so forth."

"A deterministic sort of thing?"

"Exactly. And for the Chinese I think it has to do with rivers. The great sages of Chinese thought, Confucius, Mencius, Lao Tzu, Chuang Tzu, Han-shan, were all great observers of nature, but especially rivers. Lao Tzu's whole philosophy of *wu-wei*—no action contrary to nature—was based, I believe, on the careful observation of the flow of water—the great rivers, the Yellow River, the Yangtze—and all the smaller ones as well."

"And this observation had an influence on their method of dealing with conflict?"

"A profound influence. Again, the importance of Lao Tzu, of Taoism. You watch a river and what does it teach you? It teaches you *wu-wei*, that's what—no action contrary to nature. It also teaches the healing, purgative quality of time, or the bending of time, of timelessness. This is what Lao Tzu meant by 'non-action,' which is not at all the same thing as doing nothing, as so many in the West misconstrue. Non-action means coordinating your actions with the laws of nature, knowing when to move and when not to move. It puts a premium on waiting and watching, and knowing when to exert the precise amount of pressure, or will. No action contrary to nature. So we have the Greeks with their *agon,* this great dramatic struggle between Thanatos and Eros and all the lesser side-shows carried out in the inner and outer realms with the utmost storm and fury, to the great delight of the audience, and we have the Chinese with their *yin-yang,* the patient reconciliation and merging of opposites, all things within each other, signified by the black and white dots of the *yin-yang* symbol. For Heraclitus, Hegel, Marx, Hitler, LBJ and Nixon—and let's throw in Mao while we're at it—conflict, the clash, and resolution of oppositional forces—the extreme expressions of which are war and revolution—are the producers of values in human affairs and takes place in a kind of perpetual state of turmoil and becoming. In every triumph and resolution of conflict are the seeds of further struggle, which produce the bitter fruits of human folly, which in turn must be confronted with more conflict until yet another resolution is achieved. The whole of Western history is a riotous bloody spectacle of which most are delighted observers—unless some of that blood happens to fall on their heads. Then it's not so delightful. But it makes for splendid movies, doesn't it? So. In the West we have the violent purging of our fallibilities, our sins. Observe the crucifixion. To purge. From the Latin *purus,* meaning pure. We want the clean slate, the *tabula rasa,* to start all over again. But there is no such thing as a clean slate in human affairs. It's like Lady Macbeth, 'Out, damned spot! Out, I say!' We'll never rid ourselves of it. Original sin, in a sense. Only I don't think of it as sin—"

We are at the beach and Jake and Terry, Mutt and Jeff, lit up like Roman candles, are out of their pickup and striding towards us pointing to the parking space next to their truck.

"Speaking of opposites," I say, and they are upon us in jovial excitement jabbering about where to park Rosalina and pointing to some people several hundred yards down the beach where the party is going to be. Clearly there is more than a hint of knavery in the boys, not of the malicious sort but of the type to make things interesting, adventurous, perhaps a little rough and tumble. I suspect we might be seeing officer Nichols again before the night is over. But their wildness is infectious. We are on the road with no responsibilities or schedules and an open-ended agenda that welcomes just these sorts of happenings. Paul, super-primed as always, is out of the car before I even make it to the parking space, while it is still rolling in fact, facing the blue massive ocean raising his arms and yelling at the top of his lungs, "The bleat, the bark, bellow and roar, are waves that beat on heaven's shore!" and turning to Jake and Terry, who look at him with great amusement and conspiratorial delight, having already been turned on to the singular phenomenon of this archetypal hippie-mystic-intellectual character who fits every millimeter of their fantastical preconceptions (they have finally met a *real* hippie!), yells again, "William Blake, my friends, the one and only! The greatest poet in all of English literature!" And turning once again to the sea looking like a cross between van Gogh and Poseidon, flinging his arms out like an albatross's wings shouts, "He who binds himself to a joy doth the winged life destroy—but he who kisses the joy as it flies, lives in eternity's sunrise!"

"Right on, Lao Tzu!"

"Outta sight, man!"

Paul runs around the car his hat flying off and gives each one of the boys a bear hug. "No! It's you guys who are outta sight. You have no idea! Sam! Get out here and show these boys some soul power!" Jake and Terry immediately go into a James Brown routine shouting *Soul power! Get down! Ah feeeel good, dana-nana-nana-*

nah! Ah noo that ah woood nah! boogalooing and jiving, Paul right there with them and I get out of the car and start dancing too, all of us doing James Brown and Jake the stocky one gives me a bone-crushing hug lifting me off my feet and the combination of that and the marijuana coming off him nearly knocks me out but gives me a powerful rush at the same time as if I'm doing some amyl nitrate and no sooner has he finished with me than Terry comes over, engulfs me in his gangling frame and administers another vertebrae-cracking embrace and we step back and slap palms and then Jake and Terry turn to each other and hug and so do Paul and I. I guess we do every possible combination of hugging, Jake/Terry, Paul/Terry, Paul/Jake, Jake/Sam, Sam/Paul, Terry/Sam, and no one had to figure out with paper and pencil who has been excluded from this mathematical love-fest as we are just right-on-one-for-all-and-all-for-one-the-four-of-us and I am a bit in awe of this because it isn't just the marijuana, although that is part of it—I haven't yet partaken—but every damned thing that is good about being young, vital, a little crazy and reveling in the freedom and possibility that is ours at the moment, possibly knowing or feeling in the back of our minds (*kiss the joy as it flies!*) the gathering unknowns, the fleeing moments, the future inevitables. And the goddamned party hasn't even started yet. We haven't even set foot on the beach.

Paul gets his hat, goes back to the car and hoists the cooler on his sturdy shoulders and I grab our packs and the tarp and when we see Jake and Terry take off their shoes we put down our burdens and do the same, throwing them in the car. There are a lot of people on the beach and some topless female sunbathers too, a phenomenon I am not used to as the only Easterner in the group though I notice my three mates looking just as boldly as I do. Of course it is uncool to stare and our looks are of a contrived casual nature but here it is all laid out before me: California. And what again, I ask myself, is my purpose in going back East? Well, I will stay long enough to save a little money and bring that part of my life to something of a formal close and then it is mainline back to the Golden Coast, but now the warm gray sand grips my feet resolutely as my soul is gripped by the sight of the young celebrants in the still-warm Santa Cruz spring afternoon, throwing Frisbees, body surfing, running with the Irish setters and golden retrievers, flirting, getting high, lolling on the huge colorful beach towels pressed to earth by the warm benignant weight of the one and true California god.

Paul surges ahead carrying the cooler on his right shoulder gesturing with his free hand as he speaks wild hippie words that Jake and Terry scramble to catch up with. I marvel at his strength and energy as he plows forward with a ferocious enthusiasm that carries us behind him as if riding the draft of a race car or tractor-trailer, his strong ankles and feet churning the sand reminding me of Vincent striding across some rugged terrain, *The Artist on the Road to Tarascon*, carrying easel and paints on his indomitable frame, propelled by the passion to wrest a clutch of vibrant paintings from the landscape. Paul's drive seems no less genuine or forceful only here he is driven apparently by the sheer joy of being alive and the prospect of interacting with a congenial group of fellow beings, the limits on revelry only the sky itself. Paul, I am learning, is an intensely gregarious fellow, and intensely generous too, wanting to sweep everyone in his orbit into the warm center of his good will and enthusiasm.

We march forward and quickly arrive at our destination, staked-out already by four early birds, three males and a female, slightly older than Jake and Terry, setting up a volleyball net and drinking beer. Throwing down our stuff we get right away into the provisions packed by Carmen, Paul opening a can of sardines and four bottles of Guinness, passing them around. Jake rolls a joint and we smoke, settling into the mood of the moment, loose, carefree and pitched towards the promise of something wild, which to me means females, lots of them, hopefully dancing naked around the huge bonfire sure to come. People steadily filter in, mostly of college age, decidedly of raffish counter-culture flavor and in advance of the promised kegs, bottles of wine and six-packs make the rounds, the air all the while thick with the cloying sweet musk of Mary Jane.

***

With dusk upon us most everyone gets up and scours for wood and soon the beginnings of what will grow to be a great fire are kindled and as the flames gather energy an excitement ripples through the crowd, now numbering thirty or so, and a large red truck straight out of the early fifties with a power winch on the front and vertical grill like teeth and huge tires and rumbling engine, loaded with four silvery kegs and a pile of firewood, makes its way up the beach towards the party. People move away making space next to the fire for the vehicle midst shouting and the trading of friendly insults and a giant bearded man in his thirties, a veritable Haystacks Calhoun, dressed in ragged denim overalls lowers himself ponderously from the cab and faces the fire throwing his enormous arms in the air letting out a roar that puts the revelers into a frenzy. This is the sort of fellow who would have thrown Lulu Delilah over his shoulder and carried her off that wretched night at The Canal Zone and I reflect on the vagaries of birth and genetics and envy his physical power and total lack of self-consciousness, a monster who grips life by the balls and flings it around his head like a *bola*, a Babe Ruth, Jack Johnson, or Eric the Red, the immensely physically gifted, charismatic and lustfully passionate ones. What ordinary male like myself wouldn't trade places with such heroes? Well, the guy probably won't make it past forty but while he is around he will enjoy himself and everyone else right along with him.

Another guy about the same age as Haystacks but slim in a tight black T-shirt, jeans and motorcycle boots with thickly-veined muscular tattooed arms and shoulder-length dirty-blond hair jumps down from the passenger side with the compressed power and energy of a catamount and moves silently to the back of the truck and begins unloading the kegs and Haystacks, whose nickname is something like "Jumbo" or "Mambo," goes around to get the firewood along with several others joining in, Jake, Terry, Paul and myself included and in short order the wood is next to the fire in a tumbled pile with Mambo or Jumbo's friend wasting no time intently tapping the first keg that stands in a galvanized bucket of ice glittering gold and red with the fire. After several plastic cups of foam dumped on the sand the first clear draft of the cold liquid is drawn, held up to the fire's light as a lucent amber offering and then swiftly drained by the muscular piratical fellow whose bulging Adam's apple registers emphatic satisfaction with each thirsty swallow. Then Jambo (it is "Jambo," pronounced *Jahmbo*—I have asked Terry, who seems to know him pretty well) steps forward into the light of the fire—it is quite dark now all around—and produces a pewter tankard that he fills to overflowing as the crowd looks on silently, raises the vessel to the fire as his friend has done and intones in a deep voice that reverberates off the dunes, "To the great gods of orgiastic feasting, to Dionysus, Diana—to Walpurgis Night, to the great Zulu warriors, to Greta Garbo—" Someone yells out, "Henry Kissinger!" Jambo continues, "To Henry cocksuckin' motherfuckin' Kissinger! And all of you little boys and girls gonna get good and fuckin' laid tonight!" And then with the crowd chanting, "Jambo! Jambo!" he drains the tankard in five leviathan swallows spilling a good bit of it down his beard and overalls and the intensity and volume of the crowd redoubles followed by raucous cheering as Jambo triumphantly raises the empty container to the evening sky.

This is obviously a practiced ritual and Paul, who is standing next to me, looks on as spell-struck as I, clearly ready and eager to be sucked in and overwhelmed by all of it. Jambo fills his tankard again, the crowd excitedly looking on, steps up to the fire and stretches out his massive arms, some of the beer spilling out onto the sand. His sidekick, seemingly uninterested in Jambo's theatrics, sits on the tailgate rolling a cigarette. For an expectant moment everyone is quiet and then someone yells, "Jambo!" and the crowd picks this up and the same chanting starts in again, "Jambo! Jambo!" The giant man widens his eyes, raises the tankard high and pours its contents onto his enormous unruly head, the foaming liquid dripping down his wide shaggy beard and he erupts in another Viking roar: "LET THE PARTY BEGIN!" The crowd bellows in return and a bunch of them do the same as Jambo and pour beer on themselves or each other from cans and bottles. Paul and I look at each other, hesitate, and roar simultaneously, pouring the Dos Equis we have gotten from somewhere over each other as do Jake and Terry and then they pour some onto a couple of girls standing next to them too.

Paul races off to join a group of six or so drummers, two of whom are black, I am glad to see, and starts banging a stick against his empty beer bottle and dancing in a funny, vertical almost mechanical style but with all of his signature fervor. He appears to have no rhythm whatsoever but that just adds to his charm and appeal as a person of straightforward open collaboration with the essential humanity of everyone with whom he comes in contact. And don't you know he is joined by two really sexy hippie girls in colorful Middle Eastern-looking garb, veritable *houris* both of them, with long wavy hair, one's black the other's brown and they sway back and forth in front of him as if he is some sort of priapic totem figure, a Pan with stick and empty beer bottle, the black-haired one taking away his instruments using them herself, the other boldly placing her hands on his hips and moving hers in commanding summons to vernal gyrations. I am knocked out. He has been banging on his bottle all of forty-five seconds and already two sexy chicks are dancing around him like charged atomic particles.

Jake and Terry are next to me taking hits of hashish from a long clay pipe and I gladly accept it from Jake, drawing deeply on the tarry embers and holding my breath for a long time before expelling the sweet-tasting smoke. I like hash, the smooth high it gives me with none of the roller-coaster swoops of weed and I position myself for another hit of the friendly stuff as it comes around. After the second time a profound warmth comes over me and I feel a deep connection to all of the people as the fire grows larger and hotter, casting its lambent glow on the excited happy faces so innocent, sexual, vulnerable, so intensely lovable, their shadows dancing across the sand behind them as elongated tutelary companions of whom they are reassuringly if peripherally aware. Jambo and his sidekick have set up a large grill over a section of the fire, the sweet smell of cooking meat suffusing the air, smoke rising and disappearing in the darkness all around like a layering of velvet as the drums weave everyone together in rhythmic communion. Several more drummers have joined the group which makes about a dozen people banging intently as a gaggle of ragged hippies flail their arms and churn the sand with their African dancing. I spot Paul talking animatedly with Jambo who is laughing and pointing up at the sky as if indicating the exact spot he's just seen a green whale with its flukes on fire. The two Middle Eastern girls whose outfits fairly glow in warm arabesque swirls and colors and whom I imagine have arrived on a flying carpet are belly dancing with their arms high over their heads in front of the two black drummers. Someone hands me a cup of draft beer and disappears before I can see who it is. I move in the direction of the grill thinking vaguely that I might get a piece of meat but not really caring if I do. If the forces deem so I will. People glide past, over and around me as a finely choreographed dance of colorful spirits and I am barely conscious of my feet touching the sand as I move, a month passing and still far from the grill and its sizzling meat, which, cooking in the midst of these African rhythms and swaying bodies, illuminated by the crackling bonfire, might be wildebeest or buffalo steaks while upstairs the Southern Cross winkles down on its dancing children.

3

Many (mostly) fond goodbyes > Samaritans to the rescue > Apostles'
Creed, Angel style > Sweet music of Eros > The *Murkan way > A tale*
of two butterflies

On the road again after a night of nonstop drumming, dancing, drinking, and a looping endless supply of marijuana, hashish and other things, the party still going strong at four a.m. when I located our tarp, dragged it over the dunes like a horse with the blind staggers and collapsed in a spinning blissful heap, the stars numerous, bright and close as if projected onto a planetarium ceiling. Goodbye to Santa Cruz. Goodbye to officer Nichols, who never showed though I felt his presence then and again like a toxic plume creeping around the perimeter of our gathering, goodbye to Mr. Righteous American who is really Mr. Quiet Desperation American and whom I regard with real respect and fondness, though I have my reservations about the children, especially the little demon Special Forces fucker, goodbye to The Catalyst, a really cool place that I vow to return to—breathtaking chicks!—goodbye to the mighty Jambo, still awake and holding forth as we leave the beach at eight in the morning bidding us a warm farewell and good luck, goodbye to the honeyed, sun-kissed topless girls on the beach with their

Frisbee-jumping Irish setters and golden labs, goodbye to Jake and Terry who both dropped acid around midnight and then some time later disappeared. What will happen to them in Nixon's America? Jake soon in the Marines, probably ending up in Vietnam. Terry, a little wilder and funnier than his pal, waiting on the lottery. I hope he gets a good number and if he doesn't I can't see him going. But who knows? People can have all the attitude in the world but when Big Daddy comes knocking they usually fold like beach furniture at the end of a carefree sunny day.

Paul, who hasn't slept at all, helps push Rosalina, jumps in and falls asleep immediately and snores like a chainsaw until just north of Monterey where he wakes with a start and without comment reaches into the glove compartment, pulls out my copy of *The Wretched of the Earth*, randomly picks a page and begins reading: *"This atmosphere of violence and menaces, these rockets brandished by both sides, do not frighten nor deflect the colonized peoples. We have seen that all their recent history has prepared them to understand and grasp the situation. Between the violence of the colonies and that peaceful violence that the world is steeped in, there is a kind of complicit agreement, a sort of homogeneity. The colonized peoples are well adapted to this atmosphere; for once, they are up to date. Sometimes people wonder that the native, rather than give his wife a dress, buys instead a transistor radio. There is no reason to be astonished. The natives are convinced that their fate is in the balance, here and now. They live in the atmosphere of doomsday, and they consider that nothing ought to be let pass unnoticed. That is why they understand very well Phouma and Phoumi, Lumumba and Tshombe, Ahidjo and Moumie, Kenyatta, and the men who are pushed forward regularly to replace him. They understand all these figures very well, for they can unmask the forces working behind them. The native and the underde-*

veloped man are today political animals in the most universal sense of the word."

Paul stops and scratches ferociously at his beard. "Damn! This is fantastic stuff! I've been meaning to read this book for a long time. *'The native and the underdeveloped man are today political animals in the most universal sense of the word.'* Amazing! Isn't *that* the goddamned truth! Let's face it, Sam, none of us knows a damn thing about what politics really is in any *lived* sense. It's the poor fuckers at the bottom of the barrel who know what it's all about. Here, dig this: *'between the violence of the colonies and that peaceful violence that the world is steeped in, there is a kind of complicit agreement, a sort of homogeneity. The colonized peoples are well adapted to this atmosphere; for once, they are up to date.'* The peaceful violence that the world is steeped in..."

We ride along for a bit thinking about that last phrase as Highway 1 unspools with Monterey ahead under an immaculate spring sky with a slight breeze ruffling the Pacific to our right, hard to come to terms under these idyllic conditions in the beautiful and bounteous state of California in the beautiful and bounteous United States with the oxymoronic *peaceful violence*, but I have a pretty good idea what it means and I wait for Paul as resident philosopher to make the first observations. "That's a Fanonian oxymoron that makes complete sense, like jumbo shrimp," he says.

"*Jambo* shrimp."

"Jambo shrimp!"

"What do you think it means?"

"People in the Third World live lives of routine suffering, poverty and violence that is unimaginable to us. What Fanon is saying, I think, is that we're all complicit in this suffering and vi-olence—that our pleasures, or even the rudiments of our existence are gained at the expense of others. You could look at it as a kind of world continuum of exploitation, or advantage, from the very poorest to the very richest, where the material wealth increases exponentially the further up the line you go—and of course the greater the material advantage the greater the ability to consolidate that wealth and exploit and control those beneath you. So, you don't ordinarily think of shopping in the supermarket as a particularly violent activity, unless you've elbowed someone out of the way or bent their fingers back to get to the best artichoke in the pile. I mean, look at these supermarkets in California, clean ordered environments with soft Muzak in the background, mountains of consumer goods arrayed in a dazzling wonderland. It's all like a fantastic drug, you don't even have to go out to the henhouse and grope around in the straw. There are your eggs right there in cardboard cartons, there's your meat, wrapped in plastic, there's your milk, your radishes, your tampons, your fucking gallon of Gallo wine."

"It's a dream come true."

"It's the American Dream. But the American Dream is the artichoke picker's nightmare. That's the peaceful violence. It's the ordinariness of it—cruising the air-conditioned aisles pushing our four-wheeled chromed cornucopias drugged with Muzak and giddy with abundance—think of it, Sam, the fatness of it! The obesity of it! The obscenity!

"It's as if our souls were marbled with fat, like the heart of some beef-snorting, hog-licking, pill-popping, suds-swilling, chain-smoking insurance salesman who hasn't fucked his wife in five years sitting at his desk all day with his fat little hard-on daydreaming about Ann Margaret. While we're cruising the aisles in this soulless stupor there are poor brown-skinned fuckers out there breaking their backs in the broiling sun making ten cents an hour so we can glide along in these pornographic dream palaces called supermarkets. It's the American Dream, all right, and we're sound asleep while the Third World deals with its waking nightmare. They toil and suffer while we sleep. And don't think for a moment that we aren't the recipients of a healthy dose of this peaceful violence either, the peaceful violence meted out to our pathetic, reactionary middle class souls each and every day, the deadening conformity, the mindless obedience, the desperation of one-track lives, the endless addictions, drugs, alcohol, consumerism, sex, the fear of obsolescence, debt, old age, physical decay, illness, accident, losing your job, being replaced, losing a step, falling behind, falling down, the peaceful violence done to our consciousness by advertising, television, fear-mongering politicians, the constant threat of nuclear annihilation, communism, the Russians, the Chinese, the Viet Cong. They want to scare the shit out of us, Sam. But hell, they don't have to try very hard because this system is scary enough. Lift the veil and take a look at what's going on hidden from ordinary view. Go into the nice house behind the white picket fence and look at the peaceful violence family members inflict upon one another. Take a peek in the medicine cabinet at the prescription drugs. Stick around for a while and learn what mommy and daddy have to do to put food on the table and keep a roof over their children's heads. Listen how daddy describes planting his puckered lips on his supervisor's hairy ass, hating himself every minute for it, so that he can get a promotion or simply keep from losing ground to the young buck who's hustling up behind him looking to put his foot on his neck. Hear about losing market shares to company X and the contortions, sweat and chicanery he and his fellow workers have to go through to stay ahead so that the poor slobs just like him who make up the competition lose ground, lose money, lose their jobs, lose their peace of mind, lose every goddamned thing. But nobody thinks anything about it because it's the ordinary way of things. It's like lifting up a rotten log in the forest and seeing the pitched battles going on underneath. So people lose, they fall by the wayside, they drink, take tranquilizers, succumb to depression, their marriages fall apart. But life is ordinary, no one notices, it's peacetime—peaceful violence. Winners and losers."

Paul scratches his beard, looks out the window and continues, "Go into a house in a neighborhood a few blocks over that's not quite so nice. There's trash on the front steps and in the yard that's been there for weeks because everyone's too preoccupied with surviving to pick it up, no one has the energy—the rent, the food, the busted car, the broken stove the landlord won't fix, the junkies hanging out in the alley all night keeping them awake. Both parents work shit jobs and you tell me how they manage to care for their three young children with the degree of consistency and full attention they require. But they bust their asses and agonize over it because they love their children just as much as middle class parents love theirs. Their health isn't nearly as good as it is for those in the middle class because they can't afford the same care, their neighborhood is run down and has higher levels of pollution, the food they eat isn't as fresh as it is in the fancier supermarkets and more expensive to boot so they fill up on starches and sugar, their level of stress is higher which leads to more friction in their relationships, they drink more and take more drugs, which leads to violence, spousal abuse, child abuse—they smoke more—their education is incomplete, they didn't go to college, nor did their parents and grandparents, the schools in their district are overcrowded and dilapidated with overworked teachers in packed classrooms who long ago gave up on trying to motivate ordinary students and who focus on the rare exceptions as if they were diamonds or personal gifts from god, while these so-called ordinary students are essentially neglected, passed along and marginalized, which for them will only continue a familiar pattern that they already understand will last for the rest of their lives. And on top of all the peaceful violence of their lives they're getting bombarded constantly by images in the media, television, advertising, billboards, newspapers, magazines, movies: their features aren't fine enough, their waists aren't small enough, their bodies aren't perfect enough, their teeth not white enough, their skin not white enough, their hair not straight enough, their clothes not cool enough, their cars not new enough, their deodorant not smelly enough, their sugar not sweet enough, their cigarettes not sexy enough, all the same peaceful psychic violence that the middle class suffers but worse because they're poor and it eats their guts out with a smoldering resentment and makes them hate those who have more and who live better, not realizing the shallowness of materialism and how soul-stultifying it is. How could they? When you don't even have what you *need* you don't have the luxury of contemplating the spiritual and psychological ills of materialism."

***

The day is stunning, the ocean below and to the horizon a vast, calm, overwhelming presence. We are quiet for a moment. Rosalina is running smoothly. Everything is running smoothly. California. Paul recommences. "That's why the working class hates us, Sam. They think we're spoiled rotten and haven't a clue about the real world and the cutthroat realities of survival, that it's easy for us so-called hippies to turn our backs on materialism because we've had everything we've wanted—we're biting the hand that feeds us. It's the children of the poor and the working class who are fighting and dying in Vietnam, the same people who fight and die just to survive right here—peaceful violence. We can rail all we want against the war with our student deferments, our parents' money, our connections, but the reality is that in some sense it's a luxury, this life style we've adopted, these protests, this turning away from the culture—and the poor and working class see through us like we were made of glass. They know that when it's all said and done, when the war is over, when we're through with this little rebellious phase, this little adventure, that we'll go back to where we came from with our education, our nice white skins, our money, our mommies and daddies and the same dreary values we've suckled from the beginning. They know full well that the majority of us will finish school and get our degrees, go into daddy's business, marry, have our 2.5 kids, nice homes, investments, vacations, end up voting Republican, support the next criminal war the country gets into and criticize the latest batch of protestors and rebels. They know damn well that out there in this unwashed, pot-smoking, self-righteous, libertine crowd are tomorrow's bankers, stock brokers, attorneys, car salesmen and politicians—the very same that run the system today, the system that fucks them over at every turn. Peaceful violence.

"Don't get me wrong, Sam. I'm not saying that the stuff we stand for isn't good and that a lot of us, even most of us, aren't sincere in our beliefs: ending war, racism, liberating ourselves from materialism, trying to be freer and more spontaneous in our lives, re-establish connections with the natural world, in fact, *save* the natural world, trying to break down the barriers between people, attempting to establish a sense of community, recognizing the wisdom of aboriginal cultures, understanding the importance of primordial drama, Dionysian revelry, out-of-mind experience—all those things are good, ultimately good, and they need to be pursued because if not we'll likely end up a stinking pile of radiation and industrial waste drifting through space."

Paul stops for a moment and looks out the window. I think about the earth as a pile of radioactive rubbish and industrial waste. Drifting. The earth on fire. A yellow catamaran cuts through the azure water below, bouncing on the small waves. Seagulls. A stronger breeze. A few clouds. Pale blue sky. How could we ruin this? What is wrong?

"So yeah, this is good what we're doing, absolutely, but dammit the whole thing's too big, Sam. We think we can change the world, that we've got all this power, but what happens is that the world changes us. All we can hope for is that some of our values take root, which is why it's so important not to give up. When mankind is finally up against the wall maybe some of these things will register and people will say, right! That's what we have to do! Why didn't we do this before? Well, it's this peaceful violence Fanon talks about, the mundanity of it. The ordinariness. Nothing is noticed until it's too late. Listen: *'The natives are convinced that their fate is in the balance, here and now. They live in an atmosphere of doomsday, and they consider that nothing ought to be let pass unnoticed.'* They notice, Sam—the two-thirds of the world's people who lead lives of struggle and poverty. It's like black people in the US. A colonized people, Malcolm X called them, and he was right. Black people notice everything, Sam. White people walk around with their heads up their asses, like the rest of the world didn't even exist, or existed only as a means to serve their ends. I read something recently about a study that said that black people commonly dream about whites but that it was rare for whites to dream about blacks. It's been my experience that blacks are much more sophisticated politically than whites. I'm not talking about campaign tactics and demographic analysis here, I'm talking about the realities of power. Black people know *exactly* what the realities of power are, in the same way the Algerian, Congolese or Vietnamese do.

"And what is politics but the organized, sanctioned application of power by those who already possess it? Whites take it all for granted, the peaceful violence, ordinary politics, the dream world, the walking dead, while the colonized are wide awake—*'that nothing ought to be let pass unnoticed.'* Interesting phraseology. I like it. It's like right attentiveness of the Eightfold Path, only here it's political awareness, not spiritual—a state of warfare, the passing over on the continuum from peaceful violence to actual violence, everyday violence, a state of consciousness that eats the guts right out of you, exactly the opposite of the Buddha's attentiveness, that which leads to the profound understanding of the transitory nature of reality. The colonized, the oppressed, have a heightened awareness also, but its medium is rage and violence, not love and pacifism. For the oppressed, reality is anything *but* transitory, flitting gracefully from one precious moment to the next. Reality is a tar pit, a cancer of the bowels, a generational affliction—as if one were slapped in irons at the moment of birth with no hope of liberation, freedom, ever a carefree moment, a life your children and children's children are doomed to repeat. They hate this reality but are attached to it like a sickness. They want nothing more than to smash it into a million pieces—and their oppressors along with it. But in the meanwhile they are consumed in a shit-storm of violence, chaos and ugliness, taking their anger out on each other, hating themselves but most of all hating their masters—that would be us, Sam—who sleepwalk through their lives completely unaware of being cogs in the great devouring machine grinding away in peaceful violence. We're eating the world alive, Sam, and god help anything that gets in our way."

"What is the Eightfold Path?" I ask. I have never even heard of it.

"The Eightfold Path is one of the main tenets of the Buddha's teaching. It comes out of the Four Noble Truths."

"Which are?" I am embarrassed by my ignorance. I haven't heard of the Four Noble Truths either.

"Existence is suffering. Suffering is caused by selfish craving. Selfish craving can be eliminated. Selfish craving can be eliminated by following the Eightfold Path."

"Interesting. Suffering is caused by selfish craving. It seems like this culture would be the epicenter of selfish craving. I'm thinking about those medicine cabinets full of prescription drugs you talked about, those aisles of goods in the supermarkets."

Paul stares out the window at the great ocean, whose color matches the hue of his eyes. I think they are equally matched in depth as well. He grips Fanon's book tightly, still open to the page from which he read after emerging so abruptly from his half-hour deep snoring sleep into a state of instant clarity and analysis, as if he had not been unconscious but meditating on the ramifications of Fanon's peaceful violence, opening his eyes and reaching into the glove compartment and opening the book to the exact page he had been thinking about. Turning and fixing me with a piercing look, Paul says, "Exactly. And here's where the Buddha and Frantz Fanon intersect. Our suffering—our medicine chests full of prescription drugs, our liquor cabinets full of alcohol—is brought about by a selfish craving so vast that not only does it make our lives miserable and empty but it radiates out into the rest of the world as an insatiable force, devouring resources, destroying lives, so that our suffering becomes the world's suffering, or more to the point the Third World's suffering. That's Fanon's peaceful violence again. We go about our ordinary lives of conditioned selfish craving, endlessly striving to fill an impossible void with money, status, material goods, because that's all we're ever told, that consumption and status are the keys to well-being and happiness—it's all we know.

"Consume! It all seems perfectly normal to us, this cycle of consumption-emptiness-craving/consumption-emptiness-craving, and at the same time we know dreadfully all-too-well that this cycle is moving very rapidly, centrifugally, and if we loosen our grip for a moment we'll fly off into oblivion or worse, obsolescence, and so we strive desperately to hold on to the one thing we know, or we think we know, will save us: money. And to get this money we prostitute ourselves and step on fingers so then it's the other guy who loses his grip and flies off into oblivion, off this cycle, this insane Ferris wheel spinning around so ridiculously fast. Peaceful violence, Sam. Selfish craving. Suffering. Quiet desperation for the likes of us, napalm and defoliants for the Vietnamese.

"The Eightfold Path is the Buddha's manual for good living, kind of like an instruction booklet for installing a washing machine, or putting together a model car, only it's not sequential—rather all things observed as a whole. The first step is right understanding, which means that before one starts down this path towards spiritual peace—and actually this first step does involve something of sequential order because everything else depends upon this and it includes, in a general sense, all the other steps—you have to have an understanding of what the 'problem' is, and that's clearly enunciated in the Four Noble Truths: We're in a world of pain and to eliminate that pain we need to know what lies at the bottom of it. Selfish craving."

"Do you mean that if I want to get laid I'm in for a world of pain?" I am thinking about Lulu Delilah and how she had driven me wild with her sex, how all I had wanted to do was fuck her night and day and yes indeed I am now in a world of pain. What has this to do with the Buddha's teachings?

"Yes. Absolutely. You're in for a world of pain. Because according to the Buddha, all desires, pleasures of the senses, even love of art, literature, spirituality itself, even *life* itself, are pleasures—cravings, in a sense. You pursue them, grasp at them, they give you momentary pleasure, and then they are gone. 'He who binds himself to a joy doth the winged life destroy—but he who kisses the joy as it

flies, lives in eternity's sunrise.' Blake, Sam, is a Buddhist. Not literally, of course, but in spirit."

"So I can get laid but I just can't—what—be obsessive about it?
Enjoy it and understand it for the transitory pleasure that it is? Be
willing to give it up? Lose it?"

"Yes. Getting laid is a beautiful thing. But, as you know, it's even
better—"

At that moment who should appear hitchhiking a little way
ahead, as if materialized from the pages of *The Thousand and One
Nights*, standing beneath a sign announcing the mileage to Monterey, which is six, but the two beautiful Middle Eastern-looking
girls who had danced with such sensual abandon at the party. Paul
and I look at each other and smile. He thrusts Fanon's book into the
glove compartment as if it's a copy of *Warriner's Fifth Course*. For the
time being the wretched will remain wretched. Rosalina makes a
beeline for the glittering beauties who smile and wave their thumbs
around in circles, the fabulous blue Pacific and vast horizon providing a backdrop to an image that might make a postcard to suit some
middle-American tourist's fancy or fantasy: *California Dreamin.'*

We pull up on the shoulder just in front of them and they
bounce up to the car, all colors, breasts, hips, legs, skeins of thick
wavy dark hair and smiling faces. The gates of heaven.

"Selfish craving," I say.

"Samaritanism," says Paul.

***

Their names, or so they call themselves, are Butterfly and
Datura, and they fill Rosalina's cramped back seat with an intoxicating mixture of beery, womanly, smoky odors, free and sensual
laughter, exuberant sexuality and a limitless sense of adventure and

possibility. They sit wedged together on the tarp covering the bo-ingy springs next to the cooler and bounce up and down as the little gray SAAB jumps excitedly back on the road as if she's suddenly caught a whiff of a handsome red Ferrari just ahead, all leather, clean oil, high octane and freshly lubed.

I look in the rearview mirror and catch Butterfly's dark smiling eyes, the lids lined with kohl, her high Asiatic cheekbones and splendid thick raven Pacific-wild hair and instantly my mind is wiped clean of every bit—a whole lifetime—of the jagged furniture careening around inside my skull since I had fled the dreary East Coast how long ago? A week? Two weeks? Five days? Paul and Datura, who speaks with a thick German accent, dive immediately into a manic, impassioned discussion on Hindu philosophy and he is turned around on his own piece of plywood, gripping the seat with his strong expressive hands looking for all the world as if he is about to jump into the backseat and ravage the openly receptive Datura right on the spot. They flirt outrageously, reminding me of the eat-ing scene in *Tom Jones* minus the turkey legs and oysters. Between the almost comical erotic heat radiating from Paul and Datura and mindless abyss I have fallen into looking at Butterfly's dark eyes in the mirror I lose track of the primary responsibility of the moment, which is keeping Rosalina on a life-sustaining course and I drift into the northbound lane almost colliding with a pack of Hells Angels (big mistake, that, as we will soon see) and yank the wheel hard to the right coming thrillingly close to pitching the whole game over the edge and into the indifferent rocks and waves three or four hun-dred feet below.

Naturally this causes a bit of excitement and embarrasses the shit out of me but I also think what the hell not a bad way to go though preferably Butterfly and I fucking like mad, boulders and waves coming up fast. I can see Paul riding the lustful Datura yahooing like

Slim Pickens riding the bomb over Vladivostok or wherever the hell it is. The girls with their backpacks have hitchhiked from San Francisco and are on their way to Big Sur. Butterfly is from some little town in New Mexico and Datura is from Düsseldorf. They had met in San Francisco at an Isley Brothers concert and had hit it off immediately.

Monterey is touristy and depressing though both Datura and Butterfly get excited about Cannery Row, Butterfly having read the book in sixth grade and Datura "last year." Datura waxes exuberant about Steinbeck which doesn't surprise me as I figure he is kind of an American touchstone for Europeans and of course I have to tell them both about my friendship with his son, John Jr., in my own sixth grade days and how I had once gone with him to their apartment near Central Park and had seen the great man lying down on his bed taking a nap.

I smoked my first cigarette with John Jr. in Central Park. There were about five of us in those days who hung out together and we thought we were hot shit. After school we would go to an Army/Navy store a few blocks northeast that sold us knives that we bought with our allowances and soon we had collected some pretty wicked specimens. I had three, a Cat Knife, a cheap stiletto with a sinuous eight-inch blade and a six-inch gravity knife. We had nothing much going for us in the way of real menace other than our impressive collection of knives, which we brought to school (small, private, between Lexington and Park Avenues) in our leather briefcases to show each other on the sly and more openly brandish after school. The kids who got more allowance bought more knives, some of them having as many as ten or twelve of them.

After a while with all these weapons clanking around in our briefcases we began to think we were pretty tough and so decided to turn our buyer's club into a real gang. A pudgy nasally kid named Horowitz, one of the leaders because he had an actual switchblade, though it was tiny, maybe an inch-and-a-half long, came up with *The Little Arsenals* one day as we loitered outside the Army/Navy store. The name I suppose was derived from *The Little Rascals* and had a degree of descriptive honesty as we were no tougher than the average private school kids, which is to say not very tough at all, but we did have weapons. Not only did the creative Horowitz name us he also came up with the initiation, which was to bump into an un-suspecting kid on the street and pull out a knife. We didn't think too much about what came next but since we were intoxicated with our weaponry and newly-founded status as a gang it made no differ-ence and since it was Horowitz's idea and he was the only one with a switchblade, albeit no longer than a kitchen match, it seemed right that he should be the first to initiate himself. Flushed with swagger and daring he turned and walked up to the first "strange" kid he saw, a bigger, older Puerto Rican (all Latinos were Puerto Ricans to us: "PRs") boy carrying a dry-cleaned suit over his shoulder, obviously a working kid making a delivery. I watched the impending con-frontation between the pudgy Horowitz in his blue private school blazer and the serious working-class Latino boy in fascination, un-derstanding that something extraordinary was about to happen and that it likely was not going to turn out too well for our feckless leader and his tiny knife. Horowitz bumped into the kid and pulled out his little switchblade and no sooner had it flicked open than the boy was all over him like lightning on the Empire State Build-ing, yelling in Spanish and punching Horowitz's head, all the time holding on to his dry cleaning. It was such a beating that a couple of men came over and pulled the kid off Horowitz, angrily rebuk-ing him for picking on someone smaller. We stood slack-jawed at the spectacle. The boy, shouting, roughly threw his arms from the men and moved on, hurling some last angry remarks in Spanish at Horowitz and the rest of us whom he recognized as being in some way connected to his thoroughly humiliated assailant, knowing that he had triumphed over all of us completely and righteously as we stood absolutely deflated, our gang passing from existence that very moment. *The Little Arsenals* had lasted for about twenty minutes. Horowitz's knife had gone flying in the melee and we never found it. I remember it well though, its brass body and small silver blade, a really cool knife.

The girls and Paul laugh at my story and as I look into the rearview mirror at Butterfly's beautiful eyes I catch a glimpse of four very scary-looking bikers coming up fast on little Rosalina, remembering of course nearly piling into the front of the pack of Hells Angels, probably about twenty of them, and hoping at the time that they were too intent on some marauding mission to bother with some goofy hippie and his pathetic wreck of a car. Well now here are four Hells Angels right behind us and though I want so very much to think that they are not related to the bunch I had almost plowed into, their snarling expressions and the fact that the one in front, a very large and hairy guy, is thrusting a bratwurst-sized middle finger at me and yelling something likely other than the Apostles' Creed forces me to consider the dreadful probability that yes these are indeed the very fellows I had almost smeared into Highway 1 roughly three miles ago. In fact it cannot be otherwise. How is it my fellow travelers have not detected this rumbling menace behind us so close now you can feel the heat coming off their foreheads? Paul notices.

"Oh, shit," he says.

"Oh shit is right," I say. "We have an escort. And I don't think it's the Secret Service."

"It's those guys we almost ran into. I recognize the big one. He scared me then going in the opposite direction."

"He doesn't seem to be going in the opposite direction now."

"No, I think you're right. Maybe we're hallucinating."

"Let's hope so."

The girls turn around and look at the snarling ape-like monster on his enormous hog. I hope for a forlorn second that their pulchritude might mollify the beast. We'll offer them up, I think, that might do it. Hell, we hardly know them. Datura from Düsseldorf might especially get a thrill. *Hells Angels!* Butterfly turns around quickly with a worried look and shoots me a glance in the mirror. My own fearful expression hardly serves to reassure her. I try to look composed but it's like trying to fuck under an electric blanket outdoors in a rainstorm. I can't muster it. Datura however is excited. Atavistic Hun-attraction. Actual Hells Angels. Think of telling her friends in Düsseldorf! Hilde, Kurt, Heidi, Werner. Datura's face, of a slightly rubious tinge to begin with, turns bright scarlet, her wild brown hair standing out like a freshly watered houseplant.

"Oh, my! Look at ziss fellow! He's truly a monzter! Vy iz he so ubzet? Vat duz he vant?"

The monster waves his arm in a sweeping motion and two of the riders behind him speed forward and position themselves in front of Rosalina, slowing down, forcing me to slow down too. They point at the side of the road indicating that I should pull over. I look in the mirror and the monster is pointing like his buddies in front. Another guy, swarthy and fat with a huge black mustache and wearing a red bandana and sunglasses, pulls up next to him. We are caught in a pincer maneuver and a well-practiced one too by the looks of it. The noise from the choppers is so loud that I have to yell at Paul, "What the hell should we do?"

"Pull over," he yells back. I look at the girls in the rearview mirror and they are much the same as a few moments before, Butterfly with a serious, slightly fearful expression, Datura flushed and excited. Paul seems pretty calm. I am scared shitless but balls ahead anyway I think and pull over to the side but before I can get out of the car the monsters are off their choppers and one at each corner of her bumpers hoist Rosalina into the air growling like Cossacks and carry us to the edge of the cliff overlooking the Pacific hundreds of rocky feet below, drop the little car two feet short of certain oblivion and laughing insanely pound numerous dents into poor Rosalina with their sledgehammer fists and then walk back to their idling Harleys without so much as a backwards glance and take off in a roaring, throat-ripping, bowel-pummeling thunder that shakes the very ground beneath our tiny tires and makes me fearful that the edge we precariously rest on might break off and pitch us onto the glistening boulders so many hundreds of feet down. We say nothing for about five seconds and then Datura, flushed with excitement, exclaims, "Oh my God! Dot vuz fantastic!" Yeah, I think, just fuckin' great, now you really have a story to tell your Teutonic playmates. Paul and I look at each other like holy motherfuckin' shit that was just about it wasn't it, while poor Butterfly, as shaken as if a shark or giant star-nosed mole had suddenly thrust its snout through the floorboards turns to Datura with a look suggesting her friend has seriously gone round the bend or had never arrived in the first place, says, "Are you fucking out of your mind?! We almost died!" They both shriek with laughter and hysteria and Paul and I let loose with our own whooping histrionics, screaming about how insane that was and everything is and we jump out of the car and run to the road to make sure the monsters are not coming back.

***

They are gone and we run back to poor little Rosalina with dents on her roof and hood while the girls still in the back are laughing and yelling, the bikers, the experience, having put them in a state that I find a little disconcerting, somehow pulling me back to Lulu Delilah at The Canal Zone and her own wildness and again if I had the hairiness, the size, the balls of these Angels or of someone like Jambo how I would have picked up my sweating, topless sex animal and tossed her over my shoulder and given her a good fucking on somebody's lawn right there and then and how sometimes it just comes down to the brutal *taking* of something whether it is women or land or whatever by the boldest, baddest animal on the block, with all the danger, violence and sexuality of it, how this is at least partly what's going on with Butterfly and Datura right now, how these very large crazy males have overpowered Paul and me and symbolically raped the girls and poor little Rosalina to boot and don't you know there is something pretty fucking exciting about it to these females and how maybe in some recess of their sexual souls they might not be unwilling to ride off with two of the biggest gorillas if they come roaring back right now and throw *them* over their shoulders for at least a night or two at some barbarian encampment, makings of a tale Datura's friends would not even believe.

This is what goes through my mind, at any rate, feeling very much the pencil-neck twerp as our hitchhikers have their WOW! session in the back seat tumbling out little dented Rosalina all heaving bosoms, wild hair, colorful loose garb and breathless excitement, Butterfly staying to look at the magnificent ocean and Datura running to the highway for a glimpse of the wild men on their roaring hogs. Meanwhile Paul is thirty yards away careening down a vertiginous path to the ocean whooping as he goes and I run after him figuring a different kind of wildness, this wildest thing of all that opens up before us, the only thing that can compete with the craziness of moments earlier, in fact absolutely overpowering it, thankful that we are not in some deserted lot in Elizabeth or Paterson staring at gutted buildings and leaden skies while our exhilarated companions suddenly presented with bigger more unusual kicks wonder which beer-sloshed riotous tavern the rampaging Angels have disappeared to, eyeing these dead-enders who have picked them up in the funny little starter-less, upholstery-less car with the rapidly deflating adventurism of a teenage girl on a crazy fling watching the middle-aged salesman take off his clothes in their motel room. In other words laters for this, baby, but like I say we have the biggest trump card in the world right in front of us, the Pacific Ocean, and Paul with his dead-on instincts does the only thing possible to escape the rumbling force field, wrest the energy from the hairy pan-sized paws of the rampaging Angels, which is to gambol and whoop down the declivitous, boulder-strewn path and into the belly, the cunt, the lap, of the great liquid mother down there—way down there!

So I know that when the girls see us racing down the cliff to the great ocean riding the crackpot energy of the moment they will follow as surely as flies after potato peels and I don't even have to look back because I hear them and feel them coming behind me, can feel the heat coming off them the same way we felt the heat coming off the Angels behind us moments earlier. But oh man this is a heat of a different order and I don't have to look back but I want to and do, to capture forever the image of these two magnificent creatures leaping, laughing and yelling all glorious hair, golden skin and wildly billowing accoutrements and sure as hell I see them as clear as faceted crystal shooting rainbows into the brilliant California sky (*coming, colors in the air—oh, everywhere!*) maybe the ultimate vision because nothing can ever be better, all the more indelible because I trip and fly balls-over-kneecaps cracking my head against a boulder the next image being Butterfly's worried face, all sculpted cheekbones, raven hair and soothing words with Datura just behind her and Paul coming up fast.

I don't feel badly at all just warm and extremely lazy, thinking briefly about getting up but it is so much nicer lying here staring into Butterfly's face while the sky rocks back and forth purple and blue as Paul comes skidding up breathing heavily from his exertions and stands over me with his bright red face and orange beard, blue eyes filled with concern. "Jesus, Sam! Are you all right?" I have never been happier in my life and say so, smiling goat-like at Butterfly, not really understanding who she is, slightly familiar and beautiful, and I want Paul and the other one to go away and leave us alone, which they do, Butterfly sitting down next to me, softly caressing my cheek and asking me what sign I am. I think I'm Pisces, I say, and she smiles.

It is not too difficult, graceful reader, to describe my feelings at this particular moment, having experienced yourself similar feelings in dreams and certain interludes in childhood when the twin demons of time and enterprise are annulled and everything is wrapped in a warm and protective blanket where bliss and comfort reign, even better this adult version I now experience with the sweet music of Eros coursing through my veins and the sound of the waves below corresponding to the rush of internal tides flowing to my extremities, most tellingly to that which has no conscience or vaguest notion thereof. I am sure Butterfly notices because her expression changes from one of maternal concern to something different, the softness in her eyes replaced by little gleams and flashes and the corners of her mouth twinkle and twitch. I have a distant memory of who she is which makes her even more appealing as if I have conjured her from my unconscious and it seems as if my escape from the dilapidated heartbroken East has only just happened, intervening adventures a flashing dream and now here I am awakening to a Middle Eastern beauty stroking my face, smiling, positioning herself so my head lies in her warm lap looking at her dark eyes and feeling myself falling into them bewitched once again. She leans over and kisses my forehead and what is left of my governing self flies right out into the troposphere of fools, familiar territory of course and most divine, though how I have gotten here isn't so familiar. Feeling dizzy I sit up and Butterfly explains how I have ended up with my head on her lap and who exactly she is and in the telling most of it comes back, including the last glorious vision of her and Datura leaping down the hill.

Somewhat unsteadily I follow Butterfly to the bottom where the four of us explore, I less energetically than the others, finding a warm nook, falling asleep to the sound of crashing waves and dreaming about my father who has turned into one of the Hells Angels and we grapple fiercely rolling down the cliff to the ocean. Waking, I watch Paul and Datura in the distance exploring a tidal pool. Butterfly is collecting shells. Shaken by the dream I think about Paul's book and his quest for reconciliation with his father, recalling serious issues with my own father, a dominating, self-absorbed man. Also, like Paul, my mother had died, though unlike his father mine had remarried, to a shallow, calculating woman with pretensions to art and culture. We disliked each other instantly.

Fortunately I was in college and was not around much. What little warmth that existed between my father and me rapidly cooled, which was frustrating because I'd had a desire to make things better, for us to get to know each other. I have kind of given up on the idea but coming in contact with Paul apparently rekindles it or rekindles something as the violent dream attests but then, I think, there's a shitload of stuff to deal with if the old man and I are ever going to have any kind of relationship. In truth I dream of him frequently, about ninety-five percent of them violent and I know that until I get a grip on this anger and pain I am at best half a person, half a man, that this truncated bitter misunderstanding that passes for a father-son relationship is a burden I carry around on my back, a burden that has its ugly teeth sunk into my neck. So, yes, it is kind of amazing that Paul and I have hooked up, really, and if he is older, wiser, smarter, more directed than I, it will only be to my benefit.

***

I watch lovely Butterfly intently search for shells. Being from New Mexico this is probably pretty exciting for her. It is pretty exciting for me also, being here and being with Butterfly, even though the ocean is far from a novelty—the Atlantic, that is. The Pacific though is something else and down here with the wild rocks and cold crashing waves, much more powerful than what I am used to, comfortably protected by a huge boulder that has a dense sentient power way beyond anything I can comprehend, I get a sensation of the timelessness and unity of things that Huxley and all the rest talk about though maybe it is the knock on the head or just youth, wild like the waves that plunge against the boulders, churning the ganglia-like kelp, the life in the tidal pools, the open possibilities of the great ocean itself.

Or maybe it's Butterfly. She is walking back to me clutching a pile of sandy shells and at the risk of belaboring the point, patient reader, please indulge me, perhaps recalling your own innocent, warm and glittering days as I say again what a dizzying vision she is, a kind of stunning wild animal, her strong sure feet navigating the challenging shore with its rocks, pools and rushing tides, imagining a young healthy goat nimbly gamboling about the hills and rocks of New Mexico with a freedom and rootedness that speaks of something ancient, natural and deep, a sureness of spirit that mirrors the grip of her feet on the earth, half expecting to see hooves as she gets closer but no, they are white sandy human feet connected to sturdy ankles and strong calves and thighs beneath the loose colorful pants.

There is something else under those pants I wonder about as Butterfly comes up smiling, sitting down next to me, smoothing the sand between us and laying down the glistening shells. She is excited at their beauty and sure they are nice but hell I have spent a good part of my life with the ocean and have seen a million shells but no shell or collection of shells can ever compare with this exotic female animal smelling of patchouli, campfire smoke and seaweed, filled with childlike wonder over a dozen or so sea shells, her enthusiasm so touching I feel like a jaded urbanite, but not so jaded that I don't have a good bit of enthusiasm of my own, though not over the shells, nice as they are. I try to replicate Butterfly's pleasure with the shells but the best I can muster is a kind of gurgling that reveals all-too-obviously where my true enthusiasms lie. I take her hand and she stops loving the shells, looking at me in a way that empties my mind of everything but the sound of the waves and the gulls wheeling overhead, a week and three thousand miles ago the same mind packed with razor blades and gloom. Now I am staring into the eyes of a Big Sur Guinevere who judging by the currents passing between us is ready to hand over the keys to the kingdom, circling seagulls screeching approval, the huge linga boulder bulking protectively, the wash of the Pacific moving back and forth, the warm California sun loosening and lubricating our limbs and other good parts and here is Paul, Poseidon-like, bellowing on top of the boulder scaring the shit out of us and a ululating Norse sea goddess, which would be Datura, jumping out from behind the boulder and it is fabulous because me and Butterfly are going to *get it on, Jack*, in fact getting it on already and this just a delicious *interruptus* (interrupt us), the beginning of foreplay that will last until the ecstatic, triumphant moment and then more, more and more again right here under the sun, moon stars and pounding waves of Henry Miller's own bad Big Sur and sure it is the spirit of the old Brooklyn satyr that has me by the cock and balls but sure it is more, too, of desert, mountains, cactus and sage, of a little place tucked away somewhere in the wild southwest that breeds such rare creatures as this that sits next to me throwing off enough warmth to melt all the soot-grimed crusty snow in all the chilly industrial concrete canyons of New York, Elizabeth, Paterson and Chicago put together. Butterfly! Impossible name that, but so what? Datura! So what? They had named each other in San Francisco the night they met at an Isley Brothers' concert, insinuating themselves backstage afterwards through some tripped-out connection and then to the hotel room where the party continued for many hours, days maybe, we do not ask, and nor will I ask Butterfly's real name for she is, we are, flitting, flirting and flaunting our youthful colors, fugitive, they, we know so well, and to be a butterfly now is precisely the essence of all that matters. *Kiss the joy as it flies!* Indeed!

***

This is a great place, a great place to camp, which we all want to do and in a rush clamber up the path to get our stuff, Paul and I following the girls who laugh and chirp like jungle birds in full plumage leaving us breathless behind them. We figure the car will be fine for the night in the small pullout. Who would mess with such a dowdy little maid anyway (they don't know the real sexiness and pluck of my diminutive Rosalina), all springs, dents and no starter to boot. There are no signs prohibiting camping/smoking dope/tripping/drinking wine/ running naked and/or fucking so it looks like we are safe unless the Angels come back and push Rosalina over the edge and if they do I figure she might not mind so much as this as good a place as any to take the plunge. Better than some junk pile in Elizabeth though I wouldn't feel badly about leaving her with Vanzetti and his seagulls and shotgun as I know he has a soft spot in his heart for the old girl and wouldn't he flip if he could see us now. Hell, he might with his sentimental Italian soul make a special place for her out in the lot to rust away in peace—rust in peace, little Rosalina.

Anyway there she is waiting faithfully where the snarling Angels had deposited her, looking as sure-footed as a mountain goat herself, little fazed at being so close to the edge. After closing the windows, locking the doors and giving her a goodbye pat, with backpacks, tarp and cooler in hand we negotiate the steep hill, Sherpa-like, to the bottom, walking down the rocky beach about half a mile and finding a nice spot sheltered from prying eyes above and fierce waves below. It is past noon and we are hungry so we eat some sardines dipped in peanut butter and drink the last of the Guinness. Butterfly and Datura have a good supply of fruit, trail mix, cheese and water in their packs plus sleeping bags and extra clothes, provisions enough for a couple of days at least, absolutely perfect.

After fortifying ourselves with the sardines, peanut butter and Guinness we take off down the beach, Butterfly and I walking slowly, falling behind Paul and Datura who stride ahead immersed in some kind of crazy talk, I don't know what, looking like Mr. and Mrs. Hatter late to the Queen's party. I wonder if they are going to get it on the way I think Butterfly and I are certainly going to—unless the crack on the head has rendered me delusional, a possibility, obviously, not that I need a bump on the head for that, but I feel the *vibes* you know, when the soft tumblers click into place and the safe opens, yielding its treasures. It is the female's call and we must wait like good lads until the signal is given unless it is the marauding *taking of it* like I had imagined the Angels doing or our boys in *Veetnam* defending Murka from the slant-eyed commie devils, slopes, dinks, gooks and then it doesn't matter because these are apple-cheeked Murkan boys 8,000 miles away in a war where crazy shit happens anyway.

Butterfly notices this bit of darkness sweep over me and asks what's wrong and I say ahh, nothing, not wanting to put a downer on the festivities and she says no, really, what? So I relate the Vietnam thoughts but not about my wonderings if Paul and Datura are going to fuck and the stuff about females giving the word, the signal, the wink, poor boys waiting, tales thumping, tongues hanging out and how some bad ones just won't wait, naughty fellers. She agrees that Vietnam is awful and how much she hates the architects of the war, "They're disgusting, these old white men! Nixon, Agnew, Hoover! All of them! I'm so tired of bigotry and narrow-mindedness. So many people where I live are like that. I'd love to live in a place like San Francisco where people are so open-minded. My parents aren't like that. My daddy hates the war. He fought in Guadalcanal. He knows what war is. He won't even talk about his experiences, only that he saw many a good man broken by combat. And Mama hates it to. But I don't know if I could live in a city for my whole life, I just love New Mexico too much." She describes her mother as "a Buddhist without being a Buddhist, if that makes any sense," and her father as a hard-working, hard-drinking, moody, passionate man, something of a legend around those parts, both parents respected to the point of reverence by those with the sense to know anything worth knowing. She talks about her beloved New Mexico, "As a child I used to spend summers at my uncle's ranch. Oh, god, it was so beautiful, so wonderful. I helped with chores and rode on cattle roundups. I used to sleep at night on the porch under the stars. You could hear coyotes howling, sometimes mountain lions too, and great horned owls. Sometimes a bear or mountain lion would get a taste for cattle and my uncle would have to track them down and shoot them. Maybe it sounds awful but that's life on a cattle ranch. But isn't San Francisco wonderful? And this ocean, oh my god, I just love it. Mama and daddy would love it too, especially mama. Oh, but you should see the skies of New Mexico! There's nothing like it. Before I go back to New Mexico I want to see a poetry reading at City Lights. That's always been my dream. We had a young Episcopal priest in town when I was in high school who talked about the beats and poetry and writing and Kerouac and music. It was so exciting. It opened a whole new world for us. How we loved him!"

Butterfly's connection to the place and the people in her life is obviously profound. She is a creature from a different world. As she speaks I am struck for the millionth time by my own fractured and floating existence, despite my father's money and material comforts, never trusting the solidity of anything, though I do have certain connections, to nature, the ocean, my own un-centered self. I can see why Datura has named her Butterfly, her conversation dancing and darting while she grips the earth with those hooves, connected to home, family and tradition, her wild and beautiful New Mexico.

We pass Paul and Datura perched in the rocks, smiling and waving as we walk by, Butterfly going on about the people in her town, the two grade school sisters who carried rocks in their fists on windy days so they wouldn't blow away, the little boy who called girls over to watch as he poked his penis with mesquite thorns, drawing little drops of blood, the old men sitting in town on summer days talking playfully to her as she went by, the handful of eccentrics, some of them very rich, who had made her quiet little village their home, her brother, mystic photographer of ancient Indian sites, her oldest cousin, free-spirited rodeo cowboy who died young in a fiery crash, an actual burning ring of fire, like the song and here she stops for several seconds and her eyes fill with tears and I can see that her earth-nature includes a deep aquifer of grief, someone not quite as flighty and flitting as her nickname might imply. Her talk swoops and spirals, spinning off on tangents layered with details thick as pine needles on a forest floor so that I find myself wondering if she will ever find her way back, but she has a firm grip on the thread of her discourse and always returns, invigorated by her wanderings and sidetracking, substantiated, somehow, as if verbally attending to these memories plants her roots even more deeply in the rich soil of her upbringing and traditions.

It is as if Butterfly has a dual nature, exhilarated by the rebellious energy of the youth "revolution" and the free thinking and honesty it champions, which dovetails so perfectly with her own values, and at the same time profoundly anchored in a past that is obviously disappearing and steeped in what some self-inflated charlatans call "traditional values" (the Christian, capitalist abattoir), though in her case they are real. She is a true person of the old West, not the loony, violent West of Jerome with its rearing white stallion in full erectile splendor, but the West of decent, free people where love of nature, hard work, self-reliance and a sense of justice predominated and perhaps still do. She talks of her parents as exemplars of these traits, with an element of wildness and unbreakable independence thrown in that can only come from such a vast, lonely, fiercely beautiful landscape, her father with an extra dose of this aspect and so, too, the cousin who had died and she speaks of them with special fondness. What Paul says about landscape influencing people's philosophies and personalities is true, I think, and no better example than the old West, good and bad. The bad was the urge to dominate, exploit and destroy, as if the scale of the landscape gave some the license to behave like animals, as if normal constraints didn't apply in such a sparsely populated, seemingly desolate environment. You could do what you wanted, no one was looking, there was no law. The good was the instinctive understanding of the beauty and fragility of the land in spite of its size and harshness, which brought out a reverence that was hitched to the resourcefulness and strength needed to survive. For such people, absent the usual edifice and comfort of law in this open territory, a natural morality developed that emphasized fairness, respect and trust—the basic golden rule—and a quick resolute response to those who violated this code: frontier justice, Old Testament all the way, and I picture Butterfly's family very much cast from this mold.

But of course it is not the old West any more, it is the age of Aquarius, of long hair, smoking dope and free love and as enthralled as I am with Butterfly's stories I find myself listening less, falling into a salamander haze, submerged in thick glorious waves of long black hair, the jogging of full bra-less hippie breasts beneath the cotton blouse, strong thighs and a powerful, shapely oval rump even the loose pants cannot hide, a real beauty, this Butterfly, and a mercurial personality along with the sexiness, a package that whisks old Lulu Delilah out of my thoughts like a good sweeping of the cabin on a clear spring morning.

***

But alas sweetness is always tinged with the bitter. As we walk along I am aware of a pressure inside my head that I want ever so much to associate with my growing intoxication with Butterfly but suspect it is not and as we approach a kind of small natural arch that channels the onrushing surf into a powerful flume that we dance to avoid the pressure grows to a thumping headache at the same time the brisling sardines, peanut butter and Guinness becoming embroiled in some serious disagreement in my stomach, having apparently decided they really do not get along so well after all. Along with this I begin to shiver and shake as if I have suddenly stepped into a dead zone in a haunted house, my temperature feeling like it has dropped twenty degrees and then a crazy-house rocking, the color draining from the world, the surf pounding in my ears like a battery of howitzers and I am staggering forward like Jimmy Cagney riddled by Tommy Guns, looking for some nook or natural receptacle to vomit in and finding none I slump to my knees and with all Big Sur a spinning tilt-a-whirl I retch like a dog, a beaten man, the end of the world, the knock on the head having done me in.

Alarmed, Butterfly kneels down beside me. As miserable as I feel I am more embarrassed than anything and chagrined too that I might now be too sick to do what I so much want to do, what seemed 30 seconds ago as close to a done deal as is possible to get without actually being done. A Niagara of self-pity tumbles over me. Why when things seem like they are finally going well does all have to turn to shit? What is it about me, my life? The image of Lulu Delilah, crazed, sweating, topless, dancing at The Canal Zone wildly kissing her arms, thick hair flinging around, eyes closed in some kind of weird Dionysian ecstasy, hits me in the chest like a jousting pole and I heave again, drooling bitter yellow and green bile, moaning like a gut-shot mongrel, a small dead-certain voice laughing fiendishly saying I'd be better off if old Hem himself came up behind me right here and put me out of my misery with his elephant gun one shot to the back of the head, much better, yes, as I see the tumbling, painful, wandering fiasco of future days, the futile search for meaning, love, fulfillment, etc., growing older, weaker, suffering, dying. This is as good as it ever gets right now and here I am puking myself inside out, drooling spittle and bile as the world spins like an old Rudy Vallee record, no money, no prospects, a hollow, beat-up, dented car with no starter, a stinking yellow-brown viscous puddle of sardines, peanut butter and Guinness Stout staring me in the face, so good had it tasted and with such good spirits had been eaten and now *this*, dreadful sudden jackhammer headache, spinning world, bilious, bitter mouth, burning throat, a glistening thread of snot hanging from one nostril, a degenerate, pitiful spectacle of a human being who only moments before sparkled with notions of lubricate, carnal joy with a beautiful young sexual woman who observing him now must surely be filled with disgust, loathing, contempt, embarrassment, you name it.

But no. Butterfly gently caresses my back and whispers soothing words, so soothing that despite my wretched condition a gentle heat spreads into my loins and I allow myself to imagine that perhaps there might be some purpose to my life after all. Allow yourself a smile at this juncture, all-knowing reader, as you see once again how the surge of chemicals under random stimuli affects the mood and philosophical outlook as much as Paul's mountains and rivers ever do. A few caresses and sympathetic words from Butterfly have me as centered and secure as a sumo wrestler. Where seconds before I had been staring into a pile of cruel, mocking, ugly, meaningless vomit, that very same now becomes reassuring proof of my substance, my humanity, a symbol of the suffering that binds humans together in sympathy. Butterfly whispers she'll be right back and I feel good enough to sit up and admire her beautiful ass as she walks knee-deep into the water and bends over to wet the lower half of her blouse, walking back to me like a mermaid emerging from the ocean into what I am not quite sure is dream or reality, a subtle smile on her gypsy face as if to say let's take care of this small matter as we've got more pleasant things to attend to. She sits down next to me and has me put my head on her lap, taking the wet part of her blouse and pulling it forward to place on my forehead and as she does I have a good look at what lies underneath, far and away the best I have ever seen.

This is a different category of image than the beautiful, exuberant picture of Butterfly and Datura running down the hill just before I cracked my head against the boulder. My eyes roll back as if swooning and I sigh deeply, my body at once limp and electric, a current of amphibian bliss surging through my limbs into my help-less brain. The mystics can have their nirvana, Hillary his Ever-est, Willie Sutton his banks. I'll take my head on Butterfly's lap and one glimpse under her cotton blouse. It is everything I can do to keep my hands off her and I groan, my legs moving back and forth. Interpreting these pathetic sounds as caused by my sudden, mys-terious illness, as if snatched from sea level I have been deposited at the summit of Annapurna, convulsed with hypoxia, and to be sure my head still pounds and my stomach feels like I have swal-lowed a pint of fish emulsion, Butterfly murmurs soothing words and strokes my forehead as I fervently hope she'll lift her blouse again, my eyes closed in innocent, delicious agony. She stirs, get-ting up to wet her blouse once more but I catch no view to my dis-appointment, though returning, positioning herself as before, she holds her blouse out an extra bit as if inviting me to look which I unabashedly do, not caring if she sees.

There are moments in one's life that stand out like pepperonis on a sea of melted cheese, those stabs of erotic intensity that stay with you forever, cherished as much if not more than anything else, your first car, high school graduation, the birth of a child. I was eleven the first time I saw a girl's breasts, summertime, blossom-ing wonders, a neighbor of thirteen, red-haired freckled girl wear-ing a loose pullover, bending over to pick something off the ground. They were pointy, substantial, startling, and it took my breath away. I was obsessed with her for two years. Then there was the hot day on the New York subway around the same time when a young woman wearing a sleeveless blouse lifted her arm to hold on to the strap, revealing an armpit of black bushy hair, just about knock-ing me over. I had never seen anything like it, never *imagined* any-thing like it—women weren't supposed to have armpit hair. I had seen pictures of the magic triangle before and I had seen my poor mother's on occasion and of course it fascinated me and turned me on, young goat that I was, still am, but in those days white middle-class women—the only ones I knew about—shaved their armpits as assiduously as they mopped and waxed their kitchen floors and to see a mass of hair under this woman's arm came as a shock, as if the beautiful bush itself had migrated. I have loved hairy armpits on women ever since and wonderful to relate magnificent Butterfly has two dark lovely tufts of the sweet-smelling stuff herself as I can see clearly the second time she enticingly tents her blouse over my supine, semi-delirious form.

She continues to press the cool cloth against my forehead, sitting quietly, the ocean's rhythmic pounding putting me to sleep. I must have been out for some time because when I wake the sun is heading out over the ocean and the tide has receded. I look up at Butterfly staring off in the distance, a touch of melancholy in her eyes, perhaps looking in the direction of her beloved New Mexico or some other wild primitive place where her spirit feels more at home, like North Africa or the Peruvian highlands or wild Patagonia. As untamed and beautiful as Big Sur is, a marvelous revelation to an East Coast boy like me, it is still California and I get the feeling that for someone like Butterfly, as much as she likes its openness and energy, it is pretty civilized business, a bit sterile and safe—too modern.

Sitting up slowly—my stomach feels better but I still have a headache—I look around at the amazing scenery, the most amazing part being Butterfly who regards me appraisingly with a sympathetic smile. Paul and Datura are nowhere to be seen and I imagine them making love in some warm sheltered spot though perhaps not as maybe Paul will remain faithful to the extraordinary Carmen. As far as I am concerned it doesn't make a bit of difference either way. Zorba said the one unforgivable sin is when a woman calls you to her bed and you don't go and maybe Paul follows the same credo. I certainly do. But if I have a woman like Carmen—or Butterfly—I might remain faithful. Or maybe not. After all it is free love, stoned groovy vibes and *connecting*, the apotheosis of course being the old in-an-out and to hell with anachronistic staid middle-class morals, impediments to the dawning age of which we are the self-assured vanguard, the midwives, stoned trumpeting Blakean heralds on golden wings fucking whomever we please, whenever. For sure! *Why can't we go on as three? Four? Five?*

I want to kiss Butterfly but I feel gross and stink of vomit so I stand up and go to the water, the world still spinning, cursing the bang on the head (and feeling the lump above my right ear) as no doubt the cause of my illness as I have been knocked out a couple of times before and have had similar reactions, the worst part being the splitting headaches that last for long miserable hours. I duck my head into the water, almost getting knocked over by its surprising force, so much more powerful than my grumpy little Atlantic, and then cup three or four mouthfuls of seawater, gargling, swishing and spitting out the cleansing liquid along with bits of sardine and peanut chunks, feeling better in spite of the headache that still clangs like a bell tower, looking out at the vast blue ocean to the horizon beyond which lies an even more unfathomable expanse of water and on and on until you sail into what, China? Japan? The East, for sure, Asia, the land of wisdom that Paul talks about with such reverence and enthusiasm. Will I ever get there? Does it matter?

***

Well, what matters now is Butterfly and getting rid of this terrible headache. Getting over to China and Japan can wait for another day. We walk back to the campsite where Paul and Datura are gathering driftwood, apparently in meager supply as there is only a small pile. I make a couple of half-hearted forays and manage to dig up a few twigs but enervated in the extreme all I want to do is lie down, which I do in the shelter of our little camp. My three companions go farther afield climbing the cliffs behind us and I drift off again, soon awakened by the laughter of the wood-gatherers each with an armload of dried twigs and branches they throw in a pile and after checking on me they scramble off for more. Paul is particularly solicitous, which is touching, kneeling down and putting his firm hand on my shoulder. Datura advises more rest and Butterfly says she will make peppermint tea for my headache when the fire gets going.

Fortified with warm feelings and thoughts of Butterfly's peppermint tea, and Butterfly, I fall asleep and dream of camping with a small band of Indians somewhere in the Colorado Rockies in the middle of winter. I know it is Colorado because searching for firewood I come across a road down which roar logging trucks and camouflaged military vehicles passing a sign that says Denver 63 miles. Hurrying back to the campsite to warn the Indians I find it abandoned with a hastily smothered campfire, the ground littered with beer cans, pieces of rusted metal and bundles of old newspapers. I wake up and the sun is dropping fast into the Pacific, the horizon a blazing orange-yellow. Judging from the pile of wood they must have come by with a second load and have gone for another. The chilliness, encroaching twilight and long shadows fill me with loneliness and I yearn for the return of my mates. It is the first time I feel this way since taking off from Long Island. Driving across I was so filled with heartbreak, sexual humiliation and the excitement of heading towards California there was no room for feeling lonely. I still have a goddamned headache which really pisses me off but seeing Butterfly, Paul and Datura inching their way down the hill carrying wood and talking quietly makes me feel better. The odd, seemingly random events, the collapsing line of dominoes, the Goldbergean perpetual motion machine that constitutes a life, one occurrence begetting another and so on, blows me away as I sit watching the three figures descending in the twilight, their arms laden with fuel, their voices a soft murmur. If Jake and Terry had not come by when they did, if, say, Terry's friend Taylor the mad chemist had not had the ingredients for a new batch of LSD spilled by his cat who had jumped onto the table chasing a fly they might have been tripping in Jake's basement listening to *Disraeli Gears* when we got our flat tire. Surely we would have gotten the tire fixed relatively quickly and been on our way, passing the spot where eighteen hours later our beauties waited with their lovely thumbs and other parts hitched in the air, providing some random occurrence had not changed the course of *their* adventures. No party, no Jambo, no Butterfly. Something else. What?

The closer they get the more freaked out I become thinking about the tenuousness of everything, the unpredictability, the *unreality* of it. I try to hide the strangeness I feel as they arrive, their faces pale and ghostly in the diminishing light. As strange as they seem to me I feel I appear even stranger, lurking among the rocks like Gollum, addled and sickly, a total weirdo freaked out by the pure randomness of events and lack of control over one's life. I begin to think I am losing my mind and for a moment I panic, impulsively reaching out to grasp Paul's shoulders in order to ground myself, to snap out of whatever it is that's getting me, at the same time saying, "Hey!" Paul, startled, looks at me as if a tarantula has jumped out of my mouth and landed on his shoulder, but the actions of speaking and grabbing hold of my friend make me feel instantly better. Resolving to make myself useful rather than stand alone like a whirling assemblage of meaningless particles I ignore my headache and help Butterfly and Datura with their loads, hoping they won't pick up on my on my weirdness, though I suspect Paul already has. Soon enough we are quietly sitting around a nice fire, Butterfly having made a cup of peppermint tea from her stash of herbs that I slowly sip while Paul and Datura talk about reincarnation. Sitting by Butterfly, holding the warm tea, watching the dancing fire and vaguely following Paul and Datura's conversation, my feeling of insubstantiality subsides. I have had these sensations as long as I can remember, of floating away or becoming invisible and they have always been disturbing, causing me to doubt the reality of everything. It is not that I doubt my existence but it is just that in a way I am like the sisters in Butterfly's village who held the rocks during windstorms. I have known myself to spin out of control with this, sucked into a self-diminishing vortex that leaves me feeling like *The Incredible Shrinking Man*, a movie that had an inordinate impact on me as a child. Sometimes with the shrinking sensations comes a loss of voice which is why I shouted Hey! to Paul—to arrest my fading away, using the sound of my voice to re-establish my own reality. Often the only reason I speak is simply to confirm my identity, to reassure myself that I exist, to keep from drifting away.

I suppose this is some sort of psychological condition, affecting me less now, but as I sit comfortably, though still with a headache, next to Butterfly and listening to Paul and Datura, I begin to get the fading again—I am having a real run of this bullshit, maybe because of the knock on the head—and so I speak, my voice sounding to me like it is coming from the back of a cave. From my companions there is an expectant, slightly anxious silence, as if they are not sure who I really am or if in my right mind, but I plow ahead, more for my own orientation and reassertion of being. "Do any of you," I ask, "ever feel like you have no control over your lives? Like everything we do is determined by events, and those events have been determined by other events and on and on until you don't really feel like you have, like, any free will at all?"

I feel better as I speak, existing, part of the company. This is my intention and it is good enough. I know where I stand on the issue, that is, I don't think we have much going in the way of free will. Sometimes it freaks me out, sometimes it doesn't. I am interested however in what everyone has to say about the matter. There is silence—I am sure Paul is holding back to give Butterfly and Datura a chance to speak—and then Datura says, "Vell—I agree vid you gumbleedly. Only I would take id even vun step fhurzer."

Datura leans forward, eyes shining, hair sticking out with Medusa-like intensity, staring into the fire, its light dancing across her forehead. I am noticing her really for the first time. A genius like Paul? "I sink vee haf no free vill vudzoever," she says, her eyes growing wider. "Nussing. Searo. Even za vurds I speak are coming from zumvhare elze. I haf no guntrol over zem. Everything iz preconditioned, deturmund. I haf no guntrol over za circumstances of my burse und my bayzik kemistree. All zis from za start haz deturmund my personality, my moods und my philosophical owdlook. Zairfore id follows zat everysing stems from zeeze initial conditions. Und zats just za beginning! Az Hamlet said, 'Vee are forchund'z foolz!'"

Paul laughs. I think of Jerome. Essential bodily fluids. Datura continues. "Since vee haf no free vill zen zare iz no such thing as reincarnation, since zat prezupposes moral agshun, vich iz za only way vee can affect za karma. Za beleef zat vee haf joyzes iz an eeloozhun."

I stare at Datura. It is the first time I have heard her speak at any length. Being of the generation to follow the ghastliness of WWII there cannot help but be certain responses to her thick accent. She is a phenomenon, surely, obviously intelligent and full of passion, but the accent just kills it for me. That and the intensity. I guess it doesn't affect Paul and Butterfly the same way because he is smiling and she looks on with interest, though I wonder what is really going on with her because she has her foot against mine and seems to be applying some pressure with it, perhaps some kind of message. I find myself beginning to dislike Datura, but, poor girl, it is not her fault, and then I have the thought that maybe her extreme take on determinism has something to do with her country's nightmare, god only knows what poison reaching out for how long, decades, centuries, declaring herself a victim, innocent of the sins that preceded her. Of course she has no "guntrol," but is she then absolving her antecedents of their heinous acts? Did they "haf no guntrol"? What about her parents? What did they do during the war? Were they Nazis? Fortune's fools my ass, I think. Her position, I decide, is absurd. There *has* to be some place for conscious action, for going against the grain on an individual level. But of course she would argue that even those acts of conscience are determined by the circumstances of birth that shaped us, by our "bayzik kemistree."

I can't say anything to refute or dissuade her philosophically and her personal history is a loaded gun that I will stay away from. Paul however jumps right in, scratching his beard briskly, his blue eyes glittering in the firelight. "Well, you're together with Hobbes on this one," he says, smiling at the wild-haired Datura. By the way she smiles back it is pretty obvious there is some "kemistree" between them. In spite of her accent or maybe, perversely, because of it, Datura is a sexy chick, with her energy and crazy hair. Some powerful vibes this one. Butterfly has her own power but different. I see Datura in leather smacking a riding crop in her palm. Paul goes on. "Hobbes believed that humans were controlled by unyielding causality, and that in the way we normally think of it there is no such thing as freedom, or free will. There is motion to our lives, like flowing water, but that's as free as it gets. Otherwise," he says, smiling, "it's solitary, poor, nasty, brutish and short. And Spinoza said almost exactly what Datura's saying about the illusion of choice, that there are factors we are unaware of that dictate our thoughts and emotions, though we may believe differently. Take a step back and view a person's life. There are very few surprises. Voltaire, who valued freedom and rationality above everything, granted a measure of choice, but not much, and only if the conditions are right. We have just a tiny bit of free will. A tiny, tiny bit."

"But," I say, "can the exercise of free will alter the course of a life? Can we decide to do something radically different? Can we change?"

"Only outside events, which are themselves determined by previous events, can change the course of a life, and of course how one responds to those events has essentially been predetermined. This reminds me, since we have a butterfly in our company—have any of you read the short story by Ray Bradbury, *A Sound of Thunder*"?

"Oh, I haf!" exclaims Datura. "Zat'z a great story!"

"What's it about?" asks Butterfly.

"It's all about determinism, how events that happened eons ago affect the course of history. Even seemingly inconsequential things, like in this story the killing of a butterfly—" he looks at Butterfly and smiles, "don't worry Butterfly, we're all here to protect you—have subtle but profound reverberations that affect the course of history. What this shows also of course—and I firmly believe this—is the interconnectedness of all things. We may not have free will, but we are all definitely connected."

When Paul says we will all protect Butterfly I put my arm around her and give a squeeze. In Bradbury's story history has been changed by the elimination of a butterfly. A different sort of Butterfly has flown into my story and has already affected my life, the question of the moment how to get this Butterfly back into her cocoon—she is sitting on its downy baffles—and me along with her.

4

Cavorting with Krishna's maidens > Breaking fast at El Capitan >
Documenting Datura's American thrill > A nasty, brutish encounter >
The zilch explained > A happy goddess

Well, no lovemaking for Butterfly and me this night in the
pounding ghostly caverns of Big Sur. I fall out and sleep like a sack
of ball bearings and when we wake, scruffy, rumpled and yawning,
it is immediately agreed that we are hungry as hell and what we all
want more than anything is a hearty sit-down breakfast at a nice little restaurant, one of these redwood rustic deals we have seen along
the way. Ham 'n eggs! Coffee! Hot buttered toast! Big Sur is spectacular but spooky, but not so spooky as to prevent Butterfly and
Datura from running down the beach about fifty yards, taking their
clothes off and diving into the screamingly frigid water and pounding waves, whooping and cavorting like Krishna's own maidens, yet
another beautiful sight provided by these fabulous creatures, glistening in the morning sun. Too much! Paul and I look at each other
and, following suit, de-suit, yelling and running into the ocean like
berserkers, a thing we would never do but for the inspiration only a
long touchdown pass down the rocky beach.

We drift down to the yelping females who stand waist deep in the frothy water, covered with huge goose bumps, fabulous nipples sticking out aggressively in the cold. Roaring, Paul grabs a mound of kelp and, lunging forward, heaves it on top of Datura and I do the same to Butterfly and they go charging out of the ocean draped in the rubbery stuff screaming like Sabines. Paul and I cover ourselves also and run towards the girls bellowing and chasing them down the beach, all good fun of course but not a shred of innocence as underneath the kelp is good, goose-bumped naked flesh of a slightly bluish tinge and we are still freshly-minted boys and girls driven by the usual glorious impulses, not chasing too hard of course, after all, what will we do if we catch them? A few teeth-chattering moments later we are dressing at the campsite eyeing each other unashamedly. Their bodies are fit and well proportioned, firm arms, shoulders, thighs, calves—strong-boned savage females looking for some strong-boned savage fun. No doubt! Paul, who has a good muscular Viking body, stares at these whooping voluptuaries with the intensity of an arc light, looking like a satyr too long denied. I wonder if he has any thoughts of Carmen. Lulu Delilah is not even on the horizon. We finally pack our things and trundle up the trail to Rosalina who, waiting faithfully, seems to be smiling at us though she is closer to the edge than we remember.

We pile the stuff in haphazardly and Butterfly gets behind the wheel as the three of us push Rosalina to the highway, unfortunately uphill going south, our direction, so we roll the little car the other way and Butterfly pops the clutch and Rosalina is animate and rumbling once again. After about a mile we find a place and turn around. My headache is gone and the sourness in my stomach has been replaced by a rioting hunger. Butterfly drives Rosalina as if they have been together their whole lives, drives like Neal Cassady, popping the clutch at just the right time to get us going, accelerating to the proper rpm in each gear, shifting smoothly and handling the dizzying curves like a Formula One driver. It is the West—growing up with competent, self-reliant people—that accounts for her expertise. When I note her skill she says she's been driving since she was ten. I picture her in daddy's pickup jouncing down some country road, her cute buttocks tense with the effort, little hooves barely touching the pedals, little hooves turned to strong ankles and white sandy feet that confidently pump Rosalina's own tiny pedals.

Paul and Datura gabble excitedly about food, what they love to eat: pancakes, waffles, maple syrup, blueberry syrup, butter, bacon, ham, steak, corned beef hash, hash browns, grits, muffins, whole-wheat toast, sour dough, bagels, omelets, scrambled eggs, eggs over easy, sunny-side up, boiled, poached, eggs benedict, strawberry cheese blintzes, hot coffee, hot tea, hot cocoa. Datura luffs Amerigan breggvaztzz! We are a wild-looking bunch, salty and crazy-haired, almost giddy with hunger and stoked by our morning polar bear plunge into the cold Pacific that does nothing to dampen the charged particles that crackle from one set of loins to the next. It makes us a little self-conscious and shy, this crackling, but don't you know how nice it is.

After about twenty minutes we find our rustic redwood restaurant, "El Capitan," set back from the road in the midst of a dungeon of trees where the temperature is at least ten degrees cooler and the hills in back ascend into a shadowy unknown. There are only two vehicles in front, a baby blue Cadillac convertible, top down, and a monstrous chromed Harley with handlebars set so high only a trained orangutan could reach them. Paul and I exchange glances and open the tinkling door, the four of us standing for a moment adjusting our eyes in the dark interior. There are two men seated at a table who look at Datura and Butterfly, not even wasting their energy with so much as a glance at Paul and me, and then resume eating, talking intensely. One is a biker, a huge, mean-looking dude with a long ponytail and a dark, pockmarked face, wearing an absurd puffy Liberace-style red shirt with white polka dots (not a problem, sir!) and a cowhide vest, but he is not from the day before, thankfully. The other guy is lanky and strikingly handsome in a fine-featured way with combed-back shaggy brown hair and a mole on his upper lip, dressed in a denim shirt, blue jeans and cowboy boots. There is something familiar about him.

We face a long log cabin style wooden counter behind which a middle-aged woman with a haunted, sensual face and dark hair turning to gray pulled back in a bun tells us to take a seat, coming around the counter clutching four menus, walking slowly towards us. "Isn't she fabulous?" whispers Butterfly. "She's like an oracle or something." She does have a mysterious quality that is slightly forbidding but as she bends over and places the menus on the table, leaning close to us with an unexpected intimacy, she smiles slightly as if appreciating our youthful carnal exuberance, behind the apparent severity a beautifully aging sensualist herself, the top buttons of her dark blue denim shirt opened revealing a strip of black lace bra and the soft twin mounds of her breasts, her skin clear with agreeable crow's feet around knowing, crystal-gray eyes, only the suggestion of sagging under her strong chin, a wisp of hair hanging down her cheek that she brushes back when she stands up. She wears loose jeans and a black unbuttoned sweater over the shirt, blue sneakers and no socks. There is, like the handsome lanky guy sitting with the hulking Liberace biker, something familiar about her, and then I think of course, she is Paul's Carmen about fifteen years from now, still a real beauty, a Big Sur beauty, and damn wouldn't I like to have a woman like that some day. In fact she also reminds me of Butterfly and I wonder what life would be like in New Mexico with a passel of kids, painting, growing vegetables, raising chickens and pigs, the beautiful Butterfly by my side, growing old together. The woman looks at us for a moment with the same enigmatic smile, a dignified, powerful, sexual presence. We stare like children. "Can I get you some coffee?" she says.

We order three coffees—Butterfly asks for a pot of hot water for her herbal tea—and the woman leaves. Paul and I look at each other. Meanwhile, Datura, who has been looking at the lanky guy across the room, leans forward and whispers, "Dot's Glind-Eeezd-vood," and returns her gaze to the man. It takes a moment to figure out what she has said but sure enough it is the actor himself who, feeling the energy from Datura's attention, looks at her and smiles. The waitress returns with our coffee and Butterfly's hot water and answers affirmatively to Datura's question about the actor's identity, adding that he is a frequent visitor at El Capitan. Datura is excited and as we eat our food—avocado, Gruyere and mushroom omelets, pancakes with whipped butter and fresh blueberry syrup, smoked ham, Canadian bacon and homemade sour dough toast with apricot jam, all of which we share—she continues to stare at the actor, smiling openly, every now and then putting her fork down and running her fingers nervously through her frizzy brown hair as if primping herself, and when the two men pass our table to leave Datura surprises us and blurts out, "Excuse me, but are you Glind-Eeezdvood, za agtor?" Eastwood, extremely tall, a toothpick sticking from the corner of his thin lips, fixes Datura with his blue eyes and with a hint of a smirk but utterly polite he answers that yes, he supposes he is and asks her name and where she is from. Datura, responding with a brassy enthusiasm that makes us all cringe a little bit, introduces herself and her place of origin and then introduces us. We nod and smile at the actor, who seems amused with Datura, his monstrous companion standing in the background, not interested in any of this but also staring at the ballsy German hippie chick with the wild hair.

"Vood you mind if one uf my gumpanions took a picture uf uz togezzer?" As she asks the question Datura opens her backpack and withdraws a thirty-five-millimeter camera, a Pentax, and hands it to me and we go outside where Datura calls to Butterfly to come get her picture taken and they pose next to the Cadillac, the actor towering in the middle with his arms around them, all smiling broadly as I take a couple of pictures and then a few with Datura and Eastwood alone and then Datura asking the biker if she can photograph him and his Harley and after that I take a picture of the two of them standing next to the chromed hog with its crazy handlebars. Datura's enthusiasm, chattering on about her "American eggsperience," puts everyone at ease. Even the biker is smiling. Eastwood is thoroughly relaxed—a nice dude, I think—and he surprises us all by yelling for Rebecca, the waitress, to come out and take a group picture, which she does, Paul, me, the biker, whose name is Ray, Datura, Butterfly and Clint Eastwood, all brightly smiling, El Capitan in the background. Next he is hugging the girls and shaking our hands and a moment later is driving the baby blue Cadillac convertible out the gravel driveway smiling and waving goodbye and Ray the biker kick-starts his Harley and rumbles off down the highway in the opposite direction. We go back inside and finish our breakfast and Rebecca, the waitress, tells us about a nice little campsite with some hot springs about fifteen miles to the south.

***

Things are humming along nicely, Datura buzzed from the encounter, not only with the actor but also with the biker, both quintessential American types, and we are all buzzed from the good food and our growing familiarity with one another, the girls up for spending at least one more night with us at this cool-sounding campsite with the hot springs. Rosalina, always sensitive to the prevailing vibes, starts with barely a push despite the gravel driveway, puttering down the winding highway trailing just a hint of blue smoke, her pheromones, while we take in the amazing scenery, quietly excited to be together, eager to find the campground and relishing the maximum promise of the hours to come.

The natural pairings solidify, Butterfly sitting in front as I drive while Paul and Datura squeeze together in the back with all the stuff, the great ocean blue and calm as Neptune's eye, blinking waves against the shore through eyelashes of floating kelp. We jabber about Clint Eastwood and his movies. Datura is a huge fan, thus accounting for her boldness and excitement at the restaurant. To the east dry hills like elephant hide give way to denser, steeper terrain, more canyon-like and finally, thrumming with anticipation, we spot the road to the campground, marked only with a small, barely noticeable sign and I pull Rosalina cautiously onto the dirt road that leads to a dark, bosky and narrow canyon whose sides close over us like the wings of a manta ray. Everything becomes suddenly quiet and dense, sealed off from the open, blue, vast Pacific with its marvelous freedom and light. We find ourselves silent and a little spooked, with no way to go but forward, but before too long we come to a grassy clearing surrounded by trees with room enough to pull Rosalina over to the side, the space about the size of a gymnasium, a kind of meadow with yellow and blue wildflowers and tall grass and to the east, uphill through the woods, a small trail, probably the way to the hot springs.

We unload our gear at the northern edge of the campsite where we discover a fire ring, by all appearances not used for some time, and Paul immediately goes into the woods looking for fuel and comes back with an armful of dry branches, dumping them next to the ring. The clearing is warm, shielded from breeze, overhead a few puffs of white clouds hanging motionless in a blue sky. We decide right away to look for the hot springs, pulling damp towels from our packs along with some trail mix and water and with

Paul leading we walk single file, uphill, my eyes fixed on Butterfly's mind-bending hindquarters flexing provocatively with each step under her loose white cotton pants. Datura, following Paul, wears cut-off dungarees and a colorful peasant blouse, in contrast to Butterfly's black tank top. The trees, mostly oak and pine, close around us thickly, the air still and cool and on the ground to our left a glint of light and subtle murmuring becomes a stream that grows larger as we advance. On an impulse I walk over and stick my hand in—it feels warm. The forest floor is covered with leaves and pine needles, reminding me of woods in the East, evoking thoughts of vague and ancient things, of people walking quietly in a forest that is their home, of shelters built from bark and animal hides, of encroaching winters and the taut, anxious demands of survival, of a black-haired, dark-eyed beauty, perhaps the very same with me now, one of our tribal fantasies to disappear into the deep woods and live in the old way, as Indians, in teepees huddled with our plump children wrapped in furs around small fires, living out our own atavistic dreams in communes and such things, fleeing from an irredeemably corrupt and brutal society to live forever in renegade youthful splendor, growing corn and marijuana, fucking like nymphs and satyrs, communing with animals.

The hot springs are a series of stepped pools, four altogether, the highest the warmest and cooler on down. All of the pools are large enough to accommodate the four of us and soon enough we are cozy, warm and naked in the second pool from the top, able to see the grand Pacific horizon, though it is the lesser of magnificent sights to be sure. There is a wide, flat ledge next to the pool below us and Butterfly gets out after a while to sunbathe, soon followed by Datura, both lying on their stomachs, pale bottoms soaking up the sun and I say a quiet thank you to Lulu Delilah for landing me, of all places, in the Garden of Eden. There isn't enough room to join them on the ledge, nor is the comfort level at this point quite high enough to do so, though if one of us tried I doubt it would be a problem. The air is slightly cooler than the water, which makes things just about perfect. My companion has been relatively quiet the last several hours and I wonder if he has been thinking about Carmen. Wearing his battered straw hat, blue eyes flashing under the brim, his skin reddening in the sun, he looks more like van Gogh than ever and sure as hell the old color-mad marauder would be right here with these beauties had he the chance, the glory roaring in his ears. Vincent is just like us, only more so. "So, what are you thinking?" I ask.

"Not a goddamned thing," replies Paul. "But if I were it would be that I am in heaven. We'll not see the likes of this again, that's for sure. At this rate it'll take us five years to get to Jacksonville, but who cares? Hell, I'd rather be here than staring into my old man's tortured mug in that plastic, godforsaken house in wretched Florida. Poor bastard. This here is what he needs, Sam."

Paul spreads his arms out to take in the whole scene and looks around in a kind of wonder, his gaze resting finally on Butterfly and Datura. He shakes his head ruefully. "What is it, Sam? Why do people insist on beating themselves up so?" I have no answer for this, just shake my head with a sad smile, reduced to an elemental state by the warmth of the pool, the extraordinarily blue, gracefully curving horizon stretched out below, the wild deep foliage surrounding us like druids, the sunlight breaking over the hills at our backs, the murmur and purl of the hot descending mineral-laden water, filling, falling, filling, finally absorbed in the cool dark forest ground, the naked sensual women languidly sunning themselves on the warm rock ledge. A grunt and dreamy, mindless smile is the extent of my communicatory power.

"Don't you know people have been coming here for millennia, just like us now, exactly the same," says Paul. "A couple of Indian dudes sitting here like you and me with a couple of mind-boggling

Indian chicks stretched out just like them, thinking the same thoughts, feeling the same things."

Paul seems kind of wistful and I wonder what he is really thinking. He has mentioned his father so maybe he is having second thoughts about the whole venture, like leave well enough alone, no sense in trying to salvage something or reach an "understanding," that probably his father is pretty far gone, drinking more than ever, bitter, wound up in himself and his miseries to such a degree as to be unapproachable, that the effort will only come to frustration, anger and grief. Or maybe he is thinking about Carmen and wrestling with his conscience about the roll-around to come with Datura, because it sure as hell seems to be in the offing. But Paul is a serious guy and I feel hesitant to pry overly much, in fact even to pry at all, though I am keen to know what is going on. So I venture, "I've had big problems with my own father, just like you've had with yours. After my mother died I was shipped around to all sorts of schools, a total misfit, failing all my classes, getting into trouble, angry as hell, the whole time hardly ever having a meaningful conversation with him. I boarded with a family on Long Island and went to a public school where I played sports, partied, duck-hunted and just generally yahooed my way along. It was great fun but it did nothing to resolve the conflict with my father, only bury things more deeply. He's a successful man, a powerful man, but like your father, or so it seems, very much wrapped up in his own concerns. Actually, I pretty much hate the sonofabitch. I have violent dreams about him all the time."

"Like what?"

"Like literally killing him. Like bashing his head in with a rock. Like beating the shit out of him with my fists."

Paul chuckles. "I've had those dreams myself. They're not good. Maybe they're partly Oedipal. I don't know. You must go through some pretty heavy emotions in those dreams. I know I do."

"Oh, man," I say, shaking my head. "I'm in such a rage it's frightening. A lot of times I'll wake up sweating, with my heart pounding like a freight train."

"Ever get into any fights with him?"

"No, but he slapped the shit out of me once in a public place. All over a misunderstanding. I was ten or eleven, too embarrassed to do anything but just stand there and take it, crying like a baby. People just walked by, afraid to say anything, but I remember how appalled they were. I had this fear of him my whole childhood. And then when I was sixteen, on the advice of a shrink I was seeing, I forced a confrontation."

"What'd you do?"

"It was during a time, briefly, when I was living with him and his new wife, a terrible, shallow person, a complete phony and gold digger. I was having a lot of problems and moved back in with them to see this shrink for a while. This was in New York City. One of my big issues was being dominated by my father, my fear of him. The shrink suggested that I force a confrontation, physically stand up to him, deal with my fears. So I did."

"So what happened?"

"I did my homework on his desk one night and refused to remove my books when he asked me. It was totally unreasonable on my part but I was following the shrink's advice. I was scared shitless but I did it, stuck to my guns. Sure enough, my father went into a rage. We were an inch from coming to blows. You should have seen the sonofabitch. I thought he was going to blow an artery. He's a stocky, powerful guy. A welterweight quarter-finalist in the Golden Gloves in his day, a rough and tumble guy, a street fighter—grew up in Hell's Kitchen. We were standing nose to nose. I wouldn't back down, even though I thought he was going to kill me. His wife and my younger brother were flipping out, running around, squawking like chickens, trying to get between us. It was a real scene, believe me."

"Damn," says Paul, "That's some heavy shit. I had some bad scenes with my old man too, even worse than that. Violent, scenes, physical scenes—really bad news. I actually came close to killing him once. I'll tell you about it, but not now. This is too nice. I don't want to ruin the vibes. Besides, I gotta take a leak." Paul stands up slowly, looking like Pan, the water dripping down his hairy body. He hops onto the ledge behind us with a strong, agile motion and quickly disappears into the woods. Even though I have been around Paul almost a week and am getting to know him as a distinct personality—very much his own person—he still reminds me, at least in appearance, of van Gogh. I have spent a lot of time with Vincent during these last few years and I know, or fancy I know, pretty much everything about the adventures, calamities and triumphs of his eventful life, though I am certain that what happens next is something Vincent never experienced, else we surely would know about it.

***

Among the many branches of the tree of the occult that casts its aura over "the counter culture," numerology is a fairly big one if you're into such things. I am not, but it is obvious that different numbers possess different energies, for example the number three, which is what I gradually become aware of the longer Paul stays in the woods. Under the circumstances three seems unstable and slightly foreboding, as opposed to the usual smooth, sensual flow of energy that passes through our agreeable quartet. Maybe fifteen or twenty minutes have passed and Paul has not returned. At first I think he is probably digging walking naked in the woods but as time drags on I begin to worry, finding myself playing a little with the numbers: three and four, seven, lucky; three and four together, thirty-four or forty-three; four times three, twelve, the apostles; four minus three, one, the loneliest number; three minus four, negative one—bad. Paul is in trouble. The girls stir. Datura asks where is he and I say in the woods to piss but he has been gone a while and I am going to go look for him and if I am not back in half an hour call the California Highway Patrol or the Maharishi. I pull myself out of the pool, a little self-consciously as both females are looking, and walk into the woods, which are dark and chilly and immediately spooky in the way this whole area seems to be, as if with each step farther in another door silently closes behind me so that I quickly lose sight of the hot springs and am enclosed in another world, a Grimm brothers' Hansel and Gretel world, or something like it.

Leaving the pool I had briefly considered putting on my pants but would have felt silly because everyone is naked and enjoying the easy eroticism and what is more I like the idea of walking in the woods without clothes even though I feel immediately vulnerable, increasingly so the deeper I get. This is not your warm and fuzzy Bambi type forest. Not only is it chilly and dark it has a creepy vibe as if inhabited by Donner Party ghouls or bears like the one on the state flag. I begin to wish I was wearing camouflaged garb and carrying an M-16 instead of shivering in my skinny white skin and shrunken testicles.

I am pretty far in by now and turn to see if I can find my way back to the hot springs and it seems I have been following a trail of sorts so I am reassured, at the same time noticing the ground all around me oddly stirred up, unlike the smooth carpet of leaves and pine needles around the hot springs or next to the trail. This spooks me even more and I call out Paul's name, my voice swallowed up as if I am shouting into the mouth of a whale. I call out again a little louder and after a moment hear him call my name, to the left, maybe fifty yards away, something odd about it, a fearful almost desperate tone as if he is immobilized somehow, fallen into a pit or bitten by a snake and I move quickly in the direction of his voice, noticing that the ground is really roiled as if churned up by mortar fire with small craters everywhere, leaves and pine needles scattered wildly. I call again and Paul answers, closer, "Sam, be careful. There's a bunch of wild pigs around here. I'm up in a tree. There's a big fucker right under me. Watch out. I think he's coming after you! Climb a tree, quick!"

So that's why the forest floor is riled up as if a marauding army of Orcs has passed through. Pig country. Of course! I've heard people talk about the wild pigs around here, nasty, brutish motherfuckers with tusks like scimitars, able to run faster than Bob Hayes. If they get you cornered or on the ground they can turn you into sausage, kill you, that's what I've heard, some of these fuckers weighing three hundred pounds. I look around frantically for a tree to climb and in the same instant a big, bristly, black monster with curving tusks trots into view about twenty yards away and, spotting me, charges, grunting loudly. There are a bunch of trees around but as I don't have time to pick the ideal one with nice limbs where I can wait comfortably until the beast gets tired of the game and trots away I choose the larger of the two scraggy scrub oaks nearest me, the trunk at most four inches in diameter, the worst of it being the skinny brittle limbs that snap like stale Tootsie Rolls as I pull at them but my adrenaline pumping such that I could climb a flag pole covered with petroleum jelly in the time it takes to sneeze or fart, a good thing too because the pig is at the tree bumping it with a snout the size of a football, its yellow tusks covered with mud, slime and pine needles, a drooling, ill-tempered beast that looks up at me with malevolent, brown, startlingly human eyes.

I'm only about six feet above him, clutching the topmost and flimsiest part of the tree, my toes gripping the remnants of the branches I've broken in my frantic scramble. "Get the fuck outta here!" I yell, my unstable perch swaying, the grunting boar up on its hind legs like Napoleon in *Animal Farm*, front hooves pawing at the slender trunk, its slathering tusky mouth no more than ten inches from my feet, powerful smell of humus, urine, musk and pig breath wafting up at me. Then Paul appears running through the trees, a whooping, hairy, pale, naked apparition flapping his arms wildly and the pig turns, grunts and chases after him but Paul is up a tree in a scampering instant about thirty yards away laughing like a lunatic. "Sam! Are you okay?" he yells. I'm so hyped climbing the tree that I haven't felt a thing but I'm covered with scratches and there's a small cut on the inside of my left thigh. "I'm fine," I say. "Where the hell are the rest of the pigs?"

"They took off a few minutes ago. For some reason this fucker decided to stick around. He's having a little sport with us." The pig grunts and rears up on his hind legs like he did with me, his hooves on the trunk of Paul's tree, at the same time unloading a pile of steaming yellow-brown shit, the sloppy, fibrous turds smearing the back of his straining hocks. "Get the fuck outta here, you disgusting satanic swine!" Paul yells. At that moment six or seven grunting pigs come into view from the surrounding forest as if they've been watching the fun but have taken umbrage at Paul's words. They're all ugly as Republicans but not as big as the one who has run us up the trees, the leader probably. They mill around seemingly confused, grunting anxiously, trotting back and forth between our trees, their hairy snouts lifted, sniffing the air. For a second they stand still and then in a burst of coiled pig energy race off into the woods.

A voice.

"Hey. Vair are you guys?"

Datura, at fifty yards, has scared the pigs.

"Over here," we yell, jumping down, warily looking around.

Datura and Butterfly, both dressed, come into view looking at us like shocked anthropology students and we stare at each other for a surreal moment, as if standing on either side of a 20,000-year chasm. They remind me of the naval officers in *Lord of the Flies*, Paul and I Ralph and Jack complete with pigs and we turn tail and run back to the hot springs laughing hysterically, yelling, "They're coming! They're coming! Run! Faster!" expelled from the forest by cloven-hoofed demons of the underworld, delighting in the absurdity, danger and pure sexiness of it, Paul and I practically diving into the pool, the laughing shrieking girls scrambling out of their clothes and following us in—kerplash!—looking back expecting to see an army of pigs charging out of the forest up to the hot springs, all of us laughing crazily especially Datura and Butterfly whose out-of-control mirth doubles and re-doubles as they recall the sight of our pale bottoms and swinging scrotums in fearful flight from the hell-hogs who they hilariously note are undoubtedly hauling freight in the opposite direction.

A few hours later we are at the campsite, dry, sunburned, clothed and still bubbling from our encounter with the pigs and dash through the forest, scouring the woods for fuel, ever alert, by now late afternoon, the sun disappearing behind the trees and with a decent stash of dry wood we decide to find a way to the beach to catch the sun's melodramatic sizzling plunge into the Pacific, packing our stuff safely away in Rosalina, back down the road, finding a route to the beach and a sheltered spot from which to watch the pounding surf, much larger than the day before, sitting in silence until the huge sun meets the horizon, casting a glimmering path that seems to invite us to walk its length as if into a blazing orange-yellow portal, awesome and beautiful.

Paul and Butterfly, who both know something about Kerouac and revere him, talk about his book, *Big Sur*, and how the ocean had unnerved him, the whole of Big Sur for that matter and we agree that yes it is a powerful place and we can understand how such a thing could happen. As she talks about Kerouac Butterfly looks wistfully out to sea. I had read *On the Road* a few years earlier and loved it but that is all I know of his work. Paul and I are doing our own version of Sal and Dean's trip. Anyone worth their salt has to do it at least once just as anyone worth a damn has to go a little crazy once in awhile. We all agree on that. Trust no one over thirty and no one who has not gone crazy. Paul says that as how he is twenty-eight and been crazy more times than he can count he is an "eminently trustworthy fellow," the sort of expression Vincent might use and I think of him, Vincent, chased up a tree by a wild boar, his paints, canvas, easel, palette trampled by the brute, maybe a masterpiece destroyed, the boar symbolizing thick-boned violent society and Vincent laughing just as we had, providing it was not during that shattered period of his life when nothing was funny at all. Thinking these things I look down at Butterfly's hand resting on the warm smooth rock between us and I cover it with mine as we look at the sunset. Datura is sitting in front of Paul leaning back on his raised knees. It seems kind of amazing really how close and comfortable we are after only two days but what a two days they have been, Hells Angels, a tumbling minor concussion, camping on the beach at Big Sur, a hearty breakfast, Clint Eastwood, naked hot springs, a run-in with a nasty pig and now this magnificent sunset—and so much more, the second-by-second sensory monitoring of a life so full we need Huxley's "reducing valve" to remain operable, all the thoughts, glances, motions, feelings, stimuli, memories, complexes, sounds, tastes, random occurrences, unceasing even to our dreams. No wonder we need sleep! And what a horrifying curse insomnia would be, no respite from the inexorable, gnawing work of the human brain. I have never read Proust but I can see how a whiff of something could produce a book as thick as a cantaloupe. To do justice to moment would take dozens of pages.

At this moment of course I have no interest in channeling my libidinal energies towards something socially acceptable such as writing a book. My only desire, healthy and fully American, is to make love to the delicious Butterfly. We make it back to the campsite and light a fire and after a nutritious if spartan supper of peanut butter, trail mix and herbal tea, Butterfly and I lie down next to each other on our sleeping bags looking up at stars spread across the night as if jewels hurled from a bucket onto a black velveteen surface. Datura and Paul move away a bit and lie on their bags murmuring about reincarnation and Hinduism while shooting stars go zilching across the sky. I explain the zilch to Butterfly, the cheap college thrill of hanging a tightly-rolled knotted plastic garment bag from the ceiling of a darkened dorm room and lighting it over a bowl of water, producing a toxic light show, making the odd onomatopoetic "zilch" sound as the blazing napalm-like knots fall through the air, landing with a sizzling splash in the water. Stoned to begin with, we would be thoroughly wigged after breathing the burning plastic fumes that choked the air like cigar smoke in a den of Chicago ward heelers.

Butterfly talks about sleeping on the porch during summer nights at her uncle's ranch, the mind-drenching flush of stars, yelping coyotes running amok, the smells of sage, creosote, wild roses, honeysuckle, the *hoohoo!* of great horned owls and as she talks of these things I run my fingers through her hair and she moves her legs and puts her hand on my thigh, rubbing close to my groin. Paul and Datura have stopped talking. The next thing I know the sky has turned and Butterfly and I are spinning through each other like pinwheels on an axis of stars, sliding down some hurrying slope with no exit and no power to resist, everything I have imagined, our clothes peeling off in an instant under cover of my bag, her strong body moving urgently beneath me fabulously hot and moist, a healthy animal with no hesitation or hang-up, opening so completely with such natural abandon that she carries me along with her, no hang-up or hesitation myself, no thoughts of Lulu Delilah and the humiliating fiery sexual crash that I had mistaken for a broken heart, no thoughts of sad shattered mother, domineering father, self doubts, nuclear war, Vietnam, silent majorities, Hells Angels, Kerouac, Cassady, Kennedy or Khrushchev—only the red, green and yellow explosions on the insides of my eyelids as Butterfly caresses and strokes (full erectile splendor!) and spins around and takes me in her mouth as she covers mine, the whole dripping, sweet-smelling tropical mass so deep and intoxicating that I might swoon or even die but Butterfly is having more and she spins again, moaning that awesome animal female sound as I ease into her strong and grip her flanks and do my best not to come too quickly as she writhes and bucks beneath me while I stuff my head with futile thoughts of baseball, football, carpentry, breakfast at El Capitan but then Apollo Eleven and a groaning launch inside her warm and beautiful as she moans deeper and sticks her tongue into my mouth and tightens her legs around my hips while stars fall on Alabama, the world turns cartwheel and Johnny comes marching home. I don't know if she comes and don't ask but she breathes softly and happily and I fall asleep on top of her, awakening maybe twenty minutes or half an hour later to see her smiling at me as I kiss her gently all over her face. "Baby kisses," she whispers.

Paul and Datura have moved with their sleeping bags about twenty yards to the south and seem to be conducting their own explorations though it is hard to tell how far they have traveled or at what speed. I get the impression they are going at a slower rate than Butterfly and I had. If our journey was a subway ride we had definitely taken the express. I am already thinking of the next ride on the local. Both have their pleasures. Lying next to Butterfly, the smells of our juices clinging like sexual syrup, the universe shifted to an agreeable, sensible shape for the moment, it is hard to refute the notion that really in the end it is about two human beings clutching each other under rioting stars, preferably but not necessarily sucking and fucking to their wild hearts' content. Sex and more sex! Get it while you can because the grave is a cold and onanistic ride and lasts for a long time. Butterfly's head rests on my arm as we silently look at the stars as Jefferson Airplane's "Somebody to Love" plays in my head and I think why not Butterfly as my somebody to love but it is at the moment impossible, though maybe not later. There are always more stories to tell.

***

Meanwhile familiar sounds are coming from Paul and Datura's direction that definitively answer my questions about his fidelity to Carmen. I wonder about hers to him. I know damn well that should the opportunity present itself I would probably have a roll with the fabulous Carmen, friendship with Paul be damned, the musk-monster obliterating all sentiment and good sense.

Butterfly and I sleep in each other's arms and before the sun warms our little meadow we make love again, going at it with fabulous early-morning intensity. After that we sleep for a while. During the night Paul and I take turns stoking the fire as at one point think we hear pigs snuffling around and so between yeoman love-making with our beauties and intrepid guard duty we are pretty tired come daybreak but pleased as pudding to be sure. Obviously sexual healing is where it's at. Paul and Datura stir and go naked up to the hot springs with only their towels and come back minutes

later in great laughing spirits, dressing quickly, Paul starting a new
fire for some Butterfly tea as we now call it. As Paul nurses the fire
Butterfly and I run up the trail through the chilly woods and jump in
the warm water, a bit shy with each other but happy also to be like
this, young, healthy, beautiful and kind of amazed at what is happening. She sits across from me in the pool looking like something
out of Tolkien and it strikes me sort of dumb just to look at her long
black hair plastered to the sides of her strong cheekbones—she can
easily pass for Native American—the ends floating in the water like
luxurious dark moss, the water half-covering her buoyant breasts so
that her nipples bob in and out of view. I don't know what she sees
looking at me but I doubt it is anything like the strong wild creature she surely is and for a moment the old miasma goes over me,
mocking and sinister, *hoohoo!* like the great wicked horned owl as I
swallow and try to beat the bastard back. There has to be something
about me she likes—a lot, apparently—but I am damned if I can understand it, this rather half-baked aimless stick figure I have come to
know all too well, which makes me think of Yeats' tattered coat on
a stick, a mortality that hovers around us like the stench of an au-
topsy with weekly death counts pasted on Friday night news screens
like football scores: we're winning! A mortar nicely placed in our
pool would transform Butterfly and me into strips of meat hanging
from the limbs of nearby trees for the crows to eat. The old tattered
sticks that run the world point their bony fingers and give the orders to turn the young into strips of meat. What is it about the old?
Is this how they get their kicks? This death-dealing lust for power?
We know they resent the hell out of our sexuality and secretly yearn
for it, the Johnsons, Nixons, McNamaras of the world and so many
more. We figure if these ghoulish bastards had more fucking and
sucking they would be less inclined to kill, maim and destroy. Is it
that they see themselves as tattered coats on sticks, more skeleton-

like day by day, absurd, anemic, on the fast track to oblivion lashing out in spite at the young, the healthy, the hopeful?

And here is Butterfly sitting across from me, a Mona Lisa smile on those sensual lips that have kissed me passionately and made love to me—the great wonder of it—and she is the very natural and healthy antithesis of the violent blood-splattering bastards who shit all over the world with their B-52s, napalm, agent orange and nuclear weapons. She is a miracle, a miracle that likes me. I am a fool to question or hesitate, to taint this moment with the poison of a sick world made sicker by tattered old men and their castrated lives. I slip under the water and surface next to her, taking her in my arms and kissing her and she reaches down and takes hold of me. Somewhere I have heard or read that you can't make love in the water but it must have come from a Bedouin or Inuit because within a minute Butterfly and I are doing it hot and fast once again and this time she moans and cries out loudly so all the creatures and spirits of the forest can hear and rejoice. Of the four of us Butterfly is the wildest and truest animal of the woods. *I love making love in nature* she says when we finish and she wraps her legs around me and clings to my neck licking and biting my ear as I look over her shoulder into the woods imagining the pigs and birds grunting and chirping approval: the goddess Butterfly is happy.

5

Pubic pleasures of the inferno > Jackboot misogyny > White tits
versus the racist pig power structure > Indian country, there and here

Datura and Butterfly have planned to go as far as Big Sur and then return to San Francisco but they change their minds and decide to go with us to Los Angeles to see the Watts Towers. Datura has a German friend in Santa Monica who will likely put us up for a few days. This friend, Sylvia, is doing graduate work in political science at UCLA and renting an apartment with her boyfriend who is active in "za black liberation moovemundt." About six hours later we are smack in the middle of a hot, chromed and sulfurous LA with Paul jumping into gear after a relatively quiet two days, maybe wrestling with his conscience, who knows, declaring his love for the "decadent, pubic, voyeuristic pleasures of America's Inferno," as he puts it, drawing parallels between Dante's *Inferno* and this great monstrous fantasyland. "If I wasn't so mucked-up in Protestantism and so attached to the pinkness of my lung tissue I'd live here in an instant," he declares, a goatish gleam in his blue eyes as he looks around happily at the glittering, ozone-drenched narcissism on full-frontal display. "Abandon all hope, ye who enter here!" he chortles

141

gaily. "We are in the circles of lust, materialism and gluttony! I love it!"

Datura and I are instantly and heavily digging it but Butterfly is pretty quiet and I keep looking at her out of the corner of my eye as her expression turns from mild amazement to shock to outright disgust, obviously one of the twenty-five percent immune to the toxic allure of LA. The color drains from her face and her magnificent jaw clenches as if wired shut but then on Wilshire Boulevard, not too far from Sylvia's place, we see a very elegant Sidney Poitier wearing white pants and a lavender shirt walking a little white poodle and Butterfly relaxes and joins the merriment. She loves Sidney Poitier. As wild and natural as Butterfly is she loves the movies and talks fondly of the times she and her parents would go to the drive-in theater in Truth or Consequences (T or C), a town formerly known as Hot Springs and famous, she explains, for its warm mineral baths where people went to "take the waters," especially popular as a haven for tuberculosis patients in the thirties. She speaks of the name Truth or Consequences with embarrassment, explaining how in 1950 the town was named after the radio show hosted by Ralph Edwards which later morphed into the TV show with Bob Barker and Beulah the buzzer whom I remember as a chimp with its hand covering its eyes.

Having seen one movie star and still in the afterglow of the encounter with "Glind-Eeezdvood" Butterfly and Datura are jazzed with the prospects of seeing more and Paul and I get into a thing of giving pedestrians famous names as we drive along Wilshire, the only rule being that there has to be at least minimal resemblance, shouting, "Hey, it's Tab Hunter!" or, "I see Rock Hudson!" or, "Look, it's Kim Novak!" and so forth, ascending to the more obscure highbrow end of the spectrum with, "Oh my god, Aldous Huxley!" or, "There goes Igor Stravinsky!" or, "I can't believe I just saw William Faulkner!" and then it is King Kong, Porky Pig, Flipper, Frankenstein, the Creature From the Black Lagoon, Buster Keaton, Bela Lugosi and Fatty Arbuckle. Soon we are at Sylvia's pad in Santa Monica at 3001 4th Street, right on the corner of Pier Avenue.

We find a parking space on Pier Avenue behind an abandoned red Corvair Monza convertible with its top down, filled with old newspapers, discarded clothes, beer cans and disposable diapers, a bullet or something having blasted a hole in the front windshield, hundreds of glittering shards in the driver's seat and four flat tires. The weather is hot and humid but the pollution is not bad, making it feel more like Key West than Los Angeles.

Sylvia's apartment is part of a non-descript stuccoed duplex with a patch of brown withered grass in front. Two tough-looking white boys and a pale thin girl sit at the entrance giggling and sticking chewing gum in each other's long greasy hair, moving grudgingly as Datura steps forward to ring the doorbell. The kids never make eye contact and continue to laugh stupidly, kind of rolling around on each other like they are drunk but with a weird vibe, their obliviousness to our presence disconcerting, as if we simply don't exist. Datura, clearly irritated with the youths, who are maybe thirteen or fourteen, pushes the bell impatiently and after a while a tall, very thin, light-skinned young black man with a bushy Afro, scruffy goatee and narrow face opens the door and after regarding us absently for a fleeting second yells at the kids, "I thought I told you guys to get the hell out of here!" They make a half-hearted effort to move, giggling and looking dimly at each other as if trying to come to a collective decision on an impossibly complex issue that may or may not have something to do with them. Their thick silliness and indolence angers the guy and he yells again, nudging the kids with his foot until they seem to comprehend, rising unsteadily and shuffling down the sidewalk. "Pathetic glue sniffers," he says, shaking his head disgustedly. He turns his attention to us. "What can I do for you?" he asks, and there proceeds a discussion between Datura and him, though he seems much preoccupied, and he agrees to let us stay in the living room until Sylvia returns from her afternoon class in an hour, around six-thirty.

***

We sit a bit glumly in the living room under the defiant gaze of Huey P. Newton smartly dressed in leather coat and beret sitting on his wicker throne clutching a shotgun in one hand and a spear in the other, the only thing in the little room other than the filthy gray couch which Datura, Paul and Butterfly are sitting on and the gray metal folding chair upon which I sit more or less facing them. The huge poster of Huey stares at us from the wall, impossible to ignore in the cramped space with Sylvia's aloof boyfriend in the adjoining room behind its pointedly closed door. Maybe this is a mistake but where the hell else are the four of us going to stay? Indeed, I wonder where Paul and I would have stayed in LA had we not met Butterfly and Datura. In general our plan is to find campgrounds on our way across but there seems no guarantee we will be able to stay at Sylvia's given the boyfriend's apparent coldness and the fact that we have shown up unannounced, though the code of the times embraces an open-door policy. At least we assume the guy is her boyfriend. We don't even know his name. He had not offered and his peremptory, distracted manner had silenced our own introductions. Given the tension in the apartment and Huey's dominating presence there is a certain strain on the conversation.

To fill the space I talk about the Free Huey demonstration I had gone to in Boston in 1969 where the police moved in and the crowd panicked, the fear conducted like electricity, turning the many souls of the crowd into one terrified animal in full-flight modality with no sense of where to flee, of which direction constituted safety. Few had any idea what caused the panic. It was just suddenly and overwhelmingly there, as if the mass had been sprayed with a power-ful fear-inducing chemical, the crowd surging one way and then another looking for escape, the cops surrounding us with a brutal, mindless show of force. With no exit for the expanding pressure vi-olent confrontations erupted with cops beating people viciously in isolated battles, the power of the mob finally bursting through the lines.

That day in Boston the freakish turn of the crowd's mood trig-gered the powerful sensory responses to panic, the metallic taste in one's mouth, the gush of acrid underarm fluids, the crazed look in everyone's eyes, the racing hearts and loss of reason, the feeling your body has turned insubstantial, pushed any which way at the mercy of random impulses and surges. In such situations you realize there is nothing to do but try to handle the rising flood as best you can, look for an opening and get the controlled fast fuck out of there. I had seen cops beat demonstrators before, most notably at the first Yip-in at Grand Central Station in 1968 when kids tore the hands off the big clock, but never with the brutality I witnessed that day in good old Boston. What amazed me was how the jackboots went after the females with particular viciousness—I had seen that at Grand Central Station too—pulling their hair, kneeing them in the groin, wrestling them to the ground and pushing their scream-ing faces into the pavement, pulling their arms back to handcuff them with a force that surely must have broken bones. The next step would have been rape had it not been merely a "police action," the distance between what the cops were "legally" doing and the de-pravity of actual war only a hair's breadth distance.

Paul says the cops singled out the females to emasculate the males and to eliminate any doubt as to the ruthlessness of their purpose—the obliteration of any naive middle-class notions of fair play—but Datura feels that it was a frustrated sexual brutality that drove the cops to attack the girls. There was a lot of blood spilled that day and several good battles between some of the tougher males and the cops. Not being one of the tougher males I slipped away to relative safety and took in the action, overwhelmed by violent feelings and fear, opting for spectator status and rooting for the demonstrators, though many of them by the looks of it would have felt just as comfortable on the other side. These were the crazies and bad-looking dudes, white and black, that you always wondered about, whether they were provocateurs or revolutionaries or just along for the amped-up crazy ride.

The door opens and the guy passes through the living room to the kitchen without a word, returning to his room with a can of V-8 juice, an introspective frown on his long face, the forlorn semblance of revolutionary goatee adding to the gloom. The four of us exchange resigned looks as if to say well, he hates us but what the hell can you do—we are white, after all—but I think we all wonder then what the hell is he doing with Sylvia and all the old complex poisons of black men and white women rise up and slither around the room like hissing snakes sliding in and out of our skulls, not that any of us gives a damn about black men with white women, I know I don't, just that these things get pretty twisted up sometimes and maybe that is the case in this fellow's head.

A few minutes later the front door opens and Sylvia enters the room, a short, plain, slightly overweight woman in her late twenties with cropped brown hair and bangs just above the eyebrows, wearing tattered dirty jeans and a Free Huey T-shirt with the same image of him in the chair but in this case far from resting against the flat surface of the living room wall. Sylvia is impressive enough to soften even the hardest of Hueys, or harden the softest of them. On either side of the Minister of Defense the outlines of Sylvia's nipples push through like obstinate seedlings on vernal Bavarian hillocks, making the stern Huey seem almost cuddly, and you see, or think you see, that all this man needs is some of this stuff, so much like a little boy does he look between those protective mounds. Vulnerable Huey, though of course that T-shirt, especially on a gifted untethered white girl like Sylvia, is enough to give some of the ofays conniptions or worse. Huey had risked absurdity posing like that, though I admire him and support his struggles against the "racist pig power structure" as I wouldn't hesitate calling it. At any rate things are rough for Huey and the rest of the Panthers but the fever is high and if sympathetic whites are not allowed in at least we are supportive.

But it is not always so simple. A lot of blacks, likely most, just flat out do not like whites, which can leave you in a really fucked-up position. If you are treated rudely or contemptuously, which often happens, you don't always know how to respond. I have seen it in others and in myself, the awkward shit-eating silence, the guilt so easily played upon, the humiliation, self-loathing, the hopeless irony of one's rage, the automatic, defensive triggering of one's conditioned racism like a dormant virus residing at the base of the spine. Blacks can do that to you as easily as throwing a switch, bring out the ugliness in spite of yourself, and some do it for sport, a kind of cruelty but also as the sternest sort of test, the measure of which most whites are bound to fail, the heady, dangerous days of the civil rights movement of the fifties and early sixties with its dreams of non-violence, racial justice and integration seen as so much precious cargo jettisoned as our ship navigates the rougher waters of black nationalism and white backlash. We admired Malcolm, even loved him, but could not get close. When the FBI or CIA killed King, as they surely did, the divide grew so large as to be virtually unbridgeable. The best we can do is speak and act strongly in parallel. We march in support, raise our fists and wear the colors, remembering what King, Malcolm X, Baldwin, Wright, Fanon and Ellison have said and listening closely to what Carmichael, Cleaver, Davis, Newton and others are saying, trying hard to make the connections that they see so clearly as the dispossessed and despised, seeing things from the belly up as we cannot, their theoretical grounding so much more sophisticated and experienced than ours as middle class whites.

And the cynicism and contempt are largely justified, as blacks understand few so-called white radicals are willing to step over the line and join them in their death struggle with the bone-splintering gears of the establishment. Still, the contempt and coldness is hard to handle if you see yourself as simpatico, a *why me?* sort of thing, being so nice and righteous and all, rushing naively into the breach, still connected by a golden tether like space walkers to our secure capsules as blacks are not. Only the Weather Underground and some other whites are willing to go as far and they will be ground up and blown out the other end like fertilizer, for what fallow ground remains to be seen.

***

Sylvia is thrilled to see Datura, runs to her excitedly and they embrace in delight, Huey caught in the middle, as Paul and I look at each other smiling as if to say isn't this the greatest of all possible lives but then the door opens behind us and Sylvia's boyfriend walks out looking stern and Sylvia and Datura step apart, Slylvia still smiling but a slight suck of current from her enthusiasm. She looks at him hopefully and speaking in a small, hesitant voice whose accent is considerably more North American than Datura's, referring to him as "baby," asking if we have all been introduced and so forth, with much awkwardness all around and before Sylvia can speak her friend's real name Datura jumps in and says she's going by this new hippie American moniker and that's what she wants to be called, but later a few times "Zelda" slips out, which is not a big deal be-

cause Zelda and Datura merge so seamlessly it doesn't make any difference, Delda/Zatura, Zadura/Delza, no matter, she is a legitimate
Datura and will remain that way with no problems. We are used to
it, the name "Zelda" an agreeable compliment, zany enough, and of
course we all know about Fitzgerald's wife. Just right. As for Butterfly, for the time being I don't want to know her real name because
it is all a wonderful fantasy and I don't want the spell broken and,
again, the name is just perfect. I wonder, naturally, but am content
for now and when the moment of our leave-taking arrives, which
might be sad, she will tell me or not, though of course I will ask.

Sylvia's boyfriend is named Maurice, a law student at UCLA
helping the legal team of Geronimo Pratt, a Black Panther accused
of killing a white female school teacher in Santa Monica several
years earlier. I have heard of the case but it is melded with all
the other news about the on-going war between the cops and the
Panthers, an uneven, ruthless conflict where the cops have all the
advantages, not the least of which is the overwhelming media campaign that paints the Panthers as crazed, armed revolutionaries bent
on killing whitey and raping his women. The Panthers started in
Oakland but most of the violence is happening in Los Angeles
where the police department has a unit devoted to battling them.
The cops had raided the Watts breakfast program in 1969—I remember reading about that with particular outrage—and then not
much later in early December the Chicago Police killed Fred Hampton and Mark Clark in a predawn raid and shortly after that was
the five-hour gun battle at Panther headquarters on Central Avenue
in Los Angeles where the LAPD brought in SWAT teams and he-
licopters and emptied enough rounds to wipe out a squadron of
NVA. Amazingly no one was killed in that battle but the number
of Panthers murdered by the police and killed in inter-turf battles
is growing large enough that even the most indifferent cannot help
but notice that something unusual is going on.

For those of us paying attention the slain Panthers stand out like a roll call of martyrs: Bobby Hutton, John Huggins, Bunchy Carter, Fred Hampton, Mark Clark. Huey Newton is in prison and Geronimo Pratt is on trial and likely headed there. Bobby Seale had been bound and gagged at the '68 trial. The pug-faced Negrophobe Hoover, with King's blood fresh on his hands, has branded the Black Panther Party the country's greatest internal threat, which plays well in the heartland given their image in local tabloids and living room fantasy boxes, their outlandish style and stance that straddles the line between almost unimaginable courage and foolhardiness though you know they are doomed, outgunned and outnumbered by the police, infiltrated by the slithery machinations of COINTEL-PRO and demonized and ridiculed by the country's propaganda machine. The Panthers have been from the start under the dubious aegis of St. Jude, patron saint of impossible causes, which is why so many of us admire them, even love them, from afar to be sure, for to stand face-to-face in opposition to the destructive power of the government, the insuperable weight of the culture with its crushing inertia, racism and vast resources is the very embodiment of lost causes, a wild charge into the jaws of impossibility. They are magnificent, these Panthers, standing up in their black leather jackets and berets, summoning the craziest of bravado and attitude, willing to die, most of them, for something as simple and profoundly radical as feeding children in their own neighborhoods. Imagine! They probably go too far with their weapons and confrontational tactics, which plays right into the hands of the enemy, but I am in no position to criticize because it is not my reality and their sheer courage is awesome. As far as I am concerned the picture of the Black Panthers standing at armed attention on the steps of the California state capitol is equivalent to Nathan Hale's fife and drums corps as an iconic image in American history.

Well, this is how I feel which is why though I do not much like Maurice and his sourness it doesn't particularly bother me as I know he is dealing with shit I can barely relate to and anyway after a few minutes of serious talk about the Pratt case between Sylvia and him as we listen carefully and not unsympathetically, the tension subsides and Maurice actually asks us a few questions about our travels. His manner is formal and somewhat guarded, as if deliberately maintaining the distance between our worlds as a matter of policy or principle, but it is also clear that he is not a hater of whites as I first imagined, a knee-jerk response in any case in these touchy times, though it is hard to imagine any black actually *liking* whites, and who the fuck can blame them? He is in fact a decent and very intelligent guy. He had been tense and preoccupied, obviously, when we had arrived, not in the mood to deal with distractions or bullshit like the pubescent nihilist glue-sniffers on his doorstep or the unanticipated arrival of four white hippies on a lark looking for his girlfriend. In fact, as he explains, he is doing research not only on the Geronimo Pratt case (unequivocally a frame-up, he says) but also has the pressure of a twenty-five-page paper due on the Civil Rights Act of 1964, which, he says, while good (not the paper but the Act), has weaknesses based on specificity—loopholes, in other words. Paul has some knowledge about this, which makes an impression, and they have a brief exchange on some of these points in the law.

Maurice visibly softens as we speak, much the same way Huey's warrior image is transformed by the warmth of Sylvia's womanly assets. Though he is careful not to let down his guard completely the tightness in his face dissolves, his rigid carriage loosens, and while not graceful he possesses a gangly sort of ease that implies a playfulness that will surely come out once you get to know him. Even the wispy attempt at a militant goatee becomes less disagreeable, though he can do without it, but the most attractive thing about him is the clarity of his brown eyes, which not only communicate intelligence and purpose but also reservoirs of warmth and humor that make you want to be his friend, share the mirth and sarcasm, partake in some good-natured ribbing and repartee, all the more desirable because he is black and connected to the Panthers and so many dead-serious issues that you yearn to connect to in a real way yourself—in other words the frustrations of a white middle-class hippie on the lookout for "relevance," a big word these days, the quest to make it real, to escape the white-bread world of hypocrisy, bullshit and Fanon's peaceful violence.

It is agreed we will spend a couple of nights crashing on the living room floor and we pile our stuff into the room, after which Paul and I go to a small store nearby, Samman's Market, for some spaghetti, Ragu, Kraft's Parmesan and Gallo. In the store, a dusty, gloomy hole in the wall, an overweight balding Middle-Eastern guy behind a glass display case filled with horrible-looking pastries sells diapers and beer to a black kid in exchange for food stamps. A half-minute later a tall older drunk black man, barefoot and wearing a tattered black overcoat, comes in and demands wine, getting belligerent when refused, the Middle-Eastern guy reaching down and pulling out a monstrous handgun, his voice rising several octaves with the old guy retreating and threatening to come back and burn the store down. Paul and I are standing at the back of the store behind a shelf taking all this in, ready to hit the floor if the guy starts firing. The proprietor or clerk, whatever he is, takes our money in state of extreme agitation, yelling about the "fucking niggers" and how he is going to shoot somebody some day. Everything in the wretched little store is absurdly overpriced, vivid confirmation of the stereotypical situation. We get the fuck out of Samman's before the drunken barefoot guy comes back or some other crazy shit goes down. "I wonder if that was Samman himself," says Paul. We pass the old barefoot guy staring off in the distance and muttering, standing with his back against a chain-link fence surrounding a schoolyard.

In the kitchen Datura, Sylvia, Butterfly and Maurice are seated on a motley collection of thrift-store chairs and milk crates around an old Formica-topped table, drinking wine and talking animatedly about the harassment of the Panthers. Their bottle of Gallo is empty and with a flourish I put the new one on the table to expressions of approval and a warm smile from Butterfly that just about floors me and in the moments it takes to empty the rest of the bag I think of my life with Butterfly in New Mexico living in an adobe house with vegetable garden, chickens, pigs and plump healthy hippie children running wild and naked. Sylvia has a big, pale-blue speckled enamel pot of boiling water going on the funky mustard-colored gas stove and next to it a large green plastic bowl filled with lettuce and grated carrots sits on the counter alongside a greasy bottle of Wishbone Italian dressing, the grimy yellowish kitchen walls bare save for a small reproduction of a Spanish bullfighting poster featuring Manolete directly above the table, the bullfighter's elegant machismo reminiscent of the Panthers. I am struck by the emptiness of the apartment, as if Maurice and Sylvia are ready for a quick getaway. Sylvia gets up and empties the Ragu into a saucepan and the spaghetti into the pot while Maurice makes room and Paul and I sit down on metal milk crates. Sylvia joins us. Our odd assortment of drinking glasses filled to the brim with cheap burgundy, Ragu bubbling in the saucepan and spaghetti roiling like laundry in hot sudsy water, we proceed to get down to serious matters.

***

"And so our history is one long bloody story of oppression and betrayal..." Maurice and the rest of us are pretty buzzed, dirty plates piled in the sink, splotches of tomato sauce and spilled wine drying on the scratched surface of the Formica table, flecks of Kraft's grated Parmesan cheese sticking to our elbows, passions, revolutionary and otherwise, at a high pitch. Even Butterfly who professes not to be a drinker is in fine shape, at one point standing and cupping her marvelous breasts and offering them as weapons for the revolution. "It's za black tid zat suckled za white oppressor!" exclaims Datura/Zelda, her accent becoming harder to understand by the minute, standing up and cupping her own smallish breasts. "Now it's time for za white tid to deztroy za white oppressor!" We laugh like hell, Maurice most of all, after figuring out what she had said and then Sylvia gets up, a kind of expectant hush coming over us as these are the grandest of all and actually *are* being offered as weapons for the revolution, Huey warping in and out in a kind of funhouse perspective as she holds her enormous wares with fervid small hands and yells with all the gusto of Emma Goldman at a union revival, "And these white tits are being used to nourish the black revolutionary in his struggle against the racist pig power structure! Power to the people!" We jump up, Paul knocking over his wine glass, yelling, "Power to the people! Right on! Power to the people!" raising our fists like good White Panthers, excepting of course Maurice who raises a bony black fist and Sylvia takes his thin shining brown face and bushy Afro and pulls him fiercely between her militant Bavarian breasts and holds him there as he laughs and gasps for air and we keep on yelling, "Power to the people!" with a fervor possibly unsettling if sober but of course we are not so what the hell.

There is a quiet moment after this outburst as if we are checking ourselves for damage from an explosion, which, of sorts, has occurred with our drunken powers to the people and black tit/white tit exclamations, staring at the red pool of wine spreading across the table from Paul's overturned glass, a sobering sight, the blood of slain Panthers, blood shed by real, no-bullshit revolutionaries, the blood of Malcolm X, George Jackson, Martin Luther King and others and I wonder if we have gone too far with Maurice with our drunken power to the people jive, the spilled wine symbolic of a reality so far removed from most whites, especially us middle-class sojourners, that we really have no right to even utter the phrase unless prepared to back it with our own blood but no, as we sit contemplating the symbolic implications of the spilled wine he raises his glass and rather amazingly says, "That's the blood of RFK along with the rest of our martyred brothers and sisters." Paul is wiping up his spilled wine and we all solemnly intone *right on* and I relate how when RFK was killed by this odd little man, Sirhan Sirhan, so very odd indeed, I was alone at my parents' house in Long Island and was so shaken, especially after JFK and Malcolm and MLK, that I took my shotgun and killed a rabbit that was nibbling on some grass outside, disemboweled it and on my knees took its entrails in my hands and raised them to the sky as supplication or protest to what power I had no idea, the whole thing done in a kind of grief-stricken trance that surely had its roots in an ancient ritual that had come up through the soil and taken command of me, digging two holes beneath a pine tree and burying the rabbit's body in one and its entrails in the other. I had no idea why I did this. Butterfly looks at me noncommittally as if she is not quite sure about this but Sylvia and Datura say *wow* and Maurice says it is heavy, and Paul, rinsing out the dishrag, says it was a sacrifice, obviously, to a greater reality that I had the fine instincts to recognize and a cathartic gesture in the face of madness, the entrails, he explains, thought to be a source of evil in some ancient cultures, removed from the bodies of those who had died of sickness and buried separately or burned, a solid and healthy gesture he says, meaning mine, and wishes he'd done it himself but there weren't any rabbits around at the time. Instead he had gotten drunk.

"Robert Kennedy was a good man," says Maurice, "The best of the white politicians. Even though he was rich he knew what it was to suffer. He knew death and loss. And most important he knew the real meaning of class and the unequal distribution of economic power in society, how it destroys the conscience of the rich and the lives of the poor. Somehow he had the burden of conscience, which is very unusual in the wealthy, or even the middle class for that matter." He says this with a hint of bitterness, looking down at the table.

"I sink even za middle class has less conscience zan za wealthy," says Datura, rummaging through her backpack and pulling out a tin of marijuana and pack of Zig Zag rolling papers. She holds a paper with the thumb and forefinger of her right hand and tapping the container, a white throat-lozenge tin with red German lettering, with her left, distributes a nice even stream of the stuff, licks the gummed edge with her wine-soaked tongue and seals it up, then sticks the whole thing like a little white cock in her mouth for a good coating of Saxon female saliva. Perfect. So Datura is left-handed. Makes sense. She rummages some more, retrieves a chromed Zippo lighter, clicks it open, lights the joint, inhales deeply and passes it to Sylvia on her left, everyone taking a decent hit but when the joint reaches Butterfly she says no thanks and passes it along. Paul fills his empty glass and the bottle makes the rounds, following the marijuana.

Maurice speaks. "Nevertheless I fully expected to be betrayed by Bobby had he been elected. There's only so much a decent person can do in a system that's rotten to the core. This is a system that chews you up and spits you motherfuckin' out, no matter how well intentioned you are. As a black person I deal with racism every day, but that's not the main problem. It's the rotten, corrupt, capitalist system that's the true culprit and we've got to bring it down—not reform it but bring it down. And besides, Bobby was no socialist, he was a scion of the ruling class and a capitalist through and through himself."

"Agreed," says Paul, characteristically stroking his beard, "Capitalism is a dead end. But what particularly interests me these days is the patriarchal structure of the culture and how it works together with the ruthless, hierarchical demands of capitalism, with its reliance on power and domination. It's all about brute masculine force, a complete distortion of the essence of the real masculine principle, which is in my view creative and communitarian and not about domination. This leads to a question. My impression of the Panthers is that it's a completely patriarchal movement, dominated by the image and reality of aggressive masculine power—in this sense no different than the forces against which it struggles. The question, two parts, is, a: Is this an accurate perception? and, b: If so, is this the wisest path to pursue in achieving your goals?"

All eyes turn to Maurice for his response.

"Good question, good observation," says Maurice.

The joint comes to him from Sylvia and he waves it off, looking down at the table and pausing for a moment with a thoughtful, composed expression that communicates thorough familiarity with these issues and much more, as if Paul's points are elementary, a slightly rueful smile creasing his slender intelligent face, a bit of Stokely, I think, without the razor's edge. I am sitting between him and Paul and as he is about to respond directly to Paul I pull my crate back a few inches so they can see each other clearly.

"First of all," he says quietly, still looking at the table, "I'm not a member of the Black Panther Party. The fact of the matter is, I don't have their courage—nowhere near it. These are some serious people we're talking about, dead serious—and a lot of them are seriously dead. These are people who've crossed the line and made a commitment from which there is no turning back. They are revolutionaries, plain and simple, and I don't think most of us, black or white, are capable of truly understanding what that means—the seriousness of that." He pauses and looks up at all of us, his jaws clenched. He breathes deeply and takes a sip of wine. Behind the rigid expression lie his youth and vulnerability, and more than a hint of fear, the kind of fear incommunicable to those not having shared his experience. He may not be officially a Black Panther but he is close enough.

"I sure as hell didn't understand the seriousness until I became involved with Geronimo Pratt's case. I come from a middle-class background, educated parents. My reality has been as removed from the ghetto as all of yours has. There's just no way of describing or understanding that reality unless you've lived it. Just no way. So to answer your question, yes, the Panthers are patriarchal and militaristic and yes, they're falling right into the trap of emulating a more powerful adversary and fighting the war on his terms. But for all the mistakes and tragedies that have occurred I don't criticize the Panthers. I mean, I'm on their side, I'm helping them, I can relate to them.

"There's an ongoing tension within the party between the more conscious sisters and the male chauvinists and that's being resolved within the party itself. Part of the problem is that basically there's a war going on, and war, at least in this culture, is fought by males, so consequently the party is dominated by males. Like I say, this is serious business. You would not believe the aggressiveness and provocation and racist ugliness of the police, the Metro Squad, the war against the party. It's unrelenting and vicious. People are getting provoked and set up all the time, from constant surveillance to traffic stops to in-your-face motherfucking racist insults to infiltration to dirty tricks to you name it—constant, cruel and never-ending. And it comes from the top, the FBI, the White House, all the way down to the racist pig on the beat. The pressure these people are under is beyond belief. I couldn't take it. I'm halfway flipped out as it is from all the pressure and I'm just on the periphery. They've been backed into a corner and maybe some of that's their own doing, but there's no turning around. And all this really from the desire to control their own communities and having the audacity to act on it instead of just mouthing revolutionary platitudes. And they're smart, these guys, from the brothers off the street to the leadership. They know exactly what the game is, and it's called capitalist exploitation with a nice vicious element of racism for good measure."

Maurice takes another drink of wine and looks at Sylvia, who gives him a serious look in return.

"And dig this. These are some righteous brothers standing up for black males in this racist country everywhere, for the Emmit Tills and the Herbert Lees and the Lamar Smiths and all the nameless brothers strung up, burned alive, skinned alive, buried alive, strung out, humiliated and forced to eat the white man's shit for four hundred motherfucking years. Yeah, it may be a suicide mission but goddamn, we love those crazy motherfuckers—those beautiful brothers standing up and saying fuck you! We aint taking you and your racist, inhuman system any more! Fuck you! And we're willing to die for our manhood and take out some pigs in the process. And dig this. No doubt there are some crazy motherfuckers in the Panthers—some scary motherfuckers—but they're also some of the bravest, most beautiful people I've ever met or ever hope to meet, beautiful cats, and understand, their motivation is pure—pure righteous anger and pure righteous love for their people, their beautiful black brothers and sisters, their children and their elders. It's love, like Che Guevara said, that motivates the true revolutionary, and believe me, the Panthers have it."

Maurice empties his glass. I refill it and the bottle passes around the table without anyone speaking. Paul offers a toast to the Panthers. We clink glasses. Maurice takes a deep breath and exhales.

"What can I say? It's a process. The Panthers are probably going down. The forces against them are too great, too vicious. The pigs have killed or locked up most of the leadership. Internal divisions are rife, most of them fomented by COINTELPRO and their counterrevolutionary tactics. But I really believe that the Panthers will survive in spirit and will be remembered as an inspiration for future movements."

Maurice sips his wine and strokes his wispy goatee. Reaching out with a long thin arm he picks up the cold joint from a round glass ashtray and lights it with the Zippo, casual incendiary of Vietnamese hooches, and clicks it shut. He inhales, looking like the modern urban revolutionary, and, holding the joint between his left forefinger and thumb, examines the lighter in the palm of his right hand, contemplating its substance, then clicks open the lid and cranks the thumbwheel, the spark catching the wick, the soft pale yellow flame drawing our silent attention. As the spilled wine has reminded us of blood, the Zippo's flame, at least for myself, conjures visions of flaming villages and the hell-thumping of helicopter rotors, from there to the burning of US cities, burn, baby, burn. Maurice snaps the lid shut.

"What I mean to say is that we're all learning. The Panthers will die but out of the ashes will come something better, more effective. Their courage will inspire and their experience will teach. They are the vanguard, the leaders of a movement, even if only symbolically, that will carry on past our lifetime and past the lives of our children. What I've learned from some of the older brothers is to take the long perspective. We're young, we want change now, revolution now, but it's all a process, a long struggle, with victories and defeats, but I firmly believe that history is on our side, the side of the people, and the revolution will succeed. It may take two hundred years but the revolution *will* succeed."

"I'll drink to that," says Paul. He raises his glass and we toast the revolution.

"All of the dysfunctions of the dominant society are magnified in the ghetto," Maurice continues. "But the worst thing is what happens to the black male. That's what's so significant about the Panthers, and why white America is so threatened. It's the image of black masculine power that enrages whites and elicits the violent reaction. For the males of the party it's a double-edged sword, a vicious cycle. The more power they display the more violent the response. They follow Mao's dictum about political power coming out of the barrel of a gun but they're up against the greatest Maoists in the world in that regard, The United States government."

"Did the Panthers make a mistake by taking their guns to the capitol steps?" asks Paul.

"In my opinion, yes. A great act of political theater but guaranteed to unchain the beast, which is exactly what happened. The point has always been the legitimacy of self-defense in our own communities, which is why the original name was the Black Panther Party for Self-Defense, but the tactics of proving the point through the imagery of armed, black-clad, militant Black men symbolically invading the state's seat of authority was waving a red flag in the beast's face. Now, some of the party members would come down on me for this but I don't think the Panthers have the strength or recognition to be the leaders of an armed revolution in this country or the world. To think otherwise is delusional, but unfortunately there's a delusional element in the party."

"Like Eldridge Cleaver?" asks Paul.

"I would say so, yes. Look, Eldridge is a great writer but apparently he's got the idea that armed revolution can succeed in

America, which is pretty unlikely. And he's saying all this stuff from exile, in places like Cuba and Algeria. I mean, let's get real. My opinion is the Panthers should do a better job of publicizing the peaceful, community-oriented programs they've instituted that are really significant and not make a deliberate public spectacle of being armed revolutionaries. More of the Black Muslim model. I mean, the Muslims are really a low-profile, highly-disciplined organization. They have guns, they'll defend themselves, and everybody knows that—even the pigs respect that. Listen, if you go to the ghetto you'll see that the police really are like an occupying military force. It's a colonial situation, no question. The Panthers and all black people have the legitimate right to defend themselves in this colonized, highly militarized environment. They have the right to police and control their own communities the same way any group of people has the right. The legal right. Now, unfortunately, the cops, the pigs, see themselves as not just the law, but above the law, meaning that they feel they can get away with anything, and most of them are just stoned fucking racists, thugs with badges and weapons, backed up by the biggest crime syndicate in history, the US government.

"So you take these guys, these racist thugs with badges and weapons, and put them in an impoverished, dysfunctional black community and you are guaranteed a recipe for disaster. In Oakland you have a situation of extreme poverty and a high crime rate with the added element of an aggressive, mostly white, police force just basically running roughshod over what was, and is, to them, an alien community, an antagonistic community, and the result is a kind of low-level war where the entire population is regarded as hostile and suspect—'Indian country,' as they call it in Vietnam."

There is quiet at Maurice's last words, "Indian country." Datura and Sylvia, while not connected to this particular historical ugliness have their own burden of shame, the holocaust less than two decades removed. They look uncomfortable, Datura more so than Sylvia, who seems on the verge of saying something. I feel a mixture of shame, disgust and anger. The most visibly upset though is Butterfly. "Racist bastards!" she spits. "I'm fucking ashamed to be a white person sometimes."

"It's a profound betrayal, is what it is," says Paul. "We're spoon-fed a bunch of myths as children starting with the tooth fairy and Santa Claus and one-by-one they're stripped away and more ugly truths are revealed: America as a force for good in the world; everything we learn in school is true; the Judeo-Christian heritage as the paragon of human morality; free enterprise as the one and only system; our leaders never lie; every person has an equal chance to succeed; a beneficent deity watches over us and salvation is possible. These betrayals stem from male-dominated capitalist, hierarchical social structures that rely on fear, lies and coercion for their continuance. It's the great white father, god the father, the father of our country, the all-conquering powerful male, whether up in the sky or right down here on earth, spinning lies and fairy tales with one hand and slipping money under the table to his hired guns with the other. It's an authority based on brute force, physical intimidation, which is why it jibes so perfectly with what they call 'free enterprise,' meaning competition for wealth and power, an inherently unfair contest that reinforces the selfish and brutal tendencies of human nature."

Sylvia, who has been waiting impatiently to speak, breaks in, "Yes! We all know about the fatherland. The thousand-year Reich has become the thousand-year shame for the German people. And don't think it couldn't happen here! Of course males—black males who have been persecuted by the racism of this country, by the sick, hung-up sexual insecurities of white people—dominate the Panthers. It doesn't bother me that strong, intelligent black males who have the courage to stand up to this racist system lead them. These men are incredible, an inspiration to oppressed people everywhere, and most of all to young black men in their own neighborhoods. It's like Huey says, a people oppressed for so long has to stand up and make the oppressor take notice, even at the risk of death—a question of living on your knees or dying on your feet. These men have chosen to die on their feet. I'm not necessarily criticizing your points, Paul—I mean, they're valid. But you do understand the significance of what these black men are doing, don't you? It's incredibly courageous and I respect them completely."

Before Paul can respond, Maurice speaks, "I agree with most of what you say, Paul. What Huey is saying, ultimately, is that the guns are the necessary and justifiable first step—but only a first step. The emphasis from the start has been on self-defense—with weapons—both to protect our own communities and to raise revolutionary consciousness in terms of a statement of power—power on its most basic level, the level of physical force, the level that the Man comprehends. I reiterate the point I made earlier and it's related to what Sylvia says. The Panthers are standing up for all black people. And yes, the party *is* dominated by males but a lot of us don't have a problem with that because this is a society that places a terrible, genocidal burden on black males and therefore we recognize the special significance and importance of the black man standing up in the face of his oppressor. It is, as Huey would say, a historical necessity, and believe me, though a lot of black people won't admit to it, the Panthers are widely admired in the black community. What I am saying is that a necessary precondition for revolution is the psychological emancipation of the black male in this repressive, racist society. We recognize this. Most of our women recognize this. The emasculated, fetishized, stunted black male must free himself if we are to advance our cause, which is nothing less than the emancipation of all people everywhere, irrespective of color or anything else."

"Spoken like a true Panther," says Paul, smiling.

"Just another brother tryin' to make it in a strange and hostile land," replies Maurice.

"Stranger in a strange land," says Paul.

"And getting stranger all za time," says Datura.

***

I get up to take a leak in the small bathroom that badly needs a paint job but is otherwise clean. A framed print of Ben Shahn's Sacco and Vanzetti poster hangs on the wall above the toilet, the one with Vanzetti's words at the bottom: *"If it had not been for these thing, I might have live out my life talking at street corners to scorning men. I might have die, unmarked, unknown, a failure. Now we are not a failure. This is our career and our triumph. Never in our full life could we hope to do such work for tolerance, for joostice, for man's onderstanding of man as now we do by accident. Our words—our lives—our pains nothing! The taking of our lives—lives of a good shoemaker and a poor fish ped-dler—all! That last moment belongs to us—that agony is our triumph."*

Another crucifixion. I think of Vanzetti in Elizabeth shooting seagulls and if the death of the two anarchists means anything at all to him. Probably not, unless they are related. It seems extraordinary that these two humble workers had such consciousness, a rare thing to find in the modern working class, at least the white work-ing class, but then in those days people knew something about pol-itics and alternatives to capitalism. Now the white working class is about the most reactionary element in the country. I think of the hardhats who beat up anti-war protesters on Wall Street a couple of years earlier, an attack seething with resentment against the middle-class and their soft, spoiled and self-indulgent children. After all, it's the youth of the working class and poor who are fighting and dying in Vietnam. Again our rulers have divided us. Where are our Sacco and Vanzetti when we really need them?

When I return Paul has taken my seat and is talking to Maurice. I sit in Paul's old seat next to Sylvia. Datura has rolled another joint and it is being passed around, everyone feeling pretty friendly. A nice combination, the wine and the pot. I feel like leaping across the table and jumping on the delicious Butterfly. I am very lucky to be in the company of these beautiful people. A week ago I was Gregor Samsa broke down on the Jersey Turnpike, rescued by a squat Italian-American man who amused himself shooting seagulls with an expensive shotgun and who left me with the notion that I just might have a guardian-fuckin'-angel watching over me. Just might. Breaking down on the Jersey Turnpike on a bleak Sunday morning, my head and heart in shambles, balls in retreat, is certainly a low point in a young life that has seen its share but then how quick the reversals, or so I feel at this moment in Sylvia and Maurice's apartment, securely entrenched in a universe of fellow travelers that have materialized almost as if in a dream. Here is a lesson I recognize even in the dimness of my self-absorbed lights, a connection, a companionship, a friendship can turn the most desolate corner of the universe into something like a spot in front of the living room fireplace with your golden retriever's head resting lovingly in your lap, no one, I figure, knowing this better than those who have nothing, the drifters and outcasts, the hobos hopping freight cars and so forth, striking up friendships that have the duration of a signal flare, nonetheless diving in openly and intensely. Meanwhile Paul and Maurice have their heads together and are talking about parents, Maurice starting in on the subject of his own, all ears turned in his direction.

"My father and mother have a nice love story," says Maurice, and for the next half hour tells of his parents' relationship, his mother white and Jewish, his father black and Christian, his mother's family's rejection of the relationship, more for religious reasons than racial, the lovers' long separation, continuing love and incredible reunion, the makings of a tale straight out of Cervantes or Henry Fielding. I am astonished and once again struck by the wilderness of events that determines our lives, the riotous, random crashing and mingling of subatomic particles. Or was something else at work here? The women have no doubt.

"To luff," says Datura, holding up her wine glass for a toast.

"And love stories," says Butterfly.

"Amen," says Sylvia.

6

Smug reassertion of the true condition > Command to terminate >
Our burdens lightened > Cheap thrills and trapdoors > Goat's milk and
Ambu Bags for the beach lizards > A bad case of lupus interruptus

"Listen," says Maurice, "there's a Panther function tonight at a church in Watts, kind of a potluck with some poetry and speeches and some music later on. The dinner's probably over but the rest of the stuff will go on for hours, and you *know* there's going to be some good music. I need to talk to some people about the Pratt case and you all are welcome to come. Get to see some real live Panthers up close."

Now this is a little different. It is one thing to sit around a friendly kitchen table and talk about the Panthers and radical politics and voice all kinds of sympathy to the cause. Yes, that is great, uplifting and *simpatico* and makes one feel like the kick-ass revolutionary with all the "power to the people" jive, but to actually go into the heart of the ghetto to a Panther function is something else altogether. Maurice smiles at our hesitation and says, "If you have any misgivings, don't worry about it. These people are cool. Besides, you're with me, and a lot of the people working with Geronimo will be there, maybe even Geronimo himself. Just make sure you put some money in the kitty. We can go in my van."

We say okay and in a few minutes are stuffed in Maurice's pale green 1963 VW microbus on our way through the city and into Watts. As we ride along I remind myself that I am a good guy, foursquare behind liberation movements of all kinds, that I love soul music and had played baseball one summer with an all-black team, but I am still a little nervous as Maurice parks the van while across the street in front of the church black people mill about on the sidewalk, including several leather-coated Panthers who seem to be standing guard. We get quietly out of the van and walk across the street, Maurice leading us towards a large room attached to a white wooden church of the Baptist variety, loud music and laughing voices issuing from the room's dark interior, heads turning as we approach, silently watching the tall young light-skinned African-American male with five varyingly self-conscious pale faces in tow, a relatively curious sight but not so curious as to cause any particularly overt response, just kind of cool with only a few hostile expressions. Maurice walks up to one of the Panthers and does some of the business with the hands, the dap thing, and he introduces us as "comrades in struggle" and the Panther at the door, a stocky menacing-looking guy wearing shades and an Eldridge-style goatee shakes our hands in a formal manner and says, "Power to the people," to each of us and we all respond in kind. This is a step up from earlier at the kitchen table. My revolutionary portfolio is expanding. I have shaken hands with an actual Black Panther and uttered the talismanic words.

Inside the large dimly-lit room about a hundred people stand around in clumps talking animatedly as Billy Stewart plays loudly from two huge speakers on either side of a long table upon which sit great numbers of empty tureens, bowls, platters, crock pots and such, testament to what must have been a considerable feast. At one end of the table stands a collection of liquor bottles, gin, vodka, whiskey, along with an array of soft drinks, 7-UP, Coke, Canada Dry, Schweppes, cranberry juice, a large green plastic ice bucket and a pair of chromed tongs. Plastic cups are scattered about the table with stacks of fresh cups next to the ice bucket, next to which is a woven basket full of money to which we go directly and put some in. I have thirty-five dollars in my wallet, the rest of my money, about $300, in my backpack at Maurice and Sylvia's, and put in five. Though there is no big deal about our presence you know that everyone is immediately aware of us as strangers, the only whites in the place, but I don't feel too nervous or self-conscious and none of my companions appears very much so either. I had not known what to expect but the vibe is pretty mellow. Other than the huge iconic poster of Huey on the wall and the handful of leather-jacketed Panthers apparently on guard at various locations around the room and outside, it seems like an ordinary party or get-together, relaxed and happy, Billy Stewart's beautiful voice bringing me back to more innocent high school days when friends and I would hang out at a bar, Arthur's, owned by a much-respected elderly black man that was as fine and friendly a place as one could imagine.

This gathering in the church's meeting room with the music, food and warm vibes is, then, familiar, and I feel relatively comfortable, but of course Arthur's was not in the middle of an urban ghetto and the sixties had not yet exploded in violence and polarization. The four of us, Paul, Datura, Butterfly and I, trail Maurice and Sylvia as they make their way to a group of people bound together in deep discussion who greet Maurice warmly, no one in the group particularly friendly but it is not too bad either though after acknowledging us they fall back into their discussion, with one of the people, a thin dark woman with fine features and a large Afro, filling Maurice in on the latest news about the Pratt case. From what I can hear things are bad. The feeling seems to be that the government is in on this in a way they don't quite understand yet, perhaps an informant, and that Geronimo Pratt has about as much chance of getting off as his namesake had a hundred or so years earlier.

We are definitely excluded from this group, understandably, our tenuous ease diminishing correspondingly, but then someone puts Wilson Pickett on and people start dancing, at the same time an older friendly man with a Gordon Parks mustache coming over, insisting we all get drinks, leading us to the table where I help myself to a whiskey and soda, Paul having the same, while Datura pours herself some vodka and cranberry juice. Butterfly has juice. The music is loud and we try to answer the man's questions as best we can with lots of non-verbal communication, smiles, nods, arm-grasping and so forth and then Datura grabs Paul's hand, pulling him out onto the dance floor, Butterfly and I hesitating, both of us being a little more shy than our friends, but the man with the moustache enthusiastically encourages us to dance, practically pushing us onto the floor, "Don't be bashful now, come on, time to boogie!" and we self-consciously go out and start moving around to the music, getting into it, Paul and Datura already going strong, Paul thrashing around in his signature jerky style that has little to do with the actual tempo of the music but enthusiastic and energetic enough so that you can't deny him—he certainly doesn't care—and my initial embarrassment at his almost total lack of rhythm and bizarre style, which elicits all the responses from the other dancers and onlookers that you might imagine, amazement, smiles, laughter, condescension, derision, disgust, indifference, soon gives way to amusement as most people are smiling at Paul's complete lack of self-consciousness, his absolute fidelity to himself and his own style, which of course will win you points in virtually any environment or situation save the religious or political and who gives a swill for that anyway. It is tremendously clear that Paul has soul and crazy style and any white motherfucker who comes into this place and starts dancing like *that* has to have balls and a guardian-fuckin'-angel just like old Antonio had said about me. Datura, Butterfly and I just laugh and start dancing crazy ourselves, the wine, pot, whiskey, cranberry juice, Wilson Pickett and pure strangeness of being in Watts in a Baptist church filled with Black Panthers and their supporters kicking us into overdrive and we are shaking and shimmying like pale Zulus on poppers. There never was much dancing at *Arthur's* so this is the first time I have ever danced with a large group of blacks. As a kid in New York I would come home after school and watch *American Bandstand* on ABC with Dick Clark and it was cool, but sometimes I would switch over to WNTA and check out *Jocko's Rocket Ship* with the fast-talking Jocko Henderson and watch the black teenagers dance, so different from the whites on *Bandstand* it might as well have been another planet, a real head-twister for a young white boy up to that point with no experience of blacks other than Amos 'n Andy, Buckwheat, Eddie "Rochester" Anderson and a hero worship of Willie Mays. Now everyone including country cousins dances in the style of blacks or tries to anyway and apart from Paul, who is in his own unassailable realm, we try like hell to dance with as much style as we can, with varying degrees of success. Datura, full of eyes-closed abandon, has her own German funk style with her arms raised, pumping her wide hips back and forth, crazy hair flying out like a covey of flushed partridges. Butterfly is much smoother than her friend, with lots of shoulder and hip action, attracting the admiring glances of males in the vicinity who nudge each other and comment. White hippie girls are in the bra-less vanguard and this is a wholesome sight for some of the brothers, though I am not sure how their girlfriends are taking it. The woman with the fine features and puffy Afro is not wearing a bra, always one of the first things observed, so at least some of the sisters have abandoned the nasty straps which means that Butterfly and Datura won't be considered wanton freaks but I am still conscious of the stares from some of the males. What the hell, we are having fun and who could blame any red-blooded Murkan male for looking.

***

About the third or fourth song when we are all feeling good and Paul dancing crazier than ever with most people in the room seeming to accept us good-naturedly if not with open arms and Maurice and Sylvia (her Free Huey T-shirt working overtime) dancing next to us, just when everyone is letting it all hang out, working up a sweat, gettin' on the good foot (whatever the good foot is), the flashing red lights of a police cruiser outside pulse like a cancer ray and all the sweetness and fun instantly drain from the room, replaced by a terrible, bilious current that grips everyone. Someone yanks the arm from the Wilson Pickett record with a ripping sound. People shout and curse. Paul, Datura, Butterfly and I instinctively draw together, at the same time edging towards the door to get a better look at what is going on. Maurice has pushed his way through the dancers and is already outside with two Panthers talking to two beefy white cops who despite the growing crowd are posturing like storm troopers.

"Pig motherfuckers got some jacked-up motherfuckin' balls comin' down here like this!" a large woman in a black tight-fitting dress yells next to me.

"Yeah, motherfuckin' pig balls what they got," says another woman with an angelic café au lait freckled face and blond Afro. "Cut them motherfuckin' pig balls with a razor and feed them to my dogs!"

A ripple of angry laughter goes through the crowd. With Maurice outside we are feeling a little uneasy and then, shockingly, Paul is shouldering his way through the crowd excusing himself as people mutter and gave him dirty looks, wondering just who the hell this red-bearded, herky-jerky honky motherfucker is. Butterfly and I look at each other in alarm. Torn between following Paul and staying with her, Datura and Sylvia, I move slowly towards the door with the girls following me, pushed forward by loyalty to my friend, in some possibly suicidal way feeling a responsibility as a white who claims to believe in all these righteous things to step forward when stepping forward is the only thing that counts under the circumstances, when all the revolutionary slogans and sentiments (and thinking of all the times in the last four or five hours I have said, "Power to the People") finally need some substance as not to become the merest of contemptible bullshit. I am certain this is the reason Paul has plowed through the crowd and is now standing behind Maurice and the two Panthers who have confronted the burly, smirking cops. If nothing else a couple of white faces will serve as witness to the harassment and intimidation and might possibly moderate the cops' behavior, though I doubt it. I am scared shitless but move ahead anyway, not knowing if I am doing the right thing but going through with it as if in a dream or an out-of-body experience and not feeling particularly proud of myself either since had Paul not gone forward I would probably still be in the back of the room as far away from danger as possible.

People move aside and let us through, the girls going outside but holding back as I stand next to Paul, who is watching as the two Panthers and Maurice talk to the cops, one of the Panthers the guy who had greeted us with "power to the people" at the door, strong and fierce-looking, though not as tall as the cops, the other I now see for the first time, tall with a very black, chiseled face, a strikingly handsome guy. Being right up in the middle of things is like being on stage, with the same mixture of unreality and fear, though there is nothing unreal about this for the Panthers and the rest of the people. Even in the middle of a hostile crowd in enemy territory with Panther muscle on display the cops are as cool and confident as a couple of Mafioso at a PTA meeting, this in itself unnerving, bringing home immediately the larger issue of the psychological burden blacks, especially blacks like Panthers who take a militant stance against the white establishment, have to deal with virtually every waking minute of their lives. When all is laid on the table the real power equation in the country is as subtle as a pallet of bricks falling out a fifth story window. It is easy to get caught up in the rhetoric and ideology and perhaps, understandably, acquire an inflated sense of power and historical mission as, say, someone like Eldridge Cleaver has (then, maybe it is just sheer bravado), but the attitude of these cops is a real deflator, their strutting certainty reflecting the whole glistening, overwhelming edifice, of which they are an integral part, backing them up. I am reminded of the time coming out of the MTA in Harvard Square when I saw this little old Irish-looking fucker get up real close to a couple of militant-looking young blacks selling *The Black Panther*, raise his fist mockingly and sneer, "Black power," then walk away laughing. It was all right there in that mean little tableau, the smug reassertion of the true condition, the silent tension between races surfacing in a fleeting encounter at an urban subway station. The black kids looked straight ahead without reacting. The wicked confidence of the old bastard had unmanned them. In the *everyday* war being waged, the peaceful violence that Fanon had talked about, it was obvious who had the upper hand. All this is evident in the demeanor of the cops, their swagger backed up by the conviction that theirs is the baddest gang of them all and you niggers better goddamned not fuck with us or the wrath of the White Amerikan/world-stomping/power-storming/steel-booted/merciless engine of destruction will rain suffering and death on your Black Sambo/jungle bunny/spear-chucking/slum-dwelling asses.

There is an element to the way these arrogant bastards are acting that also suggests they know about something the rest of us don't, like maybe the six or seven squad cars waiting out of sight around the corner to come roaring up at the first intimation of trouble, or the SWAT team ready to do their own little My Lai thing right in the middle of Watts. The larger of the two cops, another one of those weight-lifting, hemorrhoidal, wife-beating ex-high school football stars, is repeating some story concerning neighborhood complaints about the noise, which is a good one because there are not any houses near enough to hear anything unless it might be the gunfire that lays at the basis of their commands which in our minds' ear we can hear all too loudly and how the "proceedings needed to be terminated," citing some statute about noise after a certain hour, clearly jerking everyone around with their jackboot bullying nonsense. The two Panthers are furious and frustrated in the face of these brute representatives of the omnipotent order, at least partly because it *is* getting a little bit late, around eleven o'clock, and there seems no point in pushing something that might lead to battle as it is likely that pig reinforcements are only a squeal away. Since this is a fund-raiser for the Pratt case and being held on church property with as many if not more women than men in attendance any escalation can only have horrific consequences, which usually happens anyway even under relatively favorable conditions. Checkmate. Pigs win.

Maurice and the two Panthers stand glowering at the cops, who look around contemptuously and lock eyes on Paul and me, giving us a particularly malevolent stare. I can sense Paul's rage and pray silently he won't say anything, as he had with Officer Nichols. Though the cops scare me more than I care to admit I try my best not to show it and return their savage looks with a neutral, even gaze that I hope communicates a certain objective cool, my own woefully counterfeit version of grace under pressure. If you have ever been the recipient of an appraising look from a large predatory animal then you have some idea of what it is like to stare into the eyes of these white officers of the Los Angeles Police Department this night in Watts. As arrogant and ugly as they are towards the blacks, they seem to summon a special sort of venom for Paul and me, and if something goes down in the way of violent conflict I have little illusion about the usefulness of our white skin in protecting us from harm. The cops look around once more with disdain, repeat their order to disperse, saying they will be back in fifteen minutes, casually get in their car and with a gratuitous, infuriating YAWP! from their siren, drive slowly off.

***

The rage the crowd has been holding in now comes bursting out. Angry curses erupt. Bottles are thrown in the direction of the disappearing car, smashing on the pavement like small bombs. Maurice, around whom we have gathered instinctively, writes rapidly in a notepad retrieved from his front pocket. There is talk of guns and ambush of the police when they return. There are fearful threats against pigs and a few against whites—nothing directly towards us but obviously meant to be overheard. Maurice says goodbye to the two Panthers and the one who had greeted us at the door, the one with the Eldridge goatee who had said, "Power to the people," comes up and says, "I'm sorry this had to happen. But now you see just a little bit of the kind of bullshit black people have been putting up with for three hundred years and put up with every day of their lives in the ghetto. For your own safety you'd better leave. No telling what kind of crazy shit's likely to go down. Some people around here aren't too happy right now—you know what I'm sayin'? Go back to your community and tell people what you saw tonight—folks having a good time, a peaceful gathering—at a motherfucking church, no less, and still the pigs come down here and harass us. It aint motherfucking right."

"It's a fucking outrage is what it is," says Paul. "People were just having a good time, talking and dancing. It's pure harassment and intimidation, plain and simple. I hope you and others don't think all whites are like those cops, because they're not. We're with you all the way, believe me, we're with you. We all know what the Panthers are trying to do for the community and it's a positive thing, a constructive thing, not what the media portrays. That's bullshit."

"Ya, ziss iz boolzhit!" Datura is extremely agitated. "I am frum Chermany und I vill tell zem vat I zee here tonight. Beleef me, I vill!"

"Well, thank you," says the man, who seems taken aback by Datura, though his face remains impassive. "Now you all better get going before some crazy stuff happens like it usually does around here." He makes a point of shaking our hands, again saying, "Power to the people." We follow Maurice to the van, get in, and sit for a moment. "Motherfucker!" he yells, and bangs his bony fist against the dashboard. "Motherfucker!"

He starts the little VW engine, guns it angrily and drives into the dark streets. A couple of blocks away in the parking lot of a supermarket four squad cars sit with their lights turned off. As we drive past one of them pulls in behind us and after following a moment comes up closer and hits the flashing lights and gives another of those sharp YAWP! sounds with his siren. "Fuckin' pigs," says Maurice, pulling the van over. "Don't make any sudden movements and do exactly what they tell you. These motherfuckers look for any excuse to pull some shit. Don't say a fuckin' thing unless they ask and don't say anything more than necessary because it will *definitely* be used against you. I'll do the talking."

We are parked next to a weird, sinister-looking set of tall spires that I think at first is some kind of church complex or missiles in somebody's back yard but Paul whispers, "It's the Watts Towers," and sure as hell, much taller than I had imagined, looking like something from the planet Mongo or the set of "Lost Horizon," it is them, silent and forbidding in the darkness, a surreal accompaniment to the ugly reality of the two cops unbelievably rushing towards us in a semi-crouch with their guns drawn yelling, "KEEP YOUR HANDS IN VIEW! GET OUT OF THE VEHICLE! NOW! MOVE! GET OUT OF THE FUCKING VEHICLE!"

For a moment we sit in stunned silence, our hands rising slowly to window level as if they might explode if we move them too quickly, then moving carefully out of the van with our hands up as one cop crouches on the sidewalk and the other on the street, their guns trained on us. "TURN AROUND AND PUT YOUR HANDS AGAINST THE VEHICLE!"

We do as told. With the towers, the silent and empty surroundings, it feels as if we are on a back street in Ankara or Islamabad or some other equally strange place next to a mosque with no lights, no traffic, no nothing, just dead silence and the harsh, angry commands of the cops. It appears one of them is black but I can't tell because I am terrified to even look lest interpreted as a threatening move and my body riddled, Hampton-like, with bullets. If it is the South we might very well be sucking our last breaths of earth's sweet air and though I am too frightened to think about anything but doing exactly what these maniac cops tell us to do, later I think about Schwerner, Chaney and Goodman and the countless others murdered, brutalized or abused in just these situations where one is completely helpless and any attempt at self-defense or even a wrong move is met with a fusillade of small, streamlined metal objects traveling 800 feet per second ripping through your body exploding internal organs and splattering blood and tissue over all and everything, questions, if any, resolved later, or never at all.

Small comfort though that we are not somewhere like Philadelphia, Mississippi on a country road some steamy summer night, the air thick with swamp and croaking bullfrogs, twin beams of light growing larger in the rearview mirror: This is Watts and that's bad enough. And this forlorn street we find ourselves on might as well be the Deep South for all the assurance we feel in the fair-minded application of the law as meted out by these zealous defenders of our constitutional rights. Maurice is in the street with his hands against the van, the rest of us on the opposite side, I standing at the end next to Butterfly who is looking at me out of the corner of her eye, a very unhappy expression on her beautiful face and Paul next to her, staring at the roof of the van. Datura stands stiff and pale with fear. Born fifteen years earlier she might have seen something like this in Germany. Sylvia is calmer, as if she has gone through this terrifying business before, an attitude mirrored by Maurice, who begins talking to the cops in a regular tone, though his voice is pitched higher than usual. "Look, we're just on our way home. We don't have any weapons or drugs or anything like that. Feel free to search the van if you want. We don't have anything to hide. I was just showing my friends here the Watts Towers. They're leaving in the morning and this is the only chance to see them."

I glance at the cop on the street behind Maurice and I see that indeed, he is black, an older guy with a hard expressionless face. He reaches into Maurice's back pocket for his wallet and examines it with his flashlight. The cop behind us, seeing me look at his partner, yells, "KEEP YOUR HEADS DOWN AND DON'T LOOK AT ANYTHING! DO AS YOU'RE TOLD AND YOU WON'T GET HURT!" He comes up behind me and reaches around, patting my chest and stomach, then reaches into my back pocket and pulls out my wallet. "You're a long way from home, Sam. What are you doing in Los Angeles? Where are you staying?" I explain that I am visiting my friends in Santa Monica and that I am leaving for the East Coast tomorrow. He snaps my wallet shut and shoves it roughly back in my pocket. He goes over to Paul and does the same, examining his wallet and putting it back. For some reason they don't search the females. The black cop opens the door on the driver's side and looks around inside the van with his flashlight. Finishing his search he stands up and looks at the white cop, some kind of signal passing between them, and they step back. The black cop yells, "NOW GET BACK INTO THE VAN AND DRIVE AWAY SLOWLY. STRAIGHT TO SANTA MONICA. DO NOT STOP. DO NOT MAKE ANY QUICK MOTIONS AND KEEP YOUR HANDS IN VIEW AT ALL TIMES. DO NOT EVEN LOOK AROUND. DO NOT SO MUCH AS LOOK AT US OR YOU WILL BE SORRY! NOW MOVE!"

Thoroughly freaked and humiliated we move like sheep into the van. When we are inside we put our hands down and the cops go berserk. "KEEP YOUR FUCKING HANDS WHERE WE CAN SEE THEM!" they scream. "KEEP YOUR EYES STRAIGHT AHEAD!" Shaken, we raise our hands and look straight ahead. Maurice starts the engine, puts it in gear and drives off slowly, saying, "I swear to god I'd like to blow these motherfuckers away. Now you see how all this shit goes down around here. This fuckin' shit happens all the time. A regular motherfuckin' thing around here. Now you see. Now you fuckin' see!" He picks up speed and is soon going at a good clip through the grim streets wanting as we all do to get the hell out as quickly as possible. People wonder how so many Jews could have been led passively to the camps. This incident lays it out clearly. When you have large lunatics in uniform raging at you with guns pointed at your heads you basically do what you are told, hoping that somewhere down the line rationality and fairness will prevail.

It can never be as bad as it seems, which is what we tell ourselves all the way to the doors of the gas chamber.

The ride back to Santa Monica is quiet, all of us deeply shaken, utterly humiliated, violated, as if we have been raped. However, excepting Maurice, we have the ultimate comfort of slipping into the safe anonymous cloaks of our white skins and all of us, including Maurice, can go back to our relatively affluent neighborhoods. There is no way of really knowing, as much as we try, the burdens some people are forced to carry and the damage it causes. As for our own burdens, we discover, Paul, Maurice and I, that they are somewhat lighter. The police, checking our IDs, have relieved us of our money.

***

Simon Rodia might have wished we could have seen his inimitable creation under more favorable circumstances but as an immigrant he would have understood the necessary restraints imposed by the defenders of constitutional rights on unfettered passage in this Woody Guthrie's land for the comfort and safety of the larger property-owning citizenry. As such, these necessary restraints have the likely desired effect of inhibiting our enthusiasm for returning to the old tower-constructor's neighborhood for a more illuminated view of his "vernacular masterpiece," as the arbiters of cultural standards refer to it. As far as negotiating a redress of grievances concerning crimes perpetrated by the LAPD, disbanding a perfectly peaceful and legitimate gathering and committing highway robbery, well, you might as well return to the lion's den to politely request if you can please retrieve the remains of your arm his excellency chewed off, you know, for sentimental reasons.

Our monetary setbacks are significant enough to sting but not so dire as to demand action or justice, as Byzantine and absurd an undertaking as can be imagined. Maybe if we had Philip Marlowe on the case and one of us was Sam Yorty's cousin we could pull it off. My thirty-dollar loss is ten percent of my holdings. Paul lost twenty and Maurice twenty-five. I, the poorest, at the hands of the law, have lost the most, substantiating the truism that in legal transactions it is those who can least afford it get the hardest kick in the nuts. But the worst of it is the abject humiliation, as if we had bent over and taken the splintery nightstick. Maurice is the angriest, in a cold retributive sort of way, and he is determined through his legal connections to at the very least file a formal complaint with the LAPD or DA (later we all laugh, including Maurice, at the absurdity of this) about both incidents and to publicize these outrages to the greatest possible extent, though in the scheme of things they are absolutely minor. But, as he points out, even the smallest offences need the light of day lest their cumulative disregard plunges the whole world into darkness. On the other hand, he says, with so much going on one has to pick the right battles and perhaps this is one you just have to forget about and take your fight to the enemy all the more fiercely the next time. All of us volunteer to testify or sign statements right in the middle of lion's den if that's what he wants but Maurice says no, he'll take care of it himself, and after that we stop talking about it.

Despite our outrage and sensible talk of fighting the right battles we are all in a state of shock and pretty much thoroughly depressed and hang around most of the following morning staring at Maurice and Sylvia's living room floor. For Maurice this turn of events is relatively unsurprising, though he admits he has never heard of anyone getting *robbed* by the cops. Killed, yes, but not robbed. Somehow this seems unusually shocking, similar to the public's reaction, as someone once remarked, to the dead in Vietnam being dogs instead of people. The war would end immediately. All those dead dogs. The horror! Maybe, we joke, it was a couple of cop impersonators.

Hungry and needing to get out we pile into Maurice's van and motor about ten blocks to a pizza joint already open at ten AM with customers two deep at the counter, ordering slices and cups of bad coffee and repairing to a filthy round metal table outside with a hole in the middle but no umbrella to gnaw at our pizza and burn our tongues on the scalding coffee, blinking in the oppressive glare of the Los Angeles sun, the smog, particularly thick this morning, descending like a defoliant. This is not Sidney Poitier's LA, the six of us sitting around a cheap metal table in a shabby neighborhood eating bad pizza at ten in the morning surrounded by a bunch of strange people who look ahead at the coming hours with all the enthusiasm of death-row inmates. At least the inmates have the possibility of appeal. Fortunately for us this dread condition is not incurable, and while this flat and unprofitable state will pass it is also clear that we have reached some sort of terminus, that is, the end of one road and the beginning of another. Farther south we will not venture. Paul and I have a continent to traverse and it beckons like a sea voyage, Rosalina more Queequeg's coffin than the Pequod, providing just enough buoyancy and space for us ride the current towards less than mythical sounding Jacksonville. But we do have purpose, I guess, Paul with his quest to connect with his father closer to Ahab's, having already lost a psychic leg to this white sperm whale progenitor and I more like Ishmael, subject to the vagaries of a somewhat aimless existence, going along for the adventure, just as likely as the next person, maybe more, to be pitched over the side to sink or swim.

Sitting next to me Butterfly is nibbling distractedly on her crust, a hint of tomato sauce at the corner of her mouth, a few crumbs resting on her athlete's thighs. Butterfly! This might be the last day we will ever spend together. She has talked about having to return to San Francisco to meet a close friend and then travel back to New Mexico. At the very least I am blessed to know her and doubly blessed to have tasted her sweetness. What kind goddess has looked down on me to bestow this fortune? I don't dare think we might have some sort of future together, I of disheveled soul and worn, wandering boot heels, she of sure mountain goat hooves and sturdy ankles, rooted to the New Mexico earth, a beauty to launch the flight of a thousand desert ravens, set the great horned owls to *hoo hooing*, the coyotes to yipping. She looks at me and smiles with those strong white Eskimo-like teeth that could easily chew a mate's frozen morning mukluks to a pliable steaming mass of utilitarian walrus-skin comfort. Could I ever be Nanook to her Nyla? Surely, ultimately, she would require a companion made of sterner stuff than I, some intrepid lancer of walruses (walri?), hewer of ice blocks and lyric poet of arctic wilderness, but alas my kayak has no starter and has sprung a hundred springs. Still, you never know. Maybe my feckless ways pull at her earth-rooted sympathies, touch something in her wild and open heart.

A turn in my expression must have affected her because she reaches under the table and gives my knee a squeeze and then slides her hand up my thigh towards the command center, which immediately stirs to action, no less alert than the round-the-clock vigilance of NORAD or the Strategic Air Command. If our company decides to get up and leave this instant I will be forced to tarry a few moments nibbling on my crust or sipping the wretched coffee, she having that effect on me now, similar to Lulu Delilah or adolescent encounters with Playboy, only she hasn't taken too much LSD and there's not a staple to be found in her navel. What is her real name? Of course I have wondered but until now there has been a dream-like quality about everything these last several days, but beneath this veil of youthful innocence and adventure there is some real business going on, actual lives being lived and choices being made with actual consequences. *Real people!* After all, I remind myself, I have fled for the West Coast in the throes of a crisis that is as painful and concrete as anything I have ever experienced, a crisis that has roiled up a welter of issues uniquely personal and problematic and will bedevil me, likely enough, for the rest of my life. At the same time these issues are not all, except for their idiosyncratic flavor, uniquely mine. Most everyone I know is preoccupied with the serious matter of finding love and meaning in a world beset with sorrow, a world that seems to conspire against fulfillment at every turn and always in the end grimly triumphant. Even Datura, whom I invariably find slightly ridiculous, partly because of my post-war prejudice against Germans and of course the *Hogan's Heroes* accent, is on the same portentous trip, seeking the same things as the rest of us. Indeed her cultural history fixes her with an extra burden, not that ours is any less barbaric. Datura with her wild hair and thirst for excitement will end up back in Germany to marry and pursue her career, giving birth to children and then her children the same as she grows older, grayer, smaller, her hair in corral, recalling the Hells Angels glorious California Big Sur day to her wide-eyed offspring, of the little car Rosalina perched at the precipice, dented by the hammer fists of those incredible New World Ostrogoths.

And what of Paul and his quest to connect with his father and to understand the significance, conflicts and ambiguities of this most primary relationship? I might be wrong but I have the feeling that he will meet with success, coming to some measure of understanding with his father, writing his book about fathers and sons that will be published and well-received, continuing a long and fulfilling relationship with Carmen that I can see producing two or three children, probably all girls, writing many more books and becoming more solid and sagacious with passing years, something of a legend or icon, morphing into a Tolstoyan figure, a kind of rustic, simple, Pan-like saint or wise man, much sought-after. I feel in awe of him and wonder why he has chosen me to accompany him on his journey, not having much to offer by way intellectual stimulation and about the same level of transportation reliability, poor Rosalina. I want to think he has found something of a kindred spirit in me, though I suspect he fancies me a type of character from his readings in Basho or Han-shan. I am both flattered and a bit humiliated by such supposed fancy as I suspect this character is something of the well-meaning, bumbling vagabond, tossed about a good deal more than usual by happenstance. In short, I think I amuse him, though there is not a cruel molecule in his body and he would never treat me disrespectfully or condescendingly. In any case I am pleased to play the imagined part, thinking the typecasting not too farfetched, even a bit agreeably romantic, not a deplorable station in life, if somewhat removed from the stream of conventional things. If this is a picture that captures a certain aspect of my personality however, it becomes all the more imperative, for reasons of purpose and self-image, that I develop my artistic talent. Art has an aura that tends to cover the blemishes of a less-than-perfect existence. This is what I think, anyway.

So, traveling with Paul is a treat and a privilege and I will gladly play the disheveled bumbler to his Cold Mountain sage, since I know that time spent with him is like the apes and astronauts in Kubrick's film coming in contact with the Monolith, resulting in a kangaroo leap in consciousness, though fleas probably leap farther, relatively speaking. Any time you elevate your contacts it is all to the good. Butterfly still has her hand on my thigh, speaking of elevated contacts, and Maurice is talking about the night before, a bit more relaxed about things, even finding a little humor in it, a new twist on the cops and robbers thing, and in the same breath mentioning that Howlin' Wolf is going to be at the Whisky-A-Go-Go tonight and if we have never seen him before it would be a good idea since he is getting older and has been sick. He's a legend, says Maurice, a great performer and blues artist, along with Muddy Waters the absolute best. Datura, who seems more depressed than any of us, perks up immediately. "Ah, Howlin' Voolfe! Are you kidding?! Zis iz fantastic! Uv course vee must see Howlin' Voolfe! I luff Howlin' Voolfe! He iz my abzolude favorite!"

Of the six of us only Maurice has seen Howlin' Wolf, several years earlier in Chicago, a memorable night, he says, simply no one like Wolf, the most electrifying performance he has ever seen. This is not a difficult decision. We are down and need some revival: Butterfly and Datura don't seem ready to leave: we all like each other. If this is going to be our last night together it will be a good send-off. Instantly we are stoked as hell, the old buzz returned. Howlin' Wolf! At the Whisky-A-Go-Go! Venue for the greats of the music world, The Doors, Otis Redding, The Chambers Brothers, The Mothers of Invention (whom I had seen in 1969 at the Fillmore East, before the concert a group of shrieking satyrs running across Second Avenue barely avoiding the onrushing yellow cabs as I gaped, later making their stage entrance to a rowdy mixture of adulation and faux hostility from the audience, trading varieties of insults with hooting aficionados, apparently a ritual before most Mothers' concerts, launching into a sizzling, mind-bending forty-five minute instrumental that blew everyone away, the great colorful liquid screen pulsing and blurching in the background), Jimmy Reed, Cream, Iron Butterfly, Canned Heat, Procol Harum...Who the fuck hasn't played at the Whisky? I don't know much else about it but have images of sweating go-go girls in miniskirts or maybe better, in general a great scene of music and libidinal energy, just the ticket after the previous evening's bummer with the slimy Los Angeles Police Department.

***

Recharged, we get back in Maurice's van and drive to the apartment where the same trio of kids is sitting in front of the door even more zonked-out than before. Seeing us approach they get up and walk off slowly, the boys staring at Maurice hostilely. It is around noon. Datura suggests we go to the beach, a few blocks away. Maurice and Sylvia have work to do so they stay while the four of us walk to the beach past more dangerous-looking teens. The whole Santa Monica area, at least this part, has a weird post-apocalyptic vibe. Even more of a bummer is the beach itself, enveloped in haze and strewn with litter and dead fish. About a half-mile to the north we see a pier with surfers bobbing in the swell, taking off around the pilings. In high school I surfed in the mushy Atlantic but California is Mecca and I am stoked about the surfers, the first ones I have seen since being here, quickening my pace, my companions following, picking our way through the trash, scattering the scavenging seagulls. Not far off shore is an enormous tanker that looks like a skyscraper on its side, oddly inert, as if everyone aboard is asleep, or dead. A subtle fecal smell mixes with the odors of the trash and rotting fish. The closer we get to the pier, a massive structure in vast incoherent disrepair, as if the recipient of a bombardment—I think of Tet—the more unease we feel. It is the pier itself that makes us feel this way, midst the squalor of the beach, looming over us as we slow our steps, coming to a standstill. "Cheezus. Ziss iz weird," says Datura.

Surfers in wetsuits take off on fast-moving waves and slice through the pier, not exactly the golden soft-focus image I have of

California surfing but urban and hard, with a crazy element of danger in the pilings that seems to cause these daredevils no more concern than if they are skirting highway cones. A group of scruffy teens stands quietly watching, occasionally commenting on the action, ignoring us completely. We stay for a while as unwelcome observers and then quietly leave, feeling alien and oddly humbled, deciding to head back towards Venice Beach, winding through the trash and seagulls, away from the broken down old pier and its wild surfers, the beach no less filthy as we head south but with an open, funky vibe, with people in getup, hanging out, playing Frisbee, goofing, smoking dope. We pass a couple barely covered with a blanket fucking in the sand, a pair of growling Rottweilers rolling around next to them. Freaks of all varieties proliferate the closer we get to Venice. Surfers in wetsuits ride a nice four-foot break, the tips of the waves feathering back gently in the slight offshore breeze. These surfers are nowhere near as bold and accomplished as the ones at the pier, many having difficulty even catching rides, but some are good, carving gracefully across the faces of the hollowed-out, fast-moving waves, walking up and down their boards, turning hard into the collapsing tubes, up, over and flat on their boards, paddling back for more. This is more my speed, less competitive, no killer pilings to separate you from your spleen or snap your board like a pencil. Ahead is the boardwalk with a great colorful mob.

Judging by the action at the periphery we are in for a real scene as the throbbing of three or four separate groups of drummers merge in a tribal rumble beneath a growing cacophony of shrieks, shouts, laughter, flutes, bells and clashing electric guitar riffs. Just before entering the main body of freaks on the boardwalk there is a contingent of aging body-builders in tiny bikinis outlining thumb-sized cocks, absurdly small in relation to their overdeveloped, sagging bronzed bodies, their dentures gleaming like Bakelite. Next to these hideous geezers is a group of equally old sun-baked bimbos in bikinis and stiff, bleached hair that would go like napalm if you lit a match within five yards. I wonder if they still fucked, these wrinkled beach lizards, a pint of goat's milk, a dozen oysters and 50 milligrams of adrenaline to get them going, Ambu Bags and nitro-glycerine pills when they finish. Their younger pumped and oiled counterparts are nearby in a roped-off area preening, glistening and slamming impossible weights while middle-aged tourists in Bermu-das and polo shirts snap pictures, their pre-pubescent daughters gawking in a Freudian stupor. Butterfly gives a shudder but Datura stares, apparently in a Freudian stupor of her own. Paul and I laugh and say we could lift those weights with our brains, the thread for which ordinary males grasp in such circumstances. We also make some remarks about the size of their penises, though a few of them by the looks of it have been doing some lifting there also, bull's equipment to go along with the deltoids, abdominals and glutei. Hardly an encouraging proposition for us ordinaries.

The whole place is an alderman's wet dream of swirling colors, anarchy, narcissism, eroticism, capitalism, gangsterism, Dadaism and tourism, where the freaks sneer at the Murkans and the Murkans lap it up, half their minds in Boschian riot, the other half agonizing on the bleeding cross. Violence and perversity hover just beneath the surface like sewer gas, cheap thrills for the Main Street worthies whose boundary is a yard from the edge but never farther, smart enough to keep an Argus eye on daughters who might fall through a trapdoor into a life of white slavery or simply walk away with one of the Satanists for a Manson-life of orgies, drugs and dark rituals while daddy and mommy stare at the weightlifters. There are belly dancers, fire eaters, queers galore, peanut peddlers, drug dealers, taco venders, interracial couples, drag queens, real estate agents, school teachers, skateboarders, morose, starving artists who sell paintings of fearful clowns on black velvet or of seagulls or kit-tens or fishing boats or green suns dipping into seas of molten lead and quick-draw portraitists who render their sitters with fangs and bloodshot eyes. People who look like they sleep 23 hours a day and others who look like they never sleep unroll swags of penknives, watches, medallions, buttons, earrings, incense, water pipes, mechanical pencils, hats, tweezers, posters of love and death, miniature surfboards, T-shirts, underwear, aphrodisiacs, rubber vomit, coffee cups, bumper stickers, used records, postcards, scrolls of runic symbols and framed photos of Martin Luther King, Dizzy Gillespie, Tiny Tim, JFK and Jackie. Revolutionaries hand out copies of *The Little Red Book*, *The Militant*, *The Black Panther* and The US Constitution. A toothless, pinwheel-eyed barefoot hippie in a striped sailor's shirt plays Beatles' songs on a battered clarinet for coins while his stoned girlfriend stares at him rapturously, nodding her head in time with the music. Four young blacks sing beautiful *a cappella* in a way I haven't heard since childhood visits to Coney Island and as I watch an old man weeps openly as a younger female companion, maybe his daughter, caresses his back.

We go to the water and sit down, Paul and I talking about leaving tomorrow and heading towards the Grand Canyon, a place neither of us have been, asking Butterfly and Datura to come along, Datura accepting immediately, Butterfly declining, constrained by her return to San Francisco and subsequently home, where she will be spending the summer. Butterfly's imminent departure depresses me and I am absurdly miffed that she will not come with us to the Grand Canyon, keeping this bit of childishness to myself, though in doing so I become withdrawn and my friends look at me questioningly. As we walk back to Maurice and Sylvia's apartment I know the only way for me to pull myself out of this self-pitying bog is to tell Butterfly the truth and, lagging behind the rest as she accompanies me, I explain my sour mood, my feelings dangerously exposed. This is more than being in thrall to a daft tropical animal with a mango-sweet pussy as I was with Lulu Delilah, where sanity had jumped the cliff like lemmings. Butterfly has a mango-sweet pussy of her own, in fact sweeter, but that is where all comparisons end because Butterfly has mango-sweet everything and, what is more, is solid and deep like the landscape that spawned her. Sure, I like Lulu Delilah, she is fun and whacky and turns me on every time she drawls in that way of hers but that's all it is, a little flipped-out, cock-quivering fling with my private sex kitten on a hot tin roof that was dangerous and wrong from the start and I knew it. Lulu Delilah isn't a bad person, she just isn't in the same class as Butterfly. It is now, the question on the tip of my tongue, that she tells me her real name, which for reasons of sentiment I will not divulge. It is a simple, beautiful name, a classic, and fits her as comfortably as Zelda fits Datura.

***

Telling Butterfly my feelings I am relieved of a burden whose weight has accumulated straw by straw, not realizing how deep I am into it until that moment of looking up and seeing the bit of tomato sauce at the corner of her mouth and the pizza crumbs on her thighs. It seems to me that Butterfly is the essence of the hippie chick we are all looking for these days, a connection to the earth and a healthy, natural sexuality, daughter of the rugged western US, riding horses at a young age, raven hair perfumed with the campfires of cattle roundups, a quick and sharp spirit that brooks no bullshit. Without consciously trying to be that ideal, Butterfly leaves the competition in her wake without drugs or artifice. And again, to my amazement, an amazement that crudely shoulders up against all my insecurities, she has, for the moment at least, chosen to grace me with her affections, which pulls me in different ways, some good, some not so good, an exasperating combination of the insecure, hesitant, earthy and sensual.

Though the awful tension that gripped me moments earlier has dissipated, I still feel myself to be some sort of creature, an alien possibly, whose face shimmers and pulses with the colors of a dozen conflicting emotions, feeling transparent and vulnerable, but safe with Butterfly for the moment, knowing that this sort of security, if not necessarily illusory, is but transitory, coming and going with the fluctuations of fate and fortune. With this feeling comes a deep and warm happiness, tinged with disquiet, some of which I identify as related to our parting, some of which is nameless, though it probably has to do with the issue of the larger, permanent parting we all have from each other, from life itself. The death of my mother when I was a kid put a permanent kink in my circuitry that twists things up in my relationships with females. I guess I kind of love them and hate them at the same time, the same way I felt about my mother. But Butterfly is different, or so it seems. I can unburden myself and not feel like such a freak or fool. She is like the river Ganges, or the Amazon, or the Grand Canyon, an absorbing force into which I can fall without fear, like jumping out of a plane in a dream and landing in a soft, sexual cloud rich with feeling and nurture. Obviously there is something of the mother in Butterfly, my mother, all mothers, and this astounds me, simply blows me away, because I have never met a female like this, never really believed something like this actually existed. Maybe Carmen is the same way, I have the feeling she is. Amazing! What is going on here? As an emotional wreck, driving a wreck of a car (though dear), plunging out west not knowing anything about where I would end up (I knew I would not be long at Lieberman's) or what in the hell was going to happen, I have fallen into the gravitational fields of some very far-out people. Though philosophically I am in the clutches of an obstinate determinism, this fortuitous bouncing has me wondering. Maybe there is a purpose I cannot discern. Perhaps there is.

***

Back at Maurice and Sylvia's, Butterfly and I fall out and crash for an hour together on our sleeping bags while Paul and Datura sit on the glue-sniffers' stoop and map out the next leg of the journey, destination: The Grand Canyon. Later in the afternoon Paul and I go to Samman's, where the guy who pulled the gun sells us a gallon of Gallo. Back at the apartment Datura rolls a couple of joints and all of us, except for Butterfly, who only drinks a little wine, get pretty loaded, then into Maurice's van to go to a Greek restaurant before hitting the Whisky. At the restaurant we drink a liter of retsina along with the boureki, dolmas, spanakopita and baklava and by the time we are back in the van heading towards the Whisky, Sunset Strip is gliding by like a carnival and we are in great spirits, though tempered by the prospect of Butterfly's leaving at 11:30 the following morning on a Greyhound for San Francisco.

The famous nightclub is jammed and there is great excitement in the air to see Howlin' Wolf and when he finally comes on the place erupts with howls, shouts, whistles and calls while his band starts up immediately and the singer, bigger and older than I expected, launches into "Smokestack Lightning," standing stock-still for the first few measures and staring off into the distance as if some kind of gigantic aging zombie and then beginning to sing, suddenly crouching absurdly low with his ass inches from the floor and strutting across the stage as the crowd hollers and screams. When he gets to the end of the stage he jumps up, twirls around and moves back across with a violent shimmying, eyes bulging, huge mouth wide open, his tongue slithering around like a conger eel. Never having seen Wolf before I didn't know what to expect, but this is more than I had imagined, a graying monster the size of Big Daddy Lipscomb who sings with his soul on fire and moves like Nureyev on an acid trip, the crowd going wild urging him on, the sweat pouring down his black Rushmore of a face like some aging African chieftain whose vigor is still the equal of three men. After three more numbers he sits down to sing another five or six songs, springing up once to move around in that hyper-kinetic voodoo style that makes everybody crazy, and then, abruptly, unexpectedly, it is over, Wolf getting up and walking slowly off the stage, blowing kisses and gyrating his hips in a parody of lewdness as the crowd calls for him with a collective broken heart, *Wolf! Wolf! Don't go!* But that's it. Wolf never comes back. The set has lasted for about forty minutes and Wolf is gone. A tinny blues recording comes on and the crowd, buzzed, seems at a loss, elated and disappointed at the same time, a bad case of *lupus interruptus.*

We are standing around wondering what next when Maurice comes up and says that he has heard The Watts Prophets are at Maverick's Flat on Crenshaw and that we should go see them and again we stuff ourselves into the rickety microbus, the world spinning from the retsina, Gallo, marijuana, Howlin' Wolf and the engine's exhaust fumes seeping into the interior. Maverick's Flat looks like a barbecue joint on the outside but the interior has the spacious opulence of a bordello in which a group of militant/intellectual-looking blacks and a few hip whites is intently digging the three black poets laying down their somber riffs backed up by a cello and piano in a kind of dissonant jazzy flow, some calling out in response to the poets' angry words, the whites remaining mostly quiet except for Paul immediately into it shouting out along with the blacks, "Yeah! Dig it! That's right!" heads turning in our direction wondering who in the hell this crazy ofay is and I am ashamed to say

I am a little embarrassed, then picking up on the vibe that everyone picks up with Paul, which is that here is a person spontaneously acting out of the sincerity of his true self, of being absolutely in the now, guided by impulses pure and correct. The moment of tension passes, replaced by a vibe that binds us together with a spirit full of good sizzling anger and reflection, not that the blacks and whites feel any closer but that at least we are legitimately in the room together. Before we had come in I don't think there had been the same feeling but thanks to Paul the discordant agglomeration of psyches untangles at least to the point where we can discern our common enemy, or enemies, which are the common enemies of all people, not only the sickness of racism but of a brutal system that exploits and destroys and sets brother against brother. At least that is how it's going down now, at this moment. So there is an implicit digging of Paul to a very unusual degree and it blesses everyone in the room, including The Watts Prophets. We stay until the end and afterwards have more drinks, Paul getting into a passionate discussion about reincarnation with one of the Prophets, who actually looks like a prophet, and there is a good feeling all around. Butterfly falls asleep with her head on my shoulder on the way home and I smell her beautiful black hair that is like the desert night and I wonder about the future.

7

To Yucca if lucky > Some playful and cutting calculations > Looking into a Bizarro world > Rediscovering Pollandria > Clicking a canyon Pan for posterity > Capricorn terror

Butterfly and I sleep on a cushion of blankets under our sleeping bags on the living room floor and make love all night like the young animals we are, trying to stay quiet as possible, finally drifting off around three or four in each other's arms, as deep and sweet and poignant a slumber as I have ever had, Eros and Morpheus our protective deities. Before waking I have a dream of being on an old Greek sponge boat off the coast of Montauk high in a tower with Lulu Delilah as Hokusai waves roll the boat back and forth, the seas washing over us. Her blouse is torn and she is covered with seaweed. Her eyes gleam and when she laughs her mouth opens wide exposing filed silver teeth. I am terrified and filled with lust and I wake to see a sleeping Butterfly with a hint of smile on her strong beautiful face, her long black hair piled about carelessly as if disposed by a generous goddess, breathing softly through slightly parted lips, and with the craziness of Lulu Deliah and the storm still coursing through me I lean over and kiss her softly and she smiles and reaches down takes me in her small warm hand and in a matter of seconds we are moving together, sponge divers in an ocean of pleasure.

We fall back into a deep sleep and wake to the noise of our friends walking around and Sylvia cooking bacon, eggs and coffee in the little kitchen. Butterfly casually wraps a blanket around herself and trots off to the bathroom for a shower, showing me her hindquarters like some mythical creature fleeing into the woods, the image forever stamped on the brain of the hapless shepherd who returns endlessly, fruitlessly, to the same spot for another glimpse. Equally indelible is the image of Butterfly walking up the steps into the Greyhound bus two hours later with her orange backpack and sitting by a window seat, a sad smile on her Romany features, waving back to us with a special sweet look for her stumbling, head-knocking earnest young lover seen soon enough again, Great Spirit willing, after the Grand Canyon adventure and other unanticipated happenings, no doubt. Yes, we are going to New Mexico after the Grand Canyon to visit Butterfly and I will see the wild and beautiful mountain goat in her native habitat. The huge bus pulls away in a noxious gray-blue cloud and we watch in silence as it merges with all the other gleaming metal objects issuing their own noxious spew and I am sure that Butterfly, sad as she might be at leaving us, is happy to get away from this alien, chrome-toxic, decadent megalopolis.

My melancholy at Butterfly's going is leavened by the excitement of our imminent departure for the Grand Canyon and points east, including of course New Mexico. Butterfly is headed for San Francisco and leaving two days later after spending time with a childhood friend, a talented jazz musician now living in the Bay Area and gigging at various clubs around the city. Her plan is to spend the summer at home and then start her first teaching job in a small town nearby. It is a relief to leave the bus depot, a typically depress-

200 | RICHARD WARD

ing affair, and riding back to Santa Monica in Maurice's microbus we make hasty plans to replenish our food supplies, check Rosalina's vitals and hit the open road, heading east on 40, thinking briefly about going to Las Vegas but deciding against it, and then at some point cutting north to the mighty canyon, a prospect filled with excitement as none of us has ever seen it. Paul is determined that we hike to the bottom and has a small guide book he has brought along just in case that features little-used trails preferred by hikers wishing to avoid tourists and seeking a more "natural" experience. This seems just the thing and Datura and I agree that a hike to the bottom and a three or four day's encampment there next to the river would be fantastic. Maurice and Sylvia want to come also but cannot. The thought of Rosalina steaming out to the Grand Canyon is daunting but it is best to keep these fears to myself. What the hell, maybe the guardian-fuckin'-angel is still riding shotgun, or on my shoulder, wherever it hangs out, but angel or not we are going, the Grand Canyon just the first destination of a roller coaster return across mid-twentieth century's version of Lewis and Clark's wilderness and a few more Sacagaweas along the way, most hopefully. We have already had two and with Butterfly's conspicuous absence Datura becomes Sacagawea of the moment, offering a fresh perspective if not much guidance. She is as brilliant and hyper-charged as a new BMW on the Autobahn, eyes gleaming, hair standing up as if she is carrying a portable Van de Graaff generator in her backpack. The Grand Canyon! One of the Murkan wonders children of the Old World marvel at in their Christmas View-Masters, along with Old Faithful, Jayne Mansfield and the mighty Mississippi.

Maurice lends us his van to get supplies from a nearby supermarket and we load up on fruit, dried and fresh, nuts, bread, tea, packaged soup, canned tuna, crackers, peanut butter, beef jerky, two packages of chocolate chip cookies and a large package of artificially-flavored lemon candy. All of us have water bottles but Paul says we need more, plus it is necessary to stash a container at the halfway point for the return from the bottom so we stop at a hardware store and buy two, three-gallon plastic gas cans, one of which we will cache. Paul has some basic cookware and a little Primus stove. The plan is to boil water from the river. It is already about two o'clock and with Rosalina's limited pace, 65 on a flat surface with no headwind, we figure if we leave right away we will make it to Needles or maybe Yucca by eight or a little after if we are lucky, though Paul points out that from sea level we will be climbing gradually to about 7,000 feet at the canyon's south rim, the extra passengers and supplies an unusual strain on the plucky little car whose provenance and stomping grounds is the sea level comfort of the East Coast.

A brief discussion concerning the merits of leaving right away or spending another night in Santa Monica and getting an early start results in a decision in favor of the first option, increasing the urgency to get going and we cram our stuff into the car, the little SAAB with three-quarters of a tank of gas, radiator swimming with good New Jersey water and a firm, plump spare tire, compliments of our Santa Cruz friends. We maneuver Rosalina from her parking space and Maurice, Paul, Sylvia and Datura push together down Pier while I steer and pop the clutch and the car starts right up, a healthy cloud of blue smoke belching from her tailpipe in full-throated, four-cylinder celebration of hitting the open road, more than ready to split this desolate scene, Datura getting in the front seat and Paul in back and in a matter of seconds Maurice and Sylvia are shrinking images in the rear view mirror waving goodbye. I quietly wish Maurice good luck, figuring he will be a kick-ass civil rights lawyer some day, hopefully ending up as attorney general in Angela Davis' Cabinet and prosecuting war criminals from the Johnson and Nixon administrations.

***

Rosalina hums along like the Swedish marvel she is, hurrying through the remaining wastes of LA, redeemed somewhat by the sight of City Hall visible through the smog in the distance, evocative of color postcards or National Geographic pictures of southern California in the thirties when the air was sweet and the Joads traveling hard. We head north on 15 to Barstow, stop for gas and the bathroom and join 40 towards Needles, the traffic picking up as we putter along in the slow lane, Rosalina winding down just a bit, the rising altitude adding its subtle burden, huge trucks and family sedans passing us disdainfully as if we have somehow stumbled into an Olympic track meet. But it is okay because the girl has grit and soon it is Needles 63, 48, 31, 18, 5 and we are going strong with the push to get across the state line and on to Yucca, which we reach around 7:30, deciding to go a little farther until we finally pull into a rest area and find a nice little space next to some juniper trees where we make camp for the evening, the only discordant note being a scorpion that gives Datura a fright, a nasty-looking little brown and yellow fucker that raises its tail and moves its claws menacingly as she jumps out of the way laughing hysterically. Paul takes a piece of wood and flicks it several yards away and then does it twice more until it is pretty far removed, though we kept a wary eye out after that. We ask Datura if there is anything like scorpions in Germany and, still shaken, she replies in German, "Nein, aber wir haben kakerlaken!"

"Cockroaches!" Paul exclaims, and we laugh. The night is brilliant and we spread the sleeping bags and look up at the desert sky, each with our own thoughts but mine focused on the mountain beauty now in San Francisco with her friend probably having dinner or maybe at a club listening to music. I am excited to see the

Grand Canyon but even more excited about New Mexico and making love under these same stars on a bed of sage next to some murmuring creek with this wild creature as her real name alternates with her hippie name over and over in my head like a tantric mantra where sound, memory and image merge and though having made love three times the night before I turn on my side and jerk off as quietly as possible, hoping not to attract the attention of any female scorpions, or Datura, for that matter, though it is unlikely as she has her wild head of hair between Paul's legs engaging in some tantric oral mysteries of her own (*coming, colors in the air—oh, everywhere!*) and I come thinking about Butterfly mixed together with a montage of all the unexpected good and wonderful things that have happened these last several days.

During the night the temperature drops and the wind kicks up desert grit as we bury our heads in our bags and sleep as best we can, which is not very much, the eastern sky turning all-too-soon from black to vivid purple-blue to pale, pushed westward as if a retractable dome moved by the sun and we are up and moving, urged along by Paul to get to the south rim before noon because, he says, if we hit the trail by then we will probably make it to the bottom before dark. The route he has chosen is called the Tanner Trail, named after a dusty old prospector named Seth Tanner who had plied his trade from river to rim in the late 1800s. It is considered a challenging route and recommended for experienced hikers only but we are young and healthy and Datura says she has hiked the Alps many times and that she is "strong az an ogs." I haven't done very much hiking but I am in pretty good shape and figure it can't be that bad. Paul, on the other hand, is an experienced hiker and tells us that it will be a difficult trek but he reckons we can make it and the destination, the bottom of the canyon, will be worth the rigors. He has always wanted to do this trip and now is the perfect time. We load our gear and with Paul and Datura pushing, Rosalina starts right up and heads bravely north to Kingman, where we will proceed to Williams, about 20 miles west of Flagstaff, and from there on 180 to the South Rim of the Grand Canyon.

The little car does pretty well on the way to Kingman, going about 60 mph most of the time, slowing down on the inclines, but the trip to Williams is a different story. We stop in Kingman for gas and back on 40 Rosalina makes a good charge for about five miles like the kid going hell for leather in the first round against the champ but she suddenly seems to realize where she is and slows dramatically, as if overwhelmed by the prospect of a 135 mile climb to 7,000 feet in an alien place called Arizona. We have been holding our collective breath hoping she won't notice the increasing altitude, to no avail, and the remaining journey is a rough one as she putters doggedly on to Williams, crawling along as if drugged. We urge her onward with chants and shouts while I worry about Vanzetti's weld, hoping it won't burst like an aneurysm. At Williams we give Rosalina a fifteen minute rest, fill up her tank and check her vital signs, water, oil, tire pressure and then with a final push and encouraging words it is on to the Grand Canyon, which is less of a climb and better going.

Finally after a nerve-wracking and toilsome three-and-a-half hour drive from Yucca, Rosalina limps to the parking lot at a place called Lipan Point, near an old stone watchtower overlooking the canyon. It is exactly 12:00. We jump out and run to the point for our first look at the canyon, which seems unreal, as if we are looking through our own gigantic View-Master, the river far below a thin ribbon of crystal skirted with white sand and wispy green foliage that seems to whisper a mysterious, beckoning message. Already we are in the canyon's spell. The trailhead, nearby, starts in the forest of juniper and pinion that constitutes the landscape at the canyon's rim. Back at the car we lace on our shoes—I have sneakers,

Paul and Datura, boots—hoist our packs, say goodbye to Rosalina and walk through the trees, everything cool, still and empty but for some large blue noisy jays and a couple of squirrels that chitter and puff their tails in irritation at our intrusion. After a mile or so, the trail gradually steepening, the canyon opens before us, an ochre, buff, pink and green expanse so silent and immense as to defy comprehension. We stand quietly, Paul and I waiting for Datura as visiting dignitary and explorer to utter the required propitiatory words to the canyon gods, the reality of our trip sinking in.

"Holy shit," she says.

"Goddamn," intones Paul.

"Wow," say I.

With its vastness, great spires, hoodoos, buttes and all-encompassing silence I feel as if I am looking into an antiquity with a distinctly Old Testament flavor, a sensation that increases the deeper into the canyon we travel. At this point it is more an intimation than anything but the feeling is powerful and my excitement quickens. Down there are the ghosts of Pharaohs, pyramids, camels dreamily munching on papyrus leaves, Jewish slaves plotting rebellion, great floods and miracles. That the canyon has been formed by the ceaseless digging into the past by a life-flowing river like the Nile or Jordan stokes my imagination and makes me want to take a hang glider and fly to the bottom, like Icarus in reverse. Obviously there will be no flying but rather an arduous, possibly dangerous, certainly hot and thirsty descent to the river before we experience the sacred waters and ancient mysteries and while I can't say my companions feel precisely the same Old Testament wonder they are clearly in the grip of the canyon's power and, wasting no further time, with Paul in the lead, we continue down the trail.

***

In my childhood imaginings the Grand Canyon had always appeared as a dizzying precipice from which one would fall straight to the bottom to a horrifying death on the boulders below, having no idea there was a river down there, much less negotiable paths that would lead the careful traveler to a kind of magical paradise redolent of the Hanging Gardens of Babylon or Pharaonic temples. The trail at this point is not too bad, a forgiving gradient demanding only common-sense attention in avoiding the loose rocks and gravel that will turn a careless step into a twisted ankle or worse, at the top such a misstep not too serious, but farther along a major hassle to say the least. My sneakers, of the tennis variety and much the worse for wear, offer no support for my ankles and no protection at all from the Viet Cong rattlesnakes known to inhabit the canyon closer to the river, about which Paul has warned us, though he says that they, along with all wild creatures, carry special animus for Republicans and most Democrats, with limited dispensation for those who oppose the war.

But the first steps on the Tanner Trail are a relief and a kind of revelation. The great canyon, after all, is not a frightening death-dealing monster but actually a humongous, palpably sentient creature that has been relatively amenable to grooming in certain parts by humans of the courageous and resourceful variety, in the same way a seemingly unapproachable goddess might open her treasures to suitors exhibiting the proper deference. And here is a metaphor, I think, the path that Paul has talked about as the spiritual way, in opposition to the heedless plunge taken by so many, certainly, it seems, by my own country, as if it can blast and spend its way to some twisted version of fulfillment. These canyon trails were also forged by wise people, of sorts, not unlike the spiritual pioneers who uncovered paths followed by succeeding generations of like-minded travelers. Or so I would like to imagine.

Of course, also, or most importantly, it is the path itself that is key, the journey, not the destination, and soon the friendly declivity turns challenging, as all worthwhile ventures invariably do, and we slow, our efforts increasing along with the heat and the spectacular landscape. The trail is steep and strewn with large rocks, a slippery switchback that menaces us at every step as we strain to maintain our footing, stopping frequently to catch our breath and drink from the three-gallon can that I carry, leaving Paul's full to stash for the return hike. We don't say much, silent with the effort and no small bit of apprehension as we are definitely into the canyon and committed to finishing the trek to the bottom. Paul has his straw hat for protection from the sun and Datura a chic African version that she crams onto her frizzy hair. I have nothing but with her help tie a white T-shirt around my head in the manner of a Bedouin. After a while we finish with the switchbacks and the trail gets a little easier, deeper into the canyon in the midst of huge buttes that loom over us like the biblical temples of my imagination. It is here Paul suggests we look for a spot to cache the water, finding some large red rocks at the base of a small butte-like formation and piling them around the can he has been carrying. He gallantly offers to carry my can but I refuse, though we agree to share the burden the rest of the way down and drink solely from it as well, lessening its weight. We still have our full water bottles. Not seeing the river since Lipan Point it is easy to forget, with the intense heat and harsh Sonoran conditions, grappling with the demands of the steep and slippery switchbacks and now overshadowed by towering buttes, that we are headed towards the beautiful chill waters of the Colorado with its sandy beaches and green willows.

We rest for a few minutes in the glaring sun and have some jerky, apples and water. Paul figures we have another six hours to go. We have been hiking for about two. My shoulders and feet ache and my legs quiver from the exertion. Paul looks like Vincent on a painting jaunt into the Grand Canyon, full of strength and determination, a visionary gleam in his cerulean eyes. I wonder if he has picked up the same Old Testament vibe I have or is in some completely different realm. Datura is grim but exudes a fierce exhilaration. She will make it fine, I am sure. My two companions, unknown to me a week ago, seem as lifelong friends, my original and reflexive prejudice against Datura vanished, replaced by a respect for her adventuresome spirit and appreciation of those strong Dietrich-like legs and crazy hair. I don't even mind the German accent, in fact I am beginning to like its guttural wildness, as if she, like the canyon, is a bit of an atavistic wonder herself—a sporting Hun female with savage hair plunked down among us ready to hike, fuck and generally make merry with her 20th century North American soul mates. Paul is the lucky one on this trip, that is for goddamn sure, but I don't begrudge him an iota of pleasure. I only wish my own wild thing, the luscious barbarian from the mountains of New Mexico, was here. Ah, to make merry by the waters of Babylon!

We hitch up and take off down the trail feeling refreshed if not frisky, winding our way around the buttes into a more open space but still surrounded by their massive walls and turning a corner see the river for the first time since the top, much closer now, and I experience a thrill not unlike seeing Yankee Stadium for the first time as a kid on the elevated train coming from Manhattan, the great ballpark and then the startling patch of emerald between its concrete walls and copper roof and as a kid, you know, it was enormously exciting, like nothing you had ever seen before, which is how I now feel seeing the Colorado and we stop for a moment as if the first ever to see it, as if the vision is ours alone, which, at that moment, it is. We stand a minute or so in silence and Paul says, "Let's get down there," and more than ever I want to fly like a condor straight to the bottom over the rugged terrain for a soft landing on the sandy shore, but onward we trudge, the sharp fierce sun beating down, stoically, carefully, one foot in front of the other, knowing we have hours more to travel, stopping periodically for water from my can and more dried fruit and jerky, our legs shaking from the exertion, encouraging each other as best we can, the river coming in and out of view, slowly getting closer though sometimes seeming more distant, either an illusion or in fact a reality caused by twists in the trail that take us momentarily farther away.

At one point, maybe two hours before we reach the bottom, a jet fighter comes through the canyon at an absurdly low altitude, its heart-pummeling roar echoing off the canyon walls, shattering the quiet and filling our heads with its evil medicine, even down here not escaping the demented beast that asserts its dominion over all things. I do not wish for the death of anyone, not even Nixon, Westmoreland or Kissinger, but I hope for that motherfucking jet to crash somewhere away from the canyon in an unpopulated area, its pilot safely bailed out. The noise reverberates for what seems like several minutes and it is much longer before our heads settle again into the ancient quiet of the darkening canyon. The remainder of the trail is a gentle switchback with the river now in constant view and getting closer all the time. One last steep section plunging down at a ridiculous angle puts us on high alert but after that it is easy going, the incline almost negligible as we quietly approach the river, whose murmur has increased to the deeply confident rumble of a great natural force, at once welcoming and forbidding. About a quarter mile from the river the trail becomes a creek bed leading directly to the beach. On the last stretch just before hitting the sand we all hear an electric buzz of what surely must be a rattlesnake maybe ten yards away, welcoming us to the bottom. I have never heard a rattler, nor has Datura, and we are both a little uncertain but Paul tells us right away, having come across many on his camping trips. "Welcome to paradise," says Paul. In the gathering darkness we can't see the snake but its presence is powerful, letting us know to whom this place really belongs. Yes, I think, it's your turf, we're just visiting, eminent sir. We come in peace, absolutely, peace.

As it is getting dark we walk only a short way up river and find an agreeable place near a large boulder and set up for the evening, Paul lighting his stove and cooking some chicken noodle soup as Datura makes peanut butter sandwiches. We eat quietly and listen to the river sliding past in its enormous power, this river that has carved one of the wonders of the world in whose protective depths we now sit, carving deeper yet. And how far will it go? Enough to quench the earth's inner fires? To keep going and slice the planet in half? How long would it take for such a thing to happen? I mention this wayward, childlike thought to Paul and he says, "Well, let's see. The earth is about five billion years old, or so scientists tell us. The rocks at the bottom of the canyon are about two billion years old. The depth of the canyon is about one mile. That means it's taken the Colorado two billion years to reach sea level from about a mile. The diameter of the earth is roughly 8,000 miles. If it took the river two billion years to go one mile, multiply two billion by 8,000 and you get 16 thousand billion years. A trillion is one thousand billion. Therefore, it would take 16 trillion years for the Colorado River to slice the world in half. By that time the earth will be a barren rock floating in space and the energy of our bodies will have dissipated and coalesced countless times into who knows what bizarre forms, part of the great cosmic dance in which 16 trillion years is not even the blink of an eye. And the idea of time itself, which is a construct of the very modest human intellect, takes us far away from the reality of its merging with energy and matter, a swirling, seamless constant of which this canyon is but the merest wisp of a dream, a trail of radiation vanishing as quickly as it comes into existence."

We sit quietly pondering this. Paul's calculations are playful but the rest is surely right on. All of this is difficult to comprehend, surrounded by the reality of the silent massive canyon, sitting on solid ground two billion years old with the river, the ultimate symbol of the illusion of time, moving by. I look at Paul out of the corner of my eye, sitting still with his chin resting in his right hand, legs crossed, elbow on thigh, contemplating the river. That all this is an illusion, a wisp, a neural spark, the tiniest bit of flotsam in the unimaginably vast ocean of the universe leaves me indifferent. I look up at the brilliant voluminous stars. This small conglomeration of matter right here is pretty good. If it is all a dream, I am happy to be a part of it.

***

"Actually," says Paul, scratching his beard and staring out at the darkening river rushing along like an endless liquid freight train, "according to the latest theories in physics the universe isn't anything close to a trillion years old, which is a lot different in scale than Buddhist and Hindu cosmology. Scientists say it commenced with a big bang, starting from a tight, hot little piece of matter about the size of an eggplant that exploded and has been expanding ever since, maybe for 15 billion years, and when it reaches its limits shrinks to its original size and density, back to the eggplant, where it rests for another 15 billion years before regaining self-awareness and blowing up again, expanding, creating new worlds, new matter, new life forms, new forms of consciousness, and on and on."

"Zat's interesting. But vot is outside za eggplant vhen it's small? Or for zat matter, vhen it's large?" says Datura, bending forward and touching her toes like a sprinter stretching before a race, making me think of the virile East German women's Olympic track teams and the drab, gray, monolithic, mechanical Eastern Bloc of May Day parades streaming by reviewing stands crammed with stolid autocrats stuffed in their winter coats, not that Datura is any of this, asking about the original eggplant with her hippie hair and long legs, idly stretching at the bottom of a hot and ancient canyon in the decadent West, not really caring about origins and cosmological theories at the moment but with a kind of languid playfulness taking up the thread of Paul's discourse. I feel pretty much the same, not especially concerned about cosmic bangs or what the hell, if anything, all this stuff is about, and I have the feeling that Paul doesn't either, has just verbalized a stray thought or two in response to my idle musings. We have just finished the equivalent of descending a mountain in the Sonoran Desert, exhausted and at the same time overwhelmed and profoundly comforted by the womb-like presence of the canyon and the great river. Talking about the meaning of what we are so deeply in the middle of seems beside the point, or simply wrong, violating the principle of not trying to label or analyze certain moments or experiences. On the other hand we feel a little drunk with what we have just accomplished and where we are. "There is no outside or inside. Everything is connected in the one rhythm, the one dream, the one continuous respiration—in the same way the Colorado is one river from beginning to end, though different in all places," says Paul.

Datura opens her pack, takes out her sleeping bag and lies down on top of it, looking up at the stars. Paul and I stare at the dark beast rolling by, its rumbling power transporting me to the stern of an old tramp steamer out of Conrad in the Arabian Sea, the water receding into the night, everything swallowed by a void where hope and meaning no longer exist, where death is the only reality save for the small glimpse of eternity one's brief awareness allows. Death is the hoodoo perched on the shoulder of my consciousness, a constant companion since the loss of my mother when I was eight years old. From that time the world has been for me a place of uncertainty and impending loss, sometimes throwing me into gloomy depths or the odd moments of insubstantiality, shrinking, loss of ego and self. Engulfed by the canyon's walls with the river flowing by like a restless ocean I am transported again to this disquieting place, or something like it, but the mood doesn't last and pretty soon I am feeling better, the mysterious energy of the canyon reasserting itself, reducing me to a kind of profound insignificance, a much better feeling than the ordinary wretchedness that so often plagues me. In the fathomless compass of the universe all are equal—worms, cockroaches, presidents, planets, solar systems, galaxies, all connected, all swirling as one in an endless cycle of creation, destruction and rebirth.

"You know, what you said about matter dissipating and coalescing into different forms over countless eons makes me think of reincarnation," I say, still looking at the river. "It makes sense. Matter breaking apart into gazillions of atoms and coming together in different combinations all over the universe—my atoms, or some of them, joining with other atoms to create something entirely different, a rock, a bottle cap, the tail of a comet, some bizarre animal in a different galaxy."

"Exactly. Of course the idea of reincarnation has to do with the soul existing after physical death and taking up residence in another form to experience the world and its pleasures again. Scientists put this down as merely metaphysical. To them all is matter. But soul, if such a thing exists, could be composed of matter, energy, which is what I believe. The soul exists not as a metaphysical concept but as a physical reality. The energy-matter of one's soul has great power and resonates in others whether the physical body is animate or not. In fact, once the physical body becomes inanimate the soul becomes more powerful, looking for a new place to reside, a new partner, a different perspective and, of course, the possibility of mutation."

"Evolution."

"Evolution. Evolution is a function of the soul's search for new kicks. Soul is the animating force, the spirit. The most radical societies, the so-called primitive ones that focus their existence on the corporeality of spirit, are the closest to these truths. A jaguar is the most powerful spirit-force in the Amazon rainforest because it resonates with something profound in the spirit of the tribal person. All things share the same energy-matter. A grain of sand and Mt. Everest are cause for the same wonder, have the same vibration, are connected to us in the same way. When you hold a grain of sand in your palm it is aware of you. You're holding the universe in your hand."

"A grain of sand has a soul? Awareness?"

"I believe it. We shouldn't be so narrow-minded as to think that ours is the only way of perceiving things."

The stargazing Datura interjects, "I can feel that zis whole place is aware of us. There is something very cosmic about zis place."

"There is something very cosmic about our shoelaces, too," says Paul, a comment that makes me think of van Gogh and his love of ordinary things, a chair, a pair of boots, a pipe, a dish of onions. Vincent said that to look in a baby's eye is to look into the universe, but wherever Vincent looked he saw the universe. I wonder what he would have made of the Grand Canyon and suspect it might have been too large for him, at least from the top, hard to picture him on the rim like so many weekend daubers trying to get it down on canvas. No, he would have strapped on his gear and marched down the Tanner Trail in a whirlwind of heat, dust and excitement, into the intense sunlight and harsh landscape that was so familiar to him, cacti in the place of olive trees, buttes and spires writhing towards the clear pale sky, a rattlesnake rearing its death-head to strike. Down into the rocky dry matter was where he belonged with the hot wind billowing his canvases and his easel spiked into the stony ground. Though the evening air is still we anticipate the afternoon winds howling through the canyon like the mistral that drove Vincent to such despair. Fortunately it had not been windy during our descent but Paul has warned us about it.

Paul retrieves his bag and places it next to Datura's. I move my own discreetly away and sit watching the river, clearly visible now that my eyes are accustomed to the dark. I hear Paul and Datura taking off their clothes and pretty soon they are a couple of sweating ancients breathing hard under the old stars while the slick young Colorado slithers along in its channel.

I have a dream that night of Butterfly, the two of us camping together beside some river smaller than the Colorado, its waters a roiled muddy red, with wild anthropomorphic spires and huge mesas surrounding us as we roast fat caterpillars on green willow branches over a fire, across the narrow river a squadron of soldiers bivouacked for the night laughing and singing American folk songs, lights from dozens of campfires flickering in the distance like stars scattered on the valley floor. Some of the sites are groups of youths under armed guard and others gypsy camps whose music drifts over everyone like a Siren call. I awake to see a shooting star leave a trail that stretches halfway across the canyon against a backdrop of a million stars so dazzling it literally takes my breath away. "Wow," I say out loud.

"Pretty nice, eh Sam?" says Paul.

"Did you see that?"

"Sure did."

"How long have you been awake?"

"Never went to sleep."

"Kind of puts you in your place, doesn't it?"

"It's a good thing, too."

"It *is* a good thing."

"It's a god thing too."

"It's a *good* god thing."

"It's a *goddamned* good thing."

I try to stay awake and watch the stars but drift off as if drugged, waking once more to an equally brilliant but different sky and then crashing again, sometime later opening my eyes to the sight of a naked Paul and Datura splashing each other with river water, laughing and shouting from the cold, morning well-advanced but absent the sun, still shielded by the canyon's rim. They come back shivering and gleeful and Paul announces that they have decided to remain naked for the duration of our stay at the bottom and that I am invited to do the same. I have been sleeping naked and get out of my bag and spread my arms, saying something about offering ourselves as children to the canyon spirits, though more like the children of Bacchus as I imagine Butterfly down here in her naked glory and for a moment I am with the most intense loneliness (once again alone!) but shake it off looking around at this incredible place and at the long sexy Datura with her magnificent wild hair, Paul like a stumpy Eric the Red with the water glistening on his hairy body and a feral look in his blue eyes, his equipment almost comically shrunk from the cold as mine is soon enough after walking to the river and splashing myself with the cold water, whooping like a Comanche. We sit huddled in towels as Paul fires up the little stove he calls "The Champion" and we drink ginseng tea and eat salami and dried fruit.

***

Soon the sun is over the canyon rim, the river and canyon walls waking from the shadows and coming alive with heat and color as we shed our towels and sit cross-legged around the little stove watching the river, now a deep swirling green that seems to have doubled its power with the sun's animating warmth. After a while the heat is too much and taking a towel, a small watercolor kit and my copy of *The Wretched of the Earth* upriver from our camp, I find a large statue-like boulder, vaguely familiar, for protection while Paul and Datura, carrying towels and a backpack, carefully pick their way farther, looking like a couple of tenderfoot nudists on a canyon hike. As the light increases the extremes of the landscape reveal themselves, the canyon's surreal formations contrasting with the chill greenish river. It is against the law to swim across the river because of its cold water and forceful currents but I have been gauging the possibilities since morning, wondering if at the right place such a thing might be accomplished.

As for hanging out the only hospitable spot is the stretch of white sand along the river with its growth of green supple willows, something like an oasis, but even here as the sun beats down and heats the canyon walls like a gigantic stone oven you have to find yourself a good boulder for shade. Fortunately there are lots of them and I have picked a good one that I now recognize as looking like Rodin's Balzac, a little weary and leaning slightly to the west, behind me a nice patch of willows with the river in front about twenty yards away, the only discordant note a used tampon next to the boulder which I bury, resuming the trying business of sitting in the shade and watching the river flow by, fancying myself very much the young Siddhartha letting the river fill me with its wisdom. After about an hour of this, still nicely shaded by the boulder, I open *The Wretched of the Earth* to page thirteen, continuing with Sartre's preface, and begin to read: *"Europeans, you must open this book and enter into it. After a few steps in the darkness you will see strangers gathered around a fire; come close, and listen, for they are talking of the destiny they will mete out to your trading centers and to the hired soldiers who defend them. They will see you, perhaps, but they will go on talking among themselves, without even lowering..."*

I awake some time later to the sound of low whispering and intense heat on my left shoulder, Fanon's book closed, next to me in the sand, the sun to the west, following the river. In a while it will be overhead. The low whisper is the beginning of the canyon wind, at first a few aimless puffs moving the wild grass and willow leaves, then strong enough to ripple the slower-moving water by the shore and then a sudden gust that stops abruptly, giving rise to the hope that perhaps this will be the end of it but the thought itself is a dandelion seed blown away by the blast that comes through the canyon with an onslaught of sand that strikes me full in the face when I foolishly stick my head out from behind the boulder, my hair, goatee, eyes, nostrils and ears filled with grit and I am transported to a summer high school job with a raffish crew sandblasting rusty railings preparatory to painting on the Smith Point Bridge from Mastic Beach to Fire Island and more than a few times hit, not always accidentally, by the nasty hurricane of particles that could have easily put out an eye at close range.

I sit with my back against the boulder with the towel over my head and fall into a reverie about that summer of sandblasting the rusty yellow railings that contrasted so vividly with the blue water of the bay, the incredible female foot traffic accounting for most of the errant blasts, everyone on the crew except for one crude halfwit—all county crews have at least one—making the most of it, regaling each other daily huddled around morning coffee and doughnuts with lubricious tales of conquest. My own was a blond Italian girl named Joanne Russo who lived in Shirley and was a sophomore (I had just graduated) at William Floyd High School (I had gone to Westhampton Beach High School), a real beauty and a sweet and gentle person too, who, for some reason that always slightly mystified me, liked me a lot. I always felt a little guilty about going out with a sophomore, as if I was robbing the cradle, an absurd notion in retrospect but one that added a delicious taste of forbidden fruit, making the drive from my parents' house west to Shirley two or three nights a week to take Joanne to dinner or a movie, usually ending up on the beach at Fire Island having passionate high school sex on an old stained Army blanket that I carried in the back seat of my 1940 Ford sedan which I had converted into a surfing buggy replete with surfboard rack, decals and an *aoogah* horn, sometimes never making it out of the car and fucking on the capacious back seat. This beautiful girl was blond everywhere, from the soft down on her young thighs to a wondrous patch of pubic hair that she swore she had not bleached, the first blond muff I had ever seen, not that I had seen that many of any sort, and since then only one other, on a girl so hung up she could only make love in public places. I spent the entire summer with the song "Jo-Ann" by the Playmates in my head: *"I had a sweetheart, her name was Jo-Ann..."* Her father was a brute who knew exactly what I was up to and I was so nervous every time I picked her up my palms sweated and my heart raced like a sewing machine hoping against hope he wouldn't be home but he usually was. Joanne's mother was pretty hot herself and just as sweet, another Italian blond, and the two of them looked like they could have been in one of those TV commercials where you had to figure out which was the mother and which the daughter. Of course I wondered about the mother's pubic hair. At the end of the summer I went to college and never saw Joanne again.

Well, Butterfly is also a hot one and while I find myself surprisingly nostalgic for those summer nights and days with Joanne I am buoyed by the thought of soon being in New Mexico with my new lover in her native habitat. After a while the wind lets up and with the sun heading west I move to the east side of Old Balzac in the shade where I take out my watercolors and little pad and proceed to do four or five quick impressionistic sketches of the canyon, full of mystical feeling and no pictorial interest whatsoever. After that I stare at the river for another hour. I have spent most of the day sitting next to a boulder with not the slightest boredom and look forward to a few more days of exactly the same thing. The canyon has the power of a thousand Yankee Stadiums, with no "action" except the wind, the river and the incalculable energy of eons of geologic change. Hours here and I am not even hungry, or, rather, I don't think about food, content as I rarely have been to sit quietly with my thoughts, absorbing the great aura of this place, facing the emerald river and playing the part of the Brahmaputra mystic.

But as I sit watching the river impressed with my cosmic consciousness another brain-busting jet fighter flies low over the canyon, shattering my equanimity. Everything I think I have gained in these few hours sitting in the shade of the great boulder next to the river, the calm, the placid acceptance of the inevitability of change, death, the endless scattering of matter and its reformations, the quiet beauty and power of the river providing sustenance with its enigmatic wisdom, is obliterated in the few seconds it takes for the screaming death machine to fly over the canyon. My heart pounds and I am filled with anger, thinking of the US jets' rain of destruction and unspeakable suffering on the Vietnamese people, the napalm, the two-thousand pound bombs, the anti-personnel explosives, the poisonous defoliants, the B-52 saturation bombings, the ghoulish nauseating bullying threats from respectable politicians, pundits and generals seconded by a distressing percentage of the population to use nuclear weapons against the North, to "turn the place into a parking lot," as if the US has not dropped enough shit, already more tonnage than World War II, on that impoverished, beautiful, agrarian society whose culture is far older and infinitely more subtle than the one from whose loins oozed the teratoid likes of Nixon, Westmoreland, Agnew, Hoover, Nelson Rockefeller. My country is the only one to use nuclear weapons against innocents, those quiet August mornings, children going to school, mothers changing their babies' diapers, workers carrying their lunches in small wooden boxes, lovers sleeping late into the morning, police directing traffic, monks sitting in meditation, men collecting garbage, prostitutes resting after a night's work, people working in munitions factories, poets staring out their windows, carpenters building things with their subtle, minimalist tools, patients resting in hospitals or undergoing operations, animals feeding or sleeping in the warming sun, old men sipping tea and reading the morning paper, criminals behind bars dreaming of freedom, a woman sitting at the kitchen table reading a letter from her son in some hellish place, an old woman watering her flowers outside, in one instant their worlds turned into a howling fiery hell, their skin turned to dripping wax, organs roasted, bones incinerated, their homes blown away like an ant hill kicked over by a careless child, as if in an instant they had found themselves plunged into a dream beyond their most gruesome nightmares, only it was fucking real, as real as US physicists, generals, politicians, industrialists and pilots could make it.

And now it is business as usual for the US in Vietnam, bombing to their deranged heart's content, as if bombing is a normal activity for the country and periods of non-bombing only a restless interlude, fallow times while the country's violent soul simmers in frustration. The full-throated exultant roar of the jet is an analogue of Kubrick's skull-smashing hominoid declaring its power and dominion over all rivals and creatures great and small. Absolute dominance. Second to none. It is an instinct, I realize, that comes from a mixture of fear and aggression, and is yet one more manifestation of man's eternal struggle against death, perhaps its greatest manifestation. Destroy your enemies before they raid your crops, rape your women and kill you. Rid the land of all dangerous predators. Become the ruling predator. One does not sleep well until the assurance of absolute dominance is attained. Of course it never is. I wonder if the pilot who just flew over feels a sense of power and domination, what the pilots who drop napalm on Vietnamese villages feel. The bombers of Hiroshima and Nagasaki. Unlikely any of them feel they are participating in the purest exercise in human folly, cruelty and cowardice imaginable. Here is the Grand Canyon, testament to natural forces almost beyond human reckoning, certainly light years beyond human enterprise, and there is the little man in his little jet making a little noise, feeling his little power, pathetic, but no laughing matter, because in human terms, which are the dear terms in which we small beings operate, our loves, joys, hates and struggles, this little man and his flying machine can deliver terrible punishment and the tribe that he represents, our tribe, The United States of America, is second to none in doling out this punishment on a regular, industrial basis all over the world. This terrible business will surely come back to haunt us, one way or another, a Niagara of rotten, merciless karma, but what can one do about it? Really, nothing except register one's small protest and try to take the river's point of view, which is aligned with something far greater, a great silence that swallows the noise of the jet's make-believe dragon roar like a single krill in the mouth of a blue whale.

***

It takes about ten minutes but my turbulence finally subsides, its ragged edges smoothed like the canyon walls worn by the river. You have to be pretty far gone not to be affected by the medicine down here and while at times I might imagine myself beyond hope it is really nothing more than youthful silliness, the strung-out existential hero in an absurd world. Yes, I have my problems, but I am not impervious to the emollients of canyon medicine or the hundred and one ways humans have to comfort and please each other. I feel good again, my stomach growling with hunger as I think about a delicious dinner of tomato soup, tuna fish and crackers and some chocolate chip cookies and fruit for dessert which, a couple of hours or so later, is exactly what we have, and most delicious too, despite the tomato soup scalding my tongue and dropping one of my tuna crackers in the sand, the usual sort of extra seasoning that comes with camp meals as well as things like a flowing river with swallows swooping and darting across its surface, canyon walls turning various shades of orange, red, green, purple, clouds glowing pink and gold, the sky fading to dark, the first stars twinkling overhead, the relaxed palaver of companions as happy as you to be in such a place, the thought of another night nestled in a warm sleeping bag beneath a cold sky saturated with stars and no worries about jobs, deadlines, broke-down cars, unpaid bills, nuclear war, pollution and ass-ugly politicians.

Of course these worries, or some of them, will reappear as soon as we return to the canyon's rim, especially broke-down cars, but Rosalina has made it this far and I am confident she will get us across in her typical courageous fashion. The three of us hardly speak at all and when we do it is a light bantering sort of thing but later, sitting around a small fire as the stars come out in full force the conversation takes on a more serious tone and Datura, Zelda, speaks about her parents during the war, how her father, Bernhardt, a former Lufthansa pilot flying for Hitler's Luftwaffe, had spent the last two years of the war as a prisoner in England while her mother stayed in their Berlin apartment waiting desperately for the conflict to end as the situation in the city deteriorated, culminating in the Russian advance and occupation and the Fuhrer's death by his own twisted hand.

During those dreadful years Datura's mother, Gretchen, assuming her husband dead, shared their home with a younger sister, a woman of marginal stability whose mental state disintegrated as the war dragged on, given to wandering the streets during air raids, cutting her arms and legs with pieces of glass and falling into such a disheveled and fractured state that even the occupying Russian soldiers, raping every halfway desirable woman in sight, avoided her. Datura's mother never talked about the Russians, which is all Datura has say about it, leaving us to consider the possibility that the poor woman had not escaped unmolested. When Datura's father returned, a gaunt and beaten figure, his wife, having survived the horrors of bombing, the collapse of society and the brutal occupation, fainted upon seeing him. As years passed she succumbed to a depression from which she never recovered.

"My mother is a very sad perzun. But I sink in some ways my father is even vurse. He is za typical Cherman stoic, denying his feelings, silently going through za motions of his life and hating every minute of it. A bitter and resentful man. I luff my parents but I cannot be around zem for very long. It is too painful. Zey are dead already. You sink your prezident is bad. I'm sorry but you haff seen nussing."

"Well, yeah, it's true," says Paul. "We've seen nothing. At least most of us white Americans. But we could, we definitely could, which is why we raise such a stink about Nixon. Your country's been an object lesson for the rest of humanity. The question is if anyone ever really learns. It doesn't appear this country has. But we have quite a history ourselves, you know, a genocide of our own and slavery on top of it. And now Vietnam. It wouldn't take much for this country to slip into a brutal fascism, where dissenters are rounded up and put into concentration camps, where all of our so-called cherished freedoms are lost, where the media and education are completely controlled by the one-party capitalist state backed by the police. Sinclair Lewis said that if fascism comes to America it'll be wrapped in the flag and carrying a cross."

"And an M16," I say.

"Right. Or a hunting rifle. You don't even have to look carefully to see signs of it now. The hysteria over the flag, for example, what

Fromm called incestuous fixation. The backlash of white Christian America over what they consider an attack on their fundamental values is going to last for years. And not just the core values of Christian America. The core values of capitalist America are being threatened also. Wait till you see the backlash from the capitalists. Nixon is just the advance guard. No, we've seen nothing compared to what your country has been through, but the potential is there, which is why some of us are protesting right now. It could happen."

"Vell, I am sorry to say, but I agree vid you. It certainly could happen here. Ziss country has too much power right now. It is kind of scary, agchually."

Paul sighs and says in an uncharacteristically low voice, "Yes, it is scary." He hesitates for a moment and continues. "Germany and The United States are very similar in this regard—Christian countries, essentially dominionist, with the image of the father in control, God the Father, The Fuhrer, The President, with their guiding credo straight out of Genesis, 'dominion over the fish of the sea, and over the fowl of the air, and over every living thing that moveth upon the earth.' It's the White Man's Burden, which is the rationale for raising hell all over the place, especially against the so-called undeveloped world, the Third World, the non-white, marginally human people of the world. *Dominion over every living thing that moveth upon the earth.* Since the non-white person is barely human he easily slips into the category of living thing that moveth, or, non-Christian living thing that moveth."

"Of course ven vee get finished vid zem zey don't moveth very much," says Datura.

I am reminded of the thoughts triggered by the jet flying over in the afternoon, how the idea of dominion is tied up with fear of death and aggression, the two going hand in hand. "Maybe the idea of dominion is another way of sanctioning those impulses of aggression that come from fear of death or domination by competing tribes," I say. "In other words, go get it, control it, before it gets and controls you."

"I agree," says Paul. "Survival is a scary proposition. There are millions of people out there looking to do you in. God says it's ok to go on the offensive, control things, rule over things, manipulate the earth and her resources, conquer people, if necessary, convert them to your way of thinking, create colonies in the name of democracy and Christianity—onward Christian soldiers!"

I know something about this from Sunday night hymns at a boarding school I used attended and begin to sing:

"Onward Christian soldiers, marching as to war—"

Paul and Datura join in:

"With the cross of Jesus going on before,
Christ the royal master, leads against the foe,
Forward into battle see his banners go!
Onward Christian soldiers, marching as to war,
With the cross of Jesus going on before!"

We laugh and Paul continues:

"At the sign of triumph Satan's host doth flee,
On then, Christian soldiers, on to victory!
Hell's foundation quiver, at the shout of praise,
Brothers lift your voices, loud your anthems raise.
Onward Christian soldiers, marching as to war,
With the cross of Jesus going on before!"

We laugh again and I wonder if we are the first to sing "Onward Christian Soldiers" at the bottom of the Grand Canyon. Probably not. Paul explains that his mother, a quiet, deeply religious person who was dying of a respiratory disease, used to insist that he and his sister sing "the hymns" with her on Sunday nights, just as I had sung them those two years at the boarding school where a tall, energetic and likable dorm-master by the name of Mr. Ames would lead us in the fervent Sabbath singing, Jews, which I consider myself, peripherally, and Gentiles alike. Datura knows them through Sunday school at the Lutheran Church her parents belong to and admits to liking them as much as we do. I suggest "Rock of Ages" and we start in with gusto. Despite our fervor our voices are swallowed by the canyon and river, knowing a thing or two about the rocks of ages:

"Rock of Ages, cleft for me,

Let me hide myself in thee.

From thy riven side which flowed,

Be of sin the double cure,

Save from wrath and make me pure..."

The haunting, morbid hymn hangs in the air a moment, washed away by the sounds of the river, booming and gushing along, a tinkling sound close to the shore like broken glass making me think of *Kristallnacht* and my peculiar relation to the hymns as someone who, though technically not a Jew, my mother was a non-practicing Episcopalian, nevertheless thinks of himself as one, or partly one. My father's Jewish parents had come over from Eastern Europe in steerage. Datura rolls a joint and we sit starlit and stoned as the river barrels along frigid with melted snow from the Rocky Mountains.

***

The next day is a carbon copy of the first, retreating to Old Balzac and weathering the scouring wind, dashing out a few more wildly impressionistic watercolors and taking a nice long afternoon nap. Later, before returning to the campsite, I walk upriver looking for a spot where I might swim across, finding one section, wider and slower, that seems a possibility. But it is daunting. The Colorado is powerful and cold and there are some pretty sizeable rapids about three hundred yards downriver. I am a good swimmer but have never taken on anything like this before.

That evening over a dinner of chicken soup, peanut butter, tuna fish and chocolate chip cookies we decide to spend two more days and nights at the bottom and then head out for New Mexico. Datura has brought some acid and announces that she is going to trip the next day and invites us to join her. Paul immediately agrees, but I am less sure. I have decided to swim across the river tomorrow and my determination is building. Doing it on acid seems problematic, to say the least. I suppose I could wait until the day after but I think I might be too tired after tripping. I fall asleep, waking a few hours later under the startling night sky, feeling something like a soldier the night before battle, listening to the river as if able to divine some secret that might help me get across as shooting stars streak across the heavens, flaring to cinders in the earth's atmosphere. I try counting them but after a while fall asleep.

Following a breakfast of ginseng tea, beef jerky and dried apricots Datura retrieves a piece of aluminum foil from her backpack, opens it and removes a small square of blotter acid that she cuts into three pieces with her red Swiss Army knife, using a flat stone as a cutting board. Paul heats more water on his stove for another cup of ginseng tea to wash it down. I am unsure about tripping as I am resolved to swim across the river, something I have not told my companions about, fearing they will try to dissuade me. I have presented myself with a challenge and it is impossible to back down. I have only tripped a few times and the most demanding thing I have done is walk on the beach and groove on the sunset. But I want to take the acid because my friends are doing it and I cannot pass up an opportunity to trip at the bottom of the Grand Canyon. The pieces Datura cuts are unequal in size and I make sure to take the smallest, muttering something about being really sensitive to LSD. We place the paper on our tongues like communion wafers and wash them down with the earthy tea and sitting in a tight circle, naked as lizards as I try to keep from staring at Datura's long athletic body and mossy walnut-brown pubic hair, a challenge throughout, we hold hands and thank the Great Spirit for allowing us to be down here. Well, let the festivities begin, I think, and following custom I go to Old Balzac to wait for the first familiar signs, hoping it won't be so extreme I can't attempt my crossing, which has now taken on the dimensions of an existential imperative. Datura says it is good acid, made by a chemist friend (every trip I have ever taken has been with acid made by someone's "chemist friend"), lasting six to eight hours and "really mellow."

***

I sit for a while looking at the river, which seems greener and more massive than ever, listening to the rapids downriver sounding like a subway. A large blue rubber raft floats by full of canyon tourists snapping pictures and nervously eyeing the rapids ahead. Four or five of these ungainly things come by each day and I make it a point to conceal myself when they appear, partly out of modesty and partly out of playing fugitive Lakota hiding from the *Wasichu*. This time I stay in plain view, a smaller rock sitting immobile next to Old Balzac. The raft passes and no one notices except for one woman whose wave I don't acknowledge, not willing to break the connection I am feeling with the boulder, the sand, the willows bowing gently in the gathering wind, the flowing river. The raft disappears from view but I can hear the whoops and squeals of the tourists as they go through the rapids and I can see them like an eight millimeter film in my mind's eye, the bright colors of their vests, the vivid blue raft careening through the rocks in the frothy water, the happy excited faces, filling me, as if my life has already passed, with an almost unbearable nostalgia for the fleeting tumultuous ride of existence, the breathtaking innocence of it all, the images and sounds of the rafters merging with others that spool in my mind like a Technicolor movie, kids playing in a summertime pool, the happy expectant faces at a major league baseball game, walking down Lexington Avenue at rush hour on a warm May afternoon, high school football, my first sexual experience, the hurtling drive west to escape the desperate energy of a broken heart, the feeling so intense that I have to move.

Taking my watercolor kit and pad I walk down to sit at the river that now seems four or five times wider than before. I swirl my brush in the slow-moving cold water in which tiny guppy-like fish circle my bare feet like sharks and the river grass sways with the currents. The cold water settles the apprehension I always feel at the beginning of an acid trip. At the same time I am filled with portent, as if the pressure is building on fault lines below the surface of my psyche: my rendezvous with the river. I look at it now from its own level, rumbling along with mythic power. Obviously it is the height of madness to even consider swimming across, some sort of death wish. Distracted by my reflection in the water, which seems ordinary enough at first, my face begins to separate, bending, swirling, looping around and reconnecting in bizarre configurations, something like a funhouse mirror with a moving surface but instead of laughing like a kid in an amusement park I am drawn deeply into the images in a kind of Narcissus-like, Bizarro World fascination. "Me Bizarro now," I say, empathizing with the misguided fractured creature, and anyone observing a naked young man looking into the water and saying such a thing would instantly concur. But I *am* a kind of Bizarro and getting stranger by the minute, utterly absorbed in the kaleidoscopic movements of a reflection that reveals the truth of an ever changing identity, as if who I am depends entirely on the perpetually shifting currents of an external world, and in the spaces of those changes, emptiness, a nothingness as hollow as the Albert Hall. This doesn't disturb me terribly though there is the impression my hands will pass through my body if I try to feel myself, not so much disintegrating as coming slightly apart, allowing some essential perception to freely circulate, the reflection that was once a recognizable face separating and coalescing into new forms, their rainbow-like colors increasing in intensity and strangeness, no knowledge of how long sitting and staring at the water, maybe ten minutes, maybe an hour, but gradually some larger force commanding attention and with effort the camera or vision force inside some sort of projection room lifts—it seems to take several minutes—and looks out over a river that shockingly has stopped moving, as if the touch of some giant's finger has rendered it inert, as if some huge diorama in some real-life version of the American Museum of Natural History, the river a mass of green glass, the canyon walls and rocks made of concrete, the faux flora bordering the river painted a delicate green, only the sand real, trucked in from some beach. If there have been doubts before about this reflection in the water, falling apart and coming together like a light show at the Fillmore East, I, or something approximating I, am totally shaken now. Am I real or just some animated mannequin on display at a futuristic exhibit? Why isn't the river moving? Where am I? Who am I? About to turn and run away from the frozen river in a panic I remember that I am tripping. This is the LSD running amok in my brain. Get a grip, relax, go with the flow—but there is no flow, the river has stopped—of course it hasn't—impossible!

Suddenly the river starts up again, as if someone has turned on a projector. I stand naked, my heart racing, holding the watercolor brush in my hand like a knife. The remainder of my painting kit, the flat metal container of Winsor & Newton color pans, the spi-

ral binder of student grade watercolor paper, lies forlornly next to
the water. Things are moving again, thank god. Returned to myself
I take several slow deep breaths and try to relax, the emerald river
laughing like an army of leprechauns, my painting supplies beckoning. Of course! I will paint! Sitting down again I dip my brush in
the green water rampant with life, bacteria, protozoa, algae, hydra,
worms, swimming like terrible Greek monsters, hunting, devouring each other, copulating and spawning billions of young. Holding the wet brush at eye level I look at the drop at the end of the
soft bristles, marveling at the life it contains, reflecting the warm,
golden, generative sun that impregnates every animate thing with
its vital force, the *élan vital* I have read about in some philosophy
class. Putting this drop under a microscope would yield a veritable Calcutta of exotic creatures. Mixing this water with my colors would make anything I put on paper dance with life—or maybe
death—a slaughter of millions!

I spend the next several minutes contemplating the teeming life
at the tip of my brush, trying to decide whether or not to sacrifice
it for the sake of an attempt at self-expression. But I want the life
force of the river imbued in my painting and so dip the brush in the
water while saying a prayer for the demise of small organisms and
then rub it in the diminutive red color pan, *alizarin crimson*, which
blooms thickly like an open wound. I hold the brush over the paper and a large drop falls onto the white surface, shocking in its violence, several smaller drops separating from the mass and scattering
about the paper. For a while I stare at the far-flung drops, pondering the laws of physics that have dictated their pattern. But there
is something about this vivid red splatter that is outside of physics,
something magical and awesome that has to do with color and design together delivering a profound message, a sign, a signal that I
struggle to comprehend, an ancient system of divination based on

dripping different colors on blank paper. Reading the drops. Jackson Pollock as high priest. No shit.

I flick the brush and a half-circle of drops swoops across the paper. Red laughter. A big nose in the middle. A cork popping with passion and joy. I am living my life exactly as I am supposed to, naked in the sun at the side of a great life-giving river, an artery fed by a network of veins. What does that make me about to plunge in, a platelet? An amoeba? A white blood cell? I flick the rest of the paint into the water and watch the red drops transported by the currents dissolving and disappearing as the river itself will into the ocean and all things again into the greater cosmic ocean. I wash the brush clean and rub it into the yellow color pan, *bismuth yellow*, saying the name as an incantation, drawing out its electric energy, "BIZZZMUTH YELLOOWW!" The inert brick of color opens itself to the water and becomes a thick pool of stunning yellowness, saturating the brush with its brilliance like sweet lemons or liquid sunshine, and the holy name echoes in the chamber of my mind. "SUNKIST," I solemnly intone, holding the brush over the paper as a large drop of paint falls onto the red, partly covering it but producing splotches of orange bleeding through as I watch, mesmerized. I flick the brush twice more and a familiar yellow/red/orange arrangement appears. "POLLOCK," I say. The swirls of color overlap, merge and dance around the page, a loose, anarchic, pulsing boogie-woogie and I say, "MONDRIAN," and the words POLLOCK and MONDRIAN come together and I say, "POLLONDRIAN," which is a great magnificent magical word that delights me and I say it again two or three more times and it is such that I decide that I am indeed a POLLONDRIAN, from the planet POLLONDRIA, which is the earth's real name, hidden from the uninitiated by millennia of bullshit, bloodshed and babble. There was a time when the earth was fresh and green and sundrops fell from leaves like honey and small naked furry humans, something like Hobbits, swam in warm clear waters, laid about, made love, smoked strawberry-flavored ganja and played a form of badminton using their minds to direct dandelion seeds over nets woven by willing spiders. This is still Pollandria—the great suffering tragedy of it! But it doesn't take much to recapture a piece of it for oneself—simple really, anyone can do it. All you have to do is see. I think of Paul and his love for Blake. I have to read Blake. Kiss the joy as it flies. Pollandria. What had happened? A huge weight comes down on me like the walls of the canyon. What a miserable, futile business to be human, striving for light and air, separated from nature, from each other, from the awareness of some unifying transcendent reality. Like the people in the rafts floating down the river we are tourists in life, unconnected, ignorant and obsessed with point A and point B, departure and destination, the beginning of the river journey and the end. Nine o'clock and five o'clock. Instead of swimming in the river we visit as tourists. Swimming. The secret is the river itself, which suddenly seems less a murderous crush of indomitable liquid force splintering my bones on the rocks than a strong, forgiving sentience that will allow a respectful Pollandrian to enter its waters and be borne to the farther shore. The river is speaking to me. I feel no fear. The place I have chosen to swim across is wide but appears slow and gentle. Far above the rapids, I can use the river's force to carry me down and across. I will go with the flow.

***

Paul and Datura have disappeared, heading up the shore, the same trek they had taken the first two days, back to places they feel accustomed to, maybe a secluded spot where they had made love. They seem like Adam and Eve down here and I an odd character left out of the narrative, a discarded prototype for Ishmael, imperfect and unmentioned. Fine with me. Comfortable with it. Sensing a presence I look up at the rim and see the stone tower near the parking lot peering down ominously, straight out of Mordor. I feel vulnerable in my nakedness, certain that someone in there is looking at me through a telescope, maybe Sauron himself, the tower a life-sucking force pulling all the joy and color out of the canyon through its dark windows, a clear manifestation of evil, at the same time just as clearly the nature of its antagonist, good, appearing all around me, a benign suprahuman consciousness in the form of a huge pulsing mass of warm color that permeates the universe, constantly shifting and moving, seeking the conditions where it can flourish, Earth such a place, but even here it fights with its opposite, a terrifying implacable anti-consciousness, sucking the warm colors into its absolute zero void, *good* and *evil* the names given to these two primary forces of the universe, the centerpieces of every great discussion of art, philosophy and religion. Individuals war with these forces internally from birth to death, according to fate and temperament going one way or the other, some to extremes, what we call righteousness or wickedness, MLK or Hitler. Normally these powers cancel each other and most go through their lives in a muddle. A great cosmic struggle played out in our tiny beings!

The menacing phallic object on the rim fills me with foreboding and a weary depression, all energy running down like a recording losing power as the voices drag slower and deeper, nothingness and death the objectives of this malignant consciousness. As a child my parents had taken me to see Peter Pan on Broadway with Mary Martin swinging back and forth on a slender wire crowing like a rooster. Near the end of the play as Tinkerbell was dying, her light growing fainter and fainter, Mary Martin told us to clap like mad to bring little Tink back to life and I and all the other concerned children in the audience clapped until our hands were sore as Tinkerbell's light gradually grew brighter and we clapped harder and harder, the force of our collective will bringing the little fairy back to full wattage. Now I am having my own Tinkerbell moment, making it necessary that I clap my psychic hands to bring the colorful, living side of the equation back into the picture.

So there it is, forces competing for dominance in our minds and our job to recognize this, bring things into balance, the tower competing against the positive forces of the river and the canyon for my attention and, ultimately, my soul, the ever-changing landscape of our psyches, a single phenomenon eliciting different emotional responses from moment to moment or even simultaneously, one's ever-changing identity, my reflection in the river, creation and destruction and so much else embedded in everything at the same time. I look at the tower, the great life-sucker, the void, what we think of as evil, and I relax. Taking four or five slow deep breaths I smile and wave up at it. *I know you*, I think. *I can control you by choosing not to let you control me!* I imagine someone looking through a telescope waving back, Sauron himself, also smiling, knowing that this person understands. Yes, he says, I am from the dark side but I have my role to play. I am great. Greater than you. But you have your measure of greatness too, your measure of insight. Good for you!

My surroundings take on an unusual aspect, neither benign nor threatening, composed in an odd, almost mechanical equilibrium, as if everything is held together by clasps or hooks, not unlike the hooks on bras or girdles. The willows are hooked to the ground, which is hooked to the substrata. The river is hooked to its bed and the materials of the canyon walls hooked to each other, gravity a form of hookage, pushing and pulling. The study of physics is an obsessive attempt at unhooking, the bomb an instant form of this, a pyrrhic victory for the small, clever human mind. It is as if there is an agreement between the forces of good and evil not to get out of hand with each other, content with living in a permanent state of disagreement, endless antagonists whose conflict has softened around the edges after eons, or so it seems as I look around, the ground held together with an infinite number of tiny hooks elastic enough to allow for movement as the ground moves beneath my bare feet, which, I can see, are moving right along with it, hooked to the ground, the motion traveling up through my ankles, shins, calves, knees, thighs, into my groin and sex, which amazes me looking at it, alive in an erotic Shiva-like dance, my pubic hair glowing gold and red, my abdomen covered with soft hair, slowly rising and falling like a calm warm kelp-laden sea with its intricate purposeful workings inside (how busy! how intimately it knows me!) the strong beating heart like another brain connected firmly inside my chest doing its steady labor, one beat at a time, sending out vibrations that radiate like sonar, searching, seeking, merging with all other hearts. I walk along the shore feeling this amazingly true sense of belonging, this connection, knowing that not to feel this way or understand it is the illusion of ordinary consciousness, that I and most of stumbling humanity suffer under this illusion much of our lives—and what an illusion, what a burden, it is!

Now the acid is coming on like a Bombay rush hour, turning the landscape into a van Gogh of Arles, an undulating dance of masculine and feminine forces, a grand riotous sexual tumble, the whole world erotically vibrating, the river an enormous flowing green phallus sluicing through warm vaginal canyon walls, the friction creating a continual orgasm that penetrates everything. I put my hand on Old Balzac and its warmth radiates up my arm, through my shoulder, filling my chest and loins. My painting supplies lie next to the river. I turn and walk towards the place where I will swim across, leaving them behind.

***

After what seems like several hours of a meandering journey I arrive at the spot I have chosen, a jumble of small boulders and rocks, and stand for several minutes watching the river flowing towards me and beyond, a massive presence coming around a bend, flat, powerful and more vividly green than ever. I am not ready to enter this extraordinary force and so lie down on a warm stone slab thrusting out over the river a few inches above its surface, letting the water run into my mind, filling me with its glittering immensity, the flat rock becoming part of my body, creating the sensation of floating just above the river. I lie blissfully still for what must be a half-hour, I don't really know, swept away by this feeling. Now it is time. Getting up a little shakily I survey the task a moment and figure what the hell and dive in, just like that.

Taking risks always involves an element of foolishness. Once, more than a little crazy and showing off for the girl I was with, I went swimming in a small pond during a thunderstorm, tempting the gods as the lightening flashed around us. A bolt struck several hundred yards away, its current traveling through the saturated ground into the pond, giving me a jolt. I had always thought the danger came from a direct hit to the water but instantly realized that a near miss could be just as bad, the current conducted to the water by the wet ground. Almost my last Eureka! moment. Now, immersed in the river, apart from the obvious hazards of strong currents and rapids, I understand what makes this swim especially risky: cold water. The initial plunge has taken my breath away but flushed with adrenaline I swim like Johnny Weissmuller through a flotilla of snapping crocodiles and make it to the middle as the opposite shore, still far away, slips past with an air of unreality, like a home movie shot from one of those rafts. This is a bigger deal than I had figured, the surprisingly powerful and fast-moving river, the rapids coming on, my body sapped of energy by the cold water—fifty degrees, I find out later at the ranger's station.

Having experience swimming in the rough waters of the Atlantic however, I know the one cardinal rule, which is that you cannot fight that which is stronger. Water will carry you where it will and survival depends not on submission but a sort of opportunistic cooperation, though it is hard not to panic because the river is carrying me quickly along and while I cannot see the rapids I sense their closeness and hear the sound of them, a faint background noise something like an approaching street sweeper several blocks away. At the same time there is an unreality about the whole thing, as if I am a character in an adventure movie. The dissonance of this is bizarre and coldly terrifying. I have to struggle to convince myself that I am conceivably about to come to a bloody, bone-splintering end, brains dashed out on boulders two billion years old, swept along by a river that Lao Tzu would have admired for its enduring truth: A traveler in this world seeks the correct path. To find this path the traveler studies the natural world and reflects on its workings: These workings are not in harmony with dropping acid and jumping naked into a cold powerful river. I am indeed flaunting the Tao, running into the teeth of a sawmill, the river narrower and faster, the water downstream churning violently like some monstrous washing machine in permanent agitator mode. Desperate, I swim as hard as I can, the current by some fortuitous quirk sweeping me closer to the shore. But still I am swept nearer to the flashing water and crushing boulders. The tumult grows louder. I'm not going to make it. What an amazing fool! Thirty yards above the rapids my toes grip the sweet gravel of the river's bed. Encouraged, I increase my efforts, finally reaching the shore ten yards from the rocks, crawling on my hands and knees and collapsing like a shipwreck survivor, like Crusoe, like Ishmael, like a sock spun-stuck to a washing machine's drum wall, the sun slowly warming my chilled bones. Against a vivid blue sky a small green bird eyes me curiously from a nearby branch.

I lie on my back for a few minutes, drying like a dishrag in the desert heat, looking up at the Technicolor sky, the clouds so white and brilliant I am forced to shield my eyes. The green bird flies off. The rapids grumble. Terra firma. Allah be praised. No magic carpet to take me back. I need my strength.

I get up and look at the green running river and the white froth crashing over and around the glistening boulders that stand like sturdy Trappists in an onslaught of trial and temptation, a glorious sight out of some CinemaScope Western, the last obstacle for the young, weary homesteading family to overcome, the other side the realization of their dreams. One more river. Staring at this spectacular but weirdly filmic scene I grapple to find a toehold for myself in the landscape, seeking reassurance with the knowledge that I have just swum across this river, real enough that it has almost taken my life. But already it seems like days or even weeks ago. Another lifetime. How have I gotten here, naked and tangled, skin baking in the fierce desert sun, standing at the edge of an incomprehensible jade river pushing its way through an enormous canyon? On one level I know exactly what is going on but something else overrules this secondary, merely empirical understanding, something deeper happening, more real, more meaningful. A yellow raft of tourists floats by full of smiling, laughing, waving women—I seem only to notice the women—snapping pictures and filming as I smile and wave back—what else can I do? They have me, naked as Pan, in their sights and I hear distinctly as if over a bullhorn the river guide's amused, amiable voice, almost triumphant actually, as if he has been able to show the housewives and their husbands a member of an exotic species, "And there's one of our canyon hippies!" and everyone beams and clicks more pictures. In a moment their attention turns to the rapids though one woman in a floppy yellow hat keeps looking at me even as the bulky craft careens through the boulders with everyone holding on and whooping like bronc riders. In a few seconds they are past the rapids and though many turn around once again to look at me only a few return my farewell wave, which strikes me as ineffably sad. They are a boatload of prisoners floating back from where they had come. I shout and wave for them to return but they are moving quickly and are soon gone. I don't suppose many, if any at all, feel a twinge of regret or horror or sadness at being swept along in the circle of their lives that wraps around them like a chain but I feel it for them, though I forget this soon enough as another raft comes floating down, this time a silver one, and before they can gawk at me I disappear behind a willow like the wild animal I am and watch as they gird themselves for the rapids, gripping the raft's gunwales with the gleeful nonchalance of veteran rapid-runners. The river is an ultra-cool amusement park ride where you pay a couple of hundred dollars for a few days with just enough wildness to make it interesting. You even get to see naked hippies. Too bad Butterfly or Lulu Delilah aren't here so we could fuck for them. I wonder if they would take pictures of that.

It is now probably four or five hours since I have swallowed the acid. From the angle of the sun it seems maybe three or four o'clock, though perhaps I have been transported to a different solar system with a second sun about to rise from the north, maybe a blue one. Truly I am a strange creature on some distant planet's nature reserve. It is imperative that I get back to the other side where at least a memory of a former reality lies. This time, knowing the river's power, I will cross higher up, as much as a hundred yards or more, and be prepared for the cold. I slowly pick my way up the shore behind the willows, hidden from gawking tourists with their grinning libidos and soul-sucking cameras. I find it impossible to figure out where I had first jumped in but judging from the tower I am quite a bit farther along and to be doubly sure I walk another ten minutes, finding a spot that seems as good as any, though it is slightly wider than the first crossing. At least I have no misconceptions about the river's cold power, though it is a tossup if my experience swimming across makes me more or less confident. I suppose being aware of what I am dealing with is an advantage, though if I had known in the first place I would have stayed baking on the slab like a sensible reptile. But no, I am a mammal with a highly developed brain and opposable thumbs—a toolmaker and art lover whose naked body causes others of its species to smile and point image-recording devices in its direction as they risk their lives crashing through churning boulder-strewn waters. All very reasonable. But of course it is not. The whole thing is sheer lunacy. Most everything humans do seems sheer lunacy. But what else is there? Sitting on a warm rock all day? Impossible. We are doomed. Folly and concupiscence. I dive in and make it across calmly and easily, landing on a little white beach well above the rapids, shivering but happy, warming in the Arizona sun. Arizona. I am in Arizona, whatever that is.

***

The effects of the acid are diminishing, the air still warm but cooling. I am tired and eminently pleased with my little adventures of the day. Really, it is amazing how things *happen*. If you stay in one place and do nothing, things happen, even if you don't want them to happen. If you step outside all hell breaks loose. I haven't done much except a little swimming and walking and it feels like I have lived several lifetimes. Of course the acid has something to do with it but even without tripping it has still been an eventful day, a happening day. I laugh at the expression "What's happening?" An overwhelming, impossible, absurd, cosmic question. What's happening? *It* is happening! It's always happening! What is *it*? Don't you know?

My surroundings, the river, plants, rocks, have taken on an intensely stylized aspect, with heavily saturated colors and a curious flatness. The opposite shore seems close enough to touch. Objects stand by themselves, each with its own striking individuality, a vivid quality that recalls expressions I have come across in philosophy classes: *thing-in-itself—essence*. Philosophy, impenetrable and soporific, becomes profound, the human mind's attempt at communion with the external world, phenomena, an effort at the same time awesome and immensely endearing. I feel a warm rush of affection for the great philosophers, Kant, Plato, Descartes, Nietzsche, Schopenhauer, the whole pantheon, even though I hardly know a thing about them or their thinking. This is what it must have been like for them, sitting on a riverbank with externalities in full cutout, ripe for philosophical plucking. Aristotle or Kant in maximum psychedelic mode, super brains riffing like Charlie Parker in Minton's at two in the morning. Uber-hep cats! Philosophy is cool!

I begin to shiver, the sun hidden for a moment behind massive spires like something on Mars. The day, the trip, is entering its final phase, the sun's radiation and the chemical losing their punch. I am hungry and have a keen desire to see Paul and Datura. The wind hasn't blown all day, a blessing. A remarkable day. The last food I had was the tea, jerky and apricots we'd eaten for breakfast a million years ago. The usual mixture of lassitude and detachment I feel after tripping is more pronounced than ever. I have done it. Swum across the mighty Colorado. On acid. An image of the woman in the floppy yellow hat appears. Who is she? Where does she live? What is her name? What was she thinking when she looked at me? A battalion of goose bumps raises the hair on my arm like porcupine quills. Time to head back, put on some clothes, get some food.

Walking along the shore I pass a thicket of willows from which issues an odd sound, and pushing aside a branch I see Paul and Datura on a red towel making love in a contorted position straight out of the Kama Sutra. Fascinated and instantly turned on I get down on my hands and knees to watch the spectacle, the lovers glowing in the late afternoon light, an erotic carving on an Indian temple, almost motionless, a tangle of arms, legs, mouths and genitals enveloped in a golden aura, slowly undulating, male and female conjoined like some primal sex creature, their low moaning and sharp rapid breathing a sound emanating from inside the earth, a physical manifestation of a powerful sexual energy just below the surface. I feel guilty watching but it is such a turn-on, such an archetypal vision, so profound and mystical, that I remain, spellbound. They have become one being, profoundly in love with itself. The longer I stay the deeper the feeling that I am witnessing something pre-human, the sylvan deities that once ruled the earth not vanished but gone into hiding in the few remaining wild places, their spirits having taken over Paul and Datura, bringing them together in a generative ritual. The coming together of male and female humans is vital for the continuance of these ancient creatures. Maybe the woman in the yellow hat had come under the spell. But not strong enough to make her jump ship. These spells strike all the time. Mostly we resist. Maybe it is because the ancient power is diminished. Paul and Datura begin moving faster, their breathing and moaning increasing, an erotic Hindu deity with multiple arms and legs copulating through eternity, spinning through the cosmos in endless bliss. The great fucking force. I know I should leave but lack the resolve, and begin to fondle myself, at the same time aware of a powerful odor, perhaps the glandular secretions emanating from the entwined groaning deities before me, the divine musk, and then, even stranger, a weird snuffling sound that doesn't jibe with the gasps and moans of the ardent Vedic lovers hidden in the willows, a discordant noise that triggers the beginnings of a response from my perimeter defenses but before my chemically altered brain can assess these strange signals a cold object feeling like a soggy submarine sandwich presses against my neck and I jump like a man discovering a severed foot in his toilet, effecting a feline twist in the air so that when I land I am partially facing whatever this horrifying thing is that has snuck up behind me.

Now, prurient and bemused reader, you must surely wonder what causes me to react with such terrified alacrity. The powerful odor, the snuffling noise, the odd, cold pressing against the back of my neck is so unexpected, so creepily jarring to my voyeuristic reverie, that I am truly terrified, terrified to the bottom of my lascivious soul. The moment from the clammy pressure on my neck to the time I land sideways is no more than a second or a bit more but it is enough to riffle through a dozen pages of a bestiary in my mind with no match other than the dreadful certainty that it is an animal, maybe a horrible animal and, in expectation of that I am prepared to defend myself to the death, at the same time woefully reflecting on the inadequacy of my pathetic human endowments, so lacking in sinew, tooth and claw.

As my brain in full reptilian mode ricochets through this little episode of stimulus and response another weird and frightening irrationality insinuates, not as an actual thought but more as coloration or association: The large ugly pig that had treed Paul and me in Big Sur has followed us to the Canyon, and this time he is really pissed. The absurdity of this is irrelevant, for, as is well known, in times of unexpected and unclassified danger the freaked human mind will manufacture any number of ridiculous and dire things, at least until the true nature of the situation is revealed. Usually the danger is less severe and more manageable than what the hyperactive imagination dishes up. Maybe this is an evolutionary gear, like overdrive, a kind of worst-case response so that we are prepared for anything. But even for worst-case responses the notion that a wild boar has followed me from Big Sur to the bottom of the Grand Canyon on a fifteen hundred mile vendetta is bit much. I have no idea why such a thought, especially since I don't think I am that much more unbalanced than the average naked young man on LSD at the bottom of the Grand Canyon fondling himself while spying on a couple making love. But in some uncanny way the subliminal image of the crusty wild pig of Big Sur is not so far-fetched, because facing me with an air of indifferent curiosity as I crouch in terror is an obviously addled cousin of the Big Sur boar, a member of the demonic order of the cloven-hoofed, a shaggy, demented-looking female mountain goat with glassy yellow eyes.

The situation presents me with a dilemma. Though relieved I am not going to be attacked by a dangerous animal I am furious with the stupid goat for scaring the shit out of me and want to scream and chase it away, but doing so will alarm Paul and Datura and likely disrobe me for the shameless peeping Tom that I am. Despite the ludicrous scene that has just unfolded, the goat noises, my coiled leap of fright, the heavy breathing of my terror, there is no indication of awareness from within the willows, indeed, above the hammering of my heart and my own heavy breathing I can hear the familiar sweet sounds of Eros still going strong. The guardian-fuckin'-angel that has seen me cross-country and across the Colorado and back is still looking over me. I rise to my feet and with a menacing step motion violently for the goat to be off, my face twisted in a mask of carnivorous threat, but the animal flicks its tail and holds its ground, staring at me as if I am a ridiculous child. Not wanting to make any noise I do not dare actually chase the foolish animal. My only recourse is to continue towards our campsite and hope the goat doesn't follow me or stick its curious nose into the willows. I back away as the goat stands still, watching me. It seems to be deciding whether to follow me or move in on Paul and Datura. If it chooses to make it a threesome in the willows I will employ my own hooves and get the fast fuck out of here but apparently it finds me more interesting and begins to follow in a distracted amble, always about ten yards behind, stopping occasionally to nibble on some branches and once to eject a dozen brown pellets the size of mothballs in the middle of the trail.

Reaching old Balzac I go to the river to get my painting supplies but they are scattered around and I notice that some of the paper has been chewed. Fucking goat. What the hell is this beast doing here? The whole of my existence, all of existence, amounts to nothing more than a sort of bestial absurdity, as symbolized by this bizarre goat that has appeared out of nowhere. It is the essence of stupid, mocking, even sinister, futility. Everything I have done in my life is ridiculous, devoid of purpose and meaning, including the day's follies, swallowing a mind-altering chemical, staring at colors, swimming across the river, exhibiting my naked self to a group of strangers in an inflated rubber vessel, spying on others of my species in the most basic of animal acts, arousing myself and then being frightened witless by this emissary from a mythic realm with its cloven hooves and sexual associations, the pre-Christian symbol of fertility, riot and debauchery with which, under normal circumstances, I have no problem. But there is something about this mindless goat that strikes me as almost terrifying, its quality of *goat-ness*, the single-minded resolve with which it follows me, as if in sublime mockery it is offering itself for me to fuck. Since I had been so interested in watching Paul and Datura, it seems to be saying, why not fuck a goat? In the same spirit the ancients have drawn Paul and Datura together they now offer me, with wicked glee, a goat.

At the campsite the goat watches as I, feeling absurd and infantile in my nakedness, put on some shorts and a T-shirt and when I go to the river to splash water on my face it walks up to my pack and pulls out my jeans. That's it. I pick up a stone and throw as hard as I can, missing by a couple of feet but the beast drops my pants and scampers over the rocks away from the river, stopping about thirty yards off, looking at me. I throw two more stones and the goat runs away, disappearing, I am sure, into the mythic dimension from where it came.

8

A properly positioned greeting > Shuddering initiation to a fiendish concoction > A master's eye in black and white > Feeling nothing, feeling good > Siren call to a thousand-year sleep > The balls of Jesus

We spend the following day and night listless but happy at the bottom of the canyon, a place I now privately refer to as *Temple Number One*. Among the previous day's experiences communicated to each other, I mention the encounter with the goat, eliminating certain contextual details. Paul and Datura have omitted at least one of their adventures as well. The next day we leave the canyon on a brutal eight-hour hike. The water is behind the red rocks where we had cached it but we have consumed the last of our food for lunch, dry tuna sandwiches, a handful of almonds and two apples and we are reduced to eating the lemon candies for the energy to make it to the top. I am glad to see the evil tower, even with the life force being drained from us by the minute as we seek to revivify ourselves with the candies. Rosalina, dusty and covered with pine needles, is waiting faithfully as we silently drag our tired rumps over the top and into the parking lot.

Rosalina's interior is hot and covered with almost as much dust as outside despite the tightly shut windows but she comes to life the minute I pop into second gear with Paul and Datura pushing. I drive Paul to the visitor's station where he calls Carmen, likely not mentioning a few things, and then we head west on 180 through Flagstaff and Winslow, spending the night in something resembling a campground near Holbrook and in the morning curve north through a little town called Alpine, excitedly crossing the New Mexico border, driving through the San Francisco Mountains, still snow-laden, and then through the Mogollons where we see mule deer and antelope, passing through little towns named Luna, Alma, Glenwood, Pleasanton, Buckhorn, Cliff and Mangas Springs, old mining towns still populated with a few holdovers and ghosts, a small market here and there, some decrepit buildings, mostly wood, a few old adobe houses returning to the earth, and on into Silver City, a sweet little town we all instantly love, especially Datura, who can hardly contain herself with the old-western-ness of it. The weather is beautiful, warm, clean and clear, with a wild mountain freshness that makes us all a little giddy. We stop at an old adobe market with a peeling façade that reveals mud bricks and straw set back on an unusually high curb—flood protection, says Paul—for sodas and potato chips and a tall, slim, garrulous white-haired oldtimer with sideburns and wearing jeans and a blue western shirt with red stitching and pearl snaps greets us warmly with a familiarity that suggests we have been expected.

The drive from Silver City to Butterfly's village takes about two hours. We stop briefly at the huge open pit copper mine in Santa Rita, which, after a week in the Grand Canyon, seems no more than a dimple and we all laugh, thinking the same thing, then continue on with a beautiful green roller coaster ride with dark mountains all around, The Black Range, and some of the typical features we have come to associate with the West, the buff, red and yellow sandstone formations like spirits rising from the old rocky ground, a couple of creeks masquerading as rivers, a few cattle ranches and always a quality of light and air that makes you want to get out of the car and run around hooting like a lunatic. It is wild, it is strange, and Butterfly is waiting on the other side. I wonder how she will react to me.

Entering Butterfly's village we drive down a quiet main street lined with cottonwood trees that remind me of small towns I have seen in New England except that we are surrounded by a landscape that is open and grand with none of the claustrophobic, slightly spooky feeling you get in the East. The fierce desert heat is at least a month away. We make our way to Butterfly's house at the western end of town, a single-story, gray-stucco adobe with a pitched roof and when I see her outside taking clean clothes from a line wearing espadrilles on her small feet, tight bell-bottom jeans and one of her peasant blouses, a white one with short puffy sleeves, the back of which is covered with her glistening black hair, my heart does a little up-and-over.

We pull into an open yard that has an adobe shed, a pile of huge tires, a covered stone well with shoots of young asparagus all around it, an old faded red bulldozer, a green metal structure supporting a large fuel tank, a big flatbed truck, a corral with a stocky chestnut stallion with a black mane and tail and an apple tree in full silvery blossom. She turns with an armful of clean clothes and smiles self-consciously—she is terrifically endearing and cute—and I am suddenly shy and self-conscious myself. I hesitate in the car as Butterfly puts the armful of clothes into a basket and Paul as Datura pile out with smiles and hugs, I finally take a deep breath, get out and walk up to Butterfly who hugs me with her pelvis properly pulled back.

There follows a moment's awkwardness with the usual questions exchanged as I examine Butterfly's face and manner for positive signs. The screen door bangs and a small, attractive dark-haired woman with an open, honest face, wearing Levis and a colorful blouse, walks towards us with a smile that is warm and knowing, putting us all immediately at ease. It is Lila, Butterfly's mother. The door slams again and an older, agreeably-weathered, intense-looking man with high cheekbones, wearing old Levis, faded blue work shirt and a well-worn grayish Stetson casually tilted back on his head strides up frankly appraising us, seemingly reaching a favorable conclusion that softens his expression into a welcoming smile. He gives the impression of size, even though he is no larger than I am up close. I figure it is Butterfly's father, Harlow, though he is older than I expect and before his daughter can say anything he sticks out a strong rough hand in greeting, looking at each of us sharply with his clear blue eyes. He seems to get something of a kick out of Datura, who introduces herself with her real name, and has a warm smile for Paul, but for me there is a hint of challenge. Feeling a bit like the suspect suitor I try to maintain my composure as Butterfly smiles at me encouragingly, pulling the last of the clothes from the line. The man looks at me with an intensity that could melt a tire iron. This is the genuine article, the mythic character come to life and I am afraid he will dismiss me as no more than a small tumbleweed blown skipping over the hills ending up lodged under a boulder but he seems pleased that I am from New York and blesses me with an amused smile. "New York, eh? Great city! Great people from New York! I was there once. You're not going to try to sell me some bridge now, are you?"

"No sir," I say, "But maybe you'd be interested in this terrific car over here. I'll sell it to you for a good price." I point at Rosalina. His hearty laugh puts me at ease, and he turns to his wife and says, "Mama, how about some coffee for these folks? Come on inside."

***

We walk up a wide, weathered, unpainted wooden porch thickly covered on one side by vines with small white flowers. An open sack of grain rests next to the door. Inside we find ourselves in a laundry room with a yellow linoleum floor, simple pine cupboards, an old wood stove, a Majestic, and a Maytag washer. There is an agreeable smell of laundry soap and wood smoke. Warm afternoon sunlight slants through the windows, illuminating the dust and imparting a golden glow to the floor, giving the room the feeling of a small chapel. A bathroom adjoins the room in which I can see a shower stall but no tub. I sense the warmth and history of this family immediately, even in the washroom, or maybe because of it, a clean, well-scrubbed frankness of being proclaiming itself for what it is and nothing more—or less. I am not used to this kind of thing, this open, human quality, where ordinary household duties reveal themselves as something beyond the mechanical act of throwing clothes in a washing machine, adding soap and turning the dial, contrasting it with my own upbringing where a succession of maids washed and dried my family's clothes, strangers privy to our stains and secrets, where I never gave the simple, profound act of washing clothes a moment's consideration. Clean clothes showed up in my drawers as if by magic. Shirts came from the cleaners starched and folded around a piece of cardboard, wrapped with a strip of paper. Like so many essential processes in my life it was at a remove, something apart from the ordinary routines of family existence. And this, I reflect, makes perfect sense because I really had no family. Little wonder that something as seemingly inconsequential and bothersome as laundry should hardly be considered. And yet here in Butterfly's house the laundry room is the first thing you walk into, presenting itself to a visitor like the entrance to a sort of holy place, humble, utilitarian, spotlessly clean, smelling of soap and smoke, like incense, the room unashamedly revealing the character and warmth of this family, instantly putting me in a state of alert respect. We enter the kitchen, with Lila in the lead, followed by Datura and Paul. Butterfly is behind Paul and directly in front of me. Harlow is at my back.

The kitchen is a large clean room with white stucco walls, tongue and groove wood floors and ceilings, illuminated by a tall wide window that looks out onto the dark mountains to the west, the Black Range, and a nearby windmill that slowly turns. Large metal hooks hang from the ceiling forming a rectangle. Above the table is an ornate cast iron chandelier. On either side of an old-fashioned white enamel sink are two kerosene lanterns sitting on gold-colored cast iron supports attached to the wall. Butterfly comes back hefting the chairs as all of us sit down except her mother who goes over to the electric stove, a clean white Frigidaire with four burners, and carefully shovels four healthy scoops of ground coffee from a large old copper can and pours them into a stainless steel percolator with a copper base and turns on the back burner. There is an appealing grace and sureness about her movements. I like her very much.

"Now I make strong coffee," she says—I can't imagine her making anything but—and she switches on the adjacent burner where sits a small round red kettle for her daughter's tea. We are sitting around the table a little self-consciously and Harlow looks at Paul and then at me, gives a little smile, and says, "You folks been doin' some hard travelin'. How 'bout a shot of greasewood to set things right."

"Sure," says Paul, "what's greasewood?" I allow as I will give it a try too, though there is hardly a question of refusing, especially with Butterfly looking at me appraisingly with an amused twinkle in her eye and Datura jumping in, "Me alzo!" with a great smile, obviously taken with Butterfly's father. Here is the real Glind-Eeezd-vood, though to me he is a different sort of Western man, Randolph Scott if anybody, modest, none of Eastwood's violence percolating below the surface, though you know this is not a fellow to be trifled with.

"Greasewood's good for what ails you," he says, turning around and retrieving four shot glasses from an old fashioned, honey-colored cupboard with a large flour bin, next to the white sink. Well, I think, there are more than a few things ailing me. Everything here is old and comfortably worn and speaks reverently of past generations, with an obvious appreciation for quality and with an air of elegant simplicity that I imagine reflects the sensibility of Butterfly's mother—the solid round oak table, the fine, stoutly-constructed wooden chairs with their round seats polished by generations of well-centered behinds, the

impressive chandelier hanging above, the plain burnished copper coffee can on the wooden table next to the stove, the clean white old enamel sink, the simple blue glass vase holding white flower cuttings from the porch vine, the immaculate, no-nonsense stove and refrigerator, both Frigidaire, the small, simple, light blue ceramic creamer and sugar bowl placed matter-of-factly on the table by a quiet, warmly-smiling Lila, all of this illuminated by the tall, wide window that looks out on the dark mountains and the old windmill revolving like a sage in serene reflection. On the table sits the Mason jar retrieved from the refrigerator filled with an ominous amber-colored liquid: greasewood.

Harlow knocks his Stetson back a bit more and grips the jar with a strong hand and shakes the bottle four times, producing a white froth on top of the liquid. "Now this stuff the Indians used to cure just about everything—and as a preventive, too. It grows wild all around here. Some people call it chaparral, some call it creosote. But I've always known it as greasewood."

Creosote, where I come from, is the vile substance used for coating wharf pilings and telephone poles. But maybe it isn't the same stuff. I hope not. He shakes the jar a couple more times, unscrews the top and fills the glasses. "They call it greasewood because it actually has a little grease to it. Here's mud in your eye."

He raises his glass eye level and appraises it for a second, as if preparing to go into battle for the ten thousandth time, and drinks it down in one gulp. And then he shudders. We look at him. He smiles and his blue eyes sparkle. Butterfly and Lila are smiling too, looking at us. Paul picks his glass up and sniffs it, his eyes growing wide. "Whoa! That's some strong smelling stuff!" Datura and I do the same. The potent, earthy odor fills my brain with something ancient and medicinal.

"Okay," says Paul, "let's do it." We raise our glasses and clink. "Here's mud in our eyes," says Paul. Lila and Butterfly smile in anticipation. Harlow looks at Paul and me. We smell the stuff once more, brace, and swig it down. I am watching Butterfly out of the corner of my eye. She is watching me. The effect of the greasewood is an immediate, powerful and involuntary shudder, almost a convulsion. I think for a moment I might throw up. I can see why Harlow still reacts this way after thirty years, or whatever it is, of imbibing this horrible concoction. Datura and Paul have the same reaction, all of us shuddering and shaking our heads and blinking, as if we have just chugged a glass of turpentine, though once the initial reaction wears off, which doesn't take very long, a few seconds, a warmth spreads through my body and my mind feels clear, with a kind of exhilaration.

"Well," says a smiling Harlow. "Whadd'ya think?"

"Wow, zat stuff iz amazing!" exclaims Datura, blinking her eyes.

"I feel like a new man," I say. And it is true, I do feel like a new man.

"Unbelievable!" says Paul. "It felt like I was drinking the earth itself. Extraordinary stuff!" He shudders again and we all laugh. "And how much do you drink?"

"Oh, a couple of shots a day, usually. Sometimes more, dependin' on how I feel. It cures skin cancer, too. I had a spot one time and kept puttin' greasewood on it and sure enough after a while it went away. Just like that. The Indians have been usin' greasewood for thousands of years. Can't beat it. Want some more?"

"Uh, no thanks," we all say, pushing the shot glasses away from us.

Lila and Butterfly laugh delightedly. The percolator sounds like a diver's bubbles and the coffee's smell permeates the warm, softly lit room, imbuing it with a tightly sealed, underwater quality. I feel like Ned Land in the Nautilus with Harlow as Captain Nemo. Butterfly smiles at me and goes to the cupboard as I sneak a glance at her mermaid behind, coming back with six small cups and saucers, very delicate, with a light blue filigree pattern on the outside, and arranges them on the table. Lila carefully pours each of us a cup, the steam drifting off the black strong-smelling brew. "Now, who wants spoons?" she asks in a warm and quiet voice. I am the only one. "There's canned milk," she says, smiling almost enigmatically, Mona Lisa pointing to the creamer. "Pet Milk. That's how the cowboys drink it." She places a tea bag gently in Butterfly's cup and pours hot water into it from the round red kettle. I marvel at the precision and care with which she does everything, as if the concentrated center of the universe is right here, in the brewing of coffee, the pouring of hot liquid into those delicate cups, the people sitting at the old oak table. With her self-effacing manner she seems responsible for all of us. Paul gives me a meaningful look. He will have something to say about her later, I am sure. She sits down. There is a moment's hesitation while we wait for her to sip her coffee or say something but she only smiles and blows gently on the hot liquid. "Mama makes the best coffee," says Butterfly, looking warmly at Lila. "It's famous all over. It really and truly is. You can't deny it, Mama. Everyone loves your coffee."

"Yes, it's true," says Harlow. "Our Lila makes the world's best coffee. Nothin' better to wash down that ol' greasewood with. Isn't that right, Mama?" He gives her the same loving look that Butterfly had given her and she smiles and shakes her head, as if to say that is nice but not true at all, though what really counts, and how deeply she appreciates it, are the feelings conveyed by her husband and daughter. I am glad of the opportunity to wash down the awful greasewood and will do so in a minute, but really I am thunderstruck, bowled over, by the warmth, simplicity and genuine class of this small family unit. What marvels and surprises there are in this tortured world! Paul, Datura and I have the same thoughts, I am sure, you'd have to be a bar of lead not to, and we sit trying to take it in, trying to make it compute. No matter how open minded you flatter yourself to be, if you come from the city you think in some ways that you are just a little bit better than your country cousins. It is a form of racism. You have good intentions but deep down inside you feel a little superior. But each minute spent in the company of these people increasingly disabuses me of any ridiculous notions of city-superiority. What I am seeing here is a high order of human beings, no question, countrified, yes, but so rooted to a profound feeling of place and decorum, so graceful, so unpretentious, so grounded in the moment (especially the magical Lila), that it has the sublime effect of putting me almost completely at ease. But what, I ask, are those curious hooks stuck in the ceiling? Those are her grandmother's quilting hooks, Lila explains. Almost every morning in the winter her grandmother would invite three or four friends over for a quilting session (a quilting bee?), where they would quilt and drink tea, laughing and gossiping the hours away. I imagine it as an old pioneer pastime, and here it is, a living reality, though, as Lila says, they haven't been used for quite a while.

Everything I had sensed about Butterfly is turning out to be true. I can see why, though she liked California, she was not really comfortable there. This is a young woman with the wildness and home fires in her veins, someone who will always be a part of the wide-open, rugged beauty of New Mexico and the rich vein of its past, redolent of the spirits of those who had staked their survival to these mountains, arroyos and mesas. They had hung on and taken something essential, making it their own, and if Butterfly's family is even a bit typical, they have given something wonderful back as well. I would be content to sit at this table for hours sipping Lila's delicious coffee rich with Pet Milk and sugar, listening to stories, fitting smoothly into tradition as the old windmill turns connecting wind with water while the dusky mountains meditate in the background, feeling the ghosts of generations that have gathered in this very place for the same comforts.

***

We finish our coffee, taking our cups and saucers to the sink offering to wash them and are gently shooed outside by Lila where Harlow shows us the bulldozer, an International TD-18 with much turf, obviously, under its treads, laid up for a few days waiting on some clutch parts which is why he is home, apparently pretty unusual for him. He tells us he does all kinds of work, from roads to stock tanks to just "movin' things around," and we marvel at this man who by all appearances is in his sixties and yet has the energy and spirit of someone thirty years younger. I know he had fought in the Pacific as a Marine and I wish for an opportunity to sit down with a bottle of whiskey and talk. Even though I despise war it fascinates me and I hold those who have experienced it in a kind of awe. I never criticize Vietnam veterans, except the stone killers, and don't know anyone that has. I'd had friends in college who worked with groups that helped veterans. I am appalled at the lack of care they receive from their government. Everything about the war is an obscenity, from the outright brutal killing to the destruction of a beautiful land and its marvelous, subtle culture, to the disgraceful neglect of returning veterans. Butterfly had told me that her father was critical of the government and the war and I would love to talk to him about all these things, his combat experience, the military, Vietnam, but I don't dare bring it up.

I think we all feel a little bit like children standing around Harlow as he talks about his bulldozer and the jobs he does, regarding him with the kind of awkwardness people get when confronted with another human being whose experience and unusual qualities demonstrably outstrip their own. Harlow seems genuinely pleased with our company and during a pause in our questions about his work and the bulldozer he pats its thick, worn treads as if for emphasis and bids us spend the night, looking at us with his arresting blue eyes, making sure to point out that the girls will stay in the house and Paul and I in the shed. The hospitality isn't unexpected but I feel more than a twinge of remorse and frustration as the boundary between the young men and women has been firmly marked by the lord of the manor, though this, too, is not a surprise. My mind races with scenarios circumventing this barrier, but the prime mover and strategist will have to be Butterfly, and I am not sure she dares go against her father's will, or her mother's, for that matter, though the devices of Eros are various and substantial and I offer up a secret prayer, hoping he will find us a way.

The shed is roomy with the same gray stucco and tin roof as the house, with windows all around and two old solid doors on opposite ends. Inside are tools and objects related to Harlow's work, organized and beautifully worn, and a couple of cots, one already open. Harlow unfolds the one leaning against the wall and whacks it a couple of times to chase the dust, which is minimal, a few small puffs quickly disappearing and at that moment Butterfly enters carrying blankets, sheets and pillows, the vision of her laden with these soft, comforting and suggestive amenities again filling me with conflicting emotions. How nice to be sleeping in her home under her family's linens, but how far away from her I will be! She goes rapidly and efficiently about the business of fixing the cots as Paul, Datura and I retrieve our backpacks from the car, and when we return she is almost finished, bending over the cots, tucking things in, bustling around, reminding me of the little girl in the Castro Convertible commercial and the jingle, one of the better ones, pops into my head, strictly a New York thing.

We sit on the cots, looking at the shed's interior. There is a seriousness here, an attention to detail that is impressive and humbling, the same feeling as the washroom and the kitchen, but very much a man's place, smelling of smoke from the box stove, oil, leather, hay and diesel fuel, a row of huge chains hanging on the south wall. On the wall to the east is a collection of ropes, bits and bridles and directly underneath a couple of fifty-pound bags of oats and a bale of hay. Two saddles, one resting on a wooden stand built into the wall and another hanging from the rafters, give off a warm afternoon golden glow. There are hooks up on those rafters too, definitely not for quilting. I imagine deer hanging during hunting season or beef from Butterfly's uncle's ranch. The two doors on either end of the shed are old, with antique-looking knobs. There is a storage area for household things in one corner above the rafters. Underneath sits an old trunk. A single pine shelf runs along the walls supporting jars and boxes filled with nails, bolts and screws, as well as various sorts of tools and other things.

Butterfly and Datura have gone into the house. Paul and I are alone in the suddenly still shed. "You know," says Paul, "I've taken part in a few tea ceremonies and I'll be damned if that's not what we just experienced. The tea ceremony is an open door for the ancestors, about preserving what is valuable about the past. Everything about that kitchen speaks of the past, the furniture, the old sink, that beautiful cupboard, the quilting hooks, the chandelier, the old copper coffee container. Implements in a tea ceremony are revered for their age and connection to the meaningful. I bet a lot of those things have been handed down through generations, the same way bowls and cups used in tea ceremonies are passed along. They carry the spirits of the ancients.

"Lila's obviously the kind of person who recognizes the value of small things. She has the yin nature of receptivity. She picks it all up. She knows the value of ritual—the way she prepares the coffee, the cold fresh water, the old copper can, carefully scooping the grounds into the percolator's basket, the sounds of the bubbling water turning into rich, wonderful-smelling coffee, the careful pouring into the small cups, the steam rising off the coffee, the quiet time waiting for it to cool, blowing on the hot surface of the coffee—all these things are just like the tea ceremony. There must be a million families doing the same thing every day but I doubt it gets anywhere near this level. It's because Lila is a Buddhist, that's why. She's the one that makes it work. It's the process, not the end result. It's an occasion to celebrate all the things that she understands as sacred, and it's constantly repeated because she knows the importance of ritual, which is the practice of remembering. She embodies the ideal of merging life and art. And the kitchen—it has a purity, it's uncluttered. In Zen it's the empty space that has meaning—a means to facilitate focus. Focus on the small things, the profound things. The things we usually overlook."

***

The next morning after breakfast, lingering over more good coffee in Lila's kitchen, Butterfly announces that we are going to take a ride later that afternoon in Lila's car to another village several miles away. Butterfly's face shines with a kind of wonderful shy pleasure, as if she is about to unveil marvelous secrets known only to her and a relative handful, slightly anxious we might not think too much of it, after all it is only a village, and we are from much larger places. But there is really no chance of that.

Around three o'clock we get into Lila's cream-colored, four-door Mercury, maybe a '63 or '64, and Butterfly starts it up and smoothly shifts the lever on the column into reverse (I think of her driving Rosalina so expertly) and then out the driveway, guiding the powerful rumbling car down the road in the direction from where we had come, over a small bridge where, she tells us, she and her friends would go to watch the floods after summer storms. The creek, normally dry, is where she often played as a child, with her mother's constant warnings of snakes and thunderstorms embedded solidly in her little girl mind.

Past the bridge we head towards Silver City, in the direction of the neighboring village. Animated with the occasion, she talks about her family and the places we pass. The country is heavy with trees and you can feel the Black Range looming over us. Driving through the town we see worn and weathered wooden buildings from the mining days and I try to imagine what it had been like, the freshness of the landscape, the excitement of riches to be mined, the great energy brought to bear in such undertakings, the houses, stores and saloons going up bang-bang, maybe even a church slapped together in a symbolic effort to save a few fevered souls. Not all the houses are wood. Many are brick and stone, like the old bank (and here we park the car, the dirt road at the end of town, where we are headed, too rough for the Mercury), the post office and the fire department, solid structures all, and some more substantial wood structures. But the real attraction is Butterfly. She has lost all self-consciousness and bubbles along as we walk, full of stories about the village and its citizens: "Here's the place that belonged to Bill James, I don't know who lives there now—every woman in town had a crush on Bill James. That house over there is the Creeley house, oh, I just love that place! It used to belong to Rose Creeley a French woman who married a man from Ireland. And that house, the one partly on stilts, that belonged to Paula Haskins. Oh, my god, Paula Haskins! She was a funny little school-teacher with crooked arthritic fingers and painted nails. She lived in Hong Kong for many years. She was Buddhist who dressed in exotic Chinese and Japanese outfits and her house was filled with things from the Far East. Oh, Paula!" And here Butterfly pauses a moment with feelings about these people from her past and you can see the depth of her roots in this place, the depth of her, and then she recovers and goes on, describing the houses and the people, making them come alive for us, and I think again about ghosts and spirits and how this place is strong with them, how they are living through Butterfly, who is a medium or historian of sorts, full of passion and love for her home, and it hits me for the umpteenth time, our lack of connection, our problem, what is missing.

Then we are well into the forest, all of us silent now in the gathering afternoon darkness, in the company of a burbling stream that fills the auditory space just occupied by Butterfly's meandering monologue. We come to a convoluted old apple tree in full blossom and Butterfly tells us her brother had seen a black bear on its hind legs getting apples last fall from this very tree. This is clearly a wilder sort of wood than New Hampshire or New Jersey and it is not a stretch to imagine a mountain lion looking at us from some little cave in the surrounding cliffs or a bear nearby sticking its nose into the air and catching our

scent. There are hawks, eagles, owls, coyotes, wild turkeys and rattlesnakes, too. Butterfly is in her element. Lulu Delilah is a continent and lifetime away. We stay at the tree for a few minutes, sniff its blossoms, listen to the silvery murmur of the creek and then head back down the dirt path into town, still not talking very much.

Back at the house Lila is fixing dinner or, as it is called in these parts, supper. Harlow is on his back under the front end of the bulldozer and when we pull in he calls out but keeps on working. I have fallen into a quiet mood, partly because I am hungry and partly because I am blown away by the total *immersion* of everything here in the utterly serious business of living in a particular, traditional way, which is at the same time immensely attractive and completely alien.

Lila calmly goes about preparing supper, giving gentle instructions on how we can help. I assist Butterfly putting plates on the table while Paul and Datura get the silverware. Lila has prepared salmon loaf from S&W canned red salmon, the smell of which merges with the earthy sweetness of brown rice simmering on the electric stove. A large Blue Willow bowl filled with cabbage salad drenched in olive oil and lemon juice sits in the middle of the table. It is seven o'clock and I can't take my eyes off Butterfly. I am almost dizzy with hunger. Lila checks the rice and declares it done, bringing over the pot and dishing out a good helping on each plate. Butterfly with her white blouse and raven hair brings the salmon, redolent of lemon and herbs, from the oven to the table. There is a bowl of chopped green chile and a bowl of sliced lemons next to the cabbage. Harlow comes in and goes through a vigorous hand washing, playfully suggesting a shot of greasewood before dinner. We respectfully decline.

***

As we eat the topic turns to literature when Lila tells Paul that Butterfly has mentioned he is writing a book. Paul modestly downplays his efforts and steers the conversation towards Eastern philosophy. I know where he is going with this because of his conviction that Lila is a Buddhist, or natural Buddhist, as Butterfly had mentioned, and sure enough she talks about how much she loves Eastern religions, especially Buddhism, and how she has always lived more or less in the way of Buddhism, even before she knew anything about it. Lila loves Thoreau and Emerson and notes how close they are to Eastern thought and Paul says yes, absolutely, yes. Harlow says he's not much of a religious person but he respects all religions and they all have something good to teach, if only people would really live according to those teachings. He says he's just finished reading a book about Confucius and what a wise man he was, how much sense his philosophy makes. Harlow wants to see the Great Wall and the Forbidden City. I look at Butterfly and she is smiling warmly at her parents. This just blows me away and I have to look down sharply because I am a little dizzy with some strong emotion, so beautiful is this relationship and how completely opposite it is from the one with my own unfortunate parents. How lucky you are, Miss Butterfly, I think, how lucky you are!

After supper we help with the dishes, though Lila insists we not do too much, suggesting that Butterfly take us for a walk around town. Harlow sidles up to his wife and gives her a little bump with his hip and she smiles that same deep down smile I have seen so many times already. He stands solid his in work clothes looking like a man from another era, maybe the thirties, maybe even before that, like a tree growing right here in the kitchen, his rough hands handling the dish towel with an easy familiarity, carefully drying the delicate Blue Willow china and putting it in the rack, the two of them standing there like a picture in one of my father's U.S. Camera Annuals out of the late thirties, the old kitchen, the classic Western couple, the strength of the land in every humble stitch of their clothes and every pore of their skin. I think if van Gogh was here he would be beside himself with the dignity and character of these people, their *texture*, and I look at Paul and he is looking at them and then looking at me, smiling. It is the place for a master of black and white photography: Lila's hand gripping the stainless steel pot as she pours the black steaming coffee: Harlow contemplating the shot glass of greasewood with his hat tilted back in the late afternoon kitchen: The old cupboard next to the sink with morning light splashed across its surface: Shafts of mote-laden afternoon sunlight spilling through the old windowpanes of the washroom: The young beauty Butterfly serving salmon loaf on a china platter to a table of upturned faces, this last image no Norman Rockwell sentimentalizing of the quintessential American family gazing beatifically at a golden platter of sanctified comestibles, no, rather real people with complex lives forged by tradition, struggle, character, hard work and love, with no illusions about the nobility of man or his institutions.

We leave Lila and Harlow at the kitchen sink, as if leaving a time capsule, and take a walk on a dirt road up a hill to the old schoolhouse. It is a beautiful evening, a bit of a breeze, not too chilly, the lights from the town below gleaming like embers. Butterfly wears her father's Levi jacket over her white blouse, a young Greek beauty standing in front of the old building as if on some ancient Aegean outcropping, the wild-haired Datura next to her, and we stand quietly for a moment imagining Lila and her brother forty-two years earlier going to high school here, the depression gathering momentum but probably not felt as keenly here, though I don't know. It seems to me that the kind of resourcefulness and self-reliance so evident around these parts would hold them pretty steady through the hard times, though it was also the time of the dust bowl and westward migrations and I don't know how much that affected New Mexico. It was a spare, no-frills kind of life, that was certain, the kind of life that was more attuned to the vicissitudes of the weather than those of Wall Street, which seems to me a very good thing. I feel the ghosts here at the school too, the decades of young spirits, mostly innocent, some not, the time of so much poignant promise and intensity. Butterfly talks about times at school, the boy who complained to the teacher that she wasn't reading because she didn't move her lips, the boy who had a crush on her but could only express it with hostility, one time poking her with a lead pencil, a big mistake, that, as she later ambushed him, knocking him down and pummeling his back with her third-grade elbows, how much the children loved her mother, who taught at the school.

Datura tells us about her tyrannical fourth grade teacher, Mrs. Diederich, who yelled at the children incessantly and made them stand on one leg in a corner for the whole period for the slightest reason and how one day a mouse appeared in the room and she screamed and jumped up on her desk, much to the surprise and delight of the students. About a week later a boy named Fritzie snuck six of his brother's white mice into the classroom and let them loose halfway through the period. Mrs. Diederich leaped onto her desk and screamed so horribly that the students' mirth turned to terror and the girls began to cry. The principal and three other teachers burst into the room like Waffen-SS storming a Rhone farmhouse, freaking out the children even more. Mrs. Diederich, Datura smilingly relates, took a leave of absence for the rest of the year.

We sit quietly for some minutes on the school steps, feeling the spirits of grade-schoolers past, looking down over the town.

Tomorrow Paul and I leave for Albuquerque, another adventure, though tinged with sadness at the thought of leaving Butterfly and her beautiful family. Already I feel at home here. An old pickup rattles down a nearby hill. A dog barks. There are stars. Will I ever see Butterfly again? She takes my hand and pulls me up. "I want to show you something," she says, and she leads me around behind the old school house and leans against the pebbly stucco wall. She is so beautiful standing there, her long dark hair, her strong cheekbones, her lips parted, the collar of the too-large denim jacket pulled up. I stand as if in a dream, saying nothing. She reaches behind my neck with both hands and pulls my face down into her's and I feel her rapid breath on the roof of my mouth, her tongue, her sharp teeth biting my lips, her strong body moving against me, *make love to me,* she says, *make love to me,* and she takes my hand and puts it against her marvelous breasts, the image of them with my head on her lap at Big Sur, and I push her blouse up and bury my head, kissing, biting the small hard fruit of her nipples, thinking how we are such simple animals that live only for this, and how much I love this and the strong, supple animal that has me in her insistent, urging grip. The breeze kicks up and bangs the old rope against the flagpole next to us and we are unbuttoning each other's jeans and she is propped up against some kind of ledge, maybe a ledge she knows from school-yard days, maybe thinking about how she would sometimes sit on this same ledge at recess, the strangeness of life, this same familiar ledge worn by small school rumps and feet and time and weather and now for the first time, possibly not, no, possibly not, by passion. *Sam,* she says, *Sam, don't leave, don't leave, come back, make love to me all the time. I will,* I say, *I will.* But I don't know if it will ever happen.

***

The image of Butterfly, Datura and Lila waving goodbye the next morning, Monday, Harlow already at work, Datura leaving the following day for San Francisco, stays with me as we head east towards 25 and then north to the strange city where I had spent the night nearly three weeks earlier in a little adobe house where large insects rustled around in the exposed mud bricks as I restlessly slept. It could have been Afghanistan. I'd had vivid dreams that sparkled wild blue and I knew California was happening and in the chilly morning with patches of snow melting and steaming on the dark pavement my two whooping hitchhikers pushed Rosalina and I was off, headed to the golden coast, their feral cries ringing in my ears.

Now is different. We are headed east, not west, and even if the South offers intrigue and possibly danger, the fact that I am going home pulls at my guts like a dull fishhook swallowed long ago. It isn't the pain of Lulu Delilah, though I am surprised it continues to hurt, but the whole depressing matrix in which I have flailed around for so long and which I realize more strongly than ever I wish to escape. But it is still the West and we are still buzzed, driving past Truth or Consequences and the strange Elephant Butte reservoir that looks like a lake on the moon and then a long open landscape with ragged, forbidding mountains close by to the west and distant, mysterious ranges in the east. Paul and I are struck by the empty, wild strength of the land and it makes us both a little quiet though we are as excited as if we were driving through Morocco or Patagonia. About 30 miles outside of Albuquerque we pass Belen, a sleepy village of farms and adobe houses over which morning smoke from woodstoves hovers in a blue cloud. There is nothing else around but distant mountains, lonely-looking massive things that give no sense of welcome. All is wide-open space. Then to the east comes the huge, ungainly Sandia Mountains, overlooking Albuquerque, a sprawling collection of buildings with no apparent order or center and a funky outlaw strangeness that I remember from my first stop with the two roguish hitchhikers. I was in a state at the time and in no mood to stick around and savor its kitschy wildness but now we have a day or two and I am feeling much better. Paul had been a few years before to visit a poet friend, Christopher Riley, who lived in a little house near the university. Christopher had gone to Berkeley and then had landed a gig in the English department at the University of New Mexico teaching freshman composition. He's a good poet, says Paul. Some of his poems have been published in well-regarded anthologies. He had gotten his PhD in literature from Berkeley. He is also something of a lunatic.

So it is with some interest and vague unease I stand next to Paul as he raps on a bowed and ragged red wooden door with an unraveling black, red and yellow *Ojo de Dios* crudely tacked up with a rusty six-penny finishing nail. The small, dirty, one-story wooden house with its peeling white paint seems ready to collapse. Faded blue asphalt shingles layered with leaves and pine needles from surrounding trees cover the moderately pitched roof. The shades on the two windows facing the street, Silver Avenue, are pulled emphatically shut. No light shines around the edges. Cigarette butts, cat shit and various sorts of crushed cans litter the dirt yard. A cracked flowerpot with a shriveled prickly pear cactus lies on its side next to the door. Paul knocks again and a gray cat jumps onto the sill inside between the window and the shade and meows at us, the next instant joined by a heavily pregnant calico with crazy-looking eyes. "He must be teaching. Let's go get something to eat," says Paul.

We walk west on Silver a few blocks. The cross streets are named after hot shit colleges, Vassar, Princeton, Columbia, Stanford, the houses ordinary enough, none nearly as run-down as Christopher's. It seems a student area, though there are not many around. We turn down Cornell to Central, across from the university, and go into The Frontier Restaurant, a bustling place that reminds me a little of the Caffè Med, full of students and other raffish characters. Paul and I order bowls of green chile stew and fresh orange juice, sit down in a booth and immediately get into a heavy conversation about our fathers. I tell him I think he's been quiet recently and wonder what the reason is, if maybe he feels a little introspective or something because of Carmen. He says that's a little of it but mostly he's been thinking about his father and wondering about the advisability of going to see him. He and Carmen are solid and might end up together for a long time but on the other hand have no claim on each other's freedom. I am a little skeptical about the freedom part, but what the hell. We stay in the booth talking for two hours, ordering more green chile stew and glasses of orange juice as the weather outside turns gray and windy. Betrayal is the theme of the afternoon, father and country.

"We're raised with certain myths about the moral authority of father and country," says Paul, his blue eyes and surrounding whites contrasting with the darkening atmosphere outside. He leans forward slightly with some of that intensity he'd had the first time we talked at the Caffè Med. The wind gusts and blows stuff down the sidewalk. More people pile into the restaurant, seeking shelter and lunch. "The state's job is to keep its population infantilized. The father has a more difficult time. There is a direct relationship between the father's role and the culture's, especially a masculine culture like ours. The child coming of age recognizes the lies and compromises the parents have made to survive in a brutal, dehumanizing system. He rages against them and their sellout, hates them, vowing never to be the same. The father reacts violently to the child's rebellion but is helpless to suppress or contain it. The mother weeps and wrings her hands, torn between her natural female honesty and love for her offspring and loyalty to her mate. The child instinctively recognizes the process of willful self-deception carried out by the parents, the slow, profound, day-by-day swallowing of lies, humiliation, loss of spirit and creativity, the loss of happiness, and he's heartbroken and terrified at their loss, which is his loss, because, unless they've been abusive, *even* if they've been abusive, he loves them dearly, he is connected. He understands with a revelatory clarity that much of what he's been told is lies, and he's blown away by a stunning sense of betrayal. How could these people, these grownups, these adults, this country, have fed him such a crock of self-serving, self-righteous bullshit? This incredibly involved, complex web of mythology fabricated to convince the child of the nation's, the father's, strength, moral superiority and divine mission. Its manifest destiny. What he realizes is that his parents have been stripped of their souls by the uber-father, the state, the system, and their job all along has been to prepare him for the same spiritual disembowelment. And to take it sitting down, take it smiling, take it up the ass! This is a betrayal of the first order, and the child correctly recognizes it as such, and has every right to rebel and rage—every right to hate his parents and his country. This is a betrayal of the human spirit, of what it means to be alive. A betrayal of our potential as creative, self-fulfilled human beings."

This resonates with me. "I understand what you're saying. I was born on George Washington's Birthday and grew up with the whole patriotic routine, American flags, little hatchets, cherries and whatnot on my birthday cakes. The thing was, it made an impression on me. All the stories about George Washington, the father of our country, how great he was, chopping down his father's cherry tree and owning up to it, the importance of honesty. Now that I think about it I recognize the significance of *his* father in the story, how little George gained his manhood by confronting his father, the righteous authority symbol, with the most powerful weapon of them all, the truth, and really, by extension, out of this tradition of righteous truth-telling, a good part of the country's mythology was being created, right there, with little George and his father."

"George Washington's birthday, eh? I was born on August 6, 1945."

"Hiroshima."

"Yes. I came into the world with a bang."

"And there's been a lot of fallout ever since."

"And it's not over yet. It's interesting. Our birthdays are kind of the full spectrum. August 6, 1945. The day the United States officially lost its soul—if you don't count genocide and slavery. I guess you could say it was the day America lost what remained of its soul."

"Well, I grew up with all that shit. The father of our country, the Declaration of Independence, all the noble ideals—and I believed it, deeply, all the stuff about the Second World War, the evil Japs, the goodness of our cause—America the beautiful, America the goo—" A sepulchral figure, tall, very thin, long face, hollow cheeks, sickly yellowish skin, long stringy black hair, dark sunken eyes, unshaven, dirty long black trench coat over a blue sweatshirt, filthy green polyester pants, motorcycle boots, holding a cup of coffee with thin reptilian fingers sprouting long ragged nails imbedded with a substance that looks liked scabs or dead, discolored skin, a silver ankh dangling from his neck, Baudelaire, William Burroughs, Charles Manson in The Frontier Restaurant, looks down at us with a dead serious expression and says he's heard more intelligent conversation in the men's room at the Oakland Greyhound station.

"Christopher!" says Paul, jumping out of the booth and pumping the guy's hand enthusiastically.

It is Christopher Riley, the poet. He slithers in next to the wall and Paul follows, introducing us. The poet, avoiding my eyes, extends his wraithlike fingers with their Gollum nails and I shake his hand, trying to conceal my repugnance. Now that he is closer I can smell him, a sharp cheesy odor mixed with a hint of urine. "Hey, man, I dig what you're saying about George Washington and his father. Dig it, the young George, born in original sin of deplorable thought and deed, whacks the old geezer's cherry tree, wrestles with his conscience like Buddha under the Bodhi tree, setting the wheel of truth in motion and floors the old bastard with the big reality, just like presumably the old fucker did with his father before him and so on. The American truth wheel passed from generation to generation, placing the burden of sin and guilt on each of us until the end of the time. But each generation shades the truth a bit more until finally we are left with nothing but lies, our present condition, of which we are totally unaware. There are no more cherry trees to cut down." I stare at this apparition that has appeared out of nowhere.

"I see you've just come from church," says Paul, smiling.

"Actually, I've just attended my third black mass of the day. The last one presided over by Anton LaVey's dwarf factotum from Philadelphia. We sacrificed three UNM co-eds after they'd been ravaged by a monster chimp liberated from the animal lab on campus. The chimp, by the way, is now living with me. His name is Jesus."

"Far out," says Paul. They laugh and slap palms. "You're as sane as ever, I see," says Paul.

"Actually, I've been far too sane. I've been trying to mitigate this unwanted clarity with increased volumes of scag, reasonable quality, readily available around this little shit berg. You're welcome to partake."

"I think we'll pass on the entertainment," Paul says. "But we do need a place to crash for the evening, if that's okay. Are you still teaching?"

"Of course it's okay, if you don't mind Jesus. And fuck no, I stopped 'teaching,' if that's what it's called, over a year ago. I'm devoting myself to more serious pursuits now."

"Jesus? The chimpanzee? It lives with you?" I ask.

Christopher looks at me for the first time. There is a deadness in his eyes. "That's right. Jesus, the chimpanzee."

"Oh, fuck! You weren't kidding!" says Paul. "You were probably telling the truth about the black masses too."

"C'mon, it's time you fellas let Jesus into your lives."

***

It takes less than five minutes to get to Christopher's house, the weather nasty, dark and surprisingly cold, the wind blowing grit into our eyes, the neighborhood so empty it seems quarantined. On the way Paul and Christopher talk animatedly as I lag behind, feeling strange and left out, anxious about the scene we are getting into, but curious too—the rundown dark house, the chimp Jesus—hopefully it's in a cage—the cats, heroin, god knows what else. This is not going to be a scene that would play well in Butterfly's neighborhood. At the door Christopher curses while searching futilely for his key, knocking four or five times and finally going to the back of the house. A minute later he is letting us in. "Had to break one of the windows in the kitchen door," he says, sucking blood from a dirty knuckle.

The living room is dark and foul. The stagnant, heavy air, which I am reluctant to breathe, is a stew of awful things I don't want to think about. As soon as we enter a horrible screeching and rattling commences from the corner and something in another room hits the floor with a heavy thud. A door opens throwing a shaft of light into the room and a tall skinny female wrapped in a long red bathrobe shuffles into the room. She is as pale and sickly looking as Christopher. Her black hair is cut short, around the ears. But the real interest is Jesus, a small chimp in a cage in the corner of the living room. Christopher flicks a wall switch and a ceiling light illuminates a chaotic scene that I am prepared for though still taking my breath away, but nothing to match the strangeness of the screeching chimp that sticks out a large supplicating human-like hand attached to a long hairy muscular arm and the pallid, waxen female that stands dully staring at us seemingly trying to speak but thwarted, as if missing her tongue.

"Fellas, this is Jesus," and then motioning towards the female, "and this is Elaine. Elaine's from Boston. She's staying with me for awhile. Elaine's a model. But not a model citizen." She smiles vapidly, looks sadly at Christopher and goes back into the room, closing the door. Christopher goes into the kitchen and comes back with an apple for the chimp, who takes a few delicate nibbles and then drops the fruit to the ground, starting in again with the insane hooting. Christopher opens the cage and the chimp hops out like a homunculus and wraps its arms around his legs, pressing its head against his calf with a forlorn expression on its small puckered face. "It's okay, Jesus, these are nice people—friends," says Christopher soothingly. The ape looks at us questioningly with its little red eyes, lets loose of Christopher's legs and comes over to me in a rolling Popeye walk and takes my hand in a cold, leathery-soft, powerful paw and pulls me into the kitchen. Though the creature is small, no higher than my waist, I know about the superhuman strength of chimps and I am careful not to communicate anything less than total agreement with this little game of show-and-tell.

Jesus jumps up onto a chair in the dark kitchen, still holding my hand, and with the index finger of his free hand taps a cigar box on the table repeatedly, pulling me closer with a tightening grip that could crush my bones like balsa wood sticks. "What's that, Jesus?" I ask stupidly. He pulls me closer so that my hand is next to the box, obviously wanting me to open it. "Do you want me open the box, Jesus?" I ask, as if talking to a 400-pound cretin holding a sawed-off shotgun, hoping that a simple question might trigger some sort of deep, incapacitating introspection. Jesus grips tighter and taps his finger on the box, agitated, his eyes like tiny bags of blood shifting rapidly between the object and me. This is ridiculous. "Hey, Christopher," I blurt, "what the fuck am I supposed to do here?" Christopher comes into the kitchen, turning on the light. Jesus jumps down and bounds to the corner next to the door where he huddles with his hands over his eyes, making little smacking noises with his lips.

"He wants to show you my works, man. The dream factory." Christopher opens the box as Paul comes into the room and joins us at the table. Inside the large Dutch Masters cigar box are hospital syringe and needle, Zippo lighter, darkened tablespoon, clump of cotton, industrial razor blade, blackened piece of aluminum foil, metal cigar tube with the closed end sawed off and a garlic clove-sized lump of a dark substance in a glassine packet. Black tar. I have heard about it but never seen it. I look around the kitchen at a horrific scene, overflowing garbage, crusty dishes piling up and out of the sink, open, empty cabinets, reeking kitty litter box filled with hardened shit and the looser variety, disgusting blurches of foul stuff looking like butterscotch syrup. The stench of the kitchen is thick like soup. I try to breath through my mouth, feeling as if I am inhaling disease directly into my lungs. I take shallow breaths and feel light-headed. Paul seems completely comfortable. The cats are nowhere around, maybe freaked with the visitors or the unbound Jesus. Christopher's eyes take on a tight, hungry glint. "Let's do this, boys," he says. I look at Paul, who seems to be considering. I am way out of my depth here. Paul says, "Maybe a little smoke, but no needle. Ever done this, Sam?"

"Hell, no," I say. A few hours ago Butterfly, Lila and Datura were in the rearview mirror waving goodbye, our souls vivified by the wholesome goodness of our visit, vernal spirits fluttering the leaves of the cottonwood trees, the dry brilliant clarity of New Mexico light and air filling us with exhilaration. Except for the hint of dread we both feel at the prospect of our ultimate destination, the dismal East with its family demons and cultural decay, we still have a marvelous adventure ahead of us, perhaps danger too, but I am by now convinced that I really do have a guardian-fuckin'-angel riding with me that will see us through safely to the end. But here is as dramatic a reversal as I can imagine, this bizarre scene with the wraith woman, sick junky poet and a chimp named Jesus that is probably into the junk itself. Paul says, "What the fuck. This is an adventure, right, Sam? Let's do a little smoke. We have nothing going on for the rest of the day, what the hell. Are you game?" Fuck it. Only live once. A little smoke can't hurt. I've always been curious. "Let's do it," I say.

Christopher clears some garbage off the table and we sit down. Jesus ambles over and grasps the back of Christopher's chair with his large hairy paw and does a weird trembling thing with his thin lips, showing his yellow teeth. "Easy now, my little friend, easy now. Help is on the way. Jesus was liberated from the animal lab two years ago by an ex-girlfriend and was, through a series of events too unseemly and tortuous to relate, passed along to me. He already had a habit when I took him. She turned him on to junk. He's a very mellow chimp most of the time but can get a little edgy if he goes without for too long. It's been since yesterday, hasn't it, Jesus? Sometimes he goes for days without it but that usually doesn't happen because I'm here and doing it so he gets involved. He can raise hell if he knows I'm slamming and he doesn't get a piece of the action, so I usually include him." Jesus seems to know Christopher is talking about him and lets out with some anxious hoots, twirls around, races to the corner, then back to Christopher's side, clapping his hands and looking up at Christopher with anxious red eyes and does the trembling thing with his lips again, showing his yellow teeth. Smoking pot or tripping I am not able to handle this scene.

There is a theme developing here, the wild pigs, the addled canyon goat and now this. Maybe my guardian-fuckin'-angel has an odd sense of humor. A wicked commentary on the catastrophic sexual origins of my odyssey. Pigs, goats and apes. Heroin, I suppose, is just the thing for dealing with this freak show.

***

Christopher retrieves a ring stand, one of those things you see in a high school chemistry lab, from the counter behind him, and places the blackened piece of aluminum foil on the ring. Watching him do this Jesus begins patting his wizened little head rapidly with both hands, barring his yellow teeth in that huge trembling smile. Christopher calmly takes the stuff out of the glassine bag and cuts a tiny piece with the razor blade and places it on the aluminum foil. He hands the sawed-off cigar tube to Paul, who with ease of manner and subtle aura of anticipation is obviously no stranger to the ritual. The door in the living room opens and the wraith shuffles into the kitchen, a wan smile on her thin, waxen face, her red robe loosely tied with a sash. Immediate, impure, bestial thoughts. Only hours from the wholesomeness of Butterfly and her family. Pigs, goats, apes abiding companions for life. She stands silently next to me, inches away, her navel at eye level. I can feel her sad junky heat. A reverential quiet takes hold as Christopher clicks open the silver Zippo and trips the thumbwheel, the distinctive blue-yellow flame delicately mushrooming against the bottom of the foil. The brown piece begins to liquefy and bubble, giving off a trail of smoke with an acrid, sweet smell as Paul leans forward, puts the tube in his mouth, inhales, slightly grimacing, almost choking, his eyes closed. He hands the tube to Christopher and leans back in his chair, eyes still closed, exhaling, his face instantly relaxed, slack, a van Gogh death mask. I am trying like hell to be cool about it but my mind is definitely blown. Fuck me. Heroin. I am scared and excited. Christopher takes in the last of the smoke and leans down and blows into Jesus' cavernous, awesome mouth which clamps shut after receiving the smoke and with his little rolling gait he goes back to the corner and sits down, sticking his thumb in his mouth like Little Jack Horner, staring at the ceiling.

Elaine leans forward in anticipation, her robe slipping open, revealing a small white breast. She really is quite pretty in an unwholesome Warholian way, with that weird zombie strung out vibe. She hasn't looked at Paul or me once, everything an inward focus on the craving of her junked-out cells. I wonder about her story. I wonder about her parents. She is probably no more than twenty but looks much older, her pale, dry skin tightly drawn around the bones of her face, accentuating the blackness of her short hair, which seems dyed. There are dark circles around her eyes. She is ghastly, erotic. The hip death goddess. I am fascinated. "Ok, sir, it's your turn," says Christopher, snapping me out of my brief reverie and back to the jaded ritual taking place at the table. Paul is sitting in his chair with his head thrown back and his eyes closed, a serious, peaceful expression on his strong face. "Take it slow and deep," says the poet, handing me the tube. My heart thumps. He cuts another piece, smaller than the first, puts it on the foil and clicks open the Zippo. I feel self-conscious as a first-timer with these two addicts but my presence hardly registers with them. The flame jumps up with the first turn of the thumbwheel and brushes against the foil. The little piece melts quickly, bubbling around the edges, giving off a wisp of smoke with that same smell. "Do it," says Christopher.

I lean forward, feeling as if I am going down the wrong end of a telescope, everything focused on the tiny smoking black dot on the foil. Putting the cold tube in my mouth I inhale the bitter smoke. It burns my throat, almost choking me, but I get most of it, taking it down deep and holding my breath. "Good," says Christopher, taking the tube and inhaling the last of the smoke. Immediately I feel a warm sensation spread through my body, followed by a deep relaxation and loss of anxiety. A virgin no more. I have done it—junk, scag, horse, smack, shit. Mellow and cool. I close my eyes and lean back into the chair, enclosed in a warm cocoon. The disgusting kitchen is now the nicest place in the universe.

But then something unexpected. I start to sweat and my head begins to spin. Feeling sick, I push back the chair and stand, asking Christopher where the bathroom is. He doesn't respond, absorbed in his works, picking through stuff. I am getting more nauseous by the second. Finally he replies, "Through the bedroom, man." I turn and make it as far as the bedroom, letting loose a rich mixture of Frontier green chile stew and orange juice all over the grimy blue carpet. I step over the mess and lurch into the plaster wall. Turning, my back against the wall, I slide to a sitting position and watch as both cats appear from under the bed and commence eating my vomit.

This makes little impression on me. The nausea eases and the warmth and good feeling take over, though my mouth tastes like the inside of some diseased internal organ, spleen, pancreas, gall bladder. No surprise when Jesus drags his stoned simian ass into the room as the cats race under the bed and tips himself forward and slobbers up the rest of my puke. Good for you, Jesus, I think. These poor animals must be starving and I am glad the carpet is being cleaned. When he finishes Jesus sits down to the right of me and puts his right hand over his stony brow and leans forward in meditation for awhile and then with his left hand takes hold of my right hand and moves it up and down rhythmically against my leg. I am aware of the puke on my goatee and have to blow my nose but I lack the will and feel just fine where I am. I hope Jesus' appetite has been sated and he won't start licking my goatee because I won't be able to resist. The image is funny.

Elaine walks into the room and folds herself slowly onto the bed, sighing, apparently not aware of me, Jesus, or my vomit, which is mostly gone anyway. After a while Jesus lets go of my hand and goes into the bathroom where I hear him get up on the toilet and let loose with a torrent of piss. So he is toilet trained. He flushes the toilet and goes back into the living room, walking on all fours. With effort I rouse myself and go into the bathroom to wash out my mouth and blow my nose with my fingers. Everything is rubber. I could fall out of a four-story building with no pain or worry. The shit is good, no doubt about it. I can see why people get into it. I wipe my face on a musty-smelling towel and turn to look at Elaine from the bathroom. She is on her back with her forearm slung over her eyes, the red robe loose and open, showing her small breasts and brown pubic hair, an erotic and pathetic sight, but I have neither desire nor pity. Basically I feel nothing, which feels good.

Paul is sitting on the sofa in the living room and Christopher is on the floor going through his albums. There is a down and heavy vibe but it is all very comfortable. I sit next to Paul and he nods at me. "Do any more?" I ask. "Nope," he replies. That's it for about another half hour. Christopher holds the same album the whole time, nodding. The weather picks up outside, the wind tearing at the house. All very good. I figure Christopher and Elaine have shot up. Jesus is somewhere else. Idly, I think about Butterfly. What a chick. She wouldn't like this though. I still feel nauseous, but it's not too bad. I want to stay like this for a long time. It's good.

After a while I start coming down but Christopher just sits there playing with his albums and Paul is in his own world. Jesus the chimp has come into the room and lies down at my feet, idly fondling his huge balls. What a comfy scene. But as the junk wears off the freakiness takes hold and I want to get out. I stand up and Jesus reaches out and grabs my ankle in a lover's clamp and won't let go. I sit back down hoping he will go away. After a while he does, hopping into his cage and leaning his head against the side. Jesus is one depressed chimp. I cautiously get up, afraid Jesus might jump out after me and go to the door. I go outside, the dry gritty wind tearing down Silver. I figure I will go back to the Frontier for some orange juice. I button my old ripped Macy's short-sleeved shirt to the top, turn up the collar and walk down Silver, turning on Cornell. It is mid-May but cold and by the time I get to the funky restaurant I am shivering and the hair on my arms stands up like an army of tiny erections. I need to find a smooth co-ed to rub arms with. The clock in the restaurant says ten after five. I order a large fresh-squeezed orange juice from an older woman who gives me such a funny look that I go into the bathroom to check myself out. Sure as hell I am a wreck, wild hair, face drawn and pale, pupils tiny dots like the archetypal addict's, flecks of dried puke in my goatee. I put my cup on the sink ledge and wash my face. The cup falls into the sink and juice sloshes onto my shirt. What the fuck. I look at my shirt, drenched from the stomach down and covered with pulp. I look in the mirror. The same sad sack who had jumped in his beat-up car running from broken heart and balls three weeks earlier. Nothing changed. This same character with me the rest of my life.

***

No matter. I get another orange juice and sit in an empty booth and look out the window at a forlorn street, Central Avenue, the wind blowing all sorts of shit, a million miles from Butterfly, another lifetime, another universe. Expect less and less, someone I read a while back had said. Then you won't be disappointed. Anyone looking at me sitting in that booth would not expect much either. But what the hell. I am depressed in an odd way that isn't so bad. The world is nothing, a big zero, no meaning, no hope. No one gives a shit and neither at that particular moment do I. There is a dull ache at the base of my skull. The orange juice tastes sweet and metallic. The Frontier, so busy several hours ago, is quiet, waiting for the dinner rush, if there is one. I don't know. I don't care.

Two hippies, boy and girl, walk in out of the wind falling all over themselves in silliness. Obviously stoned out of their gourds. Raggedy Ann and Andy. The girl even has on a thin sweatshirt with red stripes like Ann' socks. She wears a Greek fishing hat and has fat red cheeks. Maybe it really is Ann. I expect a trail of straw as they flop up to order their food at the counter. They seem too wild to be students, but who knows? The boy is tall and gangly with pimples, a frantic thatch of curly blond hair and a wispy mustache. A country boy run away to the city. But then Albuquerque is as much country as city. He wears a jean jacket over a white T-shirt. His filthy jeans are ragged and dirty and he is barefoot. His eyes look as if they had been plucked out, sent into orbit around Saturn and returned to their sockets a few minutes ago. What sights has he seen? Is seeing? What sort of mind is behind those interplanetary eyeballs? The girl, a bit chubby, big loose Raggedy Ann breasts, hangs on his every gesture and word, silly with laughter and god knows what else. They both stand flopping around with loopy mirth as the young Hispanic woman behind the counter in her Frontier uniform stares at them with bored hostility, waiting for their order. Suddenly I become intensely bored with them myself. I can't stand looking at them. The restaurant is a weary place. Outside the wind blows harder and it starts to drizzle. More detritus skitters down Central. The university looks like a prison camp. A city bus drives by with one passenger. I leave The Frontier.

Shuddering in the cold I walk past a house with an open window. Someone is playing "Eight Miles High" by the Byrds. I am eight miles low. The immediate effects of the heroin have worn off. I am in a weird sort of downer, no melancholy or blackness of mood but terribly flat and dull, a leveling out of everything, meaninglessness without despair. Maybe this is how it feels to be lobotomized. The rain stops but the wind continues. Going back to Christopher's house is like going back to a disturbing but familiar dream. There is a certain comfort to it. I knock on the door and Paul lets me into the dark, foul-smelling dungeon where Jesus is on his back with the cats playfully attacking him, pouncing and racing off as he takes bored, slow motion swipes at them. Jesus ambles over and wraps his arms around my legs and puts his head lovingly against my thigh. Jesus is a nice chimp. I rub his head and he sighs, lets go of my legs and rolls over on his side. Poor little Jesus. Paul is in the kitchen staring into an empty refrigerator. "I'm not hungry anyway," he says. Christopher and Elaine are in the bedroom. They have been fighting, Paul informs me. Elaine comes out, looking terrible, wasted, her eyes bloodshot, pinpoint junky pupils, wearing faded jeans, black T-shirt and flip-flops. She really is quite pretty. She sits down on the couch with her head in her hands. Normally I think I might leave her alone but I am in a weird mood and feel a junky kinship, so I sit next to her. Paul comes in from the kitchen and sits in a chair opposite. Jesus' battle with the cats recommences. "Everything okay?" I ask. At first she doesn't answer and I think, oh, fuck, I don't make it on the junky meter, hopeless square that I am, but she really seems a lost soul wanting sympathy or companionship and of course she is still good looking, though I have no desire at the moment. Finally she speaks, the first time I have heard her voice. "No, everything's not okay," she says quietly. "I need to get the fuck out of here. Can you help me? Please? Please?" She still has her head in hands, looking down at the floor. "I need to get away from here. From *him*." Her voice is weak, thin, pathetic. Paul is shaking his head, no, no. "You have no idea," she continues, her voice so faint that I have to lean to hear her. "He's evil. He won't let me leave. I just came for a visit. He's turned me into an addict. I just came for a visit. Just a visit. I'm trapped. Please help me."

Maybe it is the after-effects of smoking heroin, the dullness of spirit, the strange depression I am in, the alienating weirdness of the whole scene, but I feel nothing listening to this sad person. I look at her with a dim objectivity and realize that I am looking at a vampire trapped in Dracula's castle. This whole junky thing is nothing but vampirism, including the creepy eroticism—Dracula with his chalky blood-sucking temptress. The spike the vampire's fang, the thousand-year sleep, the soul of no tomorrow. Help me, please, says Elaine, and a small desperate part of her means it, the little spark that remains, but what she really wants, I imagine, is for me to fuck her like Jonathan Harker and take the fang, fall under the spell and be just like her, the walking dead. Paul is Van Helsing looking at me shaking his head no, no. Christopher is The Count, tall, emaciated, long hideous fingernails, evil genius, resting in his coffin behind the crypt door. She is under his spell. Both under the curse. We are in Transylvania, the student section, weirdly abandoned, hushed, its residents cowering behind garlic-studded doors clutching crucifixes while the Dark Prince and his girlfriend glide down alleys and streets looking for victims.

The question now becomes what to do for the evening. It is nearing seven o'clock. Aside from the flat state of my mood I have come down completely from smoking, and it appears Paul has too. Not so Elaine. She sits slumped into her elbows, head in hands, in a depressed junky stupor, her small breasts pushing against her T-shirt. It would be nice to feel them. I roil with a kind of eroticism in the abstract, appreciative but not motivated. Christopher comes into the room and gives me start, as if he really is Dracula. He looks scary and horrible and gives off a palpable energy, as if the approaching evening has brought him back to life, as well it might. "Another minute in this house and I will lose what little sanity remains to me," he says. "Let's go to Okie's." Jesus is tucked away and we go.

***

Okie's is an agreeable dive on the corner of Central and University, the sort of place where university professors get into drunken metaphysical debates with bikers and people go into the bathroom to smoke marijuana and the cops generally stay away. We get a table. Elaine is with us, somewhat more alive with the walk down Central in the cool evening. The wind has died down and the clouds have scattered, revealing glimpses of a dramatic sunset over the desert. Though it is Monday the bar is crowded and noisy. A huge blond woman wearing jeans and a tank top serves us. She reminds me of one of Crumb's women, large, sensual, flesh all over the place, enormous breasts, no bra, of course. Very friendly. Okie's is a refreshing tonic after the fetid gloom of Christopher's pad. Paul and I order hamburgers and beer, Elaine and Christopher, Cokes and French fries. Christopher talks about his experience at the university.

"I lasted less than a year teaching at the university. I tried like hell to get something going with my more attractive female students, to no avail. By the end of the second semester I was nodding in class, that is, the days I showed up. You know me, Paul. I had a minor habit before I got to Albuquerque, just chipping, but there's quite a bit of junk flowing through this dismal little town and it found me. Big time. Right here at Okie's. The English department is a joke except for a few good eggs. My students revolted and complained. I got shitcanned before the semester was up. I was relieved.

I hated teaching the pimply 4-H shit kickers, the vacuous broads in their long skirts, sweaters and Playtex bras dreaming of finding husbands or fucking the captain of the football team, or the whole football team. Before I started mainlining on a daily basis I'd drop acid and come to class and talk about the Eleusinian Mysteries and UFOs while my dumbfounded students melted before my eyes. I'd riff about being kidnapped by aliens and subjected to bizarre sexual experiments, hinting that I'd learned otherworldly sexual techniques guaranteed to drive any willing female around the bend. I was fishing, of course. No takers. Not all of my students were idiots, but I was so out of it I alienated everyone. Good riddance. For both parties. I hate college and I hate professors even more. Nowhere will you find a more noxious collection of pansies and ass-lickers. They think their shit smells like shampoo. They call themselves liberal but they're more conservative than bankers and more cowardly than poodles. A generally despicable breed. I don't know what made me think I could handle it. I had this weird idea that Albuquerque would be so strange somehow the university would be different. Well, Albuquerque *is* strange, but the university is no different. I knew it after my first day on campus, before I even taught my first class. In fact for that first class I showed up loaded."

We laugh but I can imagine having a teacher like Christopher. I'd had some doozies in my day, like the bird fresh from Harvard who taught intro to philosophy, so petrified in front of the class that he could barely speak, writing almost everything on the board, most of it in Greek, so that by the end of class the entire space, probably 50 square feet, was filled with his tiny, barely legible scratchings. It was a joke. We learned nothing. We hated it. But I got a good grade in class because later in the semester he gave a courageous, almost foolhardy speech in the quad denouncing the Vietnam War, declaring himself a hawk—for the Viet Cong—while jocks and fraternity worthies jeered and threw eggs, none of which, fortunately, hit their mark. I was so incensed by their stupidity and boorishness that I wrote a letter to the college newspaper denouncing them and defending him. I got a completely undeserved A for the course. Obviously, he had read the letter. He, like Christopher, left at the end of the year. Once in the spring a bumblebee flew into the room and buzzed around harmlessly as he froze in terror with his back pressed against the board, transferring that portion of his lesson to the back of his jacket, with virtually the same degree of legibility, though reversed. We called him Magic Morton. A complete waste of a philosophy class. It seemed most of my professors were pretty bad, mostly drab, boring, disappointingly lacking in the sort of intelligence and charisma you naively thought a college professor was supposed to have. Mostly I forgot about them immediately, but some, like Magic Morton, you remembered for their strangeness. In my sophomore year I had a sociology professor whose most distinguishing characteristics were slurred speech, heavy eyelids and tiny pupils. Everyone figured him for a junky. I wasn't so sure. Whatever the case he was a terrible teacher. The first day of class he asked what my major was and when I said philosophy he held up a piece of chalk and challenged me to a debate. Another waste of a class. So many. Then there was the English professor whose breath was so bad it drove most of the students away. The class was held in a small room and it was wintertime, the heat blasting. Those that stayed sat in the back and breathed through their mouths. I skipped most of the time and still passed, though not by much. Milton, Donne, Pope, dreary 17th and 18th century poets whose exponents developed halitosis and caused their students to flee the classroom. The few good professors stand out like geniuses or saints, avatars of humanism and learning, to be forever cherished. Well, I think, maybe Christopher's a genius but he's not to be cherished, at least in the classroom. I can understand the students' rebellion. After all, they had paid some money for the class and they probably did want to learn *something.* But maybe I would have liked him, crazy as he is.

There is no cherishing the fellow now, however. It is hard to be near him, physically repugnant, sallow skin, the long stringy hair he keeps running his filthy fingers through, the awful fingernails, the sinister vibe, his cheesy-urine smell. Despite his brilliance there is a heavy dullness about him, which I guess is a part of the addiction. He is the anti-Harlow, the anti-everything of Butterfly's world. I chew on my hamburger, which is passable, though I suspect my taste buds are misaligned, and look around Okie's, trying not to allow Christopher to burrow too far into my consciousness. I think if I ever live in Albuquerque by some Twilight Zone misappropriation of fortune I would definitely hang out at Okie's. A sort of Canal Zone, but larger, populated by its Southwest counterparts. The same funk. Instead of lobstermen and clam diggers you have professors and bikers. Lots of girls. I like it. Elaine picks at the French fries, slipping back into her pathetic morass. It seems as much a matter of comfort as anything else. She is safe in her misery. The junk has nothing to do with it. Underneath the willing surrender to the darkness that has taken hold of her is a once bright pretty little girl, the jewel of her parents' lives, or so I imagine. Though perhaps the parents are not such jewels. She is so buried in unhappiness, has so thoroughly assumed the drab vestments of depression and dissolution, that it is difficult to imagine what she had once been like. Christopher had said she was from Boston, which I associate with the blue-blooded demented descendants of the Mayflower, the not-so-gentle-bred killers who had kick-started the country and had kept on kicking, now stomping all over peasants in Vietnam. But there is a helluva lot more than that to Boston, I know, from living there several years after college. I wonder what elements of its hard reality has created the despondent cipher sitting before me called "Elaine." She barely talks and makes even less eye contact. She is very pretty but it is impossible to tell which side-of-the-tracks prettiness it is. I tend to think not working class, but you never know. Attractive and mysterious despite her forlorn, waifish, demeanor. An interesting puzzle. I find myself a little bit falling in love and entertain thoughts of saving her, even with the memory of Paul shaking his head no, no. Another impossibility. In a way she is like Lulu Delilah, damaged in spirit and mind, both from drugs, both attractive, both arousing me sexually. I really want to fuck Elaine. There is something a little sick about it and I suppose it appeals to something unhealthy in me. I am not sure. Others had wanted Lulu Delilah like mad, I know, this was part of her appeal to me, and I am certain Elaine, as strange and beautiful as she is, has the same allure. So maybe it is not so sick on my part to desire them.

But they are different in very fundamental ways. Lulu Delilah is crazy, unabashed, sexual, outgoing. She drinks. She talks. She isn't smart. She parties like a demon. She has a strong and supple athlete's body. Almost pure physicality. Aggressive. She had chosen me for a moment and I had gone along willingly for what I always knew to be a wild but ultimately disastrous ride, and though I had crashed it was worth it. Elaine is nothing like this but arouses equally strong desires. My sexual feelings are wrapped up in a weird chivalric impulse to rescue a tragic, fallen woman. Where Lulu Delilah is loud, sexual and physically robust, Elaine is silent, depressed and anemic. But underneath this I imagine the classic floundering victim desperately yearning to be rescued, sexually and existentially. Can you help me, please, please, is also can you fuck me, please, please, and there is enough unhappiness here that touches things I understand as being most definitively not healthy, which makes her perverse appeal exceptionally powerful, almost irresistible, and clearly much more dangerous than my little exploding romp with Lulu Delilah.

I stare at Elaine poking listlessly at her French fries and sucking Coke through a straw with her bloodless, dry, almost bluish lips, the outlines of her canines under the pallid, tight skin of her mouth and imagine us making slow, tripped-out vampire love on the living room couch, allowing her to pierce my jugular vein with her needle-sharp teeth as we climax, my orgasm pulsing wildly in my neck, shooting into my brain, driving me mad with visions of eternal life, endless yearning for the blood of others, dark sexual compulsion, ecstatic surrender, wild vampire orgies, submission to the master, Dracula, Christopher. And Christopher, the master, is agitated. Is he, with his extrasensory vampire perception, picking up my desire for his girlfriend? Does this mean certain death for me? Of course it is ridiculous, he is not really a vampire, but there is something about my mental state these days that causes me to be absurdly impressionable. Paul is van Gogh and now Van Helsing, Christopher is Dracula. I watch him in fascination as his eyes dart back and forth while he compulsively runs his long fingers through that stringy black hair, moving his legs rapidly up and down, the balls of his feet touching the floor. There is no denying his creepy power. Already tall, he seems to have elevated another foot above us. Even Elaine is roused from her depths, a look of muted concern on a face that is becoming more exotic and beautiful to me by the moment. "Fuck it," says Christopher. "Let's get the hell out of here." He notices that Paul and I have not finished our hamburgers and he tells us to take our time and to meet them back at the house. Elaine protests feebly that she wants to stay and I fancy it is because of me but when Christopher stands up as if ready to take flight with his vampire wings she gets up also, pulled by his magnetism. I imagine them rising in the air ponderously flapping their dark wings as the people in Okie's watch with their mouths agape. He pulls a ten-dollar bill from his pants pocket, throws it on the table and strides out of the bar, Elaine close behind, without a word.

"Phew. Strange," says Paul.

"Vampires," I say.

"Vampires needing a fix."

"Sick devil that I am, I'd like to fuck her."

"You *are* a sick devil."

"I'm ready to be a junky."

"Eat your hamburger, you crazy fuck."

I laugh, feeling weirdly elated. Paul seems vastly amused by everything that has taken place over the last several hours. He leans forward and devours his hamburger, his blue eyes flashing under the old straw hat. I look around Okie's. It is a Monday night crowd, relaxed, taking the edge off the miserable first workday with a few beers, some dinner and quiet talk. Soul music plays on the jukebox. The thought that we don't have to be at work the next day is most pleasant. Tomorrow we will head north for Taos and then turn our sights to New Orleans, the Gulf Coast and across the panhandle to Jacksonville. Though we are headed towards the East and all the old bullshit sadness and associations I am less disturbed than I might be because I have already decided to move to California, with a stop along the way to see Butterfly, who shines like a beacon of health and sanity after the Albuquerque vampires. I feel as if I am shedding an old skin, like a snake, and underneath is something shiny and hopeful. They say you can't run from your problems and, yes, it is already an old story, moving to California, but it seems like the right thing to do. A strong dose of a radically different environment might give me the boost I need. Away from the old negativity and into something new I might at least be inspired to focus on my art, which would help establish a stronger identity. I might actually start *being* somebody, feeling good about myself, and then, maybe, I might be able to deal with the nasty little termites gnawing away at my spirit. I might stop shrinking.

***

We finish our hamburgers and beer and walk back to Christopher's. Elaine is in the bedroom and Christopher sits on the couch with Jesus next to him. They are deep into Miles Davis' *Bitches Brew*, Jesus as much as Christopher. I am used to Jesus ambling up to me and sweetly hugging my legs but this time he doesn't even acknowledge our presence, which is kind of disappointing. Christopher looks at us without recognition. Paul and I go into the kitchen to discuss our plans, clearing the table gingerly as if handling contaminated material, piling it on the counter next to the sink, the Dutch Masters box with Christopher's works, dirty glasses, ashtrays, bowls crusty with old spaghetti and soup, spoons, magazines, matchbooks, and so on. Paul finds a dishrag and wipes the table. The stench from the garbage and cat litter almost makes me gag, my eyes watering from the noxious brew of gasses given off by the decaying matter in the little room that is airless but for the broken window in the door. We dare not open it lest Jesus escape. The cats must be in the bedroom with Elaine. Paul sits down across from me. "Can we handle one night here?" he asks in a low voice. Before I can respond, something to the effect of not having much choice, though I suppose we can take off for Taos right away, finding a place to sleep along the road, Jesus comes in and pulls himself into my lap and sits facing Paul, as though matter-of-factly inserting himself in the conversation, the back of his dark fuzzy little head resting right under my chin. He reaches behind with his long arm and plays with my hair, like a lover under a banana tree on a lazy spring day. His little body is warm and heavy, as if an unusually solid human child. He smells very old and earthy. His enormous balls crush against my thigh like small avocados, a weird, unpleasant sensation that per-

versely connects us, ape and human. "But hey, a guy's got *balls*," old
Vanzetti had said, and at the time it had encouraged me, but compared to Jesus' my own are back to the marble stage, back to the
M&Ms I had that blasted night slinking out of The Canal Zone. I
think of ways to get the affectionate troglodyte off my lap but I am
afraid of a violent response so I sit with his balls pressed against my
thigh as he continues playing with my hair. Christopher comes in
and pulls up a seat. "What are you fuckers up to?" Jesus' lips tremble
and he bares his teeth in the bizarre smile he seems to display only
in Christopher's presence.

"Well, I guess we'll spend the night and head out in the morning," says Paul. "We're going to check out Taos and then head
southeast, to New Orleans and points beyond."

"That's cool. A blind journey into the heart of darkness. I'm content to stay right here in this forlorn, smack-infested town. You can
have your *On the Road* adventures. Not for me. Have fun driving
through the South. I'll pray for you crazy fuckers. A guy I know,
a long-hair, went through the South a couple of years ago hitchhiking on what must have been a suicide mission and got the shit
kicked out of him in some little piss-water town in Alabama. Ended
up naked and tied to a billboard post, finally rescued by some kindly
darkies, two of whom stood guard with rifles while the others took
him down. They took him home, cleaned him up, gave him clothes,
fed him, took up a collection and put him on a bus with a ticket to
Philadelphia. He's in graduate school now, safe and sound. Swears
he'll never go to the South again. The South is no place for freaks,
believe me. If I were you I'd just drop acid and watch *Straw Dogs*.
Fuck the South."

"How about if we drop acid, watch *Straw Dogs* and *then* go to
the South?" says Paul. I think I want to do neither. "How about if

we dropped acid driving *through* the South?" I say, in a parody of bravado.

"Now there's a guy with some balls," says Christopher. Christopher Riley and Antonio Vanzetti, two perceptive guys, though Jesus has me badly beat, as the pressure on my thigh attests. As if understanding the talk about balls, Jesus turns his little head sideways and leans into my chest affectionately. "How about if we drop acid and drive through the South naked?" says Paul.

"Now *that's* an idea," says Christopher. "Even better, throw away all your clothes and possessions, donate you car to the Pentecostal Church, paint your bodies with stars and stripes, drop acid and hitchhike from Tuscaloosa to Selma singing *We Shall Overcome*."

"Terrific idea," says Paul.

"Let's do it," I say.

Mercifully, Jesus jumps down and goes into the living room, where he lies on his back and plays with his toes. "Seriously, you guys are nuts to be going through the South. There's only one thing worse than being a nigger in the South and that's being a hippie. Especially driving that funny little car with New York plates. You're going to end up in some piney woods with your balls stuffed in your mouths." More talk of balls. Maybe the South isn't such a good idea. A small razor of fear surfaces in my mind.

"That's bullshit," says Paul. "Nothing like that's going to happen. When you travel with the Tao, with a clear mind and heart, you will be safe. People intuitively recognize that. I firmly believe it."

"Tell that to the subnormals drunk on their asses on Wild Turkey and Dixie beer riding in their rusty, bottomed-out Chevy pickup truck some swamp-fuck Saturday night looking for a little fun. What are you going to do when that death wagon bangs against your rear bumper and you look in the mirror and see a bunch of crazed drunken peckerwoods howling and waving their shotguns out the window?"

"I would simply pull over to the side of the road and consult the I Ching for the best way to deal with the situation."

"And what do you suppose the I Ching will say?"

"I think it would say that it would be advantageous at that moment to cross the great stream. As rapidly as possible."

"The only stream you'll see will be yellow and it'll be running down your leg."

"The yellow river."

"By I.P. Daily."

"Well, it's not going to happen. We have Ganesh on the dashboard and Jesus in our hearts. The chimp, that is"

"And I have a guardian-fuckin'-angel watching over me. This was told to me by a very great Italian sage and anarchist living in New Jersey."

"Well, as long as he's an anarchist, that's cool. I guess you guys will be all right."

All this humorous talk masks a very real fear. The South *is* a dangerous place. Or could be. But deep down I feel that our white skins will protect us. We might get hassled but when push comes to shove, as long as we are not in the company of *Negroes* and engaged in some outside-agitating civil rights crusade, we will be okay. But still, it gives me pause. The little razor of fear is still there, and it will never quite leave as we drive through the South.

9

Sputtering past St. Francis > Howitzer ride to Hondo > A happy hippie hangout > Panhandle nightmare > Blowing the lid off with Thibodeaux & Co. > A sad encounter with war's detritus

But first things first, and that is a side excursion north, to Santa Fe and Taos. We spend the night at Christopher's, as planned, I on the couch, Paul on the floor and Jesus safely tucked away in his cage, thankfully quiet most of the night. At one point Elaine glides in like a ghost for a glass of water in the kitchen and I wake with a mixture of fear and desire, more than half hoping she will slide onto the couch for some vampire love, but not to be. After waiting for Christopher until ten o'clock we leave a note on the table and exit the mephitic gloom of that terrible place, feeling a little badly about leaving Jesus in his cage but excited to be back on the road in wide-open beautiful New Mexico, no more wind, clouds gone, the sky vivid, vast, astonishingly blue, the eye of god, gateway to the universe. Paul puts his shoulder to Rosalina, gives a roar and pumps his sturdy legs and the little car answers with her own exuberant outburst, as happy as we to be away and on the road again.

Even though I have only had Rosalina for about three months I know her valiant character, though I doubt she approves wholeheartedly of mine. It is as if she is giving me the benefit of the doubt, or maybe just has too much pride and honor to slack off, patiently waiting for this feckless owner to supply her with a new starter and some pretty upholstery, but understanding it is probably not going to happen. As Paul gets in the car I silently promise her a good cleaning, maybe a trip to the car wash, feeling guilty and unworthy of her steadfast efforts. Incredibly, I have never even given her a tune-up, never changed her plugs or points, adjusted the timing or changed the oil, though I had checked it. The most I have done was pay Vanzetti to fix the hole in her radiator. And of course I had not bothered to look closely at the tires before the cross-country dash, much less inspect the spare, which, as it turned out, resulted in our adventure in Santa Cruz with the whole gang, Officer Nichols, the attacking goblins, Mr. America, Jake and Terry, the mighty Jambo, Datura and the beautiful Butterfly. The whole determinist thing again, the result of a blasted state of mind compliments of some other bewildering convergence (an afternoon walk on the beach, the small waves shattering globs of mercury), propelling my broken-hearted catapult-shot across this equally bewildering and overwhelming country. Within minutes we are on 25 north to Taos, Rosalina puttering through the outskirts of Albuquerque with its nascent development that will certainly bloom like a red tide over the years until the city becomes just like every other ugly, blasted place, but it is a fleeting impression over which Albuquerque's funky outlaw weirdness still prevails, leaving us feeling properly strange, and soon enough, within minutes, we are blown away again by New Mexico's vast emptiness, a little spooked but exhilarated and curious to see the wild hippie mecca that is northern New Mexico, especially Taos.

The landscape has an effect on Paul, who bounces and swivels in his seat. "Damn! Look at this! Look at this!" he keeps saying, and then we are in Santa Fe stopping for gas, the air cooler, the snow-capped magnificent mountains all around, the green snap of spring making our blood bubble with excitement. We are at altitude, the atmosphere palpably thinner. Small rivulets of melting snow darken the ground and sidewalks. We see hippies, hipsters, Indians, old Spanish people. At the gas station as Paul pushes Rosalina a guy with long blond hair, beard and red headband joins in and helps as the little car rumbles into action. "Right on, brothers!" the guy says, and we wave goodbye, swinging back onto the highway heading north to Taos. In Espanola we pass a place named Saints and Sinners and stop at a grocery store for some Swisher Sweets and the sullen old Hispanic man throws our change on the counter with distaste.

Beyond town the landscape gets wilder, more beautiful, going through places named Alcalde, Rinconada, Velarde, Pilar with the spring-swollen Rio Grande rushing south on our left as we pass through more mind-bending scenery, beautiful green places, some with steep cliffs with old boulders on the side of the road from rockslides that could crush Rosalina like a beer can, then swooping down and up on a wild roller-coaster curve and just like that smack in the face into an armada of mountains, with the big one right in the middle, its death head of snow grinning at us, and we are immediately under the spell of wild northern New Mexico. "Wow! Look at that!" we say, "goddamn!" making you feel like Rosalina is a rocket ship about to take off up and over the mountains into some other mystic scary world, although Rosalina, after pulling herself up out of the crazy curve slows down with an asthmatic sputtering and limps along at about thirty miles per hour and indeed, there is something definitely wrong with poor Rosalina, coughing and lurching so badly that I pull over and open the hood, peering in as if I know what the fuck is going on. All around the air is crisp, the landscape dizzyingly vast. I am aware of it without looking. Paul gets out also and looks at the little lawn mower engine, which I have left running, and asks when the last time was I had given her a tune-up, just what I have been thinking about, and I kick myself because of course Rosalina is mortal after all and needs care and maintenance just like the rest of us. I reply I have no idea when she's last had a tune-up and feel stupid and guilty but mostly as if I have betrayed the doughty and loyal little car and vow to take care of her if she will only get us to the nearest mechanic.

We get back in and Rosalina bravely staggers another ten or so miles, the huge mountains getting closer as now we can see the valley below the big one, Taos Mountain, and over to the west the gorge that swallows up the river, and beyond, more vast landscape. It is with a mixture of anxiety and excitement we travel, though Paul keeps reassuring me it is no more than a matter of a tune-up and maybe a carburetor adjustment at this higher altitude and not to worry, he will pay for it. We sputter through Ranchos de Taos and see the famous St. Francis of Assisi Church that Georgia O'Keeffe had painted, with its strange lines, massive buttresses and soft fortress-like strength, the tops of the mountains all around still covered with snow and the land in the valley green and pliant with exuberant new life after what I imagine a hard long winter at this latitude and elevation. Though I am worried about Rosalina I am bowled over by the land and the wild feeling popping out everywhere, from the deep blue warm sky, the chill of the distant mountain tops, the melting snow running into the dirt turned soft and muddy, the intense green of the valley we pass in Ranchos, one small brilliant cloud right above us. "Jesus, Sam, this is the place! This is the place! Look at this place!" Paul says, and he is right, this *is* the place, more than anything we have seen yet, and we have seen a few, the Grand Canyon, Big Sur, Butterfly's village. But there is something about Taos that is different, a different kind of wildness, a northern wildness, a mystery that goes beyond those other magnificent places, a feeling that you are not in *America* anymore, a place you have never seen and never even dreamed about. The spirit and the power of the mountain dominate the valley, unapproachable, beneficent, protective, massive, softly beautiful, a grinning skull of snow beneath the soft contours of its summit.

***

As Rosalina threatens to quit completely we see a clean white structure that seems out of Greece or Mexico with the name ROMERO'S in big blue lettering. A garage. I pull the sputtering little car in front and we go inside an interior that is pitch dark after the brilliant day, though illuminated by the crackling business of an arc welder wielded by a solidly built man in blue coveralls fixing something on the front of a hood of a large green International Harvester pickup truck. We stand quietly watching and as our eyes adjust we see another person standing next to the truck, a young Anglo with a beard, about my age and size, wearing a loose kind of old military pants, hiking boots and a green wool shirt. A medium-sized dog, some kind of sheep dog, very smart and agreeable-looking, stands quietly at his side, attentive to the proceedings, wagging its tail slightly as we approach. The man stops welding and pulls back his visor to inspect his work, taking a wire brush and giving it a good raking over. He is an older-middle-aged man with a serious, mindful attitude to his movements that remind me immediately of Lila and her coffee. The object of his attention is a large nut that he has welded to the front of the hood so that it sticks out parallel to the ground. Beneath it, welded to the frame behind the grill, is a spring with a kind of hook on the end. You can see right away that the purpose of this modest but clever arrangement is to fasten the hood, the spring pulled up and hooked into the extended nut. The man, aware of our presence but yet to acknowledge us, tries out his contraption, pulling the spring up and hooking the end into the nut, then pulling up on the hood to test the device's effectiveness. Satisfied, he unhooks the spring and tells the young man to try it out. He looks at us with a smile and hooks the spring onto the nut.

"Agustín, you've done it again. You're a genius, that's all there is to it," he says, shaking the mechanic's hand warmly. The mechanic, Agustín, finally looks at us with a smile and says to the man somewhat sternly but with a note of affection in his voice, "You're lucky you didn't kill somebody with that thing." The young man replies no kidding and how crazy it was and tells us that he had been driving down the highway the day before and the wind had gotten under the hood, lifting it up and ripping it off its hinges and spinning it like a wicked metal Frisbee with jagged edges across the highway landing on the shoulder, some merciful agent seeing to it that no one was driving or walking by at that moment. "Whoa," we say, and I recognize someone else who has a guardian-fuckin'-angel riding shotgun, at least on that occasion, and I look at his big old truck and it seems like a cousin to little Rosalina. He pays Agustín twenty dollars and opens the door for his dog who jumps in with a springy launch, sitting on the seat and looking straight ahead eagerly as if to say let's get on with the next adventure. The young man shakes hands again with Agustín and says goodbye to us and tells us we're in good hands with Agustín Romero, which we don't doubt. He drives the big truck out of the garage into the exhilarating light of northern New Mexico and heads down the road towards Taos.

"Well, what can I do for you gentlemen?" says Agustín Romero, with the air of a kindly village uncle and a hint of amusement at yet another contingent of wayward hippies having troubles with yet another old beater they should know how to fix themselves. We explain the problem and go outside for a look at little Rosalina, and like old Vanzetti he is amused and amazed that this tiny Swedish ragamuffin with no starter and pieces of plywood for upholstery is on this crazy trip and shakes his head skeptically when we tell him of our plans to make it back to the East coast. Agustín is a handsome old Spaniard whom I can see on a big olive farm back in Zaragosa surrounded by grandchildren, married forty years to the same beautiful wife who probably looks like an older version of Paul's Carmen. He is reserved, even a bit shy, but with a commanding aspect that would have me running to fetch tools if requested. I open the hood and without a word he flips off the distributor cap that looks like a toy and whistles like old Vanzetti when he had touched my radiator. "Points completely worn," he says.

Coming from Agustín Romero it is like the Pope telling me I have used up most of my grace and it is kind of a mystery how I have gotten this far and that, like Vanzetti, he suspects but does not say that maybe a guardian-fuckin'-angel is at work, though as a different sort of Catholic, assuming they are both Catholic, he would hold in reserve what Vanzetti had blurted out so colorfully. In any case there is a smidgen of the miraculous or, more likely, a barrel-full of the outrageous, in this whole improbable enterprise, which you sense Agustín appreciates and which garners us some grudging respect from this solid and serious man. We look at the points silently for a moment and then I look at Agustín, trying to conceal my anxiety because it is unlikely there is anything even close to these little Swedish electronic parts in this land of trucks, jeeps and four-wheel-drives and as if to confirm my worries Agustín says, "No, I don't have anything like that around here," and shakes his head sadly. Paul and I look at each other blankly, like, oh, we're fucked now, as I think please, let there be something like this somewhere in Taos, otherwise we might really be fucked, hung up for days, though Taos is not a bad place to be hung up in, but the whole thing now is to go, get on with it. We are in the pull of the East. I

plead silently, *come on, Agustín, save us! come up with a miracle!* and after a few seconds, still looking at the points, Agustín says, "Well—I
just might have something..."

He goes into the garage and Paul and I look at each other again,
our hopes lifted, and in a few minutes the great man—I have no
doubt he is a great man, and if he can get us out of this jam I am el-
evating him to sainthood—comes out with some points, larger than
Rosalina's—my heart sinks at the sight of them—needle-nose pliers,
a small file and a thin piece of insulated wire, and he sets to work
without a word, filing, fitting, filing again, bending, going back into
the garage for a long five minutes to solder, coming out, fitting, filing, bending, fitting and then finally tightening the little worked-
over creation down, telling me to get in and start it up, and I'm so
excited I forget Rosalina has no starter, we all forget, and then he
and Paul get behind and push and the little car starts up, *kabrooom!*
just like that, better than ever. Milagro! I let out a whoop and, not
wanting to cut the engine, I pull the emergency brake, mostly a
symbolic effort as the thing barely works, but Agustín tells me to
turn off the engine because he wants to look at the plugs. Within
minutes the plugs are out, back in, cleaned, re-gapped, the spark-
plug wires checked. "Ready to go," he says with that same humorous
sparkle in his eye.

We talk for a few minutes and he tells us he has spent his whole
life in Taos with time out for the war, France and Germany, has
eight grandchildren and has been married to the same woman for
thirty years. He has never been to southern New Mexico, the Grand
Canyon or Los Angeles and seems unimpressed with our trip, as if
we should be doing more serious things at our age, though he is
amused we have undertaken the venture in such a car. "You never
know, you just might make it," he says with a smile. You can tell
he thinks we are crazy, but no more than most young Anglos, who

seem harmless enough, after all. Nice kids, respectful for the most part, larking about until they get serious and return home to take up their rightful places as rulers of the universe, which makes no difference to him. He is sorry he has no starter for us and doesn't know where to get one. Denver, he says, if we are going that far, or maybe Albuquerque, but Rosalina is easy to start and we don't think it is crucial. He charges us fifteen dollars for his service, the same as Vanzetti, and when Paul tries to give him twenty he refuses. We get two dollars of gas to top off the tank and he helps Paul push and we are back on the road. When we turn to wave goodbye he is already inside his garage.

***

We are hungry and decide to get something to eat, driving into the town, past the plaza, the Taos Inn, Spivey's Café, where we almost stop, and then to a little bakery next to the post office, Dory's, where several wild-looking hippies stand outside talking. We park Rosalina and saunter in, the big mountain looking over us.

A friendly woman we figure to be Dory stands behind a glass counter of baked goods and greets us with a smile. The place is small and warm with hippies all around, a scruffy rustic crew of back-to-the-landers, space cadets and artists with mud all over their boots who seem to be in on some great secret or conspiracy that makes them all happy and excited and above all friendly, which is nice and makes you feel immediately at home. We order bowls of barley soup and hunks of whole wheat bread and sit at a wooden table and right away are into conversation with two bearded guys at the next table named Dag and Keegan, with Paul and Dag doing most of the talking. Dag is a real talker, a gesticulator, very enthusiastic. Paul manages to get a friendly word or two in edgewise, while Keegan and I eat our soup and look at the hippie chicks. Keegan is thin with an explosion of wiry brownish-red hair and a beard much bigger than Dag's. Beards are the thing. Paul has his van Gogh. I have a goatee. Keegan wears round little tortoise shell glasses that proclaim aesthetic sensibilities. He is a leather worker, sandals, belts, bags, and has just learned how to make saddles. He shows me his belt, which he had made, a clean job with a small brass buckle that he says comes from equipment used in the First World War, the kind with two prongs that fit into corresponding holes. Very tasteful. Keegan has quick nervous movements with nicotine stains on his fingers and the same energy and enthusiasm as Dag. Everyone seems to have it. It is the place. It is the novelty. It is youth. Things are definitely happening here.

The subject turns to the New Buffalo commune and we ask if there is a chance to visit. Keegan says they always welcome visitors and in fact has made some belts that he needs to drop off there and today is as good a day as any if we want to come along, which of course we do. Saying goodbye to the declamatory Dag and smiling Dory we pile into Keegan's green 1950 GMC panel truck and head out to New Buffalo, white knuckling it all the way with Keegan's insane driving. Though he is obviously straight he drives as if he has just smoked a pound of angel dust, hitting the gas, stomping the brakes, shifting as if slamming shells into a howitzer, talking animatedly and taking his eyes off the road, swerving back and forth as he flings the rocking wagon side to side, avoiding certain death with oncoming traffic or tumbling off the shoulder into a gulley below. It feels like we are in a helicopter or cargo plane taking evasive action under heavy fire from the NVA, rolling back and forth with each lurching twist of the steering wheel, mad acceleration, stomp of brake and thrusting change of gear. Things are sliding and flying all over the interior of Keegan's truck, which, with its bare, drab metal, *looks* like the inside of a helicopter or cargo plane. A piece of leather hanging next to me hits my face every time Keegan makes one of his Cockeresque swerves or jumps. At one point Paul tumbles into Keegan, who, talking excitedly about a find of rare brass buckles in a little harness shop in Questa, suddenly yanks the wheel to avoid a head-on collision with an old truck laden with firewood. Deciding survival is the better part of politeness we start to scream and curse at Keegan to watch where the fuck he's going or he'll get us all killed which isn't so good because we're still young and have lots of dope to smoke and fine hippie chicks to screw and places like New Buffalo to see and even though we love him and his terrific leather work and Tolstoyan beard and cool little glasses we just might have to get the fuck out and walk if he doesn't pay fucking attention to his driving. We laugh and scream like schoolgirls but we mean every word and it finally registers and he slows down a bit and chides us for being such Nervous Nellies. My ass. The guy is the worst driver I have ever seen.

It is a shame he is such a bad driver because we have been passing some spectacular landscape and after Keegan slows down we can marvel again at the sheer wildness of it all, the snow-capped distant mountains, the vastness of everything, but as we approach Arroyo Hondo, getting close to New Buffalo, we go down some hair-raising turns, the beautiful valley below, and all I can think of is Keegan with some distraction or cockeyed reaction jerking the wheel and plunging us over the side, done in not by some *Easy Rider* inbred redneck motherfucker in a pickup truck with a shotgun but by one of our own. It is terrifying going down into the valley, the panel truck tipping and swaying from side to side as Keegan waxes euphoric on the beauty of the land and all the neat things he's making out of leather and brass and all I can think of is how ironic, getting out of the Vietnam slaughterhouse only to be nullified in an ugly

plummeting crash hundreds of feet over the side in this spectacular place. New Mexico and Vietnam. I feel a terrible pity for those
poor bastards in Nam, guys my age and younger, as the image of the
panel truck crashing and burning down the slope with us slammed
around inside like crash dummies morphs into a helicopter spinning
out of the sky and crashing into a jungle in a huge billowing ball of
deadly beautiful flames and black smoke.

But then we are into the valley and there are no more sides to
crash over, thoughts of the vast crime and carnage of Vietnam replaced with amazement at the landscape and intense curiosity over
this unique enterprise we are about to visit, this New Buffalo commune, built by young Americans like ourselves, a new kind of pioneer, motivated by idealism and a healthy rage and disgust with
a predacious, empty culture. Something new is really something
old and, I suppose, something very American, an old impulse recapitulated. It is exciting driving up the muddy rutted road to the
commune, Keegan providing nonstop exuberant commentary, fish-
tailing and humping along much too fast as we bounce on our seats
and hold on fully expecting the truck to tip over, somehow avoiding getting stuck while Paul and I look sharply out the windows for
signs of the wild new breed, as if anthropologists looking for a ru-
mored Amazonian tribe.

We drive as far as we can to a place where a few old pickups
are parked along with some other vehicles that seem to be abandoned. A bit farther up the road three hippies labor to free a battered old pickup that is missing its hood and axle-deep in mud. The
two pushing are completely covered in muck and seem to be having a good time despite their predicament. We get out of the truck
and go over to help and in about thirty seconds we are completely
covered ourselves from the spinning wheels that splatter mud all
over us as we push from behind. The guys pushing, a Mutt and Jeff
pair named Tip and Jim, both with beards and long hair, trade in-

sults and laugh as we take turns falling on our faces while the driver, Derrick, shirtless with a dark muscular torso and long dirty blond hair and missing a front tooth, laughs and curses good-naturedly at his friends. After a while a bearded guy with wire-rimmed glasses comes down with a tractor and pulls the truck out with a heavy chain and tows it onto the road but then it stalls and won't start so he tows it over to the side to a drier spot.

The sun shines fiercely, drying the mud like stucco on our faces and beards. Marty, the guy with the tractor, pulls out a fat joint and we sit on the tractor and smoke, the sky a brilliant blue, a few puffs of pure white clouds, the snow on the mountains so intense it hurts your eyes to look at them. The guys are friendly and ask a few questions, but not too many. Everything is cool and of the moment. The mud on my face feels like scales. We are a bunch of iguanas flicking our tongues in the clean air. Keegan goes back to his truck to get his belts. Marty fires up the tractor. The six of us follow him up to the commune.

***

New Buffalo is set down in the middle of a dramatic landscape with farm animals, dogs, feral children and their hippie parents in various attitudes of work, play and recline, straight out of a scene from Bruegel. Young men and women stripped to the waist work alongside each other making adobes, working in gardens, tanned, strong and healthy, not an ounce of fat among them, a lean, hard-working bunch with an air of erotic fun. I try not to gawk but cannot help myself. One of the adobe makers, a barefoot blond girl in dungarees and nothing else looks at us and smiles. There are three more girls in a garden next to the main house quietly working the soil and planting seeds. A couple of guys are busy taking an engine out of a truck. Tip and Jim, still laughing and insulting each other, help Marty connect a plow to the back of the tractor. Geese honk, rushing the dogs. Overhead, crows, cawing. A rooster. Ragged, runny-nosed, wild-haired urchins. A sea of mud. Astonishing sky.

I like Marty. He does not say much but he has an agreeable, thoughtful quality without being too serious. The others seem to respect him. You get the feeling he has a real stake in this place—a no-nonsense sort of fellow who allows himself the freedom to pull out a doobie and get high in the middle of the day and keep on working. He is not as stoned as Tip and Jim who, despite their goofery, work effectively, getting the plow on the old tractor and then ambling over to help with the adobes, looking like ragged, good-natured country boys ready to lend a helping hand, though the hippie girls might have something to do with their communal spirit. Anything contributing to the communal spirit seems okay to me. Looking at these girls I am ready to do some work myself. The place smells of manure, marijuana, rich dirt and clean mountain air.

Keegan takes us into the main house, a wide-open adobe structure, where he gives his belts to an older tall bearded guy with a fringed buckskin jacket who leaves and returns a few minutes later and gives Keegan some goat meat wrapped in white waxed paper leaking blood. He returns to his seat at a heavy wooden table where he has been cleaning stems and seeds from a pile of marijuana. Marty comes in and offers us some tea and we sit at the table, putting honey in our hot drinks with a little wooden honey dripper. The large warm room smells powerfully of smoke from an old cook stove. Marty is from New York and has come to New Buffalo on a quest for a radically new way of doing things, "a paradigm shift in values, brought about by physical labor, communal effort, sharing and close connection to the earth." My initial impression of him is corroborated by his warmth, sincerity and thoughtful words. There is an appealing idealism about him. He thinks it is possible for people to get their shit together, to be midwives at the birth of a new age, that the spirit and example of New Buffalo and the hundreds of other communes are going to lead people towards this inevitable, profound and utterly necessary change. The old ways of materialism and war, of urban living divorced from the land, of individual gratification, are resulting in catastrophe, environmental and otherwise, and the answer, he firmly believes, is in this back-to-the-land communal existence, basically self-sustaining and independent but part of a network of communities helping each other through barter and sharing skills. And when he speaks of needing to free ourselves of patriarchal domination Paul joins in and relates a bit of his own interests, his inquiries into the masculine nature of the culture, the ideas of "progress," "success," "power" and "freedom" as nothing more than covers for primitive male aggression packaged into a nice sounding ideology. The guy cleaning his stash looks on with interest at this turn in the conversation.

"My father was in the longshoremen's union, a big, tough guy," says Marty. "His parents came over from Eastern Europe to Ellis Island and lived on the Lower East Side, the whole deal, the poverty, the prejudice, the suffering, all of it. He left my mother when I was eight and took up with another woman. I basically never saw him again."

We take a half-hour walk with Marty to check out the fields, the goat pen and some of the buildings, reveling in the energy of the awakening earth, the electric mountain air, the landscape, the hopefulness of this project. These are our brothers and sisters and we wish them well. It seems like a profound undertaking, one possible vision of the future, even if it is isolated bands of misfits struggling to remain human in some godforsaken Brave New World with its totalitarian technology, violence and environmental destruction.

But this is hopeful, there is a chance, people are doing it. We say goodbye and walk through the mud back to the panel truck, each of us silent and still a bit stoned. The afternoon is hot. The people working on the adobes have stopped. The place seems to have cleared out. We make it back to highway without getting stuck, Keegan under control, the marijuana apparently improving his driving. New Buffalo, we agree, is good, but probably not our thing, too much chaos, too many egos, too many strange characters, likely too many drugs. But it is a worthy venture and we hope it succeeds. We all like Marty. If the majority of people on communes are like Marty they have a chance. Paul talks about Mencius and his ideas of communal living, how all are responsible for contributing to the general good before they can tend their own gardens. Satisfying the social and the individual. We don't know if New Buffalo has such an organizing principle. Keegan is not sure.

We spend the night in Keegan's apartment just off the plaza in town. It is a small place jammed with polished, worn tools, workbench, rolls of leather and samples of his work, impeccably crafted sandals, belts and handbags. A Ralph Steadman drawing hangs on the wall. One of Keegan's own drawings, a careful rendition in graphite of some kind of leather tool, lies on his bench. Keegan is obviously a craftsman of the first order. Paul and I are impressed, and tell him so. He is delighted to hear it. For dinner we go next door to a comfortable little restaurant, The House of Taos, and have good green chile, pepperoni and mushroom pizza. The place is presided over by a large friendly bearded man, Avram, and his wife, Rachel, an attractive dark-haired woman with a playful gleam in her eye. The restaurant is jammed, with a good rolling fire in the adobe fireplace—a place to make the hippies happy.

After eating we smoke a perfectly rolled joint at Keegan's and go to see "EL Topo" at the theater in the plaza, a movie that in our condition blows us away though we can't figure out if it is utterly profound or utterly ridiculous. Afterwards we go to the bar above the theater, an odd sort of airport lounge dominated by a large mural of a fox in the desert behind the bar that is somehow in the spirit of the movie and over drinks decide it was utterly ridiculous.

After another couple of rounds we are joined by a friend of Keegan's, a short gloomy guy who looks a little like Marlon Brando. He introduces himself as Dorman. Dorman speaks in rapid discharges, like a toy burp gun. "El Topo is a work of transcendent genius," he says, after hearing some of our criticisms, taking a slug of beer and setting it down firmly on the counter. "Jodorowsky is the Salvador Dali of cinema. There's so much profound imagery in El Topo it will take scholars and critics years to unravel it all. It's way over the heads of most people." His aggressiveness and authoritative manner strike me as comical. I laugh. "Whoa," says Keegan. "It's nothing but bullshit. Entertaining bullshit, but bullshit nevertheless. Or maybe we're just not on the same plane as you. We just don't get it."

"I think that's likely," says Dorman, staring at his beer, his small hands around the glass. "Artists are always the last to understand, especially Taos artists. Nabokov was right, a dismal hole full of third-rate painters and faded pansies."

With that Dorman chugs the rest of his beer, slams the glass on the counter, spins out of his seat and marches out of the bar, his little legs churning, bumping into a startled hippie on his way through the door. We sit stunned for moment and then laugh. "Who the fuck is *that* guy?" asks Paul. "That's the great Dorman. Tough guy, tortured soul, misunderstood genius," says Keegan. "Looks like Marlon Brando, don't you think?" "More like Brando's demented little brother," says Paul. We look at each other and, as if on cue, say, "I COULDA BEEN A CONTENDER!" and fall out laughing.

***

In the morning we make the mistake of having breakfast at Spivey's, bad food and even worse vibes, full of large, strange white people eating pancakes and sausages, but we are headed for New Orleans and the mountain is still powerful and grand, the spell of Taos still firmly lodged in our bones. It is, we agree, a spectacular and magical place, one of those "power centers" that people talk about, in spite of what Nabokov had apparently said, as conveyed by the angry and comical little Dorman. The crisp morning air and brilliant sky convey an exhilarating sense of promise, the ubiquitous mud frozen but softening in the warming day, a mountain breeze rustling the leaves, a subtle symphony of countless green maracas, a whispering, an urging, a kind of spring I have never experienced, a mountain spring. It is blowing my mind and I want to stay but we are pulled south to an opposite land of damp heat, swamp and red dirt, land of Emmett Till and Bull Connor, Chaney, Schwerner and Goodman, Martin Luther King and George Wallace, a languorous, violent land that stokes my imagination with a mixture of fear and fascination. If the North is the mind of the country the South is the body. Paul particularly loves Louisiana and New Orleans, having driven through ten years earlier on his flight from Florida. As we head south towards Espanola, passing Agustín Romero's beautiful blue and white garage, the spark of Agustín's arc welder sizzling in the dark interior, Paul speaks of his experience, "I left Jacksonville in February, hitchhiking with a green Army duffel bag and $145 dollars in my pocket. It was cold as hell going across Florida but I was lucky enough to get a ride all the way to New Orleans with a black trucker named Norris hauling furniture to Oklahoma City. A great guy. He put me up for the night in New Orleans with his family. The next day was Mardi Gras and I fell in with some guys from Tulane and had a crazy time. The day after that I got a ride with Norris to Oklahoma City, where he hooked me up with another trucker, a white dude this time, another good guy, and I got a ride all the way to San Francisco. I really lucked out that whole trip but the best part was New Orleans. It's a wide-open place, really cosmopolitan—Caribbean. Basically an African-American city. Pretty amazing scene. This was right around the time of the Freedom Riders, so things were pretty fucking dicey. A lot of tension just under the surface."

The drive through Espanola, Santa Fe and Las Vegas is beautiful but when we hit the eastern plains out across the Panhandle to Amarillo down towards Wichita Falls, Denton, Dallas, the landscape turns stupefying (though some of the land west of Amarillo is wild and haunting, a dipping ride through surprisingly dramatic landscape), flat, ugly and above all, windy, coming out of the north with a cold, moaning, unrelenting intensity, some kind of freak freezing spring storm that blows poor Rosalina all over the road, scaring the shit out of us with the specter of head-on collisions or going off the shoulder into some godforsaken Texas ditch or cotton field. The dust whips across the highway like an unending plague of vicious tiny insects, blasting Rosalina and coming through the windows and vents though we have them tightly shut, blanketing everything with a powdery grit, getting into our eyes, ears, noses and mouths. When the road veers north and we drive into the wind the little car slows to forty miles per hour, straining gallantly while huge semis buffet us, air horns blasting like ocean liners. We are a rowboat in gale-force winds on high seas, the worst part being that it goes on and on, mile after flat ugly Texas mile, the dirty red Panhandle sun shrouded in the dustbowl sky an alien star at our back, dipping to the horizon in the late afternoon casting long shadows before us as if pointing the way to oblivion. Oilmen, ranchers, car salesmen, insurance agents, football coaches and their beef-swollen, artery-hardened families line up behind the struggling Rosalina in their huge Amerikan cars and trucks honking their horns angrily and whoever of us is driving edges over to the side so they can pass. The Texans glare righteously as they speed by, children in the back spinning around in their seats to gawk, point, laugh and sneer.

We spend the night in a motel just outside of Dallas after driving twelve hours, the wind moaning heartlessly all night, an unearthly chorus of Texas misery and violence, speaking of vast spaces, the damned, the lost, the brutalized, plains grit slamming up against the windows and under the door so that we have to put a towel down to keep it out. Things rattle, clang and crash outside, startling us awake during the few times we manage to slide into restless sleep. Either the heat has been turned off or it is broken, and it is freezing, each bed having only a thin blanket. We huddle in fetal positions, blankets over our heads, too weary and defeated by the indomitable wind and cold to go outside and retrieve our sleeping bags, though sometime around three Paul jumps up with an angry rush and gets them for us. But the wind never stops and even with our bags we are cold, cold of spirit, haggard and unnerved. This is the Big Remorseless, The Lone Star State, badass Texas. It feels like we have been driving across a flat wasteland for days, hounded by a malevolent wind bent on punishing us for having the temerity to trespass the state's imperial red-neck sovereignty.

Driving past Dallas is the worst of all, the highway suddenly turning to four, five, six lanes, I can't tell, like an ocean of concrete with a thousand large metal objects hurtling at insane speeds cutting us off, tailgating, spewing exhaust fumes, roaring, honking, going god knows where as if it all really means something, and in the distance the dark place itself, fresh in our minds as the sacrificial blood ground where the young smiling leader with his shock of hair and white teeth and beautiful stylish wife had his brain exploded to redbone frappe that splattered over all of us, the stains never disappearing: Dealey Plaza, the Texas School Book Depository, Lee Harvey Oswald, a dead slumping president, Jackie crawling in her bloody pink coat and pillbox hat, J.D. Tippit, Jack Ruby, Lyndon Johnson, Saigon, Da Nang, Khe Sanh, Agent Orange, My Lai, Nixon, Kent State, all a progression, a connection that seems to follow with the inexorable logic of blood dripping from a transfusion bag. The city casts a baleful spell, you can feel its power, as if controlling the madness on the highways around it, bending everything to its will, radiating out from its foul center across the country and the world. Driving away is a release. Traffic thins, the landscape opens up, the skies clear, birds twitter happily and Rosalina purrs. Ahead: Tyler, Longview and Shreveport. Next in line: Alexandria, Lafayette, Bayou Vista, Houma and New Orleans.

**

We quickly forget the dreadful Panhandle, the horrible wind and the Dallas freeways and start thinking about Louisiana, that beautiful name, slow, like the molasses, pine tar, sweet potato, crawfish South—Loo-eez-ee-anna, enjoying the last stretch out of Texas, commenting approvingly on the nice rolling hills, beautiful women, friendly people, courteous drivers, huge American flags lolling in the country breeze, and delicious barbecue, knowing the gigantic state and state of mind is at our backs and receding at a leisurely pace (after all, we are driving Rosalina) in the rearview mirror. Paul opens the glove compartment and gets *The Wretched of the Earth*. "Let's try this again, shall we?" I look at the book a little guiltily. If a while ago I had calculated fifty-two years to read it I figure now I will bequeath it to my offspring to finish.

Paul commences, "*In these poor, underdeveloped countries, where the rule is that the greatest wealth is surrounded by the greatest poverty, the army and the police constitute the pillars of the regime; an army and a police force (another rule which must not be forgotten) which are advised by foreign experts. The strength of the police force and the power of the army are proportionate to the stagnation in which the rest of the nation is sunk. By dint of yearly loans, concessions are snatched up by foreigners; scandals are numerous, ministers grow rich, their wives doll themselves up, the members of parliament feather their nests and there is not a soul down to the simple policeman or the customs officer who does not join in the great procession of corruption."*

Paul holds the book open. "Open this book to any page and you'll find something good. He might as well be writing about Vietnam. Diem, Madam Nhu, Ky, Thieu, all the nefarious motherfuckers propped up by the US. Think of all the corrupt regimes in Latin America, Africa, just like Fanon says—the dictators supported by the United States: Samoza, Batista, the Shah of Iran, Stroessner, Trujillo, Tshombe, Papadopoulos, Papa Doc. Bloodthirsty bastards, all of them. The list goes on and on. Think about all the suffering this has caused, exactly as Fanon says, pockets of obscene wealth surrounded by dire poverty. Countries crippled by debt owed to huge Western institutions like the World Bank and the IMF, most of the money siphoned off by the ruling class, the rest going to the military and police to suppress the people, the economy opened up to Western businesses, exploitation. See what I mean? The whole rotten chain of repression, like Fanon says, from the policeman to the customs officer. Filthy money passed from one sweaty palm to another. The people suffer. Exactly."

I look at Paul with his rough beard, orange hair, ragged straw hat, brilliant blue eyes. He has been quieter than I have expected since leaving California, but I am deeply pleased to have him with me. There is something profoundly comforting about it. We pass a sign that says 220 miles to Shreveport and we both moan, Jesus Christ, a lifetime away and more dreary miles through Texas. Though we have adopted a temporarily magnanimous attitude as we are on our way out it is still Texas, with the memory of our drive across the Panhandle and the oppressiveness of Dallas still throbbing like a swollen gland. But soon we are outside of Tyler and after that Longview and then the glorious Louisiana state line where Rosalina fairly leaps forward and I honk her horn triumphantly as Paul and I whoop, at the same time looking around for Klansmen, dangerous looking pickup trucks, swamps and other unusual things, but the only difference is the highway, worse, and a noticeable change in vibe, better.

Past Shreveport heading south on 71 the land grows swampier, more mysterious and wild, with huge fields of cotton and sugar cane, passing places with fabulous names like Coushatta, Natchitoches, Alexandria, Lecompte, Cheneyville, Bunkie, Big Cane, Ville Platte, Opelousas, Port Barre, Grand Coteau and finally over to Lafayatte, where we pick up 90 headed east to New Orleans. Paul and I marvel at the graceful, lush counterpoint to what we have been through across the Panhandle, equal in an opposite way to the beauty of New Mexico. We are in the uterine zone of the country, the humid region where vegetation grows dense like pubic hair and rivers move in continual menstrual flow, emptying into the Gulf. Paul says all of this is the Atchafalaya Basin, fed by the river of the same name, and that it is the biggest swamp in the country. A swamp, he says, is a forest covered in water. There are bayous everywhere. A bayou is a stream or a channel in a marsh. A marsh is a wet, or boggy land. There are all kinds of crazy animals in the wetlands, like alligators, water moccasins, nutria (a huge rodent, introduced by accident, a terrible pest), giant catfish, snapping turtles, shrimp, pelicans, beautiful snowy egrets with their brilliant white plumage and yellow toes. All of this Paul relates.

The names of places we drive through, like so many in southern Louisiana are French-sounding and evocative. Forget trying to pronounce them as you might in France, says Paul, for here it is different. Atchafalaya is Indian, obviously—Choctaw, Paul says. On the map before bending east 90 drops south past New Iberia, Jeanerette, Bayou Vista, Morgan City, to its low point, Houma, where it bounces northeast towards New Orleans. This is wild country, with the Gulf over yonder just out of view but very much present with its warm salty expanse, a large body of turquoise blood, calm, but capable of hellacious fury. I ache to see it but we feel constrained from going outside of our planned route. Louisiana is a little spooky. It is the South. We are freaks. But even more imposing than these social barricades and minefields is the heavy, mysterious fecundity of the land itself, the terrible, fascinating life-and-deathness of it, the latent violence behind the swampy, cypress-and-magnolia allure. You know something is out there, but you don't know what the hell it is.

***

From Lafayette on down past Broussard, St. Martinville, New Iberia, Avery Island (home of Tabasco Sauce), Jeanerette, Franklin, Bayou Vista, Morgan City, is an enchanted ride past colorful rickety joints in salt-decay, heavy with smells of rotting, rank, fishy things, driveways and parking lots paved with crushed clam and oyster shells, ramshackle businesses selling fishing equipment to the local Cajun population that has been harvesting the bayous, rivers and the Gulf of Mexico for two hundred years. 1700s, Paul says, the Cajuns moved down here from Canada, expelled by the British. Shrimp, crabs, crawfish and oysters seem to be the mainstays, judging from the signs, but there is also a business for the sports-fishing tourist and the raggedy after-school angler, the bait and tackle shops that I am familiar with on Long Island and have visited myself for snapper, bluefish and striped bass under the bridges on summer evenings. Great times, those, and I figure if I lived around here I would get into it in a big way. Paul feels the same. "You know, this is one of the few places left in this Moloch-like culture that retains its traditions. Look at that. Gautreaux's Bait and Tackle. Don't you love these Cajun names? Check him out! Damn, look at that! Jesus! Incredible!"

Everywhere there are magical sights, dark water bayous surrounded by brilliant green marsh vegetation, the startlingly white snowy egrets, small boats of all descriptions, docks with, of all things, school boats, painted yellow and black like their graceless land-lubberish counterparts. At Melancon's Dockyard outside of Bayou Vista, a sprawling place covered with crushed shells next to a large bayou, several shrimp boats are up on elaborate scaffolds being tarred, caulked, painted and otherwise patched up for shrimp runs to the Gulf. One of the boats is painted with bright festive colors. It is a sight that would have got Vincent tumbling out of the car with his paints and easel in a heartbeat and I half expect Paul to demand we stop. "Wow!" he says. "Look at that! Far out!"

There are lots of bars and dance halls featuring Cajun music and drink specials and they have that hard-used, stale beer, daytime somnolence of places that you know just blow the lid off come ten, eleven o'clock and beyond. These bands have more of the great names, Thibodeaux, Arcenaux, Doucet, Broussard, Cormier. Along with the bars, dance halls and fishing joints are incongruous, ugly, square, prefab buildings selling heavy equipment for the oil rigs springing up like malignant warts around these parts, and churches, mostly Catholic. "The soul is well provided for around here," says Paul. "Dancing and drinking Saturday nights and church on Sundays. I can dig that. I bet their masses are as interesting as their dances. Damn, what a place!"

I love it too, but Paul is really stoked. I figure as appealing as it is we are still better off just driving through and looking, for obvious reasons, but the more Paul sees the more I get the feeling he is going to insist we stop somewhere, and sure enough a couple of miles past the town of Amelia as we pause for an old pickup truck making a left hand turn Paul spots a small hand-lettered sign done in red paint advertising swamp tours for $15. The sign is stuck at an angle in a yard the way certain people hitchhike walking with their backs turned to traffic, as if whoever belongs to this old, unpainted, clapboard ramshackle bayou cabin with an exterior chimney and tin roof stuck it in the ground in the off chance some Harvard anthropologist might pass by, its funky, rustic casualness broadcasting authenticity in neon.

We pull in behind an old rusty Ford pickup on a dirt driveway speckled with white shells and while I stay behind the wheel with the motor running Paul gets out, carefully climbs a couple of dilapidated steps onto a sagging porch and knocks on the screen door. The house is raised up a couple of feet, probably for flood protection, a bit better off than an Alabama sharecropper's home, but not much. There is fishing equipment strewn all over the porch and in the yard, torn nets hanging for repair, faded cork buoys, a couple of saw horses with small old outboard engines attached, their covers off, a turned-over rowboat with peeling blue paint, stacks of crab traps covered with dried moss and seaweed, old red gasoline cans, small used cans of two-stroke engine oil, crushed cardboard cans of regular motor oil, beer cans, crab nets, fishing poles, several 55 gallon oil drums filled with trash, decomposing cardboard boxes and more, and in the middle of all this the haphazard little hand-lettered sign in red paint for $15 swamp tours.

Paul stands for a few moments talking to someone inside. Belatedly, I notice at the far end of the porch a young man in a rocking chair sitting quietly and drinking beer. He is about my age, handsome with sharp features, dark curly hair, staring straight ahead holding the can of beer with about five or six empties on the floor in front of him. Paul comes back to the car and says that the guy inside,

Mr. Bujeau, will take us for a ride in the swamp in a little while for 20 bucks, but not before we come in for some gumbo. Now this is really something. I turn off the car and walk with Paul through the yard and up the creaking steps to the porch, glancing at the young man in the rocking chair, still staring straight ahead. The only thing we've had all day is potato chips and Cokes from a gas station in Longview and it is after two o'clock. It is warm, probably about 80, and you can feel the water all around you and smell the bayou, a kind of heavy, boggy decay, not unlike a fish tank in need of cleaning, but not bad, not bad at all, in fact I like it very much. I inhale deeply, filling my lungs. Louisiana.

Mr. Bujeau opens the door and lets us into his house. Contrasting with the cluttered yard, the interior is simple and clean. At opposite ends of the main room are a wood cook stove and a fireplace, both heavily blackened with use. A thick square wood table surrounded by four comfortable-looking wood chairs with worn patchwork cushions stands in the middle of a floor made of dark, smooth six-inch planks. The room's lone window looks out onto the back yard, filled with more clutter and some white chickens, and beyond, a sight that takes my breath away, a large dock and several boats, including a small white and blue shrimper, and a cut of water running die-straight to the horizon, a bayou, wide and dark, in which stands more of those snowy egrets that seem to be everywhere, enclosed all around by the same brilliant green wild vegetation. The interior walls are stretched burlap sacks tacked to the studs and bare except for a framed color print of Jesus (not the chimp) and a large colorful New Orleans Saints poster with the 1971 season schedule and a picture of their quarterback, # 8, running for his life, another in a long tradition of martyrs.

There is a small table supporting a large old-fashioned Zenith radio, beside which I imagine Mr. Bujeau passing many unhappy moments listening to Saints games Sundays after church. Football and religion are the only things recognizably mainstream in this simple rustic interior. On the blackened wood stove are a coffee pot and a large speckled blue enamel pot filled with gumbo. Mr. Bujeau, who, like Butterfly's father, seems right out of a US Camera Annual from the thirties, bids us sit at the table where he places spoons and knives and a couple of battered blue enamel bowls and ladles dark gumbo swimming with sausage, chicken, shrimp, bell peppers, onions, okra and celery. As he carries out these hospitable tasks he speaks softly in a typical Cajun patois, replete with deez, dats and doze, putting several pieces of white bread and a chunk of butter wrapped in wax paper on a green plastic dish and then a couple of heavy ceramic mugs with green stripes from an old wooden cabinet standing next to the stove, a can of Borden's sweetened condensed milk, salt and pepper shakers and a roll of paper towels. He goes to the stove and comes back with the hot coffee, which he pours into our mugs. We add generous portions of sweetened condensed, swirling and clinking our spoons.

Mr. Bujeau has dark curly hair, graying at the temples and wears a loose-fitting red flannel shirt, torn in back, tucked carelessly into heavily soiled jeans, old boots. His face is creased, tanned, fleshy, weather-beaten, with an aquiline nose, heavy jaw and green eyes. He is not especially big, but thick, with large calloused hands. There is something very gentle about him. He pulls up a chair and sticks out a warm paw in my direction, introducing himself, Gilbert Bujeau. The man on the porch is his son, Remey, badly wounded at a place called Tra Vinh, Vietnam, Mekong Delta. I think of van Gogh at the asylum in Saint-Remy in the last years of his life. There are a lot of Remy Bujeaus now sitting on porches across the country, staring at nothing, their minds and bodies ripped apart while the Kissingers of this world sip cocktails in glittering salons and smile into their double chins.

Gilbert Bujeau tells us about his son, the athlete he had been, all-district in football, basketball and baseball, his dreams of playing professional baseball now destroyed along with legs that no longer work as they had and a mind that has no rest, dulled by alcohol and pills, barely able to care for himself, barely able, even, to speak. Remey's mother died when he was eight, the same age I was when my own mother died, and Mr. Bujeau raised him alone, never remarrying. Mr. Bujeau tells us how he had hoped Remey would work on his shrimp boat after Vietnam and how it looks now like that will never happen. Even if his mind recovers his body is crippled forever, knees all broken up, body twisted in constant pain, terrible scars everywhere. He has been back since December, 1970, after a month on a hospital ship, the USS Repose, six months in Okinawa and another three months at the VA hospital in Shreveport, and spends most of his time on the porch with that thousand-yard stare, drinking beer after beer, taking his pills, sometimes with tears running down his face, and all Mr. Bujeau can do as a father is hold his son's hand and cry right along with him. Remey had joined the Marines because he felt it was his duty—joined even though his father pled with him not to go, to stay home and help on the boat. But his son would have none of it. Like a lot of kids, Remey wanted to get away from home. I wish he'd never gone, Gilbert Bujeau says in a somber voice, staring out the window. I wish he'd gone to Canada instead. I'd have helped him any way I could.

***

We sit in silence for a long moment. Eat up, says Mr. Bujeau, dat's the best gumbo you'll ever have. When you finish, he says, we'll go out on the boat. We eat with tactful enjoyment, not wanting to show too much pleasure in the face of a father's grief, at the same time feeling very comfortable in this warm and humble home, knowing we are with a kindred spirit, a person who hates the war and sees it for the bloody killer and destroyer of families it is. The gumbo is a revelation, opening my senses as much as any drug I have ever taken, so delicious, so powerful, so full of warmth, that whatever attraction I have to Cajun culture is magnified a thousand-fold. I suppose Mr. Bujeau gets some solace from his religion—I would never presume to ask—but I don't see how much more profound and reassuring a mass could be than a bowl of fresh warm gumbo, bread and butter and a hot cup of coffee laced with sweetened condensed milk. Food, I decide, as I clean my bowl with a piece of bread and butter and wash it down with a last sip of strong, sweet coffee, is the essence of culture, of its values. This is what we are looking for, a warm pot of gumbo cooking slowly on a wood stove, a comforting, wholesome meal eaten at a leisurely pace, a profound connection to the rhythms and offerings of nature, the direct relationship between work and existence. This is what Marty is trying to achieve at New Buffalo and what the dominant culture has lost. It seems as if Vietnam is a symptom, a violent, macabre venting of the pressure cooker that is American society. The more plastic, sterile and stifling the culture becomes, the more horrible the venting.

"Mr. Bujeau, I am sorry to hear what has happened to your son," says Paul. "I am vehemently opposed to this war. So is Sam. To tell the truth we are a little apprehensive driving through the South—we know how conservative attitudes are down here. But meeting you and being the recipients of your warmth and hospitality is a real treat and an honor for both of us. I'm sure I speak for Sam as well."

"Absolutely," I say.

"Well, you fellas are okay. See dat right away, I could. As for dis war, well, I'm a veteran myself, but dat was a different story. Not like dis here where I can't figure for the life of me just what the hell's going on 'cept dat it seem like a fight inside the country—more like a civil war. You know what I mean? Way I figure we should just let doze people straighten it out for demselves. You be surprised how many folks feel the same way 'round here. One thing about folks 'round here, we don't trust much the government, dat's for damn sure. An' thank you for bein' concerned about my son. It's a damned shame, it is. I thought losin' his mama it was bad but in some ways dis is worse. Just tears hell out of me to see him like dis, it does."

Gilbert Bujeau is a strong man but the suffering over his son has got to him. The person in the kitchen and the person on the porch are extensions of each other, the sadness going back and forth in some kind of exchange, like a vicious cycle.

"Everything gone to hell, to tell the truth. I use to make good money shrimpin' but now Remey hurt so bad I hardly go out no more at all, I don't. Afraid to leave him he might do somethin' to himself. It's a good thing his mama can't see him, she loved him so."

There is silence again and then Paul says in a low, measured voice, "Well, try not to despair, Mr. Bujeau. Your son's body may never be the same but with time and healing he might get some of his spirit back. This is beautiful country here, and you have a deep and beautiful culture. Does he get any kind of counseling or therapy?"

"Dis little gal come around once a month from the hospital up in Shreveport an' she stays wid him for about an hour but dat's about it. Don't seem to help much."

"How about music?" I offer. "Does he ever go to any of these dances around here? Maybe that would be good for him."

"Nah, he don't ever want to go. He got some friends, too. Dey ask him but he don't go."

"Why don't you bring the music to him? I mean, invite some musicians over for a casual get-together, cook up some gumbo, have a little party once in a while," says Paul.

Mr. Bujeau looks at us both intently with his deep weathered face and clear green eyes. He gets up slowly and asks if we want more gumbo and coffee and we say yes, of course. "Well," says Mr. Bujeau, ladling gumbo, "we got deez healers down here we call *traiteurs*, but I never much went for dat kind of stuff. But now I don't know. I might jus' be willin' to try it. There's a fella not too far from here, he's a *traiteur*. I'm a religious man an' I done a lot of prayin' but it don't seem to be doin' much good. My boy, he still sufferin'. Eat up, then, an' I'll take you boys out on the water."

When we finish Mr. Bujeau takes us out to the porch and introduces us to Remey, who, avoiding our eyes, offers a cold weak hand, and the four of us go out back to the dock, Remey lagging behind, limping, and get into a peeling old white 16 foot wood skiff with a 10 horsepower Evinrude that is tied up next to the shrimper, *Aceline*, which has raised, graceful nets spread like wings and is a lot funkier up close than it appeared from the house. Remey sits at the bow with Paul and me in the middle. Mr. Bujeau hooks up the gas line, primes the tank, wraps a large hand around the grip and with two easy pulls starts the old motor in a cloud of blue smoke. We chug off into the bayou, which, Mr. Bujeau informs us, is not a "bayou proper" but a canal dredged by the oil companies, the shrimper *Aceline* receding in the distance.

***

The whole ride passes as if some kind of dream, the motor trailing a small cloud of blue smoke, its low puttering absorbed in the dense foliage, a delicate green layer of duckweed carpeting the water, lily pads so enormous they seem unreal, large, almost danger-ous-looking red and yellow flowers, orchids, lotus, I don't know what, our wake gently pushing the huge grasses and cattails back and forth. We turn off into a side channel, a natural bayou, narrow-ing, twisting around on itself, flowing into swamps where huge cy-press trees and weeping willows stand waterlogged and mute, their limbs draped over us, blocking the sun, heading into bigger places like large ponds where ducks, herons and more snowy egrets col-lect, lots of these same egrets and other birds up in the trees, and the sun, no longer shielded, shines brilliant and hot.

Remey sits mutely in front, staring straight ahead. Mr. Bujeau points things out but otherwise says very little. We see two alliga-tors, one big one not far off, which I first think is a log, a nutria galumphing through the grass, turtles sunning themselves on old cypress stumps, slipping into the water as we pass, an occasional jumping fish, some blue herons quietly flying over that startle me, a hammering noise that Mr. Bujeau says is a pileated woodpecker ("Not many of doze left.") and several derelict old swamp houses unevenly raised on block pilings or stilts but no evidence of peo-ple. Mr. Bujeau says they are probably off fishing or trapping some-where. Mostly crawfish. Next to one of these houses is a skinny little canoe-like vessel pulled up on shore that Mr. Bujeau says is a pirogue—he pronounces it PEE-row—carved from a cypress tree. Not many of those around any more, either. He points out a lop-sided old house that belongs to a *traiteur*, and then we see the man coming out the screen door onto the porch, waving, lean and dark in a white shirt, ragged pants, barefoot, a thin beagle at his side, barking. Mr. Bujeau waves. "Hey, Jesse, *comment ça va?*"

"Gettin' on, Gilbert, gettin' on. Hey Remey, how you doin'?" the *traiteur* shouts, his dog barking. Remey Bujeau says nothing, just looks at the man. "Come see me some time, Gilbert. We'll have a little talk."

Mr. Bujeau waves at the man but does not reply. I figure the *traiteur* is talking about Remey and it seems by the tight set of his jaw Mr. Bujeau is thinking on it hard. I know if I were a parent I would do it, try anything to get a suffering child straightened out. I wonder what Remey is thinking, sitting in the bow, wraithlike and still, almost as if you can see right through him, nothing more than a bit of swamp mist gathered up in human form. The bayou curves and the tilting house, the *traiteur* and his barking dog, are gone. 8,000 miles away in a place called Tra Vinh that is not too different from here Remey Bujeau got chewed up and spit out and now it will take the rest of his life to put his crippled self together, if ever. I look at Remey as he stares off, maybe a couple of years younger than me, a little bigger, thicker, gifted athlete, good-looking guy, thin lines of pain and despair already spreading over his face, strands of gray hair that will advance like blight. Soon he will not look that much younger than his father, though Gilbert is probably aging as fast as his son with worry. The country is a destroyer, eating its young and wasting its old in grief.

Remey grips the side of the skiff tightly with his right hand, his fingers white. They are soft looking and the back of his hand is heavily scarred. There is an ugly red scar on the back of his neck. I imagine scars all over his body. I imagine knee replacements by the time he is 40 or 50. I imagine him drinking himself to death by the time he is 30. I imagine his father finding him face down in the water next week. I imagine him going crazy and killing many people. I imagine him shrinking down to a sad nothing, disappearing from the world altogether. He seems to be doing so right here in the boat, gripping tightly to prevent himself from going away. Maybe being out here reminds him of the Mekong Delta and he is freaking out.

It is an environment that resonates with me, too, my associations considerably less real, all the make-believe Technicolor WWII images of swamps and jungle warfare, blazing machine guns, heroic Marines hurling pineapple grenades, screaming Japs blown away in explosions of dirt but no blood or severed limbs, medics frantically applying tourniquets and compresses to fake wounds with sweating GIs stoically gritting their teeth, those poor indomitable bastards raising the flag on Iwo Jima, the war games I played as a kid with dirt bombs and plastic soldiers, all of it so cool, definitely cool, and here it is coming back to me in a Louisiana bayou with a real-life broken-down Marine holding the side of his old man's skiff in a death grip. What a travesty, the thrill and harmlessness of the movie version, the trumpeted glory, the sheer little boy fun and bravado. Ridiculous. I know if I ever faced live bullets in real combat I would probably be paralyzed with terror like Crane's young soldier in *The Red Badge of Courage*, shit my pants, cry for mercy. The thought of war terrifies me, and yet I cannot shake those images absorbed as a child, those rich doses of Technicolor glory, how neat it all was.

***

Poor Gilbert Bujeau casts anxious, grief-stricken glances at his pathetic disappearing son the whole time we are out on that bayou, so much like the Mekong Delta Remey must be hearing voices whispering in Vietnamese. I don't know how he had been wounded, mine, ambush, friendly fire, it hardly matters. The thing is now he looks ahead at a life in a long dark tunnel with no chance of light coming through and no one to help him. I try to imagine what it is like for him but I cannot. I have been depressed plenty in my life but looking at it now I am ashamed of its triviality. Remey is an anti-matter vortex that sucks the life out of anything close. The more time spent with him the more I am convinced there is no hope, for him, for me, for mankind, for nature itself, everything drained of purpose and energy, running down, withering away to a meaningless, infinitely sad husk. Even the beauty and abundant life of the bayou cannot compete with the spectral anti-being that is Remey Bujeau. I pity the father who has absorbed his life into his son's, each day losing another millimeter of himself, as in quicksand, going down. Succumbing to these feelings is discouraging, especially in the middle of this lush environment, but the negative side is getting to me as much as it had at the Grand Canyon battling the life-sucking force of the evil tower. In reality there is only an endgame, an absurd nothingness, decay and death, an expiring sun, a barren earth, life an odd, random spasm, a big, howling, unfunny joke.

I try to avoid the negative vibes of Remey Bujeau for the rest of the trip, focusing on the beautiful strange things in this watery world, but I can't help thinking about the masters and their wars and their infernal meddling in the lives of ordinary people. The war has stirred a bloody, lumpy stew of unspeakable things and few, except for the handful at the top, are not affected. By the time we get up next to *Aceline* I am pretty pissed at the whole thing, thinking about the injustice, the profound insult to a man like Gilbert Bujeau, who has more character in one of his toenail clippings than the whole ruling class put together. A curse, a pox, a ruination on them all, I think, except for their innocent children, rescued and sent to re-education camps in North Vietnam.

Father and son tie up the skiff without a word and we thank them profusely for showing us their amazing world and when Paul tries to pay Mr. Bujeau refuses over and over until Paul gives up and then Mr. Bujeau invites us to spend the night, just as Butterfly's father had, and partake of some more gumbo, of which there is still plenty, he says. It is not a hard decision as evening is approaching and the thought of driving through these parts after sundown is only slightly more appealing than going for a midnight swim in the swamp. Remey takes up his usual position in the rocking chair on the porch while Paul and I get our sleeping bags. The whole time Remey has not said a word.

For dinner we have the same delicious gumbo, bread and butter and strong coffee with sweetened condensed milk. Remey takes a small portion of gumbo and bread and goes back to the porch. Mr. Bujeau says he has made up his mind and will ask the *traiteur*, Jesse Thériot, for help. It is time to try, he says. Mr. Bujeau has gotten quieter as the day wears on, as we all have, under the deadening weight of his son, his strong face sagging with the day's passage, making him look ten years older. I figure it is usually like that around here. Gilbert Bujeau has rallied a bit with our unexpected arrival, if only for a moment, and just maybe we have been the catalyst for him deciding to see the *traiteur*, the thin, raggedy Jesse Thériot. I suspect the sadness of him and his son has shied people away, and both have slipped into a solitary world with only each other as reference points, a bitter and misaligned compass, to be sure.

Mr. Bujeau refuses to let us wash the dishes and we sit for a while and talk about things of small consequence, like his hapless Saints, more than balanced out by his beloved LSU Tigers, whom he talks about at some length, reminiscing about the famous 89 yard punt return by Billy Cannon on Halloween night in 1959 that beat Ole Miss, 7-3. He tells us how he had listened to that game playing poker with friends and when Cannon scored they threw their winnings in the air and then held on for dear life as the Rebels came storming back, stopped at the one yard line by the heroic Tiger defense. "Oh, lord, dat was a game I'll never forget," says Mr. Bujeau.

Paul and I decide to sleep on the porch and this is where we now go, a bit apprehensively as Remey is there doing what he always does, rocking back and forth, drinking beer and staring off into nowhere. We roll out our bags on the canvas tarp Mr. Bujeau has laid down and sit quietly for a few minutes, staring with Remey at nothing, waiting in the heavy silence for what we do not know. Suddenly Remey gets up and goes into the house and comes back with another six-pack of a cheap American beer I associate with the North. He sits down, cracks open a can, takes a swig and continues to stare. Nighttime in the bayou is a noisy affair, frogs, crickets, strange bird sounds, warm and humid, with that same fish tank smell. Remey's quiet rocking, back and forth, *creek-crick, creek-crick,* sounds like a tied-up boat rolling with the waves.

"Y'all want a beer?"

The voice comes from somewhere else, as if from a ventriloquist, disembodied. Not a deep voice—flat, without inflection, heartbreaking.

We both answer quickly in the affirmative, but with caution, not wanting to spook whatever impulse it is that has made the offer. It is a blessing, a gift, as if a wild animal has come to us, cautiously sniffing. We stay still, no sudden moves, quiet.

Remey reaches down and hands us the cardboard carton, and he is looking at us. It is the first time he has looked at us directly. In the dark it is hard to read his expression but the vibe is the same as his voice, flat and dead. Paul pulls out the beers, hands me one and gives the carton back to Remey. Thanks, we say.

"Where you guys from?" asks Remey.

"New York," I say.

"California," says Paul.

After that Remey is quiet. Neither of us knows what to say. I almost speak a couple of times but cannot summon the effort. It all seems meaningless and empty. The grief coming from Remey just stops you in your tracks.

10

Simian wreckage below the great river > Going to see the war planner > Dreadful energy of a cosseted toddler > Springboks 1, warthogs 0 > Short-order genius from Newgate prison > Thank you, masked man

The bounce is a little southwest of Houma, more of the same brilliant green, blue watery world with legions of snowy egrets flapping their wings, trailing long thin black legs as if wrapped in dancer's tights in graceful parallel, their feet extended *en pointe*, yellow like a chicken's. I love watching their white bodies against the blue water, never quite believing their reality. They seem misplaced somehow, as if meant to belong in Africa or South America. Paul says in fact their habitat extends to South America. They clump in trees by the dozens, bulky and graceless, and stalk the marshes like slightly tipsy dowagers looking for lost earrings. It is only in flight they look balletic. Seeing them flying with the marshes and swamps below and the great expanse of the Gulf in the distance triggers something primordial, almost mystical. I never tire of watching them.

Each part of the day reveals a different aspect of these wild white water birds, evening perhaps the most beautiful of all, flying silent and luminous through the darkening background as night spirits

take over and mysteries deepen. A quiet descends like the soft, terrifying mouth of a vampire and the birds move and move and finally disappear. In the morning the flying birds reflect the sun with
a fleeting, intense beauty and I think of Remey Bujeau rocking back
and forth on his father's porch. I had only got a couple hours sleep
that night on the porch and this after Remey finally rose around
two or three o'clock and walked inside to his bed where he probably stared at the ceiling for another three hours, maybe dropping
off for a bit of tormented sleep, back on the porch drinking beer at
daybreak, before we woke. Mr. Bujeau cooked breakfast, eggs, grits
and more of that good strong coffee with sweetened condensed and
Paul talked about his quest to re-connect with his father and about
the book he was working on. Mr. Bujeau listened quietly and told us
about the good relationship he'd had with his own father, how he'd
died in a storm while fishing, his body never recovered. Mr. Bujeau was 16 at the time and supposed to go that morning but instead
stayed home to take care of his mother. It was a storm that came
up suddenly, as they sometimes did around these parts. After breakfast Mr. Bujeau and Paul pushed Rosalina down the road as Remey
watched from the porch. With the little car idling at the side of the
road I got out and we said our goodbyes. We waved to Remey but
he did not respond.

***

On route 90 then, east through Lafourche Parish, Des Alle-
mands, Gretna, across another Erector Set bridge spanning the Mississippi, muddy and wide as ever, my second crossing, on into the
sinful city itself, going directly to the French Quarter to a place Paul
had been ten years earlier, the Café du Monde. The Café du Monde,
next to and actually below the Mississippi, protected by a massive levee, is an open, airy place full of tourists sipping coffee and

munching beignets (beignets? Paul has told me about beignets—bin-YAYS—warm, crispy, fresh-fried doughnuts without holes, covered with powdered sugar), blithefully unconcerned about the monster flowing by above their heads, the world's third largest river, bloated with spring runoff, carrying some incomprehensible volume of water which, if breaking through, would drown them in an instant and dissolve all the beignets, powdered sugar and coffee ever created into nothingness, sweeping the whole inconsequential mash into the Gulf of Mexico's wide waiting maw along with all the broad-beamed Germans and Texans in their polyester polo shirts and Bermudas, the latest 35 millimeter cameras dangling from their fat red necks, polishing off those last bits of beignets. Into the maw! Gone!

The place is jammed but we find a small round table in back covered with the wreckage of the previous occupants as if a pack of howler monkeys had swept through, devouring and destroying, leaving an absolute shambles in its wake, crumpled napkins flung carelessly, a few soggy as sponges, sweating, near-empty glasses of iced coffee, four or five small plates stacked precariously, discarded chewed straws, used spoons lying on the table with small congealing pools of café au lait in their bowls, scattered grains of sugar, a corner of a gnawed beignet, a Café du Monde ashtray filled with ashes and three cigarettes, all with lipstick stains (I picture them, three office girls from Nebraska, Mutual of Omaha, two busty and cheerful, one skinny and neurotic) and everywhere powdered sugar, the table, the ashtray, the top and sides of the sugar dispenser, dissolving to a glutinous paste on the sides of the wet glasses, piled up in the plates, all over the napkins, covering the seats, the floor. A couple of pigeons, bold as Bombay crows, light on the railing behind the table, flapping their pestilent wings. We dust the powder off the seats and sit tentatively, away from the table, waiting for the waiter or busboy to do his or her thing and a middle-aged, tall, light-skinned black man in a white apron and wearing a Café du Monde paper garrison cap stuck straight in the middle of his head comes over all business and dour face with the tools of his trade, a large plastic container into which he briskly deposits everything but the sugar dispenser and the ashtray, which he knocks clean and replaces, taking a dubious-looking rag out of a sudsy bucket and swabs the table down in four emphatic swipes, leaving a trail of soapy streaks that are still wet when the waiter, a stocky middle-aged white man looking like Huey Long in Café du Monde getup, his cap at a jauntier angle, takes our order, beignets and iced coffee, lickety-split and vanishes, leaving us to scope out the rest of the clientele.

We are in the middle of a happy-faced, bliss-feeding, lip-smacking, finger-licking, beignet-masticating, coffee-slurping, white powder orgy, as if this is a special corner of heaven where gluttony is smilingly tolerated, as if to prove once and for all that God is indeed from New Orleans, the Café du Monde a favored place where all types and species gather like some African watering hole in dry season. It's a timeout, get busy, eat-them-beignets, smile-on-your-brother munchfest, an open-air horizontal Tower of Babel where tongues from all lands mingle in the soft heat under the green and white canopy, my high school colors, very nice. A warm musky breeze blows in from the river and you can smell the crackling beignets frying and the rich chicory coffee. On the sidewalk an Earl Bostic impersonator plays *Ain't Misbehavin'* on a beat-up tenor that looks like it is from King Oliver's time. He is good, too. And the powdered sugar and beignet crumbs fly, like fourth of July, like Normandy, like Lindy's tickertape parade, the many brains under the café canopy a collective one-brain in thrall to a sugary, crunchy, chewy, slurpy bliss, taste buds in open lust, complete abandon, sex, power, style, class, death, mere secondary concerns, happy people, what a scene.

Earl Bostic finishes *Ain't Misbehavin'* and Huey Long comes with an easy tray compared to some of the Texas-sized orders I have seen nearby, a commercial pilot flying a kite, our two little orders and iced coffees swooped onto our still damp table, taking our money, counting change, bim-bam just like that and then splitting, whoosh! Gone! The old musician starts singing *September Song* in a rugged voice, you know, the one that goes, *"It's a long while, from May to December..."* and I think about Butterfly, how this is May, the month we have met. December. When will I see her again? What is she doing and should I call her? Does she even care? I bet she would like this place. And there right smack in front us are two plates of warm powdery beignets, three each, two glistening iced café au laits and we just look at the whole shebang for a long five seconds, saying, Wow! Sheeit! And then jumping in with some little thought of keeping the powdered sugar at bay, kind of holding the warm beignet out over the table just so but after the first bite it explodes all over you and the battle is on, the hell with it, you are just like everyone else, and you get your own style, your plan of attack, but you still end up covered from head to foot and that is just fine, deliciously fine, just don't wear black.

After the first onslaught we sit back and exhale, already covered with powdered sugar, each of us with two thirds remaining, smiling, thinking that even with grits, eggs and coffee only a couple of hours ago this is going to be a two-order affair, impossible something so good enjoyed only once. Paul and I look at each other, roll our eyes and dive in again, taking good noisy slurps of iced chicory coffee between mouthfuls of beignet. In spite of all or at least a modicum of the best Emily Post intentions the battle to maintain decorum is lost after the first bite. In my fervor I keep inhaling powdered sugar and coughing, a real Café du Monde tyro, dipping the chewed end of my beignet into the powdery pile collecting on the plate, greedy for the stuff, slurping more coffee, used napkins crumpled and scattered like the dead at Antietam, our table a battlefield, second onslaught bearing down. The people at the table next to us, an obese middle-aged white couple wearing matching green bowling shirts, red Bermudas and sandals, the woman loaded down with jewelry, ponderously rise smacking their lips and lumber off, leaving a miserly tip and a grubby *Times-Picayune*, which Paul snatches, folds and whacks against the table leg to get the powder off. Looking at the front page he exclaims with a mixture of contempt and excitement, "I'll be goddamned. Walt Rostow's speaking tonight at Tulane."

Walt Rostow is a name I am familiar with as one of the architects of the Vietnam War, one of the big-brained sluggers of the Kennedy and Johnson administrations, but apart from that I do not know much about him. Paul shows me a picture on the front page of a tight-mouthed, high-domed, middle-aged man with clear-frame glasses, dark jacket, white shirt, collar pin, black tie, exuding an aura of absolute certitude and comfort, a man used to walking on polished floors in polished shoes and eating rare sirloin three times a week. Just looking at him is enough to get my blood boiling, arousing the usual mixture feeling of fear and loathing. His topic is "The Necessity of Victory—The Realities of the Vietnam Conflict."

We devour the rest of our beignets and order another round from the squat Huey Long, who comes right back with deft movements slipping our delectables into the thick of battle, taking the money from Paul with strong, broad hands covered with black hair lush like bayou undergrowth sprouting up over thick wrists and muscular forearms. His quick sure movements have a kind of gracefulness that reminds me of Yogi Berra pouncing on a bunt and throwing out the lead runner, astonishing for someone who looks so unlike the part. He is about fifty, neatly put together, a Las Vegas croupier, tough, no-nonsense, not unfriendly. We speak briefly, laying out our stories. He has been working at the Café du Monde for fifteen years. His name is Carmen (I think of Carmen Basilio) and he was born in a little town near Natchez, from generations of farmers.

The café crowd thins as we finish our beignets and coffee at a less frenetic pace, more than a little full but satisfied, likely a normal state in this big-eating city packed levee to levee with voluptuaries and exotics. Earl Bostic is sitting down, a weary expression on his suddenly much older-looking black face, a boxer between rounds, his battered sax lying haphazardly across skinny thighs, shiny black pants rising up on his shins, black shoes, white socks. Rostow is speaking at eight o'clock. Admission is free. Paul says let's go see the sonofabitch. I say why not.

***

We consult with Carmen about a place to stay and he gives us the name of a place on Prytania, Le Bateau Rose, a rooming house run by an aunt of his. We get up to leave. The old saxophonist, back on his feet and playing *Summertime*, looks twenty years younger. He catches our eye and winks as we turn to walk down Decatur to the French Market. Decatur is filled with drooling polyester-clad zombie rednecks and their fat children shuffling in and out of stores that sell post cards, corny T-shirts, stuffed baby alligators, cheap cookbooks and confederate flags. The Market is a different scene altogether, a busy, hard-used place that might be Algiers or Port-au-Prince where funky vendors, black and white, gesture and call out in their rich Louisiana accents over stands of plump red Creole tomatoes, piles of peanuts, stacks of sugar cane, rough hills of fat sweet potatoes, plastic containers of Ponchatoula strawberries, Vidalia onions, mounds of garlic, all sorts of greens, beans, oranges, apples, colorfully-labeled cotton bags stuffed with Louisiana rice, countless varieties of pepper sauces stacked in brilliant pyramids, multi-hued snow balls, gator meat, andouille sausage, jerky, crab boil, cookbooks, trinkets and junk of all description.

Leaving the market we head up Dumaine and find a cigar shop on Royal where Paul buys a couple of two-dollar smokes and we light up on the corner, bellies full of beignets, but for the tourists, cars and electricity right back in the 19th century, a couple of misfits in any century, though feeling less so in the French Quarter, an eminently agreeable place, we agree, Royal Street in particular especially charming, the shops fancier, less touristy, easy to imagine the old life in this Caribbean melting pot of race and culture, steamy ante-bellum shenanigans, cutthroat mercantilism, cotton, sugar, slavery, fabulous wealth, all dependent on the great artery of a river that burst its banks every fifteen years or so causing massive destruction. Humans are pretty easy to figure. Give them some good water to hunker down next to and they raise all kinds of hell. And the Mississippi is one hellacious good water. You can feel its languid flowing power blocks away, smell its humid funk, a lazy anaconda as big as a mountain slithering along in its channel. None of this would exist without it. And where are the ceremonies and offerings to the great river? Surely the yearly sacrifice of a local politician's virgin daughter or eldest son wouldn't be too much to ask. Another failing of Christianity.

Yet another failing of Christianity lies a block to the north and it is called Bourbon Street, which we can smell before even getting there, a piss/vomit/beer miasma laced with aromas from a dozen restaurants opening their kitchens and cash registers for lunch, some gumbo here, catfish there, jambalaya, boiled crabs, oysters fried and raw, simmering roux, rémoulade, red beans and rice, crawfish bisque, shrimp étouffée, hush puppies, po-boys, crème brûlée, pecan pie, all the legendary dishes come to life mixed with that good tourist effluent, perfume to the nostrils of local merchants. I can only imagine what it smells like after Mardi Gras.

The foot traffic gets noticeably seedier the closer we get to Bourbon, up Toulouse, leering bleary-eyed frat boys, sad-looking soldiers, tired waitresses, strippers, hookers and their peacock pimps, bloated lecherous salesmen and conventioneers, gawking corn-fed silent majority families, one corrupt overweight Irish cop, junkies, sadists, runaways and outright crazies, the music from two-dozen jukeboxes blaring Dixieland, Cajun, zydeco, swamp pop, psychedelic, country, Al Hirt, Louis Armstrong, Jose Feliciano, Pete Fountain, Clifton Chenier, Waylon Jennings, Ray Charles, The Moody Blues. On the corner of Toulouse and Bourbon a group of hyperkinetic skinny black kids in ragged clothes with bottle caps attached to their shoes tap dance for change placed awkwardly by tourists into an old cigar box, its corners held together with grimy electrical tape. They pick up the box suddenly and race off, as if trying to keep one step ahead of something, the cops, hunger, a life too tightly-wound. Most of the clubs on Bourbon are open for business, for drinking, for eating, for ogling the sparsely clad mostly young strippers lounging in doorways or noisy bars open to the sidewalk with people already heavy into it at noontime, the regulars, end-of-the-line cats holed up at places like this and Key West and other seedy Caribbean hideaways, types in former times that might have hired on as deck hands on steamers and whaling ships, or so my overheated imagination suggests, and of course, yes, pirate ships. Jean Lafitte is everywhere, half rogue, half hero, as much a part of the fabric of this place as Louis Armstrong, Andrew Jackson and Marie Laveau, the voodoo queen. It is tackily played up for the tourists but you know at some point in the history of this hothouse, violent, fever-ridden swamp town Lafitte was a real dude who did some real things that would not go down too well in Peoria or Lindenhurst.

We decide to head back to Rosalina on North Peters Street just outside the Quarter wanting to make sure we get a room at Le Bateau Rose but poor Rosalina, looking drab, beat up and forlorn, is hemmed in between a blue '57 Chevy and a white '63 Cadillac, both convertibles, and so we walk up Canal over to St. Charles Avenue past The Pearl Oyster Bar with its great neon sign and characters inside looking like something out of a Weegee photograph and get the streetcar, throwing 15 cents apiece into the farebox, going through lower St. Charles and its city buildings past a little dive called the Hummingbird Grill that looks like fun, gawking out the windows, unabashed tourists on the famed New Orleans streetcar clattering and clanging up St. Charles around Lee Circle where the old general stands ramrod straight, arms folded, on a thin Doric column high enough to check out the happenings in the French Quarter, not looking at all pleased.

We get out and walk up Melpomene then down Prytania past Terpsichore, Euterpe and Polymnia, euphonious familiar-sounding names, though we can only guess how they would be pronounced here, Paul informing me that all but Prytania Greek muses, the only one whose realm of inspiration he can remember being Clio, the muse of history. The only Cleo I know is the droll Basset hound on "The People's Choice." As we cross Polymnia a beat up Chevy rolls up behind us and a redneck kid pokes his head out asking for dope and when we say we don't have any he calls us "fuckin' hippies" and the car speeds off, the kid leaning out the window and cursing. "That guy could use a beignet," says Paul.

Le Bateau Rose is as I had imagined, a faded pink slightly seedy two-story wooden building with beds of tropical-looking flowers on either side of the entrance. The lobby has a pay phone and smells of incense and has worn red velvet wallpaper with silver fleurs-de-lis. A red-carpeted rickety staircase with a wrought iron white banister leads to the second floor. Paul rings the bell at the office counter where the sweet incense burns and after a moment the door at the end of the hallway leading outside opens and a tall, supple-limbed young woman with full, long auburn hair and wearing a red one-piece bathing suite walks down the hall towards us with a gentle smile on her pretty, slightly tomboyish face. She is barefoot and her thighs are firm and strong and a little bit of pubic hair curls from her crotch. Tussocks of dark hair sprout from her armpits.

She goes into the office telling us she has been out back at the pool (a pool!) and appears behind the counter smiling and taking Paul's money for a room with two beds on the second floor, $18, handing over the key and eyeing us both with a touch of playfulness that flips me out. Her name is Alexandria, a law student at Tulane working part time at Le Bateau Rose and yes, she is going to the Rostow speech tonight along with several of her friends who have a little welcome planned for the war planner. With a sugar-soft drawl that reminds me of Lulu Delilah without the loop-di-loop, richly toned and intelligent, she says she hopes to see us there and don't you know all thoughts of ending the war, confronting a vile architect of imperialism and all such righteous things immediately disappear. I have only one thought and it does not have much to do with the NLF, but what the hell, everything is a revolutionary act these days. Emma Goldman said she didn't want any part of a revolution that didn't swing, which sounds all right with me. We linger at the counter as she sashays down the hall out the door to the swimming pool, long-legged and soft-swaying and Paul and I look at each other wide-eyed, smiling like drunken frat boys, as gone as we can be.

The room is a funky, wainscoted two-bed affair painted white with a window overlooking an alley with ripe overflowing garbage cans, prowling cats and a couple of forlorn, dusty banana trees. There is no air conditioning and the room is hot. I open the window and the garbage smell, the heat and tropical foliage transport me to some little dive in Saigon and I wonder for a moment if I should not be there, not for any ridiculous patriotic reasons but for the experience, for a certain comradeship with my peers, the poor bastards out there suffering and dying. After all, it is *my* war, I will never get another one, but the Remey Bujeaus of the world counsel me otherwise and the destruction and suffering caused by my country is worth no amount of extreme experience. My attraction is more like Fowler's in *The Quiet American*, which I read my senior year in college, kin to his disgust with the West and the allure of the exotic tropical. Fowler is a character I relate to in my American, Holden Caulfield sort of way. Though Fowler's world-weary sophistication is beyond me I can imagine him as an English, much older Holden, tired, low addiction to opium, Vietnamese girlfriend decades younger, the fowler with his bird, cynical, disgusted with it all but still marginally attached, still with a sense of morality. Nope, no combat for the likes of me. Better the life of journalist Fowler in Saigon, mostly out of harm's way.

***

Paul goes to the lobby to call Carmen on the pay phone as I sit watching the cats in the alley stand up to stick their heads into the garbage, coming out with things they drag into the shade and chew. There is a powerful sweet smell mixed in with the general rankness that likely comes from a squat magnolia tree against the building with its shiny, artificial-looking deep green leaves and large white blossoms.

Paul comes back. It is around four o'clock. We are concerned about Rosalina. Leaving Le Bateau Rose we walk down Felicity in the warm, pleasantly humid afternoon thick with the New Orleans smells I already love, sweet magnolias, tropical flowers, the fat rolling river, rotting garbage. Feral cats prowl the alleys. Ahead, the streetcar clacks and clangs. This is not the United States. At wide-open St. Charles Avenue we jump onto the streetcar, throwing in our 15 cents, the lovely open-air electric trolley rumbling down the tracks as we watch the conductor manipulate his bewildering shifts and levers, looping around the old general on his fluted perch, down Carondelet to Canal, jumping out and walking to North Peters where the white Cadillac in front of Rosalina has been replaced by a green Citroen with Mississippi license plates but leaving enough room to get the old girl out. We jump-start her right there and putter back to Prytania, finding a spot near Le Bateau Rose. The beautiful Alexandria is getting ready to leave, dressed in tight faded jeans, sandals and a thin white cotton sweater, no bra, her thick long hair splayed all over her shoulders. She seems pleased to see us and gives directions to Jones Hall, on the Tulane campus, where Rostow will be speaking at eight o'clock. Should be interesting, she says, hope to see you there, and out the front door she goes, smiling, a hint of magnolia herself, into the warm fragrant afternoon, a leather handbag over her shoulder, Alexandria, law school goddess. We trudge up the stairs deep in our own scandalous thoughts, then, pausing, not even bothering to go into our room, turning around and walking back down and out Le Bateau Rose onto Prytania, vaguely wondering where to eat before Rostow and glancing around for the wondrous woman, nowhere to be seen.

It is five o'clock and we figure there is time to get back on the streetcar and go into the Quarter, get some real New Orleans food and still see the fucker Rostow. Walking up Royal we spot the Acme Oyster House on Iberville and make a beeline, seating ourselves at a wooden table where a tough-looking, middle-aged, bleach-blond waitress in a tight yellow outfit takes our order for jambalaya, a dozen raw oysters and a couple of Dixie beers. The old restaurant has an open, spacious feeling and is filled with the bracing, briny smell of fresh oysters, like chilled blood. Only a handful of customers is present. It is just before the dinner rush and the cooks and waitresses are getting things lined up, as if preparing for battle.

"You know, that bastard Rostow looks a little like my father," says Paul, his blue eyes serious under the straw hat. He looks like my father too, I say, the same bald head, the same challenging expression, the same well-fed, meat-eating certitude. Paul has seen Rostow on television and has a perverse desire to see if he will become even more enraged and disgusted by the guy in person. We compare our fathers' physical descriptions and discover they are similar types, husky, bald, blue eyes, aggressive, tough, around the same height, about five-foot-eight. My father is Jewish, Paul's Catholic. Both had battled through rough childhoods, Paul's father in Chicago, mine in New York, both intelligent, self-made men, both having deferred dreams of creativity for more remunerative pursuits. My father had trained as an architect but became a photographer for a family magazine in the days when photography was taking off as a commercial medium, turning a hobby of his into a profession. Later, he became a fashion photographer. Paul's father had dreams of creating engineering masterpieces but had turned to teaching. "My father used to say, 'Those who can, do. Those who can't, teach.' But he really loved teaching and he was good at it. It pretty much destroyed him to give it up. So he had a kind of double frustration, lost dreams of becoming a famous engineer, and then sadness over giving up teaching. On top of all this his wife was dying. That's what got the drinking started."

The bleached old biddy brings two small bowls of jambalaya, which we half-finish, and a platter of cold oysters along with three packets of Saltine crackers, small bowls of ketchup, horseradish and the beers. I have never had oysters but after summer nights of high school drinking my friends and I would go to a favorite place and slurp down cherrystone clams with inebriated abandon. The clams were terrific and I loved them drunk or not, but now, looking at these large, slippery, stomach-like creatures before me I feel the need of three or four hours of boozing before consuming them. Paul notices my hesitation and laughs, showing the way with goodly amounts of horseradish and ketchup, chased with a cracker and a healthy slug of beer. After three I am bloated and a little queasy but force myself to finish the half dozen, a mistake, as you will see, and then eat the rest of the jambalaya, which settles uneasily around the six sinister bivalves lying on the floor of my stomach.

Leaving the restaurant we head back down Royal, crossing Canal and then onto St. Charles, walking past The Pearl Oyster Bar, at whose interior I studiously avoid looking, onto the streetcar past the Hummingbird Grill with its heavy, greasy aroma of hamburgers and fried onions, now manifestly unappetizing, clanging and rumbling counterclockwise around the high-up general who seems decidedly pissed-off to be stuck on top of the ridiculous column missing all the fun or maybe wishing he was back on the plantation and away from this Caribbean Gomorrah. I imagine the thin pedestal taking off like a Mercury Redstone rocket and shooting the old soldier into suborbital flight. As a kid I had been fascinated by Alan Shepard's 15-minute ride.

We keep on going, past the muses into the Garden District where the Ritz Crackers live in their white antebellum Greek Revival mansions sipping mint juleps and reading their Wall Street Journals, the avenue and recessed houses canopied with their "majestic"—no other way to describe them—oaks, stopping next to Audubon Park and stepping out into the still warm May evening, excited now, the terrible Rostow a mortar's lob away across St. Charles on Freret Street at Jones Hall. There are plenty of students walking around, straight-looking for the most part, Tulane obviously not a hotbed of radicalism, enjoying the beautiful weather, a month or two from the sweltering New Orleans summer and 8,000 miles from Vietnam, most of them likely not aware that one of the leading architects and apologists for the war is probably sipping bourbon and branch water in an oak-paneled office with some university muckety-muck or looking in a bathroom mirror straightening his Brooks Brothers tie and admiring his smug well-battened jowls, the Chateaubriand consumed at one of the city's four-star restaurants a half-hour earlier resting pleasingly in his stomach, thoroughly masticated, marinating in the high-toned gastric juices, getting ready for the dive into the small intestine and then, some time the next day, the man sitting down with a faraway look, the effluvium rising around him like rotting Vietnamese corpses. This is what I am thinking as we spy Jones Hall, a little like my old high school with some of the same feeling approaching I did as a freshman, excitement, anxiety, a bit cowed by the authority it represents with its Greek columns and red-brick solidity. This is the *establishment,* and I am about to be in close proximity to one of its hottest and smelliest shits, a bona fide flesh-rending carnivore of the first order—a *Rostowsaurus.*

"You know," says Paul, exuding some of the human cannon ball energy I have witnessed a few times before, the first conversation at the Café Med, his controlled confrontation with the sharply-creased Officer Nichols, his *Wretched of the Earth* riffs, "the closer I get to this sonofabitch the angrier I become. I just might have to say something to the motherfucker." A Young Americans for Freedom type in brown jacket, tan slacks and loafers, his short brown hair neatly parted and held rigidly in place with a slathering of Vitalis or some similar morally commendable toiletry, a corporate eagle in training, overhears Paul and gives us both a sharp look. "This guy is one of the chief strategists and cheerleaders for this abominable war. Abominable is the right word too. There's nothing he likes more than bombing the shit out of things."

None of that nastiness is evident now on this balmy magnolia-scented evening on the charming, laid-back campus, the majority of those coming to see the mastermind obviously conservative, adulatory types, the YAFers, the neatly- dressed law and government students smugly assured of their place in the golden corner of history, the older, equally conservative-looking males, professors perhaps, and their overdressed, auburn-eyed, tightly-coiffed women, all relaxed and serious, in their element. The beautiful Alexandria had said she and some friends had a "welcome" planned for Rostow. What it is I can only imagine but it creates a keen sense of anticipation and excitement, especially since virtually everyone standing around or walking into Jones Hall looks like a State Department functionary buzzing with eagerness to see one of their masters flash his teeth and godlike intellect. There are a few suspicious, possibly subversive types scattered about, individuals seemingly independent from one another, and I wonder if they are part of the contingent that has the "welcome" planned for Mr. Rostow. There is no sign of Alexandria. It is 7:45. Time to go in.

***

The room is large, airy, well-lit by high windows, a lecture hall really, with a huge blackboard and polished oak lectern at the front, the whole place redolent of high-mindedness, legions of callow, eager students, a ghostly murmur of young, serious, southern voices, debating, questioning, laughing, decades of erudite blackboard scribblings vanished to dust, and most of all an atmosphere of supremely confident moral and intellectual authority. The voices piling up in the room now are older, more sophisticated and more self-assured than the usual undergraduate cacophony, creating an intimidating aura of patrician solidity and exclusivity. The professors, lawyers, politicians and bankers, or whatever cream-crusted echelon they belong to, outnumber the freak contingent by a huge margin. The hostile stares begin right away, many of them directed at Paul and me as obvious outsiders, though there are a few others scattered around the room that look almost as un-American as we do.

About 150 wooden folding chairs fill the room, neatly arranged in two sections with an aisle down the middle, most occupied, the rest of the people standing around in conversation, peripherally aware of us and the handful of other unsavory types in their midst. Though they represent the conservative wing of the establishment and all its righteous bloodthirsty power (generalizing here, of course. Surely there are a few liberals present—the ones who originally supported the war and then changed their minds, thinking it a "mistake," provisionally anti-war until the New York Times starts sniffing the asshole of the next necessary conflict) I detect an air of unease, even defensiveness. Their country and its war have been under harsh attack on the starkest moral grounds for many years and it has taken its toll. Their certainty has been shaken and they do not like it. Rostow with his strong convictions and greasy arguments is here to reassure them. Our presence is an irritant, a disturbance in the fabric of their universe. I do not doubt that some of them, in their more forgiving moments, would gladly have us removed to a secure facility in a harsh and isolated place.

At first we don't see him but a kind of discordant energy in the corner towards the front alerts us to a tanned, neatly dressed and smiling Rostow in his Mr. Peepers glasses surrounded by a gaggle of fawning middle-aged university types and ten feet away the beautiful Alexandria eyeing him coldly, sitting next to what are probable fellow travelers, like her, casually dressed, the unofficial Rostow welcoming committee, harboring their secret plans. Looking around the room I see others who might be with Alexandria's

356 | RICHARD WARD

detachment, young, moderately long hair, informally attired, intelligent-looking and, I imagine, or it could be my own sense of impending drama, full of tense anticipation.

Rostow's resemblance to my father is more of a type than close physical similarity, a bit taller and thinner with a slightly longer face and heavier jowls, the face of a spoiled and belligerent baby. I know little about Rostow and nothing of his childhood but he strikes me as having been the love object of protective and doting parents, possessed of an inner certainty, an iron compass that never falters or admits doubt, product of a parental nest that protected, coddled and buttressed every step of the way. In this supposed regard he is unlike my father, who from the start had battled on his own and whose convictions came from hard experience at home and the streets of Hell's Kitchen. There is a softness and smugness about Rostow that I dislike immediately, and knowing he is responsible for so much violence and misery turns that repulsion into something close to hatred. He resembles my father with his tanned, strong, bald head and aura of certainty about the world's reality and his place in that tough, necessarily cruel struggle, as they both see it, though unlike my father he has bombed civilians to score his points. My father does not like the military and had not fought in the Second World War. He has talked vaguely a few times about working with the Department of War on propaganda stuff but it is all a mystery. I wonder if Rostow has seen combat. It does not look like he has. Paul is staring hard at the man, obviously having his own emotional reaction, possibly also thinking about his father. "He does remind me of my father in some ways," I say.

"Mine too," says Paul. "Only this guy's a war criminal. My old man's just a hardheaded lost soul. I'll take my sonofabitch over this sonofabitch any day. At least he's not up to his forehead in blood. Look at that smug asshole. He looks pretty fuckin' pleased with himself, doesn't he?"

As if aware of our hostility Rostow shoots us a glance, his face darkening, no doubt dismissing us immediately as inconsequential, though potentially nettlesome. Ants at his picnic. Running off with the crumbs. Getting into the potato salad. Well, fuck you, I think. You're in for a surprise, cocksucker.

It seems pretty obvious that my hatred of the authority that rules the country and the world, an authority that betrays its children and mocks and bombs to bloody pieces the moral principles to which it gives lip service is, to some degree anyway, rooted in my relationship with my father. Rostow could look like Santa Claus and I would still despise him, but the similar appearance drives the point home more deeply. My father is not a monster like Rostow but he has always been a distant, powerful figure. On the other hand looking at Rostow fills me with an ambivalence that I have to acknowledge. He is not an unattractive man and what he represents, what this setting represents, the power and glory of a certain tradition, a classical tradition, tied up with my own jumble of emotional associations, triggers a vague but undeniable desire to *belong*. This lecture hall, venue for a classically-trained intellectual arguing for the supremacy of a murderous state policy, could just as naturally the following evening be the setting for a classically-trained musician playing Bach cello suites. I am dealing with centuries of culture and class, the very thing that my father, tough son of immigrant Jews, has aspired to. These august, scholarly and WASP-ish settings with their well-heeled attendees are not foreign to me. I had gone to private schools as a child. My mother's father and grandfather had been Harvard men. My father graduated from Columbia. My mother's two sisters had gone to Smith. Though I have fallen far, my academic history a disaster, such things are ingrained. In a sense I am home, as much as Rostow. He is family.

***

But fuck all these jokers, I think, there is only one family, the human family. I can keep Bach and throw away the bombs. Bach is mine as much as Rostow's or anyone else's. And the responsibility for the bombs is as much mine as anyone's too. My stomach grumbles with a heavy anger—and queasiness—those fucking oysters sloshing around in there causing trouble. Not a good thing. It hadn't been too long ago I'd puked in Albuquerque, and before that, Big Sur. Jesus. Paul stares at Rostow, who is moving towards the front of the room, the truckling squirrels giving way. A tall, gray-haired, gray-suited man with a severe gaunt face and rimless glasses stands unsmiling at the lectern looking at the crowd. Rostow, all business now, his jaw firm, sits down next to the lectern, his pale gimlet gaze launched out over the audience, fixed on a distant spot, perhaps a new bombing target.

The more I look at Rostow the more my stomach churns. I feel light-headed and disoriented. Beads of sweat break out on my forehead. Paul's anger is palpable, heat radiating from a scorched summer road. Napalm. Children melted to the bone. Rostow's bombs. We move to a couple of aisle seats on the left side, towards the back where I have a clear view of Alexandria next to a female with red, Datura-like frizzy hair, both clutching handbags in their laps and leaning forward, staring intently at Rostow. On her other side is a black guy I hadn't noticed before, maybe just come in, medium sized Afro, black leather jacket. A Panther at Tulane? A sister sits in our group of chairs, a few rows in front of us, another mid-sized Afro, the only blacks in the place. At the exit a dim-looking cop stands rigidly, complacently eyeing the crowd. I look around again and see more young potentially troublesome types. There are only a couple of outright freaks, not counting Paul and me, if you would put us in that category, a couple sitting together two rows behind Alexandria, an unshaven Jerry Rubin look-alike with brown frizzy hair and a goatee, wearing a faded blue work shirt and small round dark glasses, and a short, angel-faced chick with straight blond hair and dumpling cheeks, wearing a red serape and those same little round dark glasses.

The rest of the people move to their seats and sit expectantly. The tall gray man at the lectern clears his throat. Rostow clasps his hands and looks at the floor. The man speaks. "Good evening. We are exceedingly privileged tonight to have with us one of the country's leading scholars and public servants. Dr. Rostow has had a long and distinguished career as an intellectual, author and advisor to Presidents Kennedy and Johnson, serving as Special Assistant for National Security Affairs to President Johnson from 1966 to 1969. His seminal book, *The Stages of Economic Growth: A non-communist manifesto*, has been instrumental in shaping the country's foreign policy for the—"

A weird sound, something between a moan and a snort, followed by giggling, comes from the freak couple behind Alexandria. Heads turn in their direction. Rostow looks up. The gray man looks sternly at the couple and continues. "—past decade. Not only have Dr. Rostow's economic theories been influential in shaping government policy—"

Another snorting sound comes from the front of the room where three of the casually dressed students sit. More giggling. The gray man looks over the audience threateningly, with a hint of apprehension, as if a substitute teacher contending with a bunch of potentially troublesome seventh-graders. Something afoot. Rostow stares hard at the students, squinting his eyes, an expression I have seen on my father's face many times. Some of the Rostow supporters look around with angry faces. This is getting interesting. Interesting except for my stomach, which feels like a bag filled with small rotting corpses. Oysters. I can feel Paul's seething energy next to me but I dare not look because I don't want to move my head too fast for fear of getting sick. I swallow hard and take a couple of deep breaths as the man goes on with his introduction, clearly now on fast-forward. "Mr. Rostow, excuse me, Dr. Rostow, is here tonight to explain, in rather truncated form, I should think (someone snickers at this), the lineaments of his economic theories and how they pertain to the US government's foreign policy and in particular its relevance to the conflict in Vietnam. So without further ado, I present to you our distinguished guest, Dr. Walt Rostow."

There is an aggressive burst of applause from the Rostow contingent as if to preempt any negative response but it is not loud enough to drown out the boos and animal noises coming from the around the room. Rostow rises from his seat with a forced smile and nods to the gray man. The cop in the back looks worried, probably wondering why his superiors hadn't the foresight to assign more officers to this seemingly innocuous event. Who the fuck is this Rostow guy, anyway?

Rostow positions himself behind the lectern, grips the sides and nods to a couple in the front. Then he looks around at whom he now knows as enemies, the goddamned bastards, and sets his jaw, smiling. Without thanking his introducer he launches in. "It seems obvious to me, and would to anyone, for that matter, who knows the slightest thing about history and human nature—"

And here he pauses, the room absolutely quiet. I have to hand it to the fucker, he looks good up there, tanned, confident, certain of his brainpower and royalty, absolute master of the groundlings in front of him, including the piddling admirers, the dark tie neatly supported by the gold collar pin, the dark tweed jacket and gleaming white shirt, glittering clear-framed glasses. The fucker is a dresser, probably sharpened up after his ascendancy to presidential ear-nibbler. Dressed to kill. How many deaths is he responsible for? How many children has he blown to pieces? He looks at the crowd with a headmaster's assurance, knowing he has the slavering obeisance of his supporters and now trying by force of will to intimidate the critics and provocateurs. We are not even beneath contempt, slugs in hibernation, but we are here so he has to deal with us, as if he has stepped in a small pile of dog shit next to the lectern. *Here I am,* he seems to say, *former advisor to presidents, their intellectual superior, in fact. You are nothing, you know nothing, you have seen nothing!* The fucker *is* intimidating, just standing there looking at us with all his contempt and all he represents, all of his experience. I suddenly feel sicker. The oysters and jambalaya surge in my gut. I swallow hard to keep the horrible mix down. The audience is silent, waiting for Rostow's next words. In the two or three seconds he pauses to look at the crowd he seems to grow several inches taller.

"—that Marxist/Leninist ideology is nothing more than a puerile fantasy, a wet dream for the disaffected and alienated misfits who occupy the margins of society." He looks around the room confidently, a subtle murmur of gleeful appreciation at the master's words rising from the suits and YAFers. The hostiles sit in stunned fury. Paul laughs. Heads turn in his direction. Here we go, I think. I am going to puke. Out of the question. Not now. I swallow frantically, my head spinning, trying not to think about Jesus and the cats eating my vomit, the crack on my skull and the puking at Big Sur. Paul looks at me with concern. Rostow, on the offensive, plows ahead.

"Though certainly the Marxist/Leninist pipe dream is philosophical and historical silliness of the highest order, I do think that it is possible to meliorate the economic condition of human beings in this world, but only through the free enterprise system, following particular stages of development, culminating in the advanced capitalist consumer societies enjoying the wealth and comfort we experience today, as in many of the European countries and of course in the United States." Rostow looks around the room challengingly. There is a muttering, a stirring, in the crowd.

"BOMB THEM INTO PROSPERITY, WALT!" someone yells.

"TELL US ABOUT THE WEALTH AND COMFORT IN MY LAI, ROSTOW!" yells another.

Rostow looks stunned, then angry, his face reddening. "Listen here. If you want to engage in intelligent debate, I'm perfectly will—"

"HOW ABOUT INTELLIGENT DEBATE FOR THE VIETNAMESE PEOPLE, ROSTOW!"

That's Alexandria.

"ONLY DEAD BABIES CAN'T DEBATE, YOU BASTARD!" screams her companion, the frizzy-haired one, full of the purist hatred with her hands cupped around her mouth as if Rostow is fifty yards away, though he is virtually right next to her. Rostow blinks and narrows his eyes at the screamer.

Suits swivel in their seats, their faces twisted in revulsion.

"SHUT UP!" they yell.

"LET THE MAN SPEAK!"

"GET THE HELL OUT OF HERE, YOU GODDAMNED COMMIES!"

A well-dressed middle-aged couple in front of us turns around and glares menacingly, though we haven't said a thing. I look at the cop, who stands leaning forward looking around the room, his hands at his sides, a bewildered and frightened expression on his dull face. He has to do something, but what? Choose one of the protesters for arrest? What about the others? Call for reinforcements? He has no communication device that I can see. He will have to find a telephone. This is a fine mess! I actually feel a little sorry for the guy. But I don't feel sorry for Rostow, who has regained his composure and is giving it back to the protesters.

"Is this the best you can do? Scream and curse? Is this the best you can do? You people know absolutely nothing about the world and reality. You know nothing about history. Your ignorance is appalling and embarrassing. Really, it is! You should all be ashamed of yourselves. You call yourselves educated people. You are a disgrace. Really, you are!"

People cheer. I am amazed at Rostow's cool. He has hardly raised his voice and looks calm as he speaks. The voice of the establishment. But this is about to change.

"FUCK YOU ROSTOW YOU MURDERING BASTARD!"

It is Alexandria again and she has an object in her hand. A red object. A tomato. She winds up girlie-style, throws it in his direction and misses by three feet. It splatters against the blackboard and drops to the floor, hitting the chalk tray on the way down. There is a moment of shocked silence as people look at the tomato and then at Rostow and then at Alexandria. Now the cop moves forward. "HEY! CUT THAT OUT!" he yells. "YOU'RE UNDER ARREST!"

People are getting out of their seats, yelling angrily. A student tries to grab Alexandria from behind but she yanks free, reaches into her handbag, pulls out another tomato and hurls it fiercely at Rostow, who ducks behind the lectern. It looks like he has practice at this. Another student tries to grab Alexandria and she slaps him across the face. "LET ME GO, YOU FUCKING PERVERT!" she screams. The black guy grabs the student by his jacket and throws him against the wall. While everyone looks at the commotion, including Rostow, who has appeared from hiding but is still wisely standing behind the lectern, a male voice behind us yells, "TAKE THIS, YOU FASCIST FUCK!" There is an explosive release of energy and another tomato goes speeding over our heads, much straighter and faster than Alexandria's misguided heaves as

Rostow's expression changes from arrogant, slightly nonplussed but essentially invincible smugness at the futile and somewhat amusing hostility, to the very sudden realization as he turns his head in the direction of the angry voice behind us that he is about to be hit flush in the face with a large red tomato, maybe one of the Creoles from the French Market, and there is not Jack Shit the largest military budget in the world, or the State Department, or the White House, or his expensive clothes, or his comfortable tan, or any of his economic theories can do to prevent it.

All this happens in a second, the voice, the flying tomato, the change in his expression, the red, pulpy, seedy explosion knocking the smart glasses sideways and splattering tomato all over his face. A gasp goes up and more angry curses as Rostow stands momentarily stunned and another tomato comes from the crowd, hitting him in the chest, completely drenching his shirt with the red stuff and then another from a different angle hitting the side of his head, knocking his glasses off completely. It all happens fast, bim, bam, boom, just like that.

Feeling like I am going to puke I stand up and walk quickly to the back of the room and double over next to the door, straining to hold on. The commotion in front intensifies and suddenly Alexandria squirts free and runs out of the room, right past me, followed by her frizzy-haired friend and the leather-jacketed black guy. The cop has apparently given up trying to arrest anyone as things are happening all over the place and instead goes up with three or four older suits to protect Rostow as if they were Secret Service agents. The protesters have vanished in the uproar leaving Paul and me pretty much the only suspects. Paul is out of his seat and backing towards the door, instinctively retreating as the odds worsen and the ugly mood intensifies.

Rostow, pale and covered with pulp and seeds, looks liked one of the pasty white colonial fools standing in shock outside the Saigon embassy after the Tet Offensive. All that is missing is the seersucker jacket. Someone pulls out a handkerchief and hands it to the war planner, who begins wiping his face. The cop hands him his glasses. Paul and I are standing at the exit, reluctant to leave, reveling in this fantastic scene with the ashen-faced Rostow wiping his face, his supporters in shocked disarray. I have beaten back the latest surge and feel better. Suddenly a pimply YAFer wearing a brown suit, yellow shirt and red tie points at us and yells, "GET THEM!" and we turn tail and run for our lives, two YAFers in hot pursuit like American pilots chasing a couple of MiG-17s over North Vietnam, tailing off as we approach the Chinese border, which in this case is the corner and the street heading towards St. Charles Avenue, laughing like giddy teenagers who have outrun a couple of pug-ugly cops with passersby staring at us as we run halfway down the street and then fall out crazy, panting and laughing, the spectacle of the bastard Rostow pelted with tomatoes, the pure, beautiful absurdity and justice of it redoubling our laughter.

"Baked ziti!"

"Scungilli marinara!"

"Eggplant Parmesan!"

We both laugh and laugh, my stomach heaving and contracting, the mere mention of food rekindling my nausea, as people walk by staring at this pair of seedy young men laughing about Italian recipes, one of them strangely bent over. We might not raise an eyebrow on Bourbon Street but up here in the Garden District near Audubon Park we are a bizarre spectacle, the realization of which makes us crack up even more. "Rostow! Fucking Rostow!" we yell, doubled over in hysterical laughter.

"Rostow the tomato man!"

"Bombs away, tomato man!"

"Let me go, you fucking pervert!"

"Take this, you fascist fuck!"

"Tomato man! Tomato man!"

"THERE THEY ARE!"

The same two guys who had been chasing us are at the end of the block and running again, loafers slapping the pavement, ties flying, murder in their eyes. "Holy shit!" we yell and take off laughing, Paul holding his straw hat with one hand, his legs churning like Tommie Smith chased by a mob of track and field-loving Alabaman patriots. The sight is so funny I almost fall down. Here is the great Paul Avery tearing ass down the street with the bloodthirsty bourgeoisie hot on his boot heels. Anyone knows how fast you can run with the predator's hot breath on your neck and Paul and I rip down the sidewalk laughing our balls off, half terrified at the same time but not really, as it is partly a game and we know it even then which is why it is so funny. We are playing our parts, springboks fleeing the warthogs. All part of the grand plan. The whole evening has turned into a hilarious farce and the richness of it propels us crazily down to St. Charles where we turn to look, the two righteous avengers having stopped halfway down the block, apparently losing interest or realizing they will never be able to catch wild hippies in flight. They flip us off in frustration and yell obscenities. "FUCK YOU, FASCIST ASSHOLES!" we yell and laugh and flip them off right back, turning to saunter down St. Charles, victory assured.

I feel a little better and right away start thinking about Alexandria, wondering where she is. We get on the streetcar, thankfully well ventilated with its open windows, soothing my condition even more, and hasten to the back where there is only one other rider, an older black woman who moves to a different seat, her face impassive, apparently a little put out for some reason. No matter. It is Thursday evening, getting dark now, not much going on, but after all that has happened doing nothing for the rest of the evening is out of the question. I have puked two times on my little cross-country trip and come close to a third, very strange, as, except for the period of temporary insanity known as high school where on week-ends I would regularly end up at two AM with my head in the toilet puking my guts out after near suicidal all-night drinking bouts, I rarely get sick to my stomach. Do I have some kind of bug? No, the knock on the head, the heroin and the oysters are not bug-related. What's it all about? Some kind of purging? Getting rid of something ugly and vile? Whatever it is I feel good and getting better riding in the back of that beautiful clackety old streetcar trundling down St. Charles on a warm late open-air May evening, glorious magnolia and rotting garbage mingling with the heavy presence of the river, elated at the wide-open prospects of a young life stretched ahead of me, both of us feeling it, laughing all the way to Felicity, all the way to Le Bateau Rose, where, sitting on the front steps is the black guy who had been next to Alexandria at the Rostow pummeling, smoking a cigarette. He has a thin goatee, strong jaw, dark skin, medium Afro and large intelligent eyes—a powerful presence.

We say our hellos and explain how we had ended up at Jones Hall, ended up in New Orleans, where we are headed, but admit having no clue as to how or why we have ended up on planet earth in the first place or what any of it means, which, all of us agree, is fine as long as we enjoy ourselves and find more occasions to throw rotten tomatoes at government officials, warmongering intellectuals and racist pigs of all variety. He is a friendly guy, his name is Aaron, and he is waiting for his old lady, Alexandria, coming soon with some of the other people who had been at Jones Hall and possibly a few other friends as well to hang out at the pool, drink some wine, smoke a little dope, listen to music. There go any fantasies about Alexandria. But what the hell, no use being greedy, though I have to admit my heart falls a little. But more power to you, Aaron, I think, more power to you. Power to the people. Maybe there will be another revolutionary sweetheart to discuss the urgent issues of the day with, listen to music, sip some wine, smoke a joint, slip into the pool, look into each other's eyes and make that cosmic connection—for the revolution, of course, all for the revolution.

***

We stay outside with Aaron for about ten minutes rehashing the festivities at Jones Hall, laughing at the crazy shit that went down, flying tomatoes, outraged conservatives, the guy Aaron pushed against the wall, everybody escaping from the place and running off like VC. The whole thing had been Alexandria's idea and Aaron is sure she will be kicked out of school but it doesn't matter because she is dropping out anyway, disgusted with the war, the hypocrisy of her professors, the law itself. There might be criminal charges but who the fuck cares. She and Aaron are splitting very soon. This society is fucked, says Aaron, and a new one is forming to take its place, he is sure of it, but not how long it is going to take, maybe decades, maybe a hundred years.

Paul mentions New Buffalo and Aaron says they have thought about communes but more likely they will leave the country, maybe Cuba, Europe, or North Africa. Aaron is from Baltimore and had a scholarship to study history at Tulane but dropped out after his sophomore year. Young, gifted and black, to be sure, and already fed up enough to get the hell out.

Along comes the beautiful and now in my eyes queenly Alexandria with four of her friends, the couple with the little dark glasses, the Datura type with frizzy red hair and a sexy, pleasantly overweight smiling Venus of Willendorf with short dark hair and pretty face with only mischief in her glittering and very stoned eyes who reminds me of someone I knew in high school. They are all in terrific high spirits, laughing and full of themselves and we go to the pool where someone has set up a record player with Junior Walker going, marijuana hanging in the air thick like Spanish moss, wine flowing fast and loose, much laughter. Paul and Aaron quickly fall into conversation and Alexandria gives me such smiles it is a wonder I don't fall into the pool. Paul tells everyone about being chased by the Republican wart hogs, which makes our new friends even happier and they welcome us as honorary members of their association.

The Venus of Willendorf, whose name is Lydia, comes over and hands me a cup of red wine, standing very close and warm and smiling and telling me how far out that Paul and I had hooked up with Alexandria and I tell her about the waiter at the Café du Monde whose aunt owns Le Bateau Rose and how we had walked over from the French Quarter and met Alexandria and so on and here we are talking and how strange it is the way things work out, one thing leading to another and how you just never know, how complicated it all is and how much we are at the mercy of chance, determinism, all determinism. No, no, says Lydia, not chance at all but powers we don't understand that control things and bring us together, like right now and she gives me a smile and brushes one of her nice breasts against my arm and says, "Wanna smoke some grass?" and before I can even reply she goes over to a tall white guy with very long straight hair and takes a joint he is holding and brings it over. "Good shit," she says, smiling and offering it to me and I take a good deep hit, closing my eyes and feeling the warm sweet vibes of this sexy woman standing next to me who just *knows* some greater force has brought us together at this moment. And who am I to disagree? I exhale, handing the joint to Lydia who sucks in the smoke, her chest swelling, pushing her nipples against her white T-shirt, smiling. "Power to the people!" she says and exhales a thin stream of gray smoke. This Lydia is looking better every minute. I think about

Rostow, the tomato man, and wonder what the slimy bastard is up to.

***

Well then. Lydia. It is really one of those nights, plenty dope, plenty wine, great comradely spirits, unbounded laughter, the sharp giddy euphoria of absolute youthful supremacy that cannot be denied, especially at that moment by the war hero, Mr. Rostow, wherever his sorry ass is, licking his wounds, nothing compared to the monstrous, hideous suffering he has caused but enough to get his attention, a little humiliation for the bastard anyway. And I hope those tomatoes stung, too.

But while we have some great laughs at Rostow's expense, who now in our minds is nothing more than a second-rate Lewis Carroll character, Lyndon's Ivy League ass licker (careful of that poison ivy, Lyndon!) throwing bombs around like playpen toys, mimicking his shocked expression, his thwarted blustering outrage, his ducking behind the lectern, the pretentious glasses flying off the precious inflated head, all of it wonderful stuff, the narcissist intellectual drowned in tomato sauce, our thoughts are mostly turned to good old-fashioned debauch, copious amounts of wine and dope, records spinning happily away, RnB, soul, local hero Fats Domino, more Junior Walker, Hank Ballard, James Brown, Wilson Pickett, Otis Redding, no psychedelic hippie stuff tonight, Joe Tex, Percy Sledge and more and while revelers dance, strip and launch themselves into the pool—bombs away!—Lydia and I stumble up the steps laughing in a high groove heading straight for the rented room where she informs me nothing turns her on more than making it in closets and why not, I think, feeling like Superman ready for a phone booth or any other compartment tiny or vast, quiet or loud, up or down, dark or light, figuring now the oysters working to my advantage. No more nausea. Into the small closet we go, all over each other like rain, like whipped cream, like gravy, secretary and shoe salesman crammed together on the rush hour A train not giving a shit for anyone or anything else, laughing, panting, our tongues down each other's throats, faces, noses, ears, knocking heads, elbows, knees, teeth, squirming and fumbling to get out of our clothes, laughing, panting, into it, after it, how I don't know, somehow, some way, the closet spinning end over end, a tumbling space capsule, weightless now, nowhere on earth, pants around my ankles, getting hers off, spreading her legs as much as she can in the tiny space, wet! Jesus, like the pool downstairs and she grabs the closet bar for lift and there it is, the cheap metal folding like a straw (Lydia is heavy) and we crumple laughing down on each other in some impossible way, still getting it, oh, mercy, still getting it, no stopping now, so good, ahhh, Lydia, crazy closet Lydia!

We lie that way for about five minutes, cooling down, breathing down, muscles cramped from the contortionist Kama Sutra tumble, laughing at the craziness, then spilling out of the closet like happy, lewd jack-in-the-box clowns, pants down, clothes off, faces flushed. I literally fall out sideways, the only way, then pull the wedged-in Lydia to her feet and out into the room. Downstairs the party is going louder than ever and we put our clothes on and return a little sheepishly where almost everyone is in the pool or has been in the pool, or half-in-half-out of the pool, some in underwear, most naked, not a bra in sight though some like the stunning Alexandria retain their panties. Paul is stripped-down Viking naked standing in the pool and drinking a cup of wine talking to the frizzy Daturian sitting next to him, like Alexandria wearing panties, red ones, no bra, her cone-like breasts sticking out like Frankenstein's bride, crazy, just crazy. Alexandria, standing in the pool next to Aaron, also naked, greets us loudly so all heads turn and I am embarrassed though Lydia takes it all in stride, unsurprisingly, and a quite drunk Paul calls out for us to take off our clothes and jump in. Lydia immediately strips and jumps in and what can I do but the same.

Later, much later, the night a wondrous spinning, it is decided the Hummingbird Grill is the place to be and we pile into strange cars, more circus clowns stuffed in tiny spaces, happy and thinking hamburgers, grilled cheese sandwiches, French fries, Coca Cola, coffee, chocolate cream pie and then the little restaurant, a place Paul and I have passed a couple of times, the last for me with no small revulsion at the heavy, greasy smells on top of my half-dozen dead oysters. But now I am strong, triumphant, and famished, for the moment the world in balance, justice served, Rostow vanquished, no puking, the glorious Lydia.

The Hummingbird is quiet when we arrive but we light the place up like new year's with our exploding energy, still giddy with the victory at Jones Hall, taking the place over and continuing the party right there, a moveable feast, someone says, and it surely is. I have a hamburger with fried onions and a side of coleslaw, coffee and a slice of chocolate cream pie, maybe the best meal I have had up to this point in my young life excepting of course Gilbert Bujeau's gumbo. The cook is a large man with long greasy black hair and huge warts on his face, an ex-inmate from Newgate Prison in 18th century London, a Gahan Wilson character to top all. He leers at the females and gives the males hostile looks and we all love him instantly, a fabulous, unreal grotesque, muttering under his breath, slamming food around like bowling pins with the mastery of a great short-order cook, a violent, graceful, stunningly fast carnival show that has us gaping. His force, ugliness and skill are such that he fits right into the evening's riotous events and relegates us to playful sophomores, amazed by as pure a display of genetic anomaly and genius as can be imagined. We are humbled, awed and overjoyed at this astounding freak. A few are worried at some of the things he might flick into our food but I watch him closely, fascinated, and see no evidence. We give him a standing ovation when we leave and he stares at us, a bemused expression on his extraordinary face.

***

The next day we are on the road after more beignets at the Café du Monde, the cooler stocked with beer, chips, muffulettas and chocolate bars from the Central Grocery, the last leg of our trip, the rest of the South, Jacksonville over the horizon, close. We will head along into Mississippi sticking to the coast, look for beaches to crash on, both of us a little apprehensive about our destinations but exhilarated by the adventures we have had, still laughing at the sublime spectacle of the saturation bombing of Walt Rostow at Jones Hall.

Leaving Slidell we cross the Mississippi line on 90 headed for Bay St. Louis, Gulfport and Biloxi, Paul talking about his last year at home and the terrible fights with his father that finally proved to be too much. He has kept in touch with his sister, Anabel, now an elementary school teacher in a rough Philadelphia neighborhood, and through her receives news of his father, though she has not talked to him in several months. For all he knows the old bastard is dead. Paul is edgy, talking a lot, more than he has for a while, since Berkeley, really, when he had blown me away with his energy and brilliance. From Slidell to the Bay St. Louis bridge he talks nonstop about his father, patriarchy, Jung's *anima*, betrayal, violence, the fatal flaws in the founding of the United States with its origins in genocide and slavery and the indomitable mindless rampage to exploit and control the land at any expense, any measure, the brutal conquest of the West, having another good laugh at Jerome's rearing white stallion in full erectile splendor, but then driving across the bridge we fall silent at the beautiful turquoise water and the Gulf beyond, a brilliant warm morning with gulls, diving pelicans and snowy egrets, boats of all kinds, people fishing off the bridge and once again we are awed by the incredible physical marvel the country is, the diversity and drama, the shifting tones and moods of landscape and culture and you have to say, yes, it is an amazing land and all the more tragic for it, such gifts squandered in what we both see as supreme folly, madness, even.

Meanwhile Rosalina putters along sweetly, happy to be pointed east, the scent of home growing more powerful with each passing mile. We stop for lunch in Biloxi, taking the cooler down to the Gulf's edge on the white sand, pelicans and gulls swooping, shrimp boats shuttling back and forth. The mufulettas, Paul's suggestion, are delicious, washed down with chips and beer. We each eat half, saving the rest for later. They remind me, I tell Paul, of a popular joint on Montauk Highway in Westhampton when I was a kid, the sandwiches with colorful signs and names to match, "Naughty Lady of Shady Lane," "Atomic Bomb," "Audie Murphy," "Meanwhile Back at the Ranch" and others. Salami, ham, peppers, cheeses, olives—all that wild stuff crammed together between Italian bread soaked in olive oil. My mother had an affair with the owner just before she disappeared. Paul talks about a deli in his neighborhood that he and his father went to on brutally hot Chicago summer afternoons for sliced meat and cheese along with pickles, beer and sodas. Koplinka's. Mr. and Mrs. Koplinka and their two daughters worked there and even when he was a little kid Paul says he had the hots for those girls, busty Polish high school wenches with braces on their teeth who teased and flirted as he shyly fidgeted, loving it.

By this time it is early afternoon and you can see the big clouds coming up on the horizon over the gulf, heavy, bad-looking things and we head back through the warm white sand to Rosalina carrying the cooler between us and two lanky white teenaged boys thick with Mississippi accents but full of curiosity and good will help Paul push and we are back on 90 again, the clouds building, driving another two hours, finally crossing the Alabama state line past darkening waters and beaches with the wind picking up, blowing garbage and bending the long grass sideways. The shrimp boats have disappeared and there are few people. With the dark sky and the first few pattering drops against the windshield we spot a small sign that says campground, driving down a sandy road into a clearing with a few picnic tables and grills but nothing else, no people, cars, trailers, which is fine with us and we sit quietly, roll a couple of smokes waiting for the storm which comes soon enough, a thundering downpour lasting for about an hour followed by a comically drenched raccoon that ambles up to Rosalina getting up on its hind legs with its paws against the door, moist little black nose sniffing, whiskers going, trying to hustle some dinner.

We manage a few chips for the beast but sharing our mufulettas is out of the question, finishing our sandwiches right then and there, rolling up the window a bit more to thwart a possible leaping mufuletta-crazed raccoon. We split the last beer and it starts to rain again, the raccoon trotting off into the bushes. For the rest of the night until about three or four in the morning it comes down slow, warm and steady. It is almost impossible sleeping in the front with the bucket seats and their exposed springs—Paul does better in the back—but I don't mind too much, the only tense moment coming when a pickup circles through around midnight and then leaves. The clouds vanish and morning comes clear, mist rising from the ground, which fortunately is hard-packed and sandy so Paul manages some traction and good Rosalina fires up and we are off down 90 again, hungry, stiff from space capsule sleeping but the day is glorious and so are we. Alabama! My childhood hero, Willie Mays, was born in Alabama. So were Hank Aaron and Willie McCovey. The Civil Rights Movement started here. Rosa Parks. Martin Luther King. Bull Connor. Selma. All of it. Birmingham Sunday.

For the hell of it and thinking of breakfast we take the bridge to Dauphin Island, a kind of dangling tooth between Mobile Bay and the Gulf, Rosalina bravely motoring along the thin strip of elevated concrete and sure as hell coming to a stop halfway across. Out of gas. I pull over as far as I can and we get out, unconcerned, really, for it is heady stuff out here looking out over the water, a slight breeze riffling the surface, a deep heavenly turquoise cut by the white wakes of small motorboats, looking down on the backs of gulls and pelicans gliding in the warm Gulf morning currents. The shoulder is narrow, just enough to accommodate Rosalina, but the traffic is not too bad and I volunteer to hitchhike to the island for gas, Paul giving me five dollars, and off I go, T-shirted, scruffy and carefree, the sparkling water below on my right, the hard brilliant concrete firm under my worn boots, the whoosh of speeding cars thumping across expansion joints (I have not yet stuck out my thumb), the warm salty breeze gently tousling my hair, a good hunger in my gut.

After a minute or so I turn around and stick out my thumb and my heart freezes because an Alabama State Trooper with his lights flashing has stopped behind Rosalina and the guy is out talking to Paul, typical with his sunglasses and creased uniform but then he gets in the car and drives up to me, leaning over and saying he will take me for gas and to get in. We speed off in the powerful car, so strange after Rosalina, the guy not talking much, older than the sonofabitch Nichols in Santa Cruz, not as tall, thicker, the rectangular silver ID badge saying Gaineswood, a cracker name if I ever heard one, but the man's vibe is not bad at all.

In a minute we are on the island at a funky tropical Mobil station where the trooper opens his trunk and hands me a red plastic one-gallon can telling me in his Alabama drawl to tell the guy inside I want some gas. I go over on the sandy, almost blinding white ground to what is no more than a shack where a young, strangely white-haired man in worn overalls sitting in a rocking chair reading an *Argosy* magazine motions to the pump and tells me to fill it up and then pay, which I do, then back in the Trooper's formidable car, a Dodge, the can on the floor between my feet and we rumble back to Rosalina where Paul sits on the bridge railing, waiting. Gaineswood stays until we empty the can, reminding us to put an ounce in the carburetor, recommends a good place for breakfast, Misty's, on Bienville, gives us a push with his potent machine and as Rosalina sputters to life he pulls out and roars past, quickly disappearing.

"Thank you, masked man," says Paul, and it is true, Officer Gaineswood is like the Lone Ranger, a man of apparent good will, few words and a kind of awesome power. We are both silent for a bit, absorbing whatever it is that has just transpired.

"Now there's a type of masculine power for you," he says, "beneficent agent of the state, proof positive of the rewards of citizenship and obedience as doled out by the enforcers. He could easily have hassled us like that other prick but chose not to, for whatever reason. An actual good cop, perchance. Had we been black it might have been a different story. I guess we'll never know."

11

Perhaps in Kansas after all > In the realm of three-legged crows >
Fleeing the knife-wielding babbler > A note for old Vanzetti > Nixon's
triumph : Prosperity and democracy, or else > Goodbye to Paul

Rosalina putters along, leaving her trademark hovering blue
cloud. True, we will never know. But had he been at Jones Hall
he certainly would have made at least one arrest, unlike the other
hapless cop. You can carry the good cop thing only so far. How
strange is the latent desire to be a part of the good cop's world,
which I think we both feel after our friendly encounter with Officer
Gaineswood, who actually did protect and serve. Paul says, "I really
think most people yearn to belong, to submit to the power of authority, the uniforms, the shiny badges, the guns and gleaming bullets, the erotic power of the state. It used to be mostly a middle
class thing but now it's the working class too, happy with their little
treats and emoluments, their new cars and sports and six packs.
The working class never had it so good—hell, their kids even go
to college, although things are looking a little shaky now with this
insane war going on for so many goddamn years, sucking everything dry. So they feel threatened—the communists, the hippies, the
blacks, the Vietnamese, the liberals. And who comes along to pro-

tect them? The fucking cops, that's who, with their gleaming bullets, shiny badges and uniforms, their masculine power, protectors of state and flag, the last refuge. It's fascism, pure and simple, misogyny, incest, hatred, violence and submission. The military, the state, our protectors. So easy to submit! It's called belonging to the state, heart, mind and balls. We'll protect you if let us fuck you and carve out your heart and steal your mind. No more worries! Tempting, isn't it? Hell, even Socrates submitted, though he didn't give up his balls and his mind. Do you think we rebel because we hate our fathers, Sam?"

Paul looks at me with his blue eyes, an ironic expression on his strong intelligent face, beard bristling, straw hat cocked slightly back—Vincent again.

I grunt in response, looking for Misty's. Do we really hate our fathers? What would Socrates do today? He had accepted the authority of the state. But what if the state was rotten to the core? I pass the Mobil station on the main drag, Bienville, the strange white haired guy still rocking, reading his Argosy, an alien magazine. Dauphin Island is unassuming and pleasant in a slow Southern kind of way, unlike eastern Long Island from where my own heart-mending odyssey commenced, beautiful but subject to the malign pressures of the big city, the naked city, pushing, always pushing. It does not seem much in the way of urban pressure pushes against Dauphin Island out here in the Gulf, tenuously connected to the mainland by the wispy filament of a bridge. A big hurricane would knock the shit out of this place. I like the vulnerability, the wildness and impermanence. Misty's is on the left between a hardware store and an empty, sandy space, a small, neat white building with a red, asphalt shingled roof and red-trimmed wood windows and a red door, a few cars in the parking lot, a little white sign that says MISTY'S painted red in a jaunty upward-slanted cursive and below, in tidy print: Dauphin Island's Finest – Breakfast, Lunch & Dinner – 7 AM - 8 PM – Seven Days a Week.

We are, at least in the standard visual sense, what passes for most ordinary Americans as "hippies" and so never know what to expect upon entering an establishment such as this, pinned immediately to the inside of the door with 12-inch knives hurled from the kitchen, set upon by rabid police dogs, tarred and feathered, a combination of all three, but to our surprise we are greeted with a hearty and cheerful, "How y'all doin'!" from a small, gray-haired, apple-cheeked, middle-aged woman looking like Auntie Em in the Wizard of Oz wearing a white blouse with a round collar, blue jeans, white sneakers and a red and white checked apron and of course we respond with all the enthusiasm and gratitude such a welcome under the circumstances merits, our response duly noted by the four or five other patrons, all males, in this trim little apple pie establishment, no-nonsense types who nod at us without any apparent murderous thoughts or hateful presuppositions. Always when such rare things happen you think that life is grand and glorious after all and humans really might be magnificent, warm-hearted creatures and for soft types like Paul and me it is all you can do not to fall down right there and weep for the joy or tragedy of it, which would of course cause everyone to think you completely insane and put in an immediate call for the men in the white coats. Poor Blanche DuBois. We may not always depend on the kindness of strangers but a friendly nod can go a long way. The woman (is it Misty?) comes up with two menus and shows us to a table for two and the others return to their meals which must be good judging by the seriousness they go at it and Misty/Auntie Em, smiling and warm as she can be, asks us if we want coffee right away and we say yes, yes indeed. She returns with two steaming cups and takes our orders for ham, scrambled eggs, toast, all very delicious and then a couple of pieces of home made cherry pie as a few others come in and nod agreeably, fishing types, and I remark that this could be Kansas in the thirties, a piece of it anyway, carried by the tornado and dropped into the Gulf though Paul reminds me of that state's violent racial past and naturally there is the question of how we would be received at dear old Misty's were we black. Of course.

We pay with a generous tip and drive east to the end of the skinny island and look out over the water, the wind picking up, chopping the surface, then turn around and head back down the island and over the bridge and up Mobile Bay towards Mobile, through the watery old city with its harbor and sleepy white ante-bellum architecture and back south along the bay until we finally reach the coast again around five o'clock, rolling into the little town of Gulf Shores where we find a public beach and get out to stretch our legs. The sand is pure white and soft, the breeze warm and gentle, the water a greenish turquoise. So far the fearsome state of Alabama has been a pussycat, the benign and welcoming Dauphin Island with the good Officer Gaineswood, everyone's kindly Aunt Misty and her delicious food, the balmy weather and gentle Gulf breezes, the brilliant white sand, and here getting ready to close for the day a green and white cart topped with a large green and white umbrella ("Fred's Fantastic Fried Foods") looking like something Ludwig Bemelmans might imagine selling fried shrimp, French fries, fresh lemonade and sodas, operated by a tall young man with a wispy moustache and wild curly hair who is not Fred but Ted, from New Jersey, staying with his uncle Fred for a while in Gulf Shores.

Ted is talkative, in his early twenties and keenly interested in our trip as well as keenly interested in getting back to New Jersey, lay-ing two plates of shrimp and French fries on us complete with hot sauce, ketchup, lemons, along with two cups of lemonade and re-fusing our money, telling us that he is AWOL from the Army and trying to figure out what to do next. His uncle Fred is from Jersey too but had married a girl from Mobile after the war, moving there to work as a ship welder, raising a couple of kids, drinking, divorcing, losing almost everything, moving to Gulf Shores and getting himself the little cart that turns out to be quite the hit around these parts. Fred, says Ted, is still a drinker and there are a lot of mornings he does not make it to work, like today, and Ted takes over for a percentage and out of obligation because his uncle is letting him crash but that is wearing thin and it is time to get moving. In the spirit of the times he asks right away if he can get a ride east with us and in the same spirit we say yes. He tells us he has a couple of hundred dollars.

***

We leave early the next morning after spending the night at uncle Fred's house, a fearful dive as bad as Christopher's pad in Albuquerque though thankfully no chimps or heroin, but empty bottles of Bacardi and J&B spilling out of the garbage and drunken unkempt Fred himself watching television all night in a Kerouac-like stupor. A half hour past the Florida state line Paul and I are already out of our minds with Ted's incessant gabbling, completely nuts, full of crazy associations, non sequiturs and esoteric, fourth-dimensional information, a mainline psycho-energy rap that bounces off everything he sees, splattering into a dozen stream-of-consciousness branches. Apparently in his crazy cunning he had withheld this part of himself—his real self—from us the day before, but now that we are on the road together he wastes no time enthusiastically adopting us as co-conspirators in his phantasmagoric, endlessly ramifying kaleidoscopic world. His first tangent, triggered by crossing the border into Florida, is the German submarine at the bottom of Lake Okeechobee. In 1941 The Boca Raton secret Kaiser branch of the Daughters of the American Revolution found a U-boat washed up in Palm Beach and spent months taking it apart, transporting it piece by piece to Lake Okeechobee, where they assembled it and launched it into the lake, where, upon reaching the middle, it sank. Very few people know about this, he explains. He wants to dive to the bottom of the lake but it is over a half mile deep—the only way to get to it would be with a diving bell. There is a salvage company in Fort Lauderdale but he doubts they have a diving bell. Maybe Cousteau would be interested. There are hundreds of sunken subs all along the Florida coast. There is also a colony of German defectors from World War II living in the Everglades. They had hooked up with the Seminoles and now there is a whole tribe of German Seminoles living there secretly, supposedly with subs, some of the old ones they had fixed up for fishing and exploring, powered by solar crystals. The government knows about it but leaves them alone, for nefarious reasons.

This is pretty amazing stuff but Ted is just getting warmed up. On and on he goes, stopping for a few seconds between riffs and looking intently out the back window, Paul and I too blown away to respond, both of us thinking of ways to ditch this character. On he goes about other things like the tunnels of Cu Chi in Vietnam (true enough), the underground tunnel from Alaska to Mexico built by the Druids, the US secret command operating inside Pacaya, an active volcano in Guatemala and a dozen other whacked-out things that mostly have to do with being inside tunnels or mountains or volcanoes or underneath large bodies of water. I resolve to head for a library and a fat psychology book when I get to New York to see just what all of this means but of course I never will. Near Pensacola I spot the turnoff for Santa Rosa Island-Fort Pickens and on impulse turn, Paul giving me a knowing look. Somehow we are going to ditch Ted, we have to, he is insane, jabbering about five thousand-mile underwater glass tunnels and other mad Jules Verne scenes that sound pretty cool when you think about them (imagine driving to Europe in a glass tunnel at the bottom of the Atlantic) but things are beyond science fiction into another realm where laughing three-legged crows dive bomb our skulls and little green people at the side of the road pelt Rosalina with dead tarantulas and as we drive across the bridges to the island Paul heroically keeps up with Ted syllable for mad syllable until I pull into a small lot at a visitors' center of some sort and say to Paul this is the place I had told him about where the submarine has washed up on shore and how Ted might really be interested in checking this out. Cool, says Ted, leaving his backpack in the car as he and Paul trudge over the sand for about fifty yards as I stay in the car with the engine running. After a minute I watch as Paul says something to Ted and he runs back to the car. As he approaches I open the passenger door, reach into the back for Ted's pack and put it on the front seat. "What do you think?" says Paul. "Should we ditch him?" We look at Ted, who is scanning the beach for the sub. "He seems harmless but he's driving me crazy. What do you think?" I ask, throwing it back to him.

"I agree, he's completely mad but I don't think he's dangerous."

We look again at the tall strange lonely figure earnestly looking up and down the beach, completely unaware that we are discussing him. If life is a series of happenings determined by previous events, as I believe, then we are presented with what seems like a contradiction. We are agents of choice and poor Ted is to have his immediate fate determined by what we decide. But are not the values, experiences and so forth that go into making this decision the product of things that had happened to us, beyond our control? If we were "fated" to meet Ted, aren't we also "fated" to ditch him (or not ditch him) on some lonely beach off the Florida coast? The more we look at him staring down the beach with his slightly crooked posture, as if he does not quite fit, as if a lifetime of being out of place has subtly warped his physical self, the less we feel inclined to leave the luckless lad alone like that. He is a doomed soul anyway, but why be among the hundreds who at the very least reject him and at worst fuck him over completely? He is in for life. Why not a modicum of kindness? He turns to us and waves. "Fuck it," says Paul. "I'll go tell him this is the wrong place."

***

It is before noon and Ted is in high spirits as we head down Fort Pickens Road towards the Civil War fort for the hell of it. Resigned to his presence we even feel a little warmth towards the old boy, whose energy and craziness make it seem like we have known him our whole lives. It is a kind of test and we have all passed, he as well as us, at least for the next fifty miles or so. Fort Pickens is an old civil war bastion with big guns and a beautiful overlook of the Gulf and Ted immediately goes off into the bowels of the place on his own subterranean quest, probably looking for a secret tunnel to the Yucatan Peninsula. Paul sits up on a rampart, a bearded Union sentinel in Melvillian reverie staring out at the Gulf, vast and deep blue with whitecaps in the distance. Though it is Florida a sign says the fort had been a Union stronghold during the Civil War and had been in use until 1947, the year of my birth. Paul was born August 6, 1945. Hiroshima. Boom.

After a while we gather at the car and Paul volunteers to drive, likely to get a break from Ted, and Ted and I push as Rosalina starts, her signature blue smoke hovering over the road as she putters along. It is about noon and we are hungry but Santa Rosa Island is a long empty stretch and we do not get lunch until Gulf Breeze, over the bridge, where Ted buys us hamburgers and Cokes in a little restaurant considerably less friendly than Misty's but the food is not bad and nobody hassles us, though we do get plenty of looks with

Ted's non-stop chatter about the inside of Fort Pickens, all the cool cells, rooms and mysterious passageways.

If we want to make our destination by evening, St. George Island, about 150 miles, we will have to push it. Hugging the coast with Paul driving and Ted in the back seat we go through little beach towns, Mary Esther, Destin, Mirimar Beach, Grayton Beach, lots of pure white sand and sparse green vegetation interspersed with glimpses of the turquoise Gulf. We stop for gas in Destin. Ted disappears and we find him about a half-mile down the beach looking for signs of old German subs. He seems reluctant to continue. We buy some food for the cooler in a supermarket and around seven o'clock cross the Bryant Patton Bridge to St. George Island and find a likely spot to camp. Ted is very excited to be on this remote sliver of land out in the Gulf, talking incessantly, a wild look in his eyes. He is certain there are subs around these parts. Our companion is wearing thin.

We go back over the bridge across the bay into Apalachicola to look for a restaurant and find a nice little place where we sit in an open area next to the docks and watch the boats come in with their catch while stuffing ourselves with fried shrimp, seafood gumbo and key lime pie. Paul pays. The good food and charm of the place are marred by Ted's crazy chatter, which, as it had in the restaurant in Gulf Breeze, attracts unwanted attention. The waitress, a blond with a sour expression and a mouth like a scar, acts as if we have leprosy. We leave a dime for a tip. As we cross the bridge back to the island an orange sun dips into the dark blue water of the Gulf and the bay takes on a reddish purple color with the beach a brilliant white slash in the middle and even Ted stops his babble for a moment. I look at Paul, who is staring raptly. Whatever arguments we have with the country are always countered by the sheer physical beauty and generosity of the land. It has happened many times on our little trip, posing no small dilemma. It would be much easier to hate the place if it was ugly, which it most assuredly is not.

After we lay out our bags and start a small fire Ted surprises us by getting some dope from his backpack and rolling a joint, which we foolishly smoke with this crazy person who gets crazier by the minute, finally reaching into his pack and pulling out a large folding knife which he opens and waives around in the moonlight babbling a stream of lunacy that thoroughly freaks us out. I get up to piss in the dunes and am startled by a raccoon as big as a dog, partially obscured in the beach grass, boldly standing his ground. In the morning we wake grainy-eyed and strange after not much sleep and spy Ted way down the beach looking for submarines and without hesitating grab our stuff, granting no more reprieves for this babbling knife-wielder. Paul pushes Rosalina and we drive off the island.

***

By the time we are over the bridge, back on 98 headed east, we are laughing about Ted and talking about breakfast and realizing how close Jacksonville actually is, a straight shot under the panhandle. "I'm a little freaked out about meeting up with the old man," says Paul. "I haven't heard from my sister in a long time. He could be dead, for all I know. Probably not, though—my sister would have told me. I wonder why she hasn't been calling. Sometimes I wonder what the fucking point of doing this is. What the fuck do I hope to accomplish? Reconciliation? Communication? Forgiveness? Then I remember, oh, yeah, I'm writing a book. Big fucking deal. I don't have a good feeling about this, Sam. I'm afraid he's not doing very well. I pride myself on knowing things, having a handle on things, but honestly, I feel like the lost little boy who wants his daddy. But daddy left a long time ago and he's more lost than the little boy. That just knocks the shit right out of me. I remember as a little kid how much I looked up to the old man. He was my whole world, Sam. We were close, too. Take me to Cubs games, play ball together, family picnics by the lake. We adored each other. Jesus! But then it all changed when I was 11 or 12. Shit was happening I didn't know about. Still don't know about. Maybe there was another woman. He started drinking. He became distant and ill tempered. We never spent time together any more. My mother and I got a lot closer. Then she got sick and we moved to Jacksonville. That was the hardest fucking time. We all knew she was dying, Jesus, I didn't want to admit it to myself—none of us did, but we all knew it. She knew it too. But she's the one who was strong and kept us all together while my father drank himself stupid and my sister withdrew and I got more and more depressed. My mother was a saint, Sam, I swear she was. She saw how things were falling apart and she tried like hell to make it better. Like singing hymns with my sister and me Sunday nights. I didn't have her faith. None of us did. It drove my father crazy to hear us singing in her bedroom. He'd sit in the living room and get fucking juiced, just listening. But he never said a word because he knew how much it meant to her. He loved her very much. Yeah, he did. Jesus Christ. Poor bastard."

Paul gets quiet. We are at a sandy little town called Panacea, which seems like a good place for breakfast. There are signs for mineral springs and cures and chartered fishing trips and old people looking stiff but happy and hopeful here in the land of Ponce de Leon—maybe this is the exact spot—and I decide that I like Florida very much indeed. There is something of the permanent holiday about it, wild, right up against the Gulf on one side and the Atlantic on the other, catching hell from monster hurricanes roaring up from the Caribbean, ghosts of sunken slave ships, pirate ships. Florida has the voodoo. I picture myself as some island character, painter of introspective, dense, van Gogh-like pictures from my seaside shack, storms, full moons and strange still lifes, a salted, weathered old man with a long white beard laced with seaweed and sand, maybe a barnacle or two, some small shells. Could be.

And what of Paul? He will meet up with his father—if he is still there—but what will happen? At least he has a beautiful woman to come home to and he will finish his book, successful reunion with his father or not. I don't know if I will ever see my own father again and don't know if I care. He is retired and living in the south of France with his wife and daughter, my half-sister, whom I hardly know. With this marriage my relationship with him has gone from bad to worse. I have never liked his wife and make no secret of it, driving the wedge even deeper. Ever the cipher to my father I was a vexing Gregor Samsa-like presence to them in my adolescence, filled with confusion and anger. Ironically that time was the most fun, if not the happiest, I have ever had, a kind of out-of-mind high school experience where I suppressed most of my turmoil and simply had a blast, playing sports and partying as much as I could, drinking enough alcohol to kill a dozen people, developing a reputation as a crazy person willing to take things a step further than most.

But things were not quite as carefree as they seemed. I fell in love with a girl and had sex for the first time, crazy sex that hurt me badly (again) but before that we had named our children and I was converting to her Episcopalian faith from my nominal Judaism, going to church, reading the bible, memorizing the Apostle's Creed, reading Lloyd Douglas, the whole soupy schmear. My goy son, my father would say, half-jokingly, and it gave me the satisfaction of being acknowledged for the first time as having a serious thought that marked me as an individual and at the same time firmly noting the Jewish part of who I was. I was seeing a Jewish shrink at the time who never said a word about my passionate interest in Christianity, but both my father and his wife thought I was trying to find a "father figure" in Jesus, which I thought was ridiculous, but maybe it was not.

Christianity was no panacea but that is where we are now and other than the anxiety of being in eastern free fall we have no pressing problems that a good breakfast cannot cure. We choose a silvery little diner that looks just about right with a parking lot of crushed shells and some palm trees and water in back with a funky dock and a couple of dilapidated row boats and over red snapper in Tabasco sauce, fried eggs, toast and coffee we talk about god the father and his boy Jesus and how our boys in Vietnam are fighting for both of them, sustained by cheerleading chaplains when they falter, yet another manifestation of insanity, Paul and I agree, in a world caught in a steel trap of its own making, chewing off its own limbs to get free. There is no justice, no sanity, no rhyme or reason to any of it. We are a mad species and there is nothing you can do but tend your own garden and attempt to unravel your own shit, which brings us back to what Marty and some like him are doing at New Buffalo and other such places. Perhaps the idea of what a revolutionary is has to be re-imagined, says Paul. The state is too powerful. You have to undermine its rotten foundation like termites, positioning yourself for its collapse. "Like Che said," says Paul, "two, three, many Vietnams, only our Vietnams will be here at home, agitating, pushing the boundaries, speaking out, living a simpler life, refusing to participate in a corrupt system, fighting our small battles every day. The system is so evil, so stupid, so unwise, that one day it will slit its own throat, collapse under its own tottering, obscene weight. We may not see it in our lifetime but sure as hell it will collapse one of these days. And what comes out of it will be something much less patriarchal, and that will be a goddamn good thing."

Paul talks with some vehemence and the waitress looks at him warily but he puts her at ease with one of his brilliant smiles and touches the brim of his hat with a gentlemanly flourish. Reassured, she comes over with some more coffee and fills our cups. She is thin and quite pretty, early thirties, a bit of Audrey Hepburn, pale, circles under her eyes, some makeup. Her brown hair is pulled into a loose bun with a pencil holding it in place. She asks where we are headed and when we jokingly invite her along, describing Rosalina, she laughs and says she would do it but has three daughters to take care of without a husband and they sure as hell wouldn't fit in the car.

She works in the diner full time and her oldest daughter, who is fourteen, helps take care of the twins, who are nine. She had come from California with a man who left after the first year. We ask why Panacea and she says because of the name, and no kidding, if we had a larger vehicle, a van maybe, she just might hitch a ride with her kids. When she is not taking care of her kids or working at the diner she writes short stories. Her favorite writer is Flannery O'Connor. She is just starting Virginia Wolfe's *To the Lighthouse*. The more she talks the more beautiful she becomes. I ask if she has ever considered living on a commune and tell her about New Buffalo and she makes a face and says the thought of living with a bunch of drugged-out hippies makes her want to puke. Done enough of that, she says, though not on communes. Her name is Loretta and by the time we leave the diner I am smitten and amazed again at the strange surprises of life. A stockbroker in New York perusing a map of Florida at breakfast spills some jam from his English muffin on Panacea and wipes it off without a thought. In the real-life town that smudge obscures resides a sensibility that would make literature of this gesture.

***

I find the post card for Antonio Vanzetti in Rosalina's glove compartment, scrawl MADE IT! on the back and mail it in the Panacea post office, a beachcomber's shack put together with weathered pine boards and raised up on short stilts, a half-dozen cats loitering in the shade beneath. The building is empty and the postal window closed but there is a stamp machine and a mail slot and I slip the card ("Greetings From Famous Fisherman's Wharf!") through, wondering if it will ever get there and if so would old Vanzetti know who the hell it was from. We are four or five hours from Jacksonville with full stomachs and a full tank of gas. Our destination has snuck up on us. The trip is about over. I do not think Paul is ready.

The ride from Panacea to Jacksonville on the narrow old highway takes us away from the water into piney southland woods that open up to small towns we would not want to be in after dark, then closing around us again for long monotonous miles. The towns are all the same, a gas station, limp American flag, broken down rusted trucks, an old store, mangy dogs, fat, mean-looking whites in overalls and everywhere dead animals, fur and tissue mashed into the baking asphalt, blood darkly congealed, raccoons, dogs, a few armadillos. There is no wind and it is hot even with the windows down. The forest is forbidding and dry. An errant cigarette would cause a disaster. We see no black people. Paul is quiet.

30 miles outside Jacksonville, around Macclenny, he turns around abruptly, rummages through his pack and pulls out an address book. He assumes his father lives in the same place, a dreary suburb on the south side with cheap ranch-style homes and struggling lawns, probably more developed and uglier since he had left. The piney woods have given way to tract houses laid out in sandy plots, more of the creeping nightmare everywhere on the East coast. I think I would rather live deep in the turpentine, cracker woods than in the new plastic boxes surrounded by zombies, but then

again maybe not. Kind of like choosing Democrat or Republican. Jacksonville appears in the distance as a concentration of more of the same, the denser middle, but you know the Atlantic is on the other side, which makes it better, though the prospect of meeting up again with the old ocean saddens me. Compared with the Pacific it is undersized, ill tempered and cold and holds a hard sack of memories I want to dispose of, though still a wild accomplice that speaks a language I love. The hot weather brings back memories of long childhood walks down a pristine beach and a warm blue ocean that holds things in place. In those days fishermen still hauled their nets from the beach. I can see the silvery flashing of fish pulled from the water, the unwanted left to die on the sand, gasping and baking in the hot sun. Since then the world has gone out of whack and senseless, the dislocations of my own life mirrored in larger events. In 1955, when I was eight, the night of a hurricane, the ocean raging, I was told my mother had died in a plane crash in South America and immediately all things were out of balance. She had left six months earlier with a new pilot's license and a plane she had bought by selling her wedding ring. I wrote hopeful post cards that my father claimed to mail. Things were never good at home but after her death they were never the same, which is a big difference in the life of a child. I suppose the assassination of Kennedy had the same effect on a nation. For me both deaths were a double blow that opened my eyes forever.

We cross the St. Johns River on another Erector Set bridge and enter the main part of the city, which is older and more interesting than I thought it would be, passing through quiet middle-class white neighborhoods of stout brick homes with white shutters and all the accoutrements, manicured lawns, flower beds, birdbaths, bicycles, two-car garages, American flags, and one equally quiet middle class black neighborhood, which is an eye-opener because I have never seen an actual black middle class neighborhood before, the buildings newer and just as orderly, though fewer flags. Downtown Jacksonville is larger and more urban than I had expected. Being from New York nothing else is really a city to me, with the possible exception of Chicago, and I am surprised at the architecture, not tall buildings but substantial, from the forties, thirties and older, redolent of a more credulous, determined spirit, ghosts, fedoras, long skirts, movie theaters, office buildings, drug stores, restaurants, newsboys shouting headlines. The palm trees fill me with the usual mysterious longing. My partner however, is not impressed, looking around anxiously as if for avenues of escape, maybe realizing at this penultimate moment that some old stories never improve with time. The city itself would not hold many memories except as a place of intense, cloistered sadness, a couple of terrible years when everything fell apart, his mother's rapid decline and death, his father's drinking and bitterness, his sister's quiet withdrawal. For the first time since we have met I actually feel Paul to be in a place with which I am all too familiar, of uncertainty and loss, and it shakes me a little because I have a kind of idealized vision of him, the older brother I have never had, grounded and wise.

But as we get closer to our destination Paul visibly steels himself and jokes about going to lake Okeechobee to dive for the old U-boat if things don't work out too well with his father or seeking contact with German Seminoles in the Everglades for an anthropological treatise. Meeting Ted, said Paul, might turn out to have been a life-altering encounter, to which I reply, yes, if we meet up with him again it might really prove life altering and I wonder at the possibility of running into him on my way to New York. I will keep my eyes open.

***

"Jesus, I remember this place," says Paul, looking at a closed down go-cart track with a driving range next to it, also closed. A used car lot glitters with colorful banners and chromed vehicles in the warm afternoon Florida sun and nearby squats an enormous Quonset hut supermarket, a monstrous white toad with a gaping mouth, its huge parking lot mostly empty. Everything is transience and commercialism. Depressing, shoddy-looking housing, much of it recently built, spreads in every direction with their barren, crabgrass lawns, busted tricycles, cheap cars and sick palm trees. Concrete and stucco everywhere reflects the white blinding sunlight. It is easy to understand Paul's escape from here and it astounds me that people actually live in such places, but then, for most, I suppose, there is little choice, and for many, it is a slice of the American dream. This is the way things are going in the land of the free and home of the brave, metastasizing cookie-cutter housing, flat dusty suburbs, closed-down go cart tracks, glittering used car lots and, for export, napalm, agent orange and Bouncing Betties. Nixon's kitchen debate, triumphant. This is the prosperity and democracy the rest of the world thirsts for, and if they don't, we'll give it to them anyway, or else.

"Well, Sam," says Paul, "it's been a helluva ride. I never told you about the terrible fight I had with my father the night before I left. He'd been drinking and I came home late. I was staying away as much as possible in those days, drinking a lot myself. He started giving me shit about coming home late and something snapped, I just blew up. We got into a horrible argument and then we were punching each other like crazy, a knock-down-drag-out brawl, and I ended up on top of him with my hands on his throat, trying to kill him. I almost did. His face got beet red and his eyes were bulging out. He couldn't breath. As he was about to pass out I came to my senses, thank god, and let go. If I hadn't I really might have killed him. I might be in prison now. Jesus. Anyway, that was it. I packed my stuff that night and left early in the morning, before he woke. Didn't even leave a note. I called my sister later and told her where I was. So you see, Sam, I have some guilt here as well. I owe him an apology. Actually, I feel terrible about it. I'm not a violent person. I hate violence. I'm opposed to it in principle. But I can get down in the mud with everyone else, no doubt about it."

"So can we all," I say

"Well, fuck, I feel just terrible for the old man. His whole life just falls apart and then his son tries to kill him and then splits without a word—without a word for ten years. I realize I haven't sorted all this out yet. Coming across was kind of impulsive. I made profound a break with my past and created this whole intellectual structure to deal with it, all this stuff about patriarchy and violence and domination, but maybe a lot of it has to do with feeling guilty about what *I've* done, not my father. The return of the prodigal son."

We enter an area that is older, if only slightly more substantial, with well-established businesses, larger houses, greener lawns, better cars, fewer broken toys and bikes in the front yards. Paul sits up straighter, looking around intently. "Turn in there," he says, pointing to a motel advertising vacancies, swimming pool and a $12 nightly rate for single rooms. I pull in and park in front of the office and Paul gets out slowly and walks inside where he talks to the clerk, a tanned, thin, balding man in his forties wearing aviator sunglasses and a red Hawaiian shirt, who keeps turning his head to spit tobacco juice behind the counter. I watch as Paul fills out the registration form for his room. Then he takes out his wallet and gives the man cash. He stands with his hands on the counter, legs slightly apart, as if for balance, as the man turns and moves his right forefinger up and down about a foot from the board of hanging room keys until he locates the right one and snatches it off the hook, turning and handing it to Paul. As Paul leaves the office the man stares at

Rosalina and then turns to spit. I get out of the car with Paul's pack and put it on the hood.

"I need your address," I say.

"And I yours."

I get *The Wretched of the Earth* and a pen from the glove compartment and he writes his address inside the front cover. "That's a good book. I'll have to get a copy," he says.

"Yeah. Maybe some day I'll finish it," I say.

"I'll stay here and get my bearings. I don't know if I'll call first or just go over. I guess I should call. It's about a mile from here. Let me have your address." He takes a small notebook from his pack and gives it to me. "If you ever get back to Berkeley you can return the ice chest. Otherwise it's no big deal. And here—to help with the gas for the rest of your trip." He hands me three twenties and when I hesitate he says it is part of the deal and if I need more he will give it to me. I thank him and say no, I don't need more. He says he will write to let me know how the meeting with his father went and that we should keep in touch and he hopes he will be seeing me soon in California. I say I will probably be in California soon, within a few months if all goes according to plan, not knowing that it will take another two years to escape from the East, that I will make it only as far as New Mexico, never to California, and that I will never see Paul again. We hug warmly and wish each other luck and Paul starts out for his room but stops after a few steps, turns and reminds me that I need a push, which I have forgotten, and he pushes Rosalina out of the driveway onto the road, churning his sturdy legs to get us going, slapping the trunk and saying goodbye to Rosalina, smiling and waving as I drive off.

12

Very good but better bad > Encounter with a prankish dolphin > No place for a handsome green fellow > Expecting terrified raccoons > Fat Anthony and little LeRoi > A glorious hood ornament

Little Rosalina seems awfully empty without my friend and it takes awhile to get my bearings, pulling over to the side with the motor running to consult my map, wanting to stick to the coast, maybe visit some of the Sea Islands where I have heard the Gullah culture is preserved. The Gullah people, descendants of slaves, maintain many of their African customs and speak a Creole dialect. I have read about them and am interested. Jim Brown is a Gullah man. It is around four o'clock and I figure I will drive a couple more hours, which will put me somewhere around Gullah territory. I will ask around and maybe get out to one of the islands.

Getting out of Jacksonville proves something of an ordeal, a couple of wrong turns, ending up on a freeway heading west, Rosalina irritated with her feckless driver but plugging resolutely along. We finally make it out, losing at least an hour, as I hug the coast, past little towns named Black Hammock, Franklintown, American Beach, Amelia City, Fernandina Beach (where I stop for gas, leaving the engine running), through a watery world, to my right the crotchety old Atlantic, behaving itself for the time being. I love the ocean and am stoked now about spending at least a day on one of the islands where the Gullah people live. Just over the Georgia state line I come to a town called St. Marys and find a funky little campground near the Crooked River that has a few Airstreams with the usual white, sunburned middle-of-the-American-road eccentrics lolling about with their beer and Jack Daniels, grills fired up for the early evening barbecue.

Leaving Rosalina running I walk up the ramshackle steps to the campground office, a shack like the Panacea Post Office, only smaller, to inquire about a spot for the night. The place is empty but for a dusty wooden counter, an open register with yellowed pages, a rusty desk bell and a mildewed poster of Mae West on the wall in a cheap black frame, *When I'm good I'm very, very good but when I'm bad I'm better.* Before I can ring the bell I hear the muffled slam of the Airstream door next to the office and a dark, barefoot, slightly plump East Indian-looking woman of about forty comes through the back door. She has a sensual face with blue makeup around her eyes and deep black hair that comes to her shoulders. She's wearing a red bikini top and tight white shorts. Her belly spills just a tad over the shorts. Standing behind the counter she looks at me with an intense, slightly amused expression in her brown eyes. Eight dollars a day, she says, shower included.

I pay the eight dollars and write my name in the guest book. She pronounces my name with her Indian accent, offering a sweaty little hand, introducing herself, Rasna. We go outside and her arm brushes against mine as she points out the bathroom and shower and then my space, a kind of enclosure surrounded by saw palmettos next to a small Airstream flying a large American flag. She smells of cooking and incense, with a hint of armpit odor. If I need anything just ask, she says. I know just what I need, I think, but

won't ask. This depresses me. Meanwhile Rosalina is clearly unhappy, heating up and threatening to stall, so I get in and drive to
our little spot.

I pass a wretched night of semi-sleeplessness, kept awake by the
patriot next door in his flag-toting Airstream watching TV most of
the night, the volume low enough that no one can legitimately com-
plain but loud enough to bother me as I slip in and out of agitated
dreams. He stays awake until two or three and soon after that some
kind of swamp bird starts in with a manic three-note warbling that
drives me to despair, stopping at first light, which is when I finally
drift off for a couple of hours until the sun roasts me awake. I need
to find a nice beach or some other agreeable place where I can lie
down and get some sleep. I get a couple of guys to give Rosalina
a push and off we go, passing Rasna's Airstream, her door tightly
shut.

***

The idea is to get out to one of the islands and I try St. Simon's
but it is obvious I am not getting any Gullah culture here as the
place has been discovered by the silent-but-deadly majority with
motels and a Howard Johnson's and an actual traffic jam caused by
an accident up the road. I pull a U-turn and get myself and Rosalina
the hell out of there, ending up almost by accident on Jekyll Island,
a bit south, a wild and beautiful place, much of it closed to development. The beach is clean and the water warm so I go for a swim and
immediately get the shit scared out of me by a dolphin that surfaces
ten feet away doing its best shark imitation. Very funny, Mr. Dolphin, ha ha.

My intention is to put down my towel and get some sleep but
I say hello to a man and his daughter and we end up talking about

the presidential election and other things for the next two hours walking down the beach. He is a political science professor at North Carolina State and helping with McGovern's primary campaign. His daughter, thin, plain and friendly, is an art major at Columbia College in South Carolina. They are intelligent, decent people, appalled with Nixon and his continuation of the war. It is refreshing to hear these liberal views expressed with southern accents. The professor tells me about Sapelo Island, one of the last true Gullah strongholds, not too far away, near a little town with the sublimely beautiful name of Eulonia. I make a mental note to consider this name for a daughter if I ever have one. He had been there several months ago. Retrieving an address book from his backpack he tears out a page and writes the number of a woman, Carmella Beasley, to contact on Sapelo for a possible tour. As we walk along the beach we see shrimp boats with their graceful winged nets and numerous cavorting dolphins, maybe one of them the prankish fucker that scared the shit out of me. I bid the man and his daughter goodbye, push Rosalina on the flat parking lot and jump in, setting out for Eulonia in search of a little campground recommended by the professor, a good location, not far from Sapelo Island.

I don't know if it is the campground the professor has in mind but I find one near Eulonia that makes the one in St. Marys look like Hyannis Port. It is hot, maybe 90. Before I get to the campground I go into a little store along the road and buy a pint of chocolate ice cream from a thin-faced unsmiling cracker wearing a dirty, sweat-stained red cap touting some brand of feed or farm equipment. The ice cream melts before I am halfway finished and gets all over the steering wheel and floor. I go back in the store and ask for water to clean up and he shakes his head no and directs me to a spigot outside ("Theya's a fawhset outsahd"), where I wash my hands as a carload of white teens in a Chevy convertible with a tattered Confederate flag on the antenna stops about 15 yards away eyeing me and talking to each other, finally peeling out with rebel whoops and chucking a half-full (I am an optimist) beer can that lands next to me. It could be worse. I soak my towel at the faucet and wipe down the steering wheel and the floor. I am in a pickle because the parking lot is gravel and I can't get traction to start Rosalina. After a couple of tries, sweating and out of breath, I lean against Rosalina, scanning the dusty Georgia landscape, worrying about the kids in the Chevy coming back. There are no houses and little of anything but baking scrub oak and pine forest, empty road and a couple of turkey vultures circling high overhead, little specs, speculating. A dusty, beat-up red pickup pulls into the lot and an old, very black man wearing a green shirt gets out wiping his face with a white handkerchief. He shakes his head and looks at me. "Whew! Hot!" he says. When he gets out of the store holding a quart of beer I ask for a push and the old truck gets Rosalina going. I do a U-turn and wave at the old man, who waves back, and head for the campground, about a mile down the road.

This time there is no East Indian to take my money but a stout middle-aged woman with peroxide hair and a fantastic mole on her upper lip that I cannot take my eyes off. In spite of the heat she wears a green sweater with red shorts. Christmas colors. Her bloated thighs are pale as suet and laced with blue veins. At her feet a dirty white toy poodle with a rhinestone collar growls. The office is her camper, next to a large olive drab tent, WWII style, presumably where she lives. My spot is next to a lake about a half-mile in diameter. It has a little dock and rowboat she says I am welcome to use. There is a shower and bathroom, similar to the other campground. I park Rosalina with her nose pointed out for an easy getaway and, sunburned from my long walk on the beach at Jekyll Island, take a shower in the little building, the water discolored, with a mild sulfurous smell. I wonder about Paul. He would have contacted his father by now and maybe they have already spent some time together. The thought of being back on Long Island depresses me but I still have a construction job and I will be able to save some money for a quick turnaround, though as it happens it will not be as quick as I imagine.

There is some shade and I roll out my towel, which, filthy and wet from cleaning the ice cream, I take to the pond and wash as best I can, open *The Wretched of the Earth* somewhere in the middle, farther than I will ever get, put it over my eyes and sleep for two hours, dreaming about giant turtles with spiky shells swimming in a network of glass tubes that arc above a city near the ocean. It is late afternoon and I have only a few pieces of fruit, some almonds and a dubious container of yogurt sloshing about in the ice chest.

Resigned to spending a hungry night in this odd, lonely place I am happily surprised when the manager invites me for some fried catfish at her tent with her sister. We sit at a picnic table outside while her sister, a slimmer and younger version with no moles, cooks the fish and French fries on an old mid-sized propane stove. We sip beers and make small talk while the poodle, Maybellene, sniffs my leg, scurrying away when I try to pet her. I am a curiosity to these people but they take me well enough in stride, on a scale of strangeness probably not far removed from the usual clientele. I think they are pretty strange themselves, northerners, or near northerners, from Delaware, traveling the country, stopping when needing the work. They have been managing the campground for a couple of months and plan to stay the summer. Their nephew had been killed two years ago in Vietnam and they are opposed to the war but they have little to say about politics. They know about Sapelo Island and tell me about the ferry landing, which is nearby. I don't ask why they travel like they do, partly because I can see doing the same thing myself and don't think it strange and partly because I am tired and not in the mood for talking very much. Dorothy and

Wanda Craig from Delaware. They seem normal and a bit lonely but there is something a little spooky about them too, something a little off. I thank them for dinner and volunteer to wash the dishes but they decline my offer, recommending that I go for a row around the lake in the morning.

It is still light, only about seven, so I walk a little nervously down the road back to the store where there is an outdoor pay phone and dial Carmella Beasley's number. She answers after the first ring, telling me to get the ferry at nine the next morning and that her son will meet me on the other side. His name is Walter and he has a brown VW bus. It will cost $20 for a four-hour tour around the island, which I can afford. I have about 200 left, counting the 60 Paul gave me, which is enough to get me home.

***

There are only two other campers in the strange little place and it is a quiet night, clear and beautiful under the Georgia stars and I sleep well, waking up at dawn to row around the lake as the sun rises yellow and hot over the forest on the other side. The lake is full of turtles poking their heads through the glassy surface. I amuse myself by seeing how close I can get to them, with little success. I have better luck when I stop rowing and drift, the water calm and everything quiet, not even the sound of birds, and the little heads pop up a few yards away, perhaps curious about the boat, and then plunge beneath the surface when they spot me.

Dorothy and Wanda invite me for some coffee and insist on feeding me scrambled eggs, toast and bacon when they discover I have not eaten, piling my plate with good food cooked on the propane stove. With a good night's sleep and fueled by the big breakfast I have the strength of a Gullah man and easily get Rosalina started. Being parked on a downgrade helps too. It takes about ten minutes to reach Meridian Landing where a boat, *Janet,* is docked as a couple of black men slowly load supplies, mostly boxes of groceries, laughing and talking softly. The pilot, an older, heavy white man with weathered sunbaked skin and blue eyes, fiddles with the engine, an inboard. He wears a dirty skipper's cap, white T-shirt and kakis. The black men are younger and very dark, one of them thin and tightly muscled, the other of medium build and softer in appearance. The thin guy has on a gray T-shirt, jeans and flip-flops. He has a sharp, fierce face but he puts me at ease right away, calling me "Walter's man," in a deep rich Afro-Georgian drawl, directing me aboard, and I jump in, trying to look as casual and nimble as possible, conscious of their appraisal. The other man wears brown shorts and a yellow and brown Hawaiian shirt, also flip-flops. The whole scene is laid back in the extreme, the morning impeccable and warm, glassy blue water, hardly a breeze, green marsh grass all around. Paradise. We wait another fifteen minutes while the captain works on the engine, introducing ourselves and making small talk. I will like Sapelo, they say, it is beautiful. They don't live there, though, nothing to do. The thin guy's name is Oliver, who does most of the talking in that deep voice. The other guy, Jim Ray, is quiet but friendly, with an easy, touchingly self-conscious smile. I like them imediately. Walter, says Oliver, knows the island like the back of his hand. He also has six children, Jim Ray says, and they both laugh.

Finally the captain finishes and introduces himself gruffly with a thick, calloused hand and we are off in a smoky blue, bubbling rumble, cutting through the glistening delicate water as dolphins swim alongside racing and breaching playfully, my heart full of excitement and wonder at the exquisite, pristine beauty of the place, first navigating through narrow water and then into a larger body called

Doboy Sound, still calm but with gentle swells, and into the mouth of the Duplin River, between "Little Sapelo" and "Big Sapelo," our destination. All this is something else, like the Grand Canyon or Big Sur or New Mexico or the Louisiana bayous and again the beauty of my country awes and humbles me. I am standing at the bow and it is a good thing too because it would be embarrassing for the others to see the sudden tears streaming down my face. It is that beautiful. There are birds everywhere, more brilliant white egrets, gulls, flitting little terns, oystercatchers, plovers and more. The water is a supple, silky, dazzling, living thing, calmly supporting *Janet's* softly shearing passage. The Vietnamese love their land as much as we love ours. It is just as beautiful and precious. The breeze from the moving boat helps dry my tears, blubbering fool. Ahead on the dock stands a black man that I guess is Walter Beasley, dressed like Jim Ray in a flowering short-sleeved shirt and shorts.

The three black men greet each other as *Janet* docks, Oliver and Jim Ray throwing the lines to Walter who fastens clove hitches over the posts. Walter is an inch or so taller than I am, solid if not muscular, dark-skinned, with a broad, untroubled African face. He wears flip-flops like the other two. I figure him in his mid-thirties. He is not particularly friendly but has a nice easy quality that reassures me. I help load the boxes into his VW, sweating with the heat, looking around the forested landscape, mostly oak, and then get in the front as he goes back to say goodbye to his friends. After a couple of minutes Walter jumps into the driver's seat and slams the door, welcoming me to his "playground."

We drop the groceries off at a store in the tiny village of Hog Hammock, no more than a few old wood buildings, and then spend the next five hours in his "putt-putt" exploring the magical island, the dense oak forests where wild hogs and cows roam free, the swampy ponds where old bull alligators and giant snapping turtles (we don't see any) preside over their harems, the "behavior" cemetery, final resting place of enslaved people and their descendants, the various buildings of tabby construction, made of oyster shells, lime, sand and water, the old R. J. Reynolds mansion, straight out of the antebellum South.

As we drive up the long oak-shaded driveway Walter talks about the island's former cotton, corn and sugar cane plantation, worked by "hundreds" of slaves, owned by Thomas Spaulding, a Georgia senator. Walter obviously loves his island and is proud of it. Young people, he says, are leaving because there is no opportunity. But I envy the people here. Walter is poor but happy with his life. As we ride around I begin to realize what an exceptional person he is, a kind of gentle, homespun Thoreau, content with a handful of beans and the beautiful place he lives. He is an herbalist and repository of island lore and folk tales, stories that, like old Br'er Rabbit, stretch back to African times. He keeps me at a psychic arm's length the whole time but I am satisfied with being in this amazing place in the presence of an American original, a treasure, straight out of National Geographic, a magazine, to my detriment, I never read.

We drive on, stopping at the lighthouse and then back to Hog Hammock—a hammock, Walter explains, is a small hill—going into the same store where we left the groceries, buying ice-cold grape soda from a vending machine with racks that hold the bottles by the necks. You put your money in the slot, ten cents, and slide the bottles along and up through the latch. Walter introduces me to a cousin, a man nicknamed Pumpkin, neither orange nor round, and an older woman, Bernice, who must have been a beauty in her time, both very friendly and warm. Outside the store he points out a small tree and a bush, toothache tree and sassafras, picking leaves from both which he ties in bundles with string from his VW and gives to me. The toothache tree leaves are chewed or made into a poultice to place against the offending tooth as a numbing agent and the sassafras is used for filé powder or tea.

Our last stop before heading back to the ferry is at a long white beach where the Atlantic, a stunning, white-capped Technicolor blue, lies in its vastness all the way to Africa. We stand there for a few minutes as Walter tells me about fishing in the old days, when the people would cast their nets into the sea, the African way, an image that will stay with me for days.

***

I decide to try for Edisto Beach that afternoon and head north into Savannah over the bridge, driving about three more hours ending up in the little touristy beach town on a hot, near full moon night where I find another of the small makeshift campgrounds that seem to be common along the coast. I am lucky because a person has just left and a spot is open, the only one available, a small clearing surrounded by huge saw palmettos and an old cypress tree whose moss droops over me as if in perpetual mourning. It is very humid and hot and the frogs and insects make a continuous racket all night as I first strip naked with the heat, the sweat rolling off me, but then mosquitoes forcing me to put my clothes back on. Either way I am uncomfortable and get very little sleep but the place is enchanted with the big moon shining over a swamp-like field in front visible through the saw palmettos, creating a mysterious silvery antebellum dreamscape where fleeing slaves flit past followed by stone-faced white men on horseback and their deadly hounds. Old southern terrors mixed with strange moonlit beauty and a riot of frogs, crickets and other mysterious noises. The fluid, dripping heat envelopes me in a uterine stupor. Drifting into something like sleep a few hours before sunrise I am awakened by another one of those pre-dawn birds in the cypress tree directly above me whistling *wait-for-willie, wait-for-willie* (a whip-poor-will?), over and over, as if perched inside my ear. I give up and go to piss in the dark green men's bathroom illuminated by a single yellow bulb and on the wall next to me is a brilliant emerald green tree frog, his little footpads splayed against the pebbly surface, red eyes watching. This is not a dignified place for a tree frog at four in the morning and I put him outside. After a while the *wait-for-willie* bird flies away and I get a couple of quiet, almost cool, hours of actual sleep.

Arising, I go for a swim in the warm calm Atlantic and then corral a teenager to help push Rosalina. About an hour later I am having coffee and a chocolate croissant at a German bakery in Charleston and in another five hours after driving through tawdry Myrtle Beach and much nicer North Myrtle Beach I am at Carolina Beach State Park, thoroughly beat, checking in for a camp site. I had earlier stopped at a market for lunch fixings and now, at the site, a small clearing surrounded by forest with a dirt road in front, sit on my sleeping bag and eat a ham and cheese sandwich, dill pickle and drink a cold beer. Finished, I walk around the campground, passing one group of stoned hippies who smile at me and then along the Cape Fear River for a while and finally back to Rosalina just in time to beat a thunderstorm with howling winds that rock the little car. In the morning one of the hippies tells me that a tornado had touched down nearby during the storm. I return to the river and walk along the bank until I find a suitable spot and wade in thigh deep and then lie back and watch the pelicans dive bomb for fish, crashing into the water like bowling balls, more often than not coming up with their flapping prey. Flying over me they seem as big as B-52s.

About four hours later I am driving Rosalina onto the "Pamlico," one of the two ferries that run from Cedar Island to Ocracoke Island, on the Outer Banks. I had driven years earlier with high school friends as far as Kitty Hawk on a surfing safari and the Outer Banks had left an indelible impression, wild and beautiful. I have to shut Rosalina down as the ferry ride is two hours but the guy behind me gives me a push at Ocracoke and I am soon at a campsite where an onshore wind is blowing at gale force, whipping the sand so viciously I can only stay on the beach for a few minutes, long enough to be awed by the roaring Atlantic which a day or so earlier had been calm. The wind blows like crazy all night confining me to Rosalina and once again I get little sleep but in the morning I go for a swim anyway and within minutes the current has swept me a half-mile to the north.

Spurred by the wind I get going, taking the ferry from Ocracoke to Cape Hatteras, this time hassled by a North Carolina trooper who scowls at Rosalina and asks for my driver's license, poking his snout into the car, sniffing. Mine is the only vehicle on this trip and I need help getting Rosalina off, reluctantly provided by a couple of deck hands who make insulting jokes about my courageous little beauty. Fuck them. Basically I have seen enough of the Outer Banks but I stop and hike to the top of the lighthouse to peer out at the wind-roiled sea, graveyard of the Atlantic, a blue-gray wickedness. I imagine the lighthouse swaying back and forth in the wind and beat a chicken's retreat to the sandy ground.

Chugging off the Outer Banks Rosalina and I travel across the amazing Chesapeake Bay Bridge. It is the first time I have ever seen the mythical bay where market gunners decimated whole species of birds early in the century. I have read accounts of hunters floating up on huge numbers of rafting ducks and letting loose with their punt guns, huge-bored affairs that shot nails and all manner of malignant things, killing dozens with one shot. The canvasback and redhead ducks were nearly eliminated. American firepower is still on the job 8,000 miles away with the latest improvements. At least this time the targets are firing back.

We are pushing it, Rosalina and I, plowing through the heat and humidity, both of us running on willpower and frazzled energy. I buy a can of STP at our last stop for gas and pour it into her blistering crankcase in the hopes of soothing her hot little innards. She barely chugs along, clearly very tired, and I am worried. Just outside of Salisbury Maryland, as I imagine a good Salisbury steak and baked potato at some nice cozy little plastic Howard Johnson's, the sky turns a baleful black and the wind whips up in sudden violent gusts, nearly pushing Rosalina off the road. It is the darkest sky I have ever seen. Thinking about the tornado at Carolina Beach I decide to get the hell off the road as quickly as possible. Spotting a motel with a beautiful yellow neon vacancy sign I pull in and within ten minutes am putting the key in the lock just as the rain begins coming down furiously, the wind almost knocking me over. It is only a moment's respite though because I have forgotten the ice chest with my food so back outside it is around the Horn in the *Pequod* with the winds howling and thunder and lightning crashing. Thoroughly soaked and safely back in his motel room Ishmael takes a deep breath and towels himself off. He is in Maryland.

***

I spend the next two hours nervously munching salted peanuts, apples, cheese, beef jerky and drinking the last of my beer as the storm beats against the hollow-core door of my motel room and billows the large plate glass window like a spinnaker. I expect some object, a tree branch, a trashcan, a metal sign, a terrified raccoon, to come crashing through the window at any moment, staying away from the glass and sitting on the floor with my back against the wall, which itself seems only a flimsy barrier. About a half-hour into it a cataract of hailstones comes hurtling out of the sky sounding like millions of ball bearings crashing and bouncing and I brave a look out the window to see a near whiteout, poor Rosalina smashed to hell by the onslaught. The hailstones are the size of apricot pits and I can hear them crashing into Rosalina. I feel puny and helpless in the face of it and think about the thousands of acres of young corn and other things I have seen growing in this part of the country, how they have surely been sliced to shreds, if not completely destroyed.

The fiercest part of the hailstorm lasts for about two minutes and when it ends I look again to see large mounds of ice packed up against the curb as if a winter storm has passed through. The wind moans and the rain batters down and I cannot see Rosalina clearly but I am dismayed to think of the damage done, many more dents now in addition to the pummeling from the Hells Angels and after the rain and wind finally relent I go outside to check and discover my little car indeed covered with hundreds of new pockmarks along with a small fresh crack in the windshield, little dents that will eventually turn into a bloom of rusty zits. She deserves a complete restoration even if I will never be able to give her one, an implicit understanding we have had from the start, though as I have gotten to know her my respect has deepened so that I feel guilty for the certain future inattention. But I am no mechanic and all the money I earn will go towards the next trip west, one that I will not make with Rosalina.

It is not late and I turn on the TV but the storm has knocked out all reception, the snowed-out screen jumping with crackling traces of distant lightning. I watch for a while anyway, a kind of perversity, something that looks like *My Three Sons* behind all the interference, images that appear and disappear as if broadcast from another planet. I wait for the screen to clear and Ming the Merciless or

Melvin Laird to deliver their ultimatums but instead only the fading and crackling and terrible electronic snowstorm that soon makes me uncomfortable and anxious and I turn it off. An ideal form of torture, to make someone sit in front of a wigged-out television screen for hours on end, but who needs wigged-out screens when clear reception effectively lobotomizes an entire nation. When I was first getting stoned an occasional amusement was to sit with friends in front of a color TV with the adjustments turned haywire and groove on the craziness—like, wow, but the bad medicine of jumbled-up-krazy-color-sizzling-electromagnetic energy would get to me pretty quickly and I would have to desist, though some of the more serious heads would watch longer. A few would do it tripping. But now extreme boredom in cubicle 16, Salisbury, Maryland. No TV and only *The Wretched of the Earth* for reading. Maryland. I know nothing about Maryland except an old Sidney Bechet recording I once had of "Maryland, My Maryland," the damnable Baltimore Colts, the Robinsons, Brooks and Frank, Gus Triandos, the Chesapeake market gunners, Edgar Allen Poe, Earl Monroe. And Aaron, beautiful Alexandria's boyfriend, also from Baltimore. I switch the TV back on, which is the same, turn it off, lie down on the bed, open *The Wretched of the Earth* and stare at Paul's address for a few minutes thinking about the incredible Carmen. My thoughts turn to Butterfly on the beach with my head on her lap, images of her life in New Mexico swirling in my fading consciousness, missing her and wondering when will I see her again.

I find a Howard Johnson's in the morning but opt for a smaller restaurant nearby where I have scrambled eggs with crab and Tabasco Sauce, toast with whipped butter and raspberry jam, two cups of good coffee, real cream, no sugar. A copy of the *Baltimore Sun* is next to me and I am amazed to see the fucker Rostow scheduled to speak that night at the University of Maryland and I wonder if he would recognize me were I there, which of course I will not be. It is the same photo that ran in the *Times-Picayune*, the smug, pampered jowls, the tony threads, the clear-framed professorial glasses. Bastard. I feel the same loathing as the first time at the Café du Monde but mixed with a guilty, giddy thrill at what had happened at Tulane, as if we had witnessed a bunch of anarchists painting *FUCK YOU!* on the side of the Pentagon and I smile, almost laughing at the memory that seems like a dream, so crazy and unreal. I think of Paul and wonder how he is doing.

I put the paper on the table and dribble Tabasco sauce on the picture, as if some Voodoo ritual, and imagine Rostow feeling the sting and pulpy splatter of the tomatoes as I do so, hoping it summons spasms of shame and rage that shake him to his rotten core. Men like Rostow quickly vanish in history's rearview mirror, their legacies hung like offal for posterity to consider and loathe, the only problem being new monsters perpetually rising to replace them. Am I wrong in thinking that things will ever be different? Is it a pipe dream to think that there might be some drift, some nice little evolutionary glide towards a more peaceful, more sensible version of *Homo sapiens*? Or are I and my ilk just a bunch of naïve squirrels perched on the far-out limb of the family tree? What is the true nature of the magnificent beast? Is it Rostow and McNamara or the Berrigan brothers? Curtis LeMay or Daniel Ellsberg? Easy to say a mixture of both but it seems the LeMays of the world are winning because they consider the use of force, of which they have supreme control, to be axiomatic, as natural as eating or shitting. This is the observed reality. Certain people run the world and these are not the squirrels sitting on the outer limb grooving on clouds or Melville's Ishmael up in the crow's nest lost in his philosophy. No, the world has its business to attend to and there is little use for the small furry rodents, the artists, dreamers and idlers, which is fine with me, loosely assigned to some category of the like, munching my acorns on the margins. I think of Butterfly's parents in New Mexico and other decent, solid people like them, not Nixon's bullshit silent majority but the country's virtuous minority, so unknown to Mr. Rostow, whose image is now completely covered with Tabasco sauce as I sip the last of my Maryland coffee. It is the good plain people that keep the world from falling apart and the Rostows and McNamaras with their murderous impulses and idiot logic that threaten to destroy it. Those who rule are without conscience. It is the only explanation. To achieve that kind of power you have to slice a bit of it away at each step until there is nothing left.

***

I leave a large tip for the young, pretty, slightly overweight waitress who walks with a limp and smiles sweetly at her customers. Outside I get a push from a guy in his pickup, a black Chevy with sideboards, a working man, maybe a fisherman, who reminds me of Gilbert Bujeau, another of the good ones. He guns it to twenty and backs off as I pop the clutch in third and Rosalina rumbles to life, a little reluctantly, I think, but it is the home stretch, maybe eight hours, and while I take nothing for granted it seems we will make it. It has been almost an exact month of traveling, longer than I had expected. I hardly think of Lulu Delilah any more. She is something like the space of gum after a pulled tooth, healing now, only slightly raw when you probe with your tongue, the pain gone, feeling not unlike a bit of the sublime female part that caused all the trouble in the first place.

Ah, Lulu Delilah! What a wild animal she is! A raw-boned slightly daft nature child traveling her own eccentric orbit—Lucy in the Sky with Diamonds. I had made a big mistake with ol' Lulu

Delilah, yessir, jumping in where more sensible young men might hesitate, but we had met under intense chemical circumstances and I have a weakness for otherworldly types, especially if they are long-limbed and, if not beautiful, possessed of some primitive essence, a sweetly-addled selkie wandering the beach covered with seaweed and dried sand, smiling at me alone in the world. She has a long almost equine face in the manner of some European actresses but her untamed vibe and laughing drawl are pure southern country USA, like some sharecropper's strange sex-hungry daughter. She is strong and supple but not athletic—maybe all the acid has disrupted her coordination—large hands and feet, a chipped front tooth and a big scar on her abdomen from an appendectomy, white and jagged against her brown skin. I imagine a country doctor operating on a kitchen table with a bottle of whiskey for himself and a rag between clenched teeth for her and indeed, as if the rag were still there, she has problems expressing herself, especially with feelings, which she mostly avoids. I chalk this up to the acid but maybe there is more to it. She will not talk about her childhood, which makes me imagine dark and sad things. It is the mystery of Lulu Delilah as much as the fabulous sex that got to me, worming its way into some callow unprotected place. She is a real number, whether lucky or unlucky I debate for the hundredth time, deciding once again on the former despite the brief crushing pain because it has been above all an experience. I've been *experienced*. Experienced with a person who is far from usual, a strange beauty in her own way and a half-dozen other young men I know wished they had been me despite the danger. I had plunged into the magnificent breach and taken the fall for all of them.

I doubt, passing Wilmington, that I will have anything to do with Lulu Delilah any more. It seems a year since I have left Long Island and she but a small figure on the horizon, especially since

Butterfly has materialized to fill the picture. Butterfly has a different sort of country charm, rooted in something deeper, a connection with strong unbroken links fastened to family and land that make my own ties wispy in comparison. Everything I know is tenuous and fractured, my own identity threatening to dissolve at the smallest disruption, the shrinking man syndrome, blown about by determinist fate. And yet there is a touching vulnerability to Butterfly, her sweet shyness, her passion for the underdog, her basic distrust of modern culture, country to the bone with just the right amount of sophistication and not without some of Lulu Delilah's wildness, though of a different sort, of mountains and mountain lions and hot dry summer washes, vast lonesome spaces and the prickly pear independence of those who settle and those who cannot stop moving. I can understand this wildness because I have some of it myself, though nothing of her grip on the land. I am just beginning to understand her strong contradictions, her hardheaded realism and deep emotional attachments, her free thinking and old-fashioned conservatism. But what really gets me is Butterfly's obvious connection to the world of the unseen, ghosts, something beyond, every passing cloud, whispering bough, call of crow, murmuring stream, distant voice, skittering lizard, splatter of rain, blooming cactus flower, grumbling thunder, a window open to the spirits that crowd like rush hour strap-hangers so close it is a wonder she has oxygen to breathe. It is nothing she ever talked about. You can just sense it.

I am going through Philadelphia and the familiar East Coast dread hits for the first time, though I had felt subtle forebodings in Jacksonville. The air is thicker and polluted with the foul hydrocarbon stink of industry and exhaust fumes, sick-sweet chemicals, the musty, depressing funk of old buildings and streets. Even the good smells, the bakeries and restaurants, the faint odor of old circuses and ballparks, the hot dog stands, the fish markets, depress me, dredging up all sorts of dreary childhood associations. What a zero, what a nothing, no parents to speak of, an alcoholic mother dead when I was eight, a father concerned only with himself, my brother and I distant asteroids, space detritus, revolving around him. The East drags me down like a decomposing corpse with its hand around my ankle. I have to shake it off, get out. Fast. The only thing that keeps me going is the sure knowledge that I will be heading back out West very soon.

Rosalina labors past Trenton, East Brunswick, Edison, Elizabeth. I think about Vanzetti and his beautiful Beretta over and under, blasting seagulls. It is Thursday so he is working, welding, running machinery, filling out forms with his thick grimy fingers, taking in old Jersey wrecks, absently looking at the gulls wheeling over the rusting metal bone yard. Vanzetti had been friendly but I wonder what his real thoughts are about the stuff that is tearing the country apart, the war, civil rights, hippies, women's rights, the sexual revolution, drugs. Is he a Nixon supporter? I had read the old anarchist Vanzetti's letters in college and had been blown away by the poetry, brilliance and compassion from a humble working man, his conviction that capitalist US was on a bobsled track to hell, the only way out revolution, which is of course what I believe completely. I have a warm spot for Elizabeth's Vanzetti, because of the name and the good deed he had rendered, but it is likely we would be pretty cool towards each other after a few beers, though there is a point, is there not, when two people can get beyond all the bullshit knee-jerk reactions that obscure their common humanity. I will never see Vanzetti again, maybe a loss. Maybe he is beyond the bullshit and always has been, but it would be hard not stereotyping each other, urban redneck, racist, pro war—hippie, commie, drugs, anti war—the same deal with Mr. Righteous America in Santa Cruz who turned out to be a sympathetic and slightly pathetic figure, poor guy, a young wife dead from cancer and two little fascist kids to raise.

***

Rosalina needs gas and we are entering Newark. Newark is bad medicine, ripped apart by poverty and racial turmoil with the fat bully Anthony Imperiale as its racist face. The city went up in black anger and flames in '67 and fat Anthony led a white working class backlash armed and ready to rumble the darkies, attracting national attention and probably a lot of sympathy from the silent, violent (white) majority. Anthony's nemesis is the skinny Black Nationalist/poet, fire-tongued LeRoi Jones/Amiri Baraka. Their battles are scathing, epic and ugly-comic, caricature-like opposites locked in bitter struggle. A huge hovering bird of violence darkens the city. Hate rises in a stench that infects the whole East Coast. Newark is a dread word, a place to be shunned like a quarantined site, the Amerikan equivalent to post-war Eastern Europe, grim as a box of dead babies, in black and white. You feel a little guilty about it, looking on in awful fascination. Poor Newark.

I would avoid the place if not for this suddenly empty tank that forces me to take the nearest exit, ending up smack in the middle of a very poor black neighborhood that looks like it had been fire bombed six months earlier. Maybe it had. It is a total reality flip, as if I have entered an alien universe. Immediately I am uptight. A lone white entering a black ghetto these days is the equivalent of a Popsicle strolling into a steel mill and compared with an ordinary ghetto Newark's temperature is closer to that of the sun. The only thing in my favor is ragged Rosalina, whose pathetic condition fits right in with the surroundings.

The place is shocking to behold and I try not to stare—buildings in shambles, boarded up or disintegrating, swaths of empty spaces filled with litter, abandoned cars stripped and ruined. In the midst of this desolation people loiter and hang out in small groups drinking from bottles concealed in paper bags. I drive around for a few minutes but the futility is obvious. Much longer and I will run out of gas. I pull over and ask an older man who looks at me sternly as if he is a teacher addressing a student who has walked into the wrong classroom. He directs me to a main thoroughfare where three stop-lights down and on the right is a gas station attached to a liquor store. It is noon and the store is doing a brisker business than the station. The price for a gallon of regular gas is seventy-four-nine, thirty cents higher than we had been paying out West. I have heard of food prices being higher in the ghetto, not to mention the shitty quality, so I am not surprised about the gas. I turn in but a woman in a white Riviera beats me to the pump. Frustrated, I back up, not seeing the Oldsmobile behind me, slamming my brakes just in time, our bumpers coming into slight contact. Faster than you can say urban renewal two scary-looking fuckers jump out, going right to the bumpers. This is it, I think, remembering breaking down in Elizabeth and thinking then it was the end of the line. The inno-cence of those days. These guys are in their forties, seasoned, hard-looking cats, one of them big, muscular, gold toothed, white tank top, do-rag. Big Cat Williams. Whitey's nightmare. The other guy wears gray sweats, big Afro, a livid Captain Ahab scar down his face. Looking for the white whale. Anything white. A white guppy. Me.

"Hey, man, you fucked up my Oldsmobile!" says Big Cat, looking in at me. "Git out the car, now! Git out the motherfuckin' car and tell me what you gonna do about this!" As he yells I can see him checking out Rosalina, the hundreds of dents, already rusting, the upholsteryless interior, bare springs, the cooler, dirty clothes. A look of disgust crosses his face.

"Hey, man, I'm sorry, I'm sorry!" I say, unable to take my eyes off his gold teeth and broad, flat nose, like some Nigerian mask. He has a scar too, on his cheekbone. Recent. I can see the pale stitch marks. As I get out his friend comes around the front yelling about a good ass-kicking for the nerve I have coming here and fucking up their car and what the fuck am I doing here anyway, while I keep saying over and over how sorry I am, it was a mistake, I should have been paying attention but I didn't want to hit the car in front, and so on, all said with the deepest heartfelt sincerity, believe me. Big Cat gets into his car and backs away from Rosalina, getting out and making a show of carefully inspecting the bumper, shaking his head at the terrible damage. His friend, watching, mirrors Big Cat's agitation.

"You fucked up, man," says Ahab. "You fucked up bad. Now we gonna have to fuck you up."

Big Cat comes back, looking at Ahab, shaking his head. "Bumper fucked up, man. What we gonna do with this motherfucker? Son-afabitch come down here fuckin' up people's shit. I've been driving 25 years and never had so much as a *scratch* on my car and this motherfucker come down here, into *my* neighborhood, and fuck up my car. Now aint that some shit!"

"Maybe white boy here needs to buy us a bottle of Crown for scratching the bumper," says Ahab. I look at the man closely for the first time. His scar runs from scalp to chin, its path crossing his eye, which has a dead milky iris.

"Go ahead, man. Go get us a bottle of Crown Royal and we might forget the damage you did to my bumper," says Big Cat.

So that's it. The white stooge forced to buy liquor for the brothers on the block. As if that has been their plan all along. In some ways it makes me feel worse than getting beat up. Humiliated, I go to the liquor store and as I open the door Ahab tells me to get a bottle of ginger ale too. "Fuck you," I say, under my breath, well under, assuredly. The store is dingy and smells like oil and stale beer. The guy behind the counter is enormous and stares at me balefully. The bottle of Crown Royal is marked $12.98 and the ginger ale $1.75. The guy charges me $20. "Take it or leave it," he says. Like I have a choice. I give the guys their bottles. Then I push Rosalina to the pump and get some gas at seventy-four-nine. Big Cat and Ahab are in their car over to the side, mixing the soda and whiskey in paper cups, happy as clams. Thanks to me these guys have settled their score with the universe for the day. Fuck it. I go over and ask for a push. They get out friendly as hell and give me a push. I half expect them to offer me a drink.

In ten minutes I am back on the turnpike and soon there is the river, the city and the two new ugly towers, freakish things that suck the poetry right out of the skyline. I have grown up with King Kong hanging off the Empire State Building swatting biplanes and clutching his little blond kicking doll. These towers signal the end for me. New York is now an alien place.

But some things are the same and soon Rosalina is rolling through the Lincoln Tunnel and out into sunny springtime Manhattan, west side, the best time of Manhattan, the great Manhattan. As much as I want to get away, am already gone, the city still thrills me, and now little Rosalina and I are into it, with it, part of the monster, rumbling, unruly animal that is my home and always will be no matter how far or long I stray. It is a beautiful day and we bump along midst the hyper-kinetic colorful flow of humans and their trucks, cabs, bikes, cars, busses, whatnot, all consumed with the greatest hustling energy on the planet, the same energy that repulses and enthralls me, the sheer amazing balls of it all. People are on the move and it doesn't matter if they only go two blocks in fifteen minutes, those two blocks are the most important two blocks in the world. Inching along in the middle of this two p.m. Garment District insanity—typical I have not thought to avoid it—I am giddy with the overwhelming reality of New York, a marvel, a historical marvel, and here we are, Rosalina and I, right in the profane, pushing, shoving, ass-thumping thick of it. In the thick of it but not part of it. Though I grew up in New York I have never really been a New Yorker in the hard-edged sense of what it means to be a New Yorker. Maybe it is a question of speed. I am just too slow, though we are not going very fast right now, a condition in which the city seems to find itself half the time. People racing like mad going nowhere. But now it is a grand exhilarating thing to be stuck in a traffic jam at two in the afternoon in the Garment District on a sunny Manhattan spring day. I think of Newark and Big Cat and his pal the badly-scarred Ahab and feel no animosity. After all, they are doing what their lives demand. I am blessed to have crossed paths with them (and blessed they did not beat the shit out of me or worse) and even feel glad I had a part in making their day a little better. I had been a temporary existential windfall for them, the stumbling white fool (what billiard ball chain of cause and effect had brought us together?) they played to their advantage, and that is not such a bad thing. We have our roles. I think if I go back to Newark and find them we might have a good laugh about it. Poor old suffering Newark with its Big Cats and Ahabs and Barakas and Imperiales clawing away at each other like crabs in a bucket. I think, lord, let them breath easier, let them ease up a little, let them understand (somehow!) that we are all knocking around together in this patched-up little boat tossed about by waves of circumstance and our own folly.

Such are my thoughts in this Garment District traffic jam on a Thursday afternoon, June 1st, 1972. It seems several lifetimes since I had stumbled across the stout little man in black blasting seagulls in Elizabeth with his shotgun. Vanzetti, the man in the middle, the pivot between East and West. My father for all his selfishness and hard Darwinian views would appreciate Vanzetti, understand his profound humor and central position in the universe. As much as the Nixons and Martin Luther Kings it is the Vanzettis who move the world, and our fate, anybody's guess, rests on all of their shoulders. Maybe even I have something to contribute. But to do so demands a sense of ownership—less the victim of circumstance and more the captain of my own vessel.

I get home around five to an empty house, my roommates still at work. A front is moving in from the west and clouds cover the sun. I sit in Rosalina for a few minutes looking at the residue of our journey, dust from the Grand Canyon, sand from the Gulf Coast, bits of trash, twigs and pieces of western weeds, chamisa, sage, not much different from when we had started but worse on the outside with the dents from Angel's fists, the cracked windshield and more dents from the Salisbury hail. Rosalina sits quietly clicking and cooling down and I feel guilty because I know there will not be much rest for my brave little beauty since I have to get back to work soon.

I sit for the next few minutes with vivid images of the Grand Canyon and the green Colorado, my cold swim, the waving rafters and the woman in the yellow hat, Big Sur and the Pacific Ocean, resting my woozy bumbled head on Butterfly's warm lap, Gilbert Boujeau and his poor crippled son, the amazing beautiful Gulf Coast, rich with life, the blue bayous, the snowy egrets, the quiet, warm visit to Sapelo Island, Paul, Butterfly and Datura, my companions and friends for life whether or not I will ever see them again and, of course, Vanzetti, the person who granted me safe passage, a mythic figure already. Maybe I will get a hood ornament made in his likeness, dressed in black, shotgun in hand, leaning slightly forward. Vanzetti leading the way, blasting seagulls and fascists. Vanzetti on the lookout for dangers and safe havens. Vanzetti spying for fine hippie chicks and ugly cops. Vanzetti, my guardian-fuckin'-angel. Onward, Vanzetti.

Ecuador
December, 2013